CAN A DESPERATE FOR...
SOLDIERS SURVI...
ANNIHILATION BY A...

THE LOST

FATEFUL LIGHTNING

WILLIAM R. FORSTCHEN

ROC ☆ 451-LE5196 ☆ (CANADA $6.99) ☆ U.S. $5.99

"SOME OF THE BEST
ADVENTURE WRITING IN YEARS!"
—Science Fiction Chronicle

ROC

AS HE CRESTED THE HILL, THE OFFICER REALIZED THAT TODAY HE WAS GOING TO DIE. . . .

A hundred yards away, a solid wall of thousands of Merki was deployed. A dark cloud rose from their ranks, soaring upward. Even before the wall of four-foot shafts came hurtling down, he could clearly hear their whispered approach growing louder. Horses screamed, rearing up, and riders tumbled, shouting, screaming, the charge disintegrating.

Another wall of arrows rose up, hurtling in, the crest of the hill a mad confusion.

"Dismount!" the officer yelled.

The bugler looked over at him in terror.

"Goddamn it, boy, we're going to die here. At least let's try and shoot some of the bastards first!"

FATEFUL LIGHTNING

"Exciting and moves like a bullet with good characters and battle scenes. . . . An excellent read."

—*Analog*

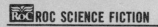

THE LOST REGIMENT

FATEFUL LIGHTNING

William R. Forstchen

A ROC BOOK

ROC
Published by the Penguin Group
Penguin Books USA Inc., 375 Hudson Street,
New York, New York 10014, U.S.A.
Penguin Books Ltd, 27 Wrights Lane,
London W8 5TZ, England
Penguin Books Australia Ltd, Ringwood,
Victoria, Australia
Penguin Books Canada Ltd, 10 Alcorn Avenue,
Toronto, Ontario, Canada M4V 3B2
Penguin Books (N.Z.) Ltd, 182–190 Wairau Road,
Auckland 10, New Zealand

Penguin Books Ltd, Registered Offices:
Harmondsworth, Middlesex, England

First published by Roc, an imprint of New American Library,
a division of Penguin Books USA Inc.

First Printing, January, 1993
10 9 8 7 6 5 4 3 2 1

Copyright © William R. Forstchen, 1993
Maps by Pat Tobin
All rights reserved

 REGISTERED TRADEMARK—MARCA REGISTRADA

Printed in the United States of America

For Sharon—
who after surviving the writing
of this series still agreed to marry me.

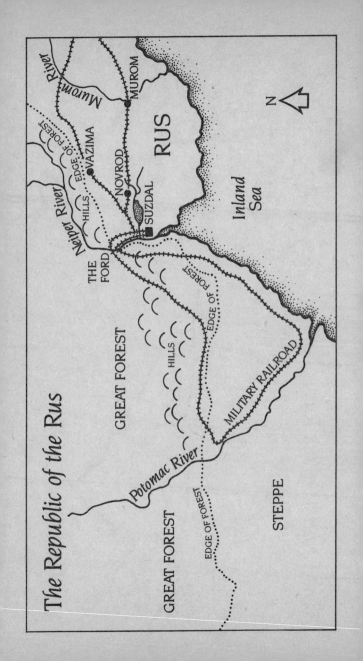
The Republic of the Rus

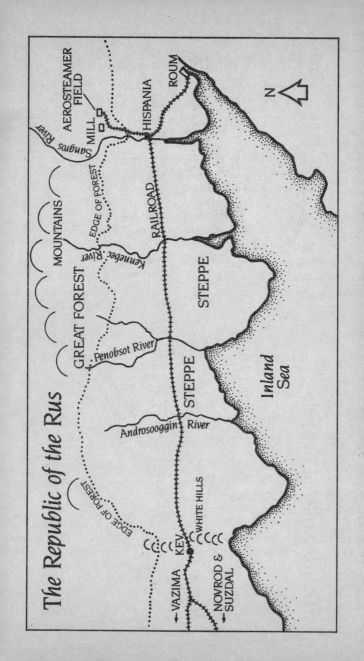

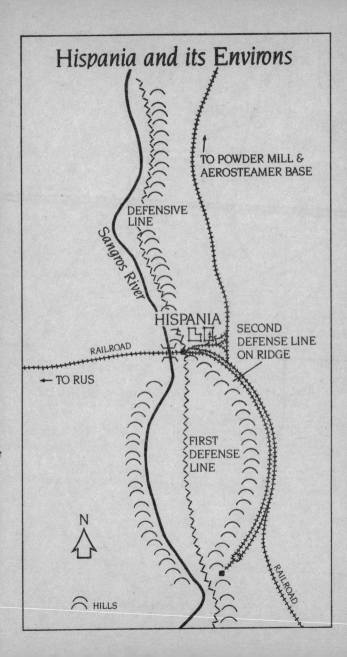

Hispania and its Environs

Sangros River

DEFENSIVE LINE

TO POWDER MILL &
AEROSTEAMER BASE

HISPANIA

SECOND
DEFENSE LINE
ON RIDGE

RAILROAD

← TO RUS

FIRST
DEFENSE
LINE

N

RAILROAD

⌒ HILLS

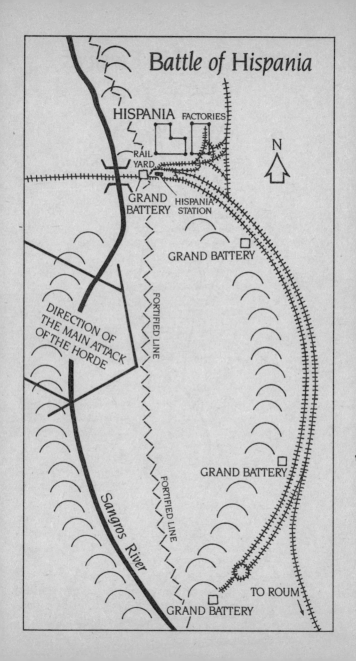

Chapter 1

He had lost a war.

Andrew Lawrence Keane, late of the Union Army of the Potomac and now commander of all human resistance against the Merki horde, could not drive that accusation out of his soul—he had lost a war.

He had known the sour taste of defeat before, the Army of the Potomac had become professionals at losing against the legions of Robert E. Lee. Yet always there had been the grim certainty in the rank and file that it had not been Lee who had really defeated them, but rather their own commanders.

He was now the commander.

He stood by the rail siding, mud-spattered, uniform reeking with the sodden smell of wet wool and stale sweat. It was raining, coming down in blinding sheets, as if the heavens were attempting to wash away the blood that had been lost in vain.

Half a corps, almost all of them veterans of the Tugar War, lost. Two other corps chewed up. Twenty thousand irreplaceable men gone. And that was another part of the difference from before. Before they could lose fifteen thousand at Fredericksburg, or twenty thousand at Chancellorsville, and within weeks the numbers were replaced, while Bobbie Lee's army slowly bled itself to death.

Now he was like Lee. The Merki horde was still numberless, upward of forty umens, four hundred thousand mounted warriors, and he with at best one-sixth that number. And Suzdal was gone, Novrod gone, the western half of Rus occupied—an entire nation going into exile down this one narrow ribbon of track.

Hans? He had fought so long to push that thought aside. The memory of Pat O'Donald describing the last minutes of Third Corps, Hans's guidon fluttering in the morning breeze, disappearing beneath the flashing swords of the Merki.

So, Hans, now what do I do? I've managed to save our people, evacuate an entire nation into exile—and for what?

A gust of wind swept down the track, driving a heavy spattering of hail before it. Lightning forked across the night sky, illuminating the tragedy. An endless column was slowly wending its way eastward, half a million people on the move, pushing on through the storm, seemingly oblivious to pain, to suffering.

"Grandma, when are we going home?"

He looked up. An old couple were walking past, half a dozen children in tow, their meager belongings piled high in a wheelbarrow, which seemed ready to break asunder from the weight. The child who had asked the question, shivering from the cold, was looking up at her grandmother.

The old woman smiled, making a hushing noise. Andrew's eyes locked with hers. He could sense a well of infinite sadness and suffering. Where were the children's parents? he wondered. Father in the army, alive, dead, God forbid a prisoner? He didn't dare ask. Guiltily he turned away.

They disappeared into the night, lost to view but not memory, part of an endless procession, replaced an instant later by another family, and another, a living stream flowing eastward, heading out into the open steppe toward Roum, and supposed safety.

"Engine's watered, sir—we're ready to move."

Andrew looked over at the young orderly, who

stood rigidly before him, canvas battle tunic plastered to his narrow chest, the bedraggled ribbon of lieutenant's rank drooping from his shoulders.

"Stop that old couple, the one with the six children," Andrew whispered, nodding over his shoulder. "Get them aboard the train."

"Sir, there isn't any room," the lieutenant said.

"Make room, dammit. Throw some of our baggage out, but make room," Andrew snapped.

"You can't save them all."

Andrew looked up to see Dr. Emil Weiss stepping down from the train.

The doctor held his hand up, in it a silver flask, uncorked.

Andrew took the drink and downed a scalding gulp without a nod of thanks.

"But bless you, Andrew, for at least trying," Emil said softly, taking the flask back and downing a gulp himself before recorking it.

Another sliver of lightning shot across the heavens, and for a brief instant he could see the column again, passing through the village, and pulled to one side an evacuation train carrying the last load of troops from Pat O'Donald's corps, now halted while a repair crew feverishly worked on repairing a cracked drive shaft. Through the sheets of rain he saw a tall, bulky form advancing, thick, muscular arms concealed by his black poncho. The man's red muttonchops and mustache were plastered down by the rain, dripping with moisture; his battered campaign hat hung limp, drooping down over his eyes. Cursing soundly as he sloshed through the mud, Pat O'Donald came up to the side of the train and wearily saluted.

"Do you have a bit of the cruel on you?" Pat asked.

A thin smile crossed Andrew's features.

"Didn't know you were on that train over there," Andrew said, extending his hand to Pat, who grasped it warmly.

"Almost didn't get on it," Pat replied, shaking his head as if clearing away the exhaustion that had become part of all their lives.

Emil handed over the flask reluctantly and watched with a sad face as Pat threw his head back and drained off most of the contents in several long gulps.

"Ah, now I know I'll live again," Pat said.

"Not if you keep drinking like that," Emil replied. "I didn't patch that hole in your stomach just for you to burn another one in."

Pat laughed gruffly, patting Emil on the shoulder.

"Come on, me friend, do you think that's what's really gonna kill me?"

"Don't talk like that," Andrew said quietly.

"Melancholia, my good colonel," Pat said, hoping to force a smile from Andrew.

Andrew did not reply.

"Andrew darlin', it certainly looks like a defeat to be certain, but no reason to be down about the mouth."

"Thanks for telling us," Emil replied.

"We might see worst even, but this war's like no other. It's no high-sounding words about glory and honor and quit when it goes against you."

He paused for a moment and sighed.

"I remember 'forty-eight, back in the old country. It looked like this, hundreds of thousands on the road, starving to death, trying to get to the boats to America.

"And we didn't know how to fight, that was our curse," he whispered.

Andrew looked over at him.

"Ah, but this one's different. It's either victory or death," Pat said sharply. "Nothing in between, only those two. And it be the same for them devils behind us. We'll most likely lose Kev when they come on, we'll be out on the steppe, chances be they'll drive us all the way to the Sangros and Hispania and take

Roum as well. But by God, I for one am gonna fight. Because there's no other way, and when I die some-one else will fight after me. We'll fight them beasties clear around this world, and come back up the other side still fighting them."

He took another pull off the flask, draining it dry, then nonchalantly tossed it back up to Emil, who looked at it glumly before pocketing it.

"You like this in a way, don't you, you damned mick?" Emil asked.

Pat looked up at him, squinting his eyes against the rain and the blinding flashes of lightning.

"Its what I live for," Pat replied, his voice slightly thick from exhaustion and the spreading effects of the vodka. "This morning my one corps held back at least three, maybe four, of their umens for an entire day in an open field fight. No fortifications this time—it was out in the open, a running fight all the way. And we still managed to get everybody out, even the wounded, thumbed our noses, waved our asses, and be damned to them. Keep me supplied with powder, shot, and canister and I'll keep killing them."

He paused for a moment.

"And besides, I hate these bastards. Killin' them goes easy on my soul. It makes it a lot easier that way. I could kill rebs, to be sure, especially them haughty officer types with their chivalry and honor and looking down their noses like a highborn noble. But they was people. I could still have a drink with them after it was over. I couldn't really hate 'em.

"Now these beasties are different. There's no alter-natives now, my good doctor. Its simple and straight-forward—we either defeat them or die."

Andrew nodded silently.

He knew it was all true. There was no honorable surrender in this war. It was unthinkable before, and more so now.

"Is it true the rumor we heard when we got in here?" Pat asked.

"About Jubadi?" Andrew replied.

"He's dead?"

" 'Assassinated' is more the term," Emil said grimly.

"Well, that ought to get the filthy buggers stirred," Pat replied, unsure of all the implications. "How'd it happen?"

Andrew briefly described Yuri's shooting of Jubadi with a Whitworth sniper rifle at a range of over a thousand yards.

Pat grinned with delight.

"I'd've given a month's pay to see it. Imagine it, over half a mile," and he shook his head. "Who'd've thought that Yuri would do it? I always suspected he was sent to kill you, Andrew darlin'."

Maybe it was a game within a game, Andrew found himself thinking. Tamuka was most likely behind it all. Had he, in fact, by turning Yuri, played out something that the Merki shield-bearer desired after all?

"God rest him, he gave us thirty days' time," Andrew said softly.

Pat nodded.

"We can play holy hell with them in thirty days. At the very least, get all of our civilians out to Roum, dig in at Kev, lay waste to everything between our lines all the way back to Vazima."

"You mean destroy our country even more?"

Andrew looked up to see Kal step out onto the train platform. The president of the Rus looked as haggard as the rest of them, his face drawn and tired, the stovepipe hat, which usually looked so comical on the short rotund Rus peasant, now slightly battered, as if it were a cast-off item picked up and saved by a servant.

"Exactly," Pat replied enthusiastically. "We've got enough captured horses to mount a regiment of scouts and raiders. Send them back up to make sure the destruction is complete. Detach a regiment or two to go into the woods to the north. Sneak out by night, get back by dawn. Make sure every well is poisoned, every scrap of food destroyed. Ambush, harass, do anything to slow them down. Leave them a desert."

"And if we ever come back?" Kal asked, his voice distant.

Pat snorted.

"Do you honestly believe we'll ever be back?"

"The land is us and we are the land," Kal said, his voice sharp. "If we're not fighting to win it back, then what are we fighting for?"

"To kill Merki," Pat replied, his voice sharp.

"Enough of this," Andrew said, looking over at Pat, who blustered for a moment and then, nodding, lowered his gaze from Kal's.

"We're fighting to win," Andrew said quietly. "To get our homes back, to give our children some kind of future. If we have to destroy our country in order to finally win, we'll do it, but by God I for one am sickened by it."

He turned away from his friends and looked off into the darkness.

He could understand what had stirred in Pat's soul, for in the darker moments of quiet reflection he knew that particular demon lurked inside himself as well. He had always strived for the dispassionate ideal of what he believed an officer of th Union Army should exemplify: a cool courage under fire, a stoic indifference to danger, a tight rein on the darker angel of destruction that lurked in every man's heart. Yet there had been moments when the destruction of war, the sheer all-consuming power of it all, had clutched at his soul, whispering its fire song of primal delight. He had, to his shame, felt such a moment at Fredericksburg, when the rebel city was in flames. He had stood watching with a perverse delight, yet horrified to truly admit that delight to himself. The city had burned through the night, and he had watched it with a dark joyful intensity.

It had happened again at Chancellorsville and at Spotsylvania, the musket volleys crescendoing through the forest, a near-apocalyptic moment, and, God forgive him, he had loved the pulsing energy within his soul, the way he imagined an opium smoker would exult as the pipe flared to life and the first acrid breath of dreams floated into his lungs. The waves of sound had beat over him like an ocean, the commingling of a hundred thousand voices, the thunder of machines of death, washing over him, beating their song of warrior madness into his soul while the red-rimmed sun hung in a sky of fire and smoke.

He suspected that those whom he had admired most in the army, men like Hancock, Kearny, and Chamberlain, had felt the same. Yet it was never spoken of—it was not the type of thing a gentleman, a Christian warrior, would admit, except in the darkness of night and to himself.

For a brief instant, now in the dark, the suffering invisible, he wondered what he would ever have done with his life if he had not known the raw passionate thrill of watching a battle line spread out across a mile of open field, advancing, bayonet tips gleaming, lit by starbursts of shells and wreathed in smoke, an entire army going into the fight, cheering hoarsely, dancing with death, and in the end defeating its dark embrace. At the doorway into that darkness, that was when he felt most alive.

Yet he hid these thoughts, never voicing them now, ashamed to admit just how little control he sometimes had. He suddenly felt his soul fill with a sick anguish for all his failings. The memory of the dream that had haunted him for so long flashed back—the field of corpses, his brother Johnnie rotting before his eyes into a skeletal specter of accusing death. He could not save Johnnie, he could not bring back any of the men of the 35th who had died under his command. Nor could he bring back all the Rus who had died since he had come to this world. How many, God forgive me, how many of them have I killed through my mistakes? he wondered. And there was a darker thought—how many more would die because of what he had unleashed with the killing of Jubadi?

He knew they were waiting for him, watching him as they always did when he became silent, lost in thought. Sighing, he looked back over his shoulder, eyes half closed against the cold sheets of rain cutting down from the black heavens.

Pat, sensing his rebuke, said nothing, but it was evident in his gaze that the unceasing fighting and above all else the fate of Hans had left an indelible mark upon his spirit.

Andrew looked at him. He had seen that all too often, an ageless look. Forty-year-olds and eighteen-year-olds looking with the gaze of old men. The same thing in Hawthorne, in a lot of the boys, especially the young ones who had come to manhood only knowing of war. They had become professional soldiers who could no longer even envision a world without war, the army, the terror, and also the moments of fierce exultation. And in Kal was the voice of the eternal peasant, working the same plot his grandsires across fifty generations had worked. He would never be the soldier. It was the ageless conflict between the warrior who did whatever was necessary to fight, and the peasant who watched his world being destroyed whenever the soldiers came. The land of Rus was the soul of the peasant; take him away from it and he starts to die. Since the collapse of the Potomac line, Kal, and all of his people, had been driven by the specter of fear, the enemy at the gates. It was that immediate concern which had driven them in the Herculean task of evacuating the people and the machines necessary to carry on the war.

Once escape had been effected, the true shock would start to settle in. It would be a problem he'd have to face. He had to get them out, and that he had achieved, especially now that the hordes were stopped by the death of Jubadi. He had thirty days before they would come on again. Now he had to fire the Rus with the will to continue the fight, even more fiercely than before, even though this first stage of the war had been a disastrous defeat.

Even more difficult, he now realized, would be to convince all of them that they could still win, and not only win but throw the Merki back and regain their homeland. If he could not do that, the next series of battles would be the final rout. If the Rus were driven back beyond Roum, their industrial bases would be truly lost once the end of the rail lines had been reached. Without factories, powder, shot, guns, the sinews of modern war, they were finished. If any Rus then survived, they would be condemned to be like the Wanderers, forever fleeing just ahead of the remorseless advance of the hordes.

It would take weeks to get the factories, now packed aboard hundreds of boxcars rolling east, back to within even three-quarters of their operational level. The depletion of ammunition from the lost campaign would have to be made good. Arms, accouterments, and supplies would have to be marshaled for the two corps training under Hawthorne. Time would have to be bought. Delay, and yet more delay. Each day to try to make themselves stronger, and the Merki ever so slightly weaker. He needed time. It seemed as if that was always the issue. The sacrifice of the 35th Maine at Gettysburg to buy First Corps fifteen minutes to pull out from Seminary Ridge, the delaying actions against the Tugars, the failed campaign on the Potomac—they were always trading precious men, and precious supplies, for the hope of getting a little more time.

"At least we still hold Kev, one small corner of Rus, to start back from," Emil said, breaking the momentary silence with a hopeful comment directed toward Kal.

"We will hold it?" Kal asked, looking down almost imploringly at Andrew.

"We'll try," Andrew said, but his uncertainty was evident. At the moment he just didn't have the strength to tell Kal the grim realization that had sunk in over the last several days. Even with thirty days of time, the numbers in the end would just not add up. The front at Kev was simply too wide to prevent a breakthrough identical to the one on the Potomac line. Kev would wind up being a delaying action and nothing more.

Kal, illuminated for a brief instant by a flash of lightning, looked down at Andrew, as if hoping to hear more. Andrew looked up at him in silence, as if imploring him not to force out yet another admission, at least not now.

The intensity of the storm seemed to rise to another crescendo, with gusts of icy wind driving the rain out nearly horizontal to the ground.

"Goddammit, Andrew," Emil finally growled, breaking the silence, "I didn't save you from typhoid just to have you die now from pneumonia. For heaven's sake get into this car so we can get moving."

"We'd best get moving," Kal said, and forcing a sad smile, he nodded to Andrew and went back inside.

Andrew looked over at Pat.

"It'll be all the way to the Sangros, to the gates of Roum, and most likely beyond," Pat said, his voice sharp and cold.

"Most likely," Andrew said.

"A splendid little war we've got here," Pat said. "One for the history books to be sure."

"Care to ride out with us?" Andrew asked, not able to respond to the bluntness of Pat's remarks.

"My staff's on the other train, and besides I want to ride out of here with my own boys. I'll see you at headquarters in Kev come morning."

Pat drew up to salute, but Andrew stopped him, reaching out to grasp his hand.

"You did well today, Pat. The way you handled the rear guard saved all of us. It was masterful, like Pap Thomas at Chickamauga."

Pat for once did not react to a compliment in his usual way. He looked straight into Andrew's eyes, his gaze serious.

"You know, Andrew, before, back in the beginning, it was mostly a game. You did the thinking, I did the fighting. Hard-drinking, head-bashing mick."

His voice dropped.

"Now, I mean with Hans gone . . ." He hesitated, fumbling for words. "It's just I want you to know, whatever you need done, I'm there for you, Andrew Lawrence Keane. Whatever it takes, I'm there for you, God bless ya, whatever you need."

Andrew, surprised, hesitated, unable to let go of Pat's hand. He squeezed it fiercely, wordlessly nodding his thanks. Pat stepped back, saluted, and then disappeared into the driving storm.

"Well, I'll be damned," Emil said. "At the age of forty he's finally grown up."

Andrew nodded, allowing a smile to trace his features.

"A Sherman for your Grant," Emil continued.

"We called Grant a butcher," Andrew said, looking over at Emil.

Emil said nothing, sensing a rebuke.

Andrew looked back down the siding. Another form was visible beside the orderly who had stood in the distance, discreetly out of hearing yet close enough to respond if wanted. Kathleen stepped away from the orderly and came up to join him.

"Just what the hell are you doing out here in this?" Andrew asked, slightly exasperated. He had to go around in this driving storm, but he wasn't amused that his wife would choose to do so as well.

"Trying to sort out those who will die if we don't get them on board this train," she replied, while reaching up to take off his glasses and then vainly attempting to dry them on the hem of her soaked dress. "I put that old couple and their six grandchildren in our berth. We've got a dozen more in our car—your staff agreed to stand for the rest of the trip."

He wanted to protest—the boys of his staff needed to get some rest—but he could imagine the rain-drenched refugees now huddling in his command car. He'd sooner walk himself than ask them to leave.

"That's why I love you," he finally said, leaning over to kiss her on the forehead while she put his thoroughly smeared glasses back on.

Extending his hand, he helped her to board the back of the train, and Emil reached down to steady him as he followed her up the slippery steps.

"Get this train moving," Emil shouted, leaning over the side of the back platform.

The brakeman, who had stood back with the orderly, unhooded his smoking lantern, held it aloft, and waved it back and forth as he ran up forward toward the engine. Seconds later the high shriek of the whistle sounded, drowned out momentarily by a rolling peal of thunder.

The train lurched beneath Andrew's feet. Slowly gaining speed, it edged through the station. On the neighboring track, Pat's train stood out, highlighted by sputtering torches and the crackling flashes of lightning, the open flatcars crowded with troops, even the tops of the boxcars covered with rain-soaked men. It was a dismal sight, made even more pathetic by the even less fortunate refugees who were strung out along the track, many of them still moving eastward through the night.

"The only thing half so melancholy as a battle lost is a battle won," Emil said.

"Wellington, if I remember my history," Andrew replied.

Emil nodded.

"Wellington never saw anything like this, though," Emil replied.

"Wellington never lost as badly as we have," Andrew said, "not even in Spain."

"Well, you got us the time we need," Emil said, trying to sound cheerful.

"At what price?" Andrew whispered.

"You mean Yuri, poor soul," Emil replied. "He was a dead man the moment the Mekri first made him a pet twenty years ago. You gave him a chance for an honorable end, and he embraced it. Don't blame yourself for his sacrifice."

"It's not his sacrifice that'll haunt me, good doctor," Andrew replied, his voice stiff and distant.

"Then what is it?" Emil asked, drawing closer, sensing a darkness that was a torture burning within his friend's soul.

"The Merki pets," Andrew replied after a long moment of anguished silence. "The Cartha prisoners, all those like Yuri who traveled with the horde."

"What about them?"

"A hundred thousand or more at the least, along with maybe another fifty thousand Cartha prisoners who are still alive," Andrew said, looking straight back to the west as if he could almost see them.

Emil waited, afraid to ask.

"When they bury Jubadi, every last one of them will be sacrificed. Yuri told me that was the custom. I brought us thirty days of time, and one hundred and fifty thousand people will die because of what I just did."

"Does Hamilcar know?" Emil asked.

"He soon will," Andrew replied.

"God help him."

"God help him," Andrew whispered, "and God forgive me, because I doubt if anyone else will."

Kathleen, trembling with emotion, put her arms around Andrew, wishing she could think of a soothing answer, knowing that reminding him that the prisoners were doomed anyhow would not be enough. She buried her head against his empty sleeve and for the first time in years began to cry.

Andrew, barely aware of her presence, watched as the station gradually disappeared into the darkness of the storm.

"My friend, it is late."

Hulagar did not move at the touch of Tamuka's hand upon his shoulder.

"You don't need to be here for this," Tamuka said.

Hulagar did not reply.

Tamuka, shield-bearer of the Qar Qarth Vuka du Jubadi, moved to Hulagar's side and knelt down. All was silent outside, except for the rhythmic beating of the great drums, timed to the tempo of a beating heart, which would roll continuously until, at the end of thirty days, Jubadi was at last sent upon his journey to the everlasting heavens. Tonight, the first of the thirty days, was the night of silent mourning, the great quiet, for this was the night when the ancestors floated through the camps, drawn by the silence. There had been no farewell chant to the evening sun, no songs of the name singers, no boasting tales rising upon the coils of ten thousand camp fires. This was the night the ancestors stirred, noticing the silence, and thus came to gather about the yurt of Jubadi Qar Qarth.

The vast golden yurt was dark, except for a single

lamp hanging in the center of the tent, its flicker of flame casting a pale light upon the naked body of Jubadi, once Qar Qarth of the Merki horde.

All fires in all the camp circles of the horde had been extinguished, except for the single lamp of mourning. From its thin tapering flame the pyre would be ignited, and the smoke of that conflagration would carry upon it the soul of Jubadi. And when that fire had at last consumed the mortal remains of Jubadi, only then would the new Qar Qarth distribute the power of fire back to his people. From that funeral pyre all fires would be lit, and they would burn until in his time Vuka Qar Qarth rode the pillar of smoke to the heavens.

Tamuka looked over at his old friend, his guide, his first teacher of the ways of the shield-bearer. There was no need to ask—he could look into this one's soul and know. Hulagar sat in silent torment, though there was not one among all the horde who would ever blame him. Yet Hulagar would torture himself nevertheless, and Tamuka could understand. For was not a shield-bearer, before all else, what his title of rank implied? Was he not protector to the Qar Qarth, carrier of the bronze shield, ever ready to place himself between his Qar Qarth and the dangers of this world? And now Jubadi was dead, and his shield-bearer had lived beyond him.

As if sensing the probing of thoughts, Hulagar looked over at him.

I should have realized it all, Hulagar's thoughts whispered back.

"You could not have realized," Tamuka replied. "The silent ones had swept the area. We did not know a weapon capable of striking from such a great distance existed."

Hulagar stirred, shifting at last after the long night of kneeling motionless before the body of his Qarth, his friend.

"But I sensed it," he said, "and you sensed it as well."

There was the hint of accusation in his voice.

"What do you mean?" Tamuka asked.

"It was your pet that was found with the weapon. The one you claim was sent to kill the Yankee leader Keane. And instead he comes back to strike down the light of our peoples. What is it that you do know, Tamuka Shield-Bearer?"

"You are overwrought, my friend," Tamuka said, his voice conveying anguish for his friend's pain, ignoring the implications of what had finally been said.

"There will be many to question you in the days to come," Hulagar said, and he shifted, still on his knees, turning to face Tamuka. He gazed into Tamuka's eyes, searching, looking for answers, and yet not wishing to know if what he suspected was true.

"Tell me," Hulagar whispered, and he rested his hands on Tamuka's shoulders, gently holding him in a fatherly fashion and looking straight into his eyes.

Tamuka returned his gaze unblinking.

"There is nothing to tell," Tamuka said. "Jubadi knew of my plan, as did you. The pet Yuri was sent to kill Keane. Keane with some devil power turned him back upon us. The evil spirits that guide and protect Keane are stronger even than the powers of our ancestors to protect us. It is an ill omen. Their power has taken our Qar Qarth from us," and he nodded toward the cold form upon the dais.

Hulagar looked away from Tamuka, gazing upon Jubadi, and his eyes clouded.

"Forgive me, my friend," Hulagar sighed, and then he looked back upon Tamuka. "And forgive me for questioning you. I had to know."

"There is nothing to forgive," Tamuka replied, his voice filled with warmth and understanding.

Hulagar let his hands drop and lowered his gaze, not noticing the momentary shift in Tamuka's expression.

"It was evil spirits, as you say."

Tamuka looked over his shoulder. Sarg, shaman of the Qar Qarth, reader of the signs, stood in the entryway to the yurt, dimly silhouetted by the approaching dawn.

"Is it already time?" Hulagar asked.

Tamuka nodded, feeling a genuine flicker of pain at the anguish in Hulagar's voice.

"The light grows," Sarg replied, and as he spoke, those who accompanied him drew back the flaps of the yurt to reveal the acolytes and the guards, who stood as they had remained through the long night. Beyond them he could see the dim outline of the city of cattle against the deep purple of the western sky, the Great Wheel of stars beyond hanging low in the heavens.

"Just a brief moment more," Hulagar sighed, and Sarg nodded.

The joints of his knees cracking, Hulagar came to his feet. Attempting to force a smile, he ascended the dais and stood before the body, looking down upon the still features. The smile flickered, and Tamuka could again sense the thoughts—the memory of two youths, riding across the steppe, laughter echoing, the joy of childhood in all its exuberance, unmindful of so much to come, uncomprehending that all such moments last but for a moment.

He reached out, brushing back the mane of hair, tinged with the first streaks of gray which would now never go to white.

"Sword in hand he died, as did his sire, and his grandsire before him," Sarg intoned. "No one of us may ask for a better death."

"Death from an unseen hand, a cattle hand, not matching blade against blade in the joy of battle, was not a good death," Hulagar replied, and Sarg fell silent.

How it has all changed, Tamuka thought to himself.

How those beasts have taken that from us, for there is no honor, no proving, in such fighting, such dying. That is why they must all die, that is the ultimate truth that Jubadi would not face. Every last cattle upon the entire world must die if we are to live. Before the cattle had even risen up in their defiance, already we had become their slaves, bound to them, to what they created, to the very meat they gave us. If we are to survive we must eliminate them all, and that is why Jubadi died, had to die, for he in the end wished to fight them in but half measures.

Yet those thoughts were gone from him as he watched Hulagar, who stood above the body of his fallen friend. This was the last moment of their being alone, the shield-bearer keeping the first silent vigil before the corpse preparers started their long ritual. Never again on this world would the two be alone, as they had been so many times across the two and a half circlings of their journey together.

Sarg interrupted with a low cough, and Tamuka looked over at him. It was getting brighter out; the first step had to be completed before the breaking of dawn. He came to his feet and with lowered head and averted gaze stepped up onto the dais.

"It is time, my friend."

Hulagar nodded.

"You know, you don't have to be here for the beginning."

"I was just remembering the night we were lost in the storm. How I dug the cave in the snow, killed my own horse, my first mount, and pulled its body over the entrance to give us warmth."

Hulagar looked over at Tamuka.

"You know in repayment he gave me a thousand horses, on the day he became Qar Qarth."

"I know."

"I loved that foolish horse, yet I did not hesitate."

He paused and looked over at Tamuka. "Would you do the same for Vuka?"

Tamuka did not reply.

Hulagar hesitated a moment. "You will be shield-bearer to the Qar Qarth. You must love him as I loved him."

Tamuka was silent.

Hulagar looked back at Jubadi. "No, I'll stay," Hulagar sighed. "I never left him before, and I will not now."

Tamuka looked over at Sarg and nodded.

The shaman came forward, the dozen acolytes behind him. Intoning the first chant of the long passage of the journeying soul, he stepped up beside Jubadi and started the reciting of the lineage, the two hundred and seven names of the Qar Qarths, starting with Grish, who first led his people out of the mountains of Nom Barkth and started the great never-ending ride about the world of Valdennia. The names rattled forth, Hulagar's lips moving in silent unison, and as the shaman spoke, the silent ones, the tongueless guardians of the Qar Qarth and the sacred treasures of the Merki horde, filed into the tent, bearing a golden ark, which rested upon the shoulders of a dozen warriors.

Fascinated, Tamuka watched as the guards placed the ark at the foot of the dais and with heads bowed withdrew. As Sarg reached the last naming of the lineage, two assistants came forward with a golden cloth. He held his arms out, and they draped it across his hands. Turning away from Jubadi, he stepped down from the dais, and with hands covered by the sacred cloth he unlatched the ark and opened it. All lowered their gaze. Tamuka, with head bowed, watched with a sidelong gaze as Sarg reached into the ark and drew out a silver urn, which rested heavy in his trembling hands.

Turning, Sarg again mounted the dais, holding the

heavy weight of the urn forward, his arms knotted with the strain, and placed it beside the body of the Qar Qarth.

Grasping the top of the urn, he ever so slowly lifted the lid, and a faint sickly-sweet smell wafted out. All were silent.

Sarg held his hands out again, and the two acolytes stepped up, removing the golden cloth from his hands. Another assistant came forward bearing a silver case, which he laid beside the urn. Sarg reached down, opened the case, and drew forth a blunt trowel-shaped dagger, its heavy blade and razor-sharp edge glinting in the light of early dawn. The shaman lifted his gaze heavenward, and there was an expectant hush.

A young shaman stepped forward, hand raised, but Hulagar stopped him, nodding for him to withdraw, and leaning forward, he extended his own hand to cover the unseeing eyes of Jubadi so that his soul would not see.

Sarg watched him and then nodded his approval.

He held the dagger up and grasped its hilt with both hands. With a lightninglike strike the dagger plunged down, slamming into Jubadi's chest. The blade entered next to his sternum, cutting in alongside the puckered bullet hole in Jubadi's chest, the place where the bullet had stolen out of his body, taking his life with it.

Sarg turned the blade sharply, and Tamuka winced as the Qar Qarth's ribs cracked open. Sarg twisted the blade again, slicing a circle around the heart, and seconds later he turned the blade yet again, scooping it down deep into Jubadi's body and drawing the heart out.

Fascinated, Tamuka watched as the heart emerged from the body. It was shattered, pierced by a hole bigger than his thumb. A thin trickle of blackening blood oozed out of the bullet hole and the severed aorta as Sarg drew it out, cupping it in his hands.

He held the bloody offering up, holding it aloft, the already decaying blood running down his wrists, staining his golden robes.

"Go now, oh heart of our Qar Qarth Jubadi, go now to join the heart of thy sire and his sires before him. Go now to rest in the ashes of what they were."

Lowering his hands, he put Jubadi's heart into the urn, a thin plume of dust rising up out of the receptacle, coating his hands. The dust of two hundred hearts, of all the Qar Qarths who had ever ridden, was now enriched by yet one more.

An acolyte now handed a silver cup to Sarg, and he scooped the cup into the open hole in Jubadi's chest and brought it out, full of the black blood of the Qar Qarth. He raised the cup to his lips and partook of its contents, then held the cup over the urn and let the dregs pour into the urn.

"Go now, oh blood of our Qar Qarth Jubadi, go now to join the blood of your sires. For as their blood coursed through your veins in life, now shall your blood mingle with theirs in death."

Dipping the cup into the chest, he drew it back out again, filled to the brim with dark congealing blood. An acolyte stepped forward, took the cup with hands wrapped in a golden cloth, and stepped back into the shadows.

Another acolyte wrapped Sarg's hands in a fresh cloth of gold. Sarg replaced the lid of the urn and resealed it. Reverently he picked the urn up and held it above Jubadi. Hulagar, who had stood motionless throughout, removed his hand from Jubadi's eyes.

"Soul of the *ka* of Jubadi Qar Qarth, see now that your heart shall always be with thy people. See now that your heart shall ride with us forever. Soul of the *ka* of Jubadi, now prepare thyself for thy journey."

Lowering the urn, Sarg bowed to the body, then stepped down from the dais and put the urn back into the ark, pulling the lid shut behind it.

Tamuka looked over at Hulagar.

"We should go now," he whispered.

Hulagar nodded and then went down, kissing Jubadi on the forehead.

"I will join you at the end of the thirty days, my friend," Hulagar whispered, "and then we shall ride together one more time."

Tamuka, placing his hand upon Hulagar's shoulder, led him out of the yurt, following Sarg, while behind them the corpse washers started upon the thirty-day ritual of preparing the body of Jubadi. The ten thousand incantations of the sacred journey would be tattooed upon his shaved body, once the washers were done with their preserving baths, which would prevent the body from corrupting. On the night of the twenty-ninth day, Jubadi would again be dressed in the ceremonial armor of his rank for the final ride.

As they stepped out of the yurt, Tamuka looked eastward. The first sliver of the morning sun cut the far horizon, reflecting off the lake which stretched out beyond the dam above Suzdal. Vuka stood there, surrounded by his guards. Sarg turned to the acolyte who had followed him and took the golden cup, then approached Vuka. The new Qar Qarth hesitated.

"Kneel," Sarg commanded, "kneel in the presence of the blood."

The companies of the silent ones, as if guided by a single hand, prostrated themselves upon the ground, while far out across the plains beyond the city of Suzdal, by the tens of thousand, the Merki warriors who had gathered about the yurt during the night went down upon the ground. To Tamuka it looked as if a vast open plain of high summer grass had, in an instant, been flattened by an unfelt wind, the only sound the rustling of their armor and the clattering of their weapons as they dropped upon their faces, arms placed over their heads.

Vuka went down slowly to his knees, and Tamuka

stepped past Sarg to kneel by the new Qar Qarth's side.

"Thus from father to son, across the endless generations of the Merki," Sarg announced, his thin reedy voice drifting high in the morning air.

Sarg nodded to one of his acolytes, who stepped forward with drawn blade. Vuka hesitantly extended his right arm, tunic sleeve rolled up to reveal the knotted muscles and matted hair. He watched the blade, nervously licking his lips, unable to control the flinch as the dagger flashed down, striking across his forearm. Fresh blood welled out. Sarg bent over, holding the cup underneath the wound, allowing the blood of the son to mingle with that of the father. The shaman nodded his approval, and Vuka let his arm drop, wincing at the flood of pain.

Sarg held the cup before Vuka. The young Qar Qarth slowly leaned forward and sipped of its contents, choking on the curdled blood and his own fresh blood as it went down his throat. Sarg next turned to Tamuka.

"Protector of the Qar Qarth, possessor of the hidden spirit of the *tu,* drink now of the *ka* of the warrior Qar Qarths."

Tamuka leaned forward, drinking in turn.

"You are bound to him as brother, as guard, as guide," Sarg said, and there was a cold emphasis on the words "guard" and "guide."

Sarg now turned back to Vuka, held the cup on high, and inverted it over Vuka's head, the blood running down across his face. Then, turning in a tight circle, he flicked the remaining drops out to the four winds.

"You are now Qar Qarth in name," Sarg announced, "and when mourning is done you shall be Qar Qarth in deed. When the war is completed you shall be Qar Qarth by law."

Vuka came to his feet and looked at Sarg, as if

unsure. The old shaman nodded and turned away. Vuka lowered his gaze to Tamuka and extended the arm still dripping blood from the ceremonial wound. Tamuka reached into his kit bag and drew out a simple unadorned silk cloth, the same as all warriors carried for the dressing of wounds. The cloth was frayed and stained. Vuka looked at it and drew back slightly.

"Should not the cloth be of gold?" Vuka asked.

"At Orki your father's ceremonial wound was dressed by Hulagar with a torn banner," Tamuka replied softly. "I thought it fitting that you should be dressed as well with a strip of your father's battle standard, since you are Qar Qarth now in time of war."

Vuka looked over at Hulagar for confirmation. The old shield-bearer nodded his approval.

"Then dress my wound," Vuka said coldly.

Tamuka took a strip of the cloth, cut it into a pad, pressed it into the wound, and then bound it tightly in place. As he dressed the wound he looked straight into Vuka's eyes. The Qar Qarth held his gaze, his suspicion evident. Finished, Tamuka remained kneeling until Vuka finally nodded, after a long pause, for his shield-bearer to arise. Tamuka stood up.

He looked over at Hulagar, who, besides Sarg, was the only one of all the Merki to remain standing throughout. Across the open fields around the city of Suzdal, Merki warriors by the tens of thousands remained prostrated. A smile flickered across Vuka's features, and he nodded to a trumpeter of the silent ones. The warrior arose, and lifting up a great narga, he sounded the long call. As if rising up out of the ground, the umens of warriors came to their feet, the fields echoing with the rattling of their armor and accouterments. On out across the fields they rose, they stood, on up to the river road. Like a vast ripple of life the Merki came to their feet up across the long miles of the road, to the Ford, across the Neiper, down along the tracks back to where battle had first been joined, and on into the steppes, where by the hundreds of the thousands the long lines of yurts waited to make their slow passage through the forest and into the land of the Rus.

There was no sound, though, other than the rustling of the weapons of war. An eerie silence prevailed. All speech was forbidden during the days of mourning, except for those commands and conversations that were essential for survival, and for war.

Vuka looked out across the multitude that he now commanded, a wolflike grin lit his features. Unsheathing his sword, he held it aloft. Scores of thousands of scimitars flashed upward in reply, catching the blood-red sun of dawn, reflecting the ruby light, rippling and shimmering as if the earth had become steel and hardened blood.

Still holding his blade aloft, Vuka went to his mount and swung up into the saddle. Kicking the stallion into a gallop, he raced down the hill, away from the funeral tent of his father, his guards racing to follow him.

Hulagar came up to Tamuka's side.

"His father did not receive a salute until the smoke of his sire's pyre had ascended to the heavens," Tamuka said coldly.

"You will have to teach him better," Hulagar replied.

"You had better to work with," Tamuka said, his voice sad.

"The blood is the blood, and we are bound to serve it."

"Let us hope the blood improves by the time we ride to war again," Tamuka replied.

Hulagar looked over at him, sensing a riddle.

Tamuka, not giving him time to ask, swung up onto his mount, and reining it about, cantered away from the death yurt.

Though it was the time of mourning, still the usual

routines of living had to be followed—horses groomed and let out to graze; weapons attended to, especially after the soaking storm that had swept through in the middle of the night; rations eaten, though cold with the extinguishing of the horde fires.

Alone, Tamuka made his way down through the encampment of the guards, the silent ones. To his left was the great city of the Rus, Suzdal, as silent and empty as the camps.

Accursed place, he thought coldly, pausing for a moment to gaze upon its spires, wooden domes, and towering log structures. He let his gaze drop to the fortification lines surrounding the city. The outer line of high earthen ramparts were dotted with Merki warriors, some on guard, others, curious, walking along the walls or gingerly moving through the open field of pitfalls, hidden traps, and brush entanglements.

Costly, but we could have taken it, Tamuka thought, studying the layout of the works, his mind already working along the lines of logic that the new weapons had created. Forward bastions to provide flanking fire along the walls, each bastion an individual fortress to hold even if there was a breakthrough.

We'll need plans drawn, he realized. If they did this here, they undoubtedly are doing the same thing elsewhere, wherever it is that they finally decide to turn and make their stand. They'll follow the same pattern yet again, and this therefore is worth studying.

Except for along the iron rails, mobility is their weakest point, he mused, pausing to look at the line of track coming out of the city. An open battle will be death the moment their flank has been turned, or a breakthrough effected. We have to catch them outside of their earthen forts, in the open, flanks exposed, and then it will be their finish. Or else we must pin them to a front and smash through the center.

The fact that he was thinking with his *ka*, the warrior spirit, troubled him not at all. The last Qar Qarth had taken war as his domain, and Hulagar did not trouble himself with its nuances and subtleties, other than for his direct concern of protecting his Qar Qarth. Was Vuka even aware of all that a study of these forts might reveal? He gave a snort of disdain. The fool was most likely in his yurt, drinking and lying with the concubine of the moment, brazenly ignoring even the most basic of strictures of mourning.

Tamuka spat disdainfully, and turning away from the city, he continued on across the field. Knots of warriors rose as he passed by, whispering at the sight of the shield-bearer, no longer of the heir, but of the Qar Qarth. He silently nodded his salute, then spurred his mount into a lopping gallop.

Crossing the fields where, unknown to him, regiments of the new army of Rus had learned their drill under Union taskmasters, he edged his way back up across a sloping hill studded with towering pines, which filled the air with their bracing scent. The sights, the smells, were so alien to him, so disquieting. Where was the open steppe, where the undulating hills, the vast open stretches, the ever-arching sky above?

As he crested the slope, half a dozen great mounds were before him, the grass rich, growing high, the tops of the mounds surmounted with tattered banners that fluttered forlornly in the early-morning breeze. It was a cold place; even the sunlight seemed pale, a place of death. He reined in hard, his horse fighting against the bit, rearing slightly.

He started to turn away from this place, and then he saw him, sitting alone against the slope of one of the mounds, which was already starting to be covered with a sprinkling of young saplings.

He nudged his horse forward. The Tugar looked up at his approach and with a nod of his head beckoned for him to dismount and sit by his side.

Tamuka swung down from his mount and approached. The look on his newfound companion's face filled him with a dark emptiness, a vastness of pain, which for an instant washed away the contempt that he usually held for the Qar Qarth of a dead race.

"You mourn your Qar Qarth," Muzta said, his voice touched with irony, "and the Qar Qarth of the Tugars sits alone mourning his people."

Tamuka looked about at the great mounds, each more than twice his height and fifty or more paces across. Through the high blades of grass and the chest-high saplings he saw shards of white, bones rising up out of the earth, here a leg, bleached ribs, bits of metal, a rusted sword, a rotting lance, the half-covered face of a grinning skull.

"All our vanities, all our pride," Muzta sighed, his gaze fixed as if on some unseen place. "Here rest all my umens, the final blood of all our ancestors. Here sits their Qar Qarth, cursed to outlive them."

He paused.

"Cursed to be the lackey of the Merki."

There was no rancor in his voice, only the straightforward admission of fact.

And he is nothing but our lackey, Tamuka thought with contempt. Reduced to sitting at our tables. Jubadi, perhaps out of some strange affection for an old foe, had acknowledged him in a way as an equal. Vuka would not be so generous.

Yet even in his contempt the bonds of race still held.

"Can you not hate them for what they have done to you, to us?" Tamuka asked, nodding back across the fields to the city, as if in those empty streets the hated foe still lingered. "Can you not see that all of them, all of them across this entire world, should die, if we are to live?"

"The cattle?" Muzta said, laughing softly and shaking his head. "They, I fear, will outlive us all. We brought them here, through the gates that our sires created when once we walked between the stars. We gave them the lands, encouraged them to breed, fed off them, allowed them to become the creators of all that we own, our weapons, our adornments, our yurts, the very sustenance of our bellies. Kill them? Kill ourselves is what you are saying."

"Are you of the blood?" Tamuka snarled. "Eighteen of your proudest umens rest here," and he pointed to the ground.

Muzta nodded, looking about at the mounds.

"You need not tell me what rests here, Merki."

"And what do you wish done?"

"I plan to survive, to have what is left of my people survive," Muzta said quietly as if finally revealing a hidden truth.

So we're all playing riddles, Tamuka thought with an inner smile, I to Hulagar and Vuka, Muzta to me, speaking the truth and yet the others not even realizing it.

"How do you plan this survival, Muzta Qar Qarth?"

The Tugar smiled innocently and with creaking joints came to his feet. He gave a low whistle. From behind one of the mounds his horse appeared, nickering a response and trotting toward its master like a loyal dog.

"Let's ride from this place," Muzta said, his tone almost that of command.

The two mounted and trotted away from the barrows without a backward glance, heading north, down the slope. Reaching the rail line that led to the factories at the base of the Vina Dam, they turned onto the track, following it as it cut across the side of the hill, dropping down into a hollow filled with sweet-scented pines and then back up again. As they rode, Muzta fell into a reminiscence of his first seeing one of the Yankee trains on this track, racing back into the city, pursued by his riders, one of whom attempted to joust with the machine and lost. Around a gentle curve through a scattering of trees, they dropped back down the slope and into the vast clearing below the dam.

The sides of the hill were still scarred from when the dam had burst years before, scoured clean straight down to the bedrock. Muzta paused for a moment, looking at the bare rock, understanding how it was thus carved. His heart felt like ice, remembering the sound of the advancing wave as it crashed into the city. The cries of exultation had been drowned in an instant, his army disappearing into the swirling night. He remembered, and closed his eyes and then rode on.

The vale below the dam was littered with the waste and wreckage of industry. Slag heaps of cinder, which filled the air with a faint metallic and sulfurous smell, were piled high. The grass grew in ragged tufts, sticking up between twisted hunks of cast-off metal, the blades gray with cinder dust. The long brick buildings of the foundries, casting shops, forges, powder mills, rail sheds, engine sheds, and shot works were all empty now, yet in his mind's eye Tamuka could imagine the bustle, the clearing reverberating with metallic clanging, the thousands of cattle voices, the smoke, the stench of their labors and sweat.

This is the future of their world, if we allow it, Tamuka thought. Valleys of smoke and stench, fiery plumes of dust soaring to the everlasting heavens, the shrieking and whirling of their engines, the clanging of their hammers and forges reverberating about the world—the sound of hooves, of the horde on its endless ride, becoming still, until it would be merely the whisper of a remembered breeze.

"By our ancestors," Muzta sighed, "what use is martial valor against these engines?"

Tamuka did not reply, not willing to admit his agreement.

He edged his mount off the rail bed, cutting across

the several hundred yards of clearing which was crossed with nearly a score of parallel tracks. His horse shied toward an engine water tank, which was dripping with moisture, the ground beneath it puddled. He let the horse wander over, easing his reins as it lowered its head to drink, Muzta's mount joining him. Atop the tower a windmill creaked with the gently freshening breeze, the pump arm rising and falling, groaning softly. He knew that such a device drew water out of the ground, but how it worked—that was a mystery.

On the next track rested half a dozen axles, the iron wheels black with soot, the track scorched, the ashes about it still smoldering. What had they burned? One of the train wagons, most likely. Unable to move it, they wouldn't even leave that, though it was useless without the machines to make it move.

A low rumbling boom echoed down from the west. He turned in his saddle. For a moment, above the line of hills he saw a trace of fire dropping down, a shell from one of their iron ships. It disappeared. Then there came another boom, another shell dropping down, this one bursting silently in the sky, seconds later its report rolling past.

"You cannot use fire?" Muzta asked.

"It is our way in the mourning," Tamuka replied, "except if survival is at stake, either from freezing or direct attack."

"Foolish."

"To shoot back at the ships is useless anyway. They are too heavily armored."

Muzta did not reply, still looking westward to see if the shelling from the river would continue.

"You should press in, stop for nothing. Give them their thirty days and it gives them time to restart the machines that once rested here."

"I know that," Tamuka said coldly. "Nevertheless, it is the way."

"And yet at Orki, even with the death of Jubadi's father you still fought."

"Because he still rode with us until the fight was done. The cattle are not here," and he pointed vaguely toward the east, "they continue to run away. If this field were still in dispute, Jubadi even now would ride."

"As did my father," Muzta replied. "We tied him to his horse, a sword blade strapped to his back to keep him erect, Qubata holding the reins and I at his side. Even as he corrupted we fought until you were defeated, and then we mourned."

Muzta tried to force the thought away, remembering his father tumbling from the saddle, yet even in death a thin smile on his features. There had been no time for final words. Only that enigmatic smile, the arrow in his chest quivering and then becoming still.

While the battle still raged, Qubata had drawn the heart out, squeezing the blood of it over the head of the new Qar Qarth. Remounting, he had pressed back into the fight, slaying even as he wept. They had tied the body to the saddle, as did the Merki for their Qar Qarth, on that same day and for two days afterward, until at last, on the third morning, the decaying body was cut loose and allowed to rest, the great battle of Orki finished.

"Sarg, Hulagar, and Vuka declared the mourning to be observed starting now, since the enemy was not upon the field before us," Tamuka said.

"And you would have done differently?"

"You know the answer to that," Tamuka snarled.

Muzta nodded.

"Did you kill Jubadi?" Muzta asked, looking straight at Tamuka.

The shield-bearer, startled, looked into Muzta's eyes.

"Tugar, you are mad even to think such thoughts,"

Tamuka said, his words drawn out as if he chose each one with care.

Muzta merely smiled and nudged his mount forward, going up over the tracks and heading for the abandoned foundry. Tamuka hesitated and with a rake of spurs followed after Muzta, coming up along-side of him.

"It's just that the cattle was your cattle. I am told that the spirit ways of the shield-bearer can, at times, direct the minds of others. It could have been a most clever plan within a plan."

He looked straight at Tamuka, who returned his gaze without a hint of emotion and said nothing.

They entered the foundry through its open cavern-ous doors, the hooves of Tamuka's horse striking sparks on the rails that went straight into the building. The building was dark, cool, a vast open shed that could have stabled the horses of an entire regiment of a thousand. The dirt floor was bare, except for the great stone foundations of the machines, the stone hearths now cold. A wooden drive shaft no longer connected to the bellows it once powered turned slowly in the air, rising and falling, driven by the thin trickle of water that continued to turn one of the wheels out-side the building, the wheel slowly creaking, groaning, its thin sound filling the vast space like the whisper of a voice, a reminder of what had once been a thunder-ing cacophony.

Tamuka looked about, filled with a vague sense of dread. He had stood countless hours in the factories that had been built in Cartha, the factories that had turned out the hundreds of cannons, the muskets, the sheathing of iron for the ships. But they were nothing compared to this.

The wheels of the Cartha factories had been pow-ered by ten thousand cattle, who walked inside of them till they dropped and died to be replaced by more. The machines had been crude, heavy, wasteful

even to his untutored eyes. Yet within here he could
see just how different his foes were.

He nudged his mount across the foundry floor. He
knew enough now of the cattle arts of metal that he
could trace out the steps. Outside the building he had
seen the long slope of earth leading to the top of the
buildings up which the wagonloads of ore, coke, and
flux must have been drawn by cables hooked to water
wheels. Inside, here, he could see where the metal
had flown out into troughs, and then moved down the
length of the building, the great frames of the hammers still embedded in the ground. Farther down were
the molds for the cannons and yet more forges, more
kilns. Overhead dangled cables for lifting. Side doors
led to yet other buildings, iron rails going down the
length of those buildings as well. All of it so orderly,
so perfectly arranged, so terrifying in its exactness.

"This is our future if we do not destroy them,"
Tamuka said coldly. "This is what I have sworn by
the blood of my ancestors to end, before it goes any
further. Not you, not the Bantag, not any of us must
ever be seduced by what this can produce, or our
world is dead. Only the perversion of cattle minds
could imagine this."

Muzta smiled.

"And when you have finished with them, I do wonder what you plan for me at the end of all of this,"
Muzta said.

"Vuka is the Qar Qarth, not I," Tamuka replied.

"But of course."

Tamuka stared at Muzta for a long moment.

"You should have died with your warriors. At least
there would have been honor in that," he said.

"Maybe you'll have the chance yourself when you
lead yours to destruction," Muzta replied. "I agree
that the cattle are our enemies. Yet our arrogance is
our enemy as well. The world is wide, the war only

beginning. Do not be blinded by your desires to destroy them.''

He hesitated for a moment.

"Or by your own desire to make yourself Qar Qarth and to use this war as an excuse for your rise to power.''

Tamuka wrestled for control, and unable to fight the rising passion, he reined his horse about and galloped out of the building.

Muzta watched him leave and then slowly followed, turning his mount northward to cross the flowing waters of the Vina and return to where the two umens still under his command were camped, while the wind carried with it the reverberation of the drums, which would beat with the rhythm of a pulsing heart for the next twenty-nine days.

"Engines stop!"

Hamilcar Baca, leader of the exiled people of Cartha, watched as the captain of the gunboat *Antietam*, named after the ship that had gone down a year ago in battle against him, edged his vessel up alongside *New Ironsides*. The two ironclads bumped gently, momentarily causing him to lose balance so that he had to grab hold of the gun carriage of the seventy-five-pound carronade mounted behind the starboard gun hatch.

"Get some lines across and watch out for snipers," the captain shouted, sticking his head down through the hatchway into the main gundeck.

The forward and aft gun hatches, empty with the two guns mounted amidships, were flung open. Half a dozen men issued out from each. Crouching low, they ran along the armored deck. They tossed lines across to the waiting crew of the *New Ironsides,* who secured the cables to their own ship. A rough gangplank was run up from below deck. Fenders made out of short woven lengths of rope were draped between the two ships while the gangplank was run across.

"It's clear."

Hamilcar, ducking low, went through the forward gunport, his staff following. Gaining the open deck, he took a deep breath, enjoying the fresh late-spring air, tinged with a cool scent of pines. Since entering the Neiper they had slowly made their way upriver against the heavy spring run, sealed inside the oven-like interior of the ship. As they passed the walls of Fort Lincoln he had seen the first of the Merki patrols on the east shore of the river. They had watched the ship pass in silence. The enemy guns, positioned in batteries on the west bank just below Suzdal, were silent, not even venturing a harassing shot. The silence had filled him with foreboding.

The shore on either side was not more than a medium arrow flight away. He could see a knot of Merki on the west bank, mounted, silent.

To the east the riverfront walls of Suzdal loomed. It brought back memories of a year ago—the final rush for the city when he had still served the Merki, ruler of an enslaved people doing the bidding of his masters. He had wanted to take Suzdal—after all, he was a warrior and that was his task—but there was no real love in it, not as if he were doing it for his own glory, his own triumph.

Then had come the realization of the Merki betrayal, that Suzdal would not be ruled as a human fiefdom of the Merki, but rather would be occupied by that horde; and that his own people would be sent into the slaughter pits anyhow. That had been the underlying reason behind his fighting the two republics, to spare his people the choosing of two in ten for the feasts.

He looked up at the city walls. They were lined with Merki warriors, who stood in silence, watching him. Strange sight. Merki in a city he had come to believe would never be taken. Behind them, the high golden domes of the churches reflected the afternoon light, the wooden walls of the houses and palaces within adorned with, to his eyes, bizarre wood carvings the Rus took such delight in, so unlike the brilliant limestone of his own palace, or the mud brick of the common people.

Hamilcar looked at them coldly. Not like them. At the very least they'd toss out some arrows just for the sport of killing a cattle or two. Merki were predictable in that. He had seen far too many cut down on the mere whim of testing a blade, or just for the sport, to alleviate a couple of moments of boredom and in the process leave a score of dead behind.

Watching the Merki out of the corner of his eye, he went across the rough gangplank, stepping onto the deck of the *New Ironsides*. A shrill pipe sounded, a Yankee custom he found annoying, the piercing cry always sending a shiver down his back. A young Suzdalian naval officer stood by the gangplank; coming to attention, he saluted Hamilcar.

"Admiral Bullfinch is waiting for you on the gundeck," the officer said, his Cartha barely understandable.

"What has been going on here?" Hamilcar asked.

"The admiral awaits you, sir. I'd suggest we move quickly—they might shoot at any moment," the officer replied, obviously drilled for this one formality and totally out of his league beyond the formal greeting.

Shaking his head, Hamilcar stepped past the officer and climbed through the bow gunport, moving fast, suspicious that a turned back would be far too much of a temptation for one of the watching Merki.

As he stood up in the stifling gloom he saw a lone Yankee officer waiting for him, dressed in a blue uniform of the same cut as the traitor Cromwell's. A jagged scar creased the young man's face from jaw to crown, furrowing underneath a black patch that covered his blinded eye.

They were of nearly the same height. But Hamilcar was bull-like, his bare arms knotted with muscles that were now, in middle age, beginning to show the first signs of the decline that so quickly transformed a muscular youth into stoutness. His black beard curled down over his chest, freshly oiled, matching the heavy matted hair that covered his body. The youth before him was nearly frail in comparison, the dark blue wool jacket and trousers hanging limp on a slender frame, the gold-trimmed sash about his waist pulled in tight, revealing just how slight the admiral of the Suzdalian navy truly was. But his gaze was hard, though Hamilcar could detect a nervousness.

"The city has fallen, then?" Hamilcar began, skipping past the usual ritual of pleasantries, driving straight to the point. Elazar, his closest friend and translator, barely through the gunport behind him, rattled off the question.

"The day before yesterday," Bullfinch replied. "We can talk about it later, though. Would you care for something to eat first, or perhaps something to drink?"

"I want some questions answered, then we drink," Hamilcar replied sharply.

Bullfinch nodded, waiting.

"Coming up the river, and here, the Merki have not fired upon us. They watch in silence."

He looked at Bullfinch, waiting for Elazar to finish. The admiral said nothing.

"And the drums—we heard them from the west shore, even before we gained the river."

He fell silent again, and as if to emphasize his point, the distant heartbeat rhythm drifted through the gunports.

"Something has happened. I suspected something; I did not know what. But I know enough of your Keane to know that he would not so meekly surrender all of your land without an action in reply. Tell me what has happened."

"The Merki Qar Qarth is dead," Bullfinch said quietly.

Stunned, Hamilcar looked away. Jubadi dead. He had no love for this Qar Qarth, yet it was hard to imagine that such a being, who wielded such power, was indeed mortal after all.

And the enormity of what might be unfolding around him struck as well.

"How?" he asked, his voice barely a whisper.

"A sniper. The pet Yuri killed him."

The translator stumbled on the word "sniper."

Bullfinch, realizing the difficulty, explained what had happened—what a Whitworth sniper gun was capable of, how Yuri had volunteered at Andrew's request, and how the Merki had stopped their advance.

Hamilcar's features flushed, and he lowered his head, the rage building inside of him, washed over with a sick sense of anguish.

"Do you realize what this means for my people?" he hissed.

"I think so, sir," Bullfinch replied, still standing stiffly at attention.

"No, you don't, you really don't," Hamilcar replied. "You've never even seen a slaughter pit, let alone the funeral of a Qar Qarth."

Bullfinch said nothing.

"Did Keane know what would happen?"

"I can't speak for the colonel, sir."

"He knew enough that it would stop the Merki for thirty days, so he must have known the rest," Elazar interjected.

Hamilcar nodded.

Hamilcar turned away and went over to the gunport. The walls of Suzdal were now barely visible in the gathering darkness. Not a single fire illuminated the city, or the hills beyond. The only sound was the drums, the ever-beating drums . . . and when they stopped, so would stop the life of every one of his people who was captive.

"It sounds horrible, sir," Bullfinch said, coming up to stand by Hamilcar, "but your people were doomed the moment they were taken by the Merki. In the end they would have died anyhow."

"Easy for you to say," Hamilcar whispered.

He looked over at Bullfinch.

"You know that my wife disappeared, was most likely taken captive by them last year. She might be dead by now—I pray to Baalk that she is. But she might be in their camps even now, listening to those drums, knowing what they mean. Oh, believe me, Yankee, the people of this world know what those drums mean, what the death of a Qar Qarth by the hands of cattle means."

"I'm sorry, sir. I didn't know."

"Keane did."

He looked over at Bullfinch, wanting to vent his rage, but for the moment unable to do so.

"I'm sorry, sir. I wish there were something we could do."

"Your sorrow won't change it. Your sorrow won't change the fact that if you had never been here, the world would be as it was. The Merki would have ridden east with this spring. Two in ten of my people would be gone, but the rest of us would have survived, to live in peace for another twenty years.

"How many have died in these wars since you cursed Yankees came! Half of all the Rus, I hear. Half of your Rus, and now you don't even have a country."

"At least we still have our freedom," Bullfinch replied, but his voice sounded hollow, unconvincing.

Hamilcar gave a snort of disdain.

"Small comfort, that word of yours. Small comfort when the Merki ride forth with vengeance in their hearts. It will be small comfort when they sweep you aside like dust before the wind and plunge through the Roum. You are a defeated people, the murder of Jubadi a last desperate bid that only delays the end.

"And what of my people?" His voice started to rise, cold and angry. "We did not want this war, I did not want it. It was your coming that destroyed our world as it was. What do you think they will do to us when this is done?"

"We are all in this together. War between humans and the hordes had to come sooner or later."

"Then dammit, it could have been later. Cromwell was right in that. He wanted to let the hordes ride through, and then come out and take twenty years to prepare, to get ready for them. I believe he dreamed that even when he attacked you last year. To buy time knowing that eventually they would ride on."

"Events forced our hand," Bullfinch replied, remembering with a twinge of guilt how he had listened to Hawthorne's impassioned speech against Cromwell's position back at the very beginning of things. Hawthorne had swayed him to vote that way, never realizing all the repercussions that would come. He never imagined that it would lead him to this moment, this telling a man that hundreds of thousands of his people were now doomed.

"Keane did not even have the courage to tell me before he planned this madness," Hamilcar said coldly.

"No one knew," Bullfinch replied, feeling a flush of anger at the impugning of the colonel's honor. "No one, not Marcus, Kal, anyone. It had to be kept a secret, otherwise it would never have worked."

He wasn't sure of the validity of what he had just said. After all, it might have been discussed. But he suspected that such a plot, which required such absolute security, would have been planned only by Andrew; and there was the other suspicion that the colonel would want such an action to be his responsibility and burden alone and no one else's.

Hamilcar gripped the side of the gunport, the iron still warm from the heat of day.

"Would you care for a drink now, sir?" Bullfinch asked, his voice filled with concern.

Hamilcar shook his head and looked over at one of his aides who waited out on the open deck.

"Get the Suzdalian engine crew out of the ship and put our people who were observing them on duty. We're leaving now."

Bullfinch, not understanding the exchange, waited until Hamilcar looked back at him.

"The iron ship *Antietam* is now mine," Hamilcar said quietly.

"That ship belongs to the Suzdalian fleet," Bullfinch snapped, his voice barely under control. "It was lent to you to help with the rescue of your people from your country."

"It's mine now," Hamilcar replied, his voice quiet but filled with a cold determination.

"Sir, I cannot allow you to take one of my ships."

"Then stop me."

He stared straight into Bullfinch's eyes, ready to pull the sword from his belt and take the young man's head if he made the slightest move against him.

"Sir, you can kill me—I know I wouldn't stand a chance in a hand-to-hand fight against you—but I can't allow you to take one of my ships."

The boy had courage, he had to grant him that.

"We can fight, you and I. I could kill you here and most likely your men would shoot me before I got back to my ship," Hamilcar replied. "You could even let me go and our ships could fight, but they are evenly matched and the spectacle would surely amuse the Merki. Either way, I am taking the ship."

"For what?"

"To go back home," Hamilcar said coldly. "Before

this is all done, the Merki in their vengeance, or even the Bantag horde to the south, will drive the Cartha, perhaps all cattle of this world, into extinction. I am going home. Your war is now your war. I am finished with it."

"Forty thousand of your people are on our land for refuge," Bullfinch replied hotly. "We gave you that even after you fought against us."

"Are you threatening them too?"

Bullfinch sighed, shaking his head.

"Our word is good. Colonel Keane offered you and your men sanctuary. He'll honor that for them even if you desert."

Hamilcar nodded in reply.

"At least you honor that. If you, if Keane honors his promise, if he does not send you and your ships to fight us, then I will not fight you. The *Antietam* will not be used against you if that promise is kept and I am allowed to go. But for this war, I am finished. I'm going home to save what I can."

Bullfinch looked at him appraisingly.

"Take the ship. I won't stop you," he finally said, his voice barely a whisper.

Hamilcar turned without comment, and ducking low started to climb through the gunport.

"But don't expect help from us after this," Bullfinch said, his anger returning.

Hamilcar paused and looked back at him.

"I never wanted it to start with," he said coldly, and disappeared from view.

Chapter 2

Running alongside the engine, Chuck Ferguson grabbed hold of the ladder, then pulled himself up. His legs dangled for a moment, just inches from the spinning wheels of the locomotive. He put his foot into the bottom rung of the ladder and clambered aboard the cab. The engineer, an old Suzdalian who looked every inch a railroad man, complete to oil-stained coveralls and peaked cap, gazed over at the young inventor and shook his head.

"Nice way to lose your legs if you slip," the engineer said calmly, while motioning for his fireman to tap off some hot water for a cup of tea.

The sound of the roadbed shifted into a hollow rumble as the engine crossed the bridge spanning the Sangros. Taking the scalding cup of tea, Chuck leaned out of the cab, looking down to the riverbed thirty feet below. From upstream a delivery of rough-cut lumber, piled high on open rafts, floated with the late-spring current, the rivermen riding atop their cargo, boating poles in hand, working to maneuver the long string of rafts over toward the east shore of the river. A gang of laborers lined the bank, just finishing up with an earlier load, hoisting the lumber off the rafts to pile it aboard a string of old narrow-gauge flatcars, which were pulled by oxen on a hastily laid track that gradually cut up the side of the embankment. Coming up out of the riverbed, the track turned east and ran across the open fields to the far side of Hispania,

where a vast city of rough shelters was going up overnight to house the ten thousand workers and their
families who were moving in with the arriving factories. The uncut lumber that made up the rafts would
be snaked up the bank later and used for field
fortifications.

"Andre Ilyavich, isn't it?"

The engineer grinned and nodded.

"Is this the train carrying the rifle factory?" Chuck
asked.

"The same."

Chuck nodded, tasting the tea and smiling a thanks
as the fireman, with dirt-blackened hands, offered him
a slice of bread covered in cheese.

The bread was fresh-baked, the cheese soft, tasty.
He wanted to ask where they had landed such a deli-
cacy, but decided it was best not to inquire. It was
always best not to ask too many questions. He looked
back into the tender car, and there sitting in the wood-
pile was a Rus family, grandparents, mother, and five
children.

Food most likely traded for a train ride out, a fair
exchange for both sides, he had to reason.

"My sister-in-law and her children and parents," the
fireman said almost apologetically.

Civilian refugees were not supposed to ride aboard the
engine and tender, but the rule was generally ignored.

"It's all right," Chuck said, and the fireman smiled
with relief.

"Where's her husband, your brother I take it?"

"With the 1st Vazima, Homula's regiment, Second
Corps. He was with the rear guard at the Ford."

"Did he get out?"

"Last we heard he was all right—slightly wounded,
but nothing serious."

"Can she cook?"

"Wonderfully," the fireman said, motioning for her
to come forward.

He didn't want to hear yet another story. Everyone had a story, ready to say anything if it meant a chance to escape into Roum territory aboard a train. He smiled at her and held up his hand for her not to speak, while she eyed him nervously, as if he might somehow send her all the way back to Kev for breaking the rules. Reaching into his vest pocket, he pulled out an order pad and jotted off a quick note. Tearing the sheet of paper out, he gave it to her.

"This is a pass for you and your family to stay on this train. You and your mother are being hired as cooks at a factory going up farther up the line. Your father can work in the factory, so just stay in this cab till your brother here tells you to get off."

The woman started to blurt out her thanks, and wearily he patted her on the shoulder and then turned away as if she no longer existed.

The fireman started to pour out his thanks as well, but he waved the man off and went to look back out of the cab. Though John Mina as chief of logistics might view the train line as his own, Chuck Ferguson felt that since he had invented it all, it was his, and he had to look out for his own people. The man wouldn't forget the favor, and he was going to need all the gratitude he could summon, and quite a bit of judicious forgetting on the part of some, in the next couple of weeks.

"But this train is supposed to turn around here at Hispania and go straight back to Kev," Andre said, looking over at Chuck, sensing something out of line in his last comment.

"A little side trip," Chuck said, trying to keep the nervousness out of his voice.

"It'll play hell with the schedule."

"I'll take responsibility for that."

"General Mina's people aren't going to like it. This train's due back in Kev at six forty-five tomorrow morning."

"I said I'll take care of it," Vincent said sharply.

The engineer, knowing better than to argue the point, turned away.

The train, having crossed the Sangros, was now into Roum territory, and they drifted past the border marker, adorned with the eagle and fasces of the newly formed Republic. A switchman in the loose-fitting tunic of a Roum peasant, who most likely a year ago had been a slave laboring in the fields, stood by the switch holding up a pole, atop which was affixed a board painted green, the signal that the switch was clear.

The train turned off the main line. The beginnings of a heavy bastion were going up to the left, and the back of the train station was on the right. Hispania Station was crowded with hundreds of refugees who had been dropped off earlier in the day and were now waiting for the train to come up from Roum and take them on the last leg of their journey into the city.

A long table of rough-hewn planks was set up by the mud-brick-and-limestone building. Half a dozen simmering caldrons were behind the table, tended by a crowd of chattering women, some Rus, others Roum, and what looked like a couple of Cartha. The mix of languages didn't seem to stop them in their conversations. Beside the caldrons was a small mountain of what appeared to be potatoes, or what passed for potatoes on this world, along with the butchered remains of what he suspected was an antelope. The refugees were lined up, patiently waiting their turn.

He had heard of the breakdown of order at a couple of places, riots to grab food. But remarkably, discipline was still holding at the rail stations. He suspected that in large part a thousand years of subservience, of following orders, even when it meant walking into the slaughter pits, had bred a resignation to privation, which at least in this situation was to everyone's advantage. Social order could too easily break down under the stress of the evacuation and the next wave of the war. If that started, they were all doomed. It was essential to get the factories up and running, the army dug in, and the remaining hundreds of thousands working in the fields and woods if they were to win this war, and beyond that have any hope of surviving the next winter. Bob Fletcher, head of food organization, struck Chuck as being something of a mad idealist, already planning out food supply a year in the future.

In twenty days the Merki move again, Chuck thought. They could be here inside of a month and a half, just around midsummer day. He forced the thought away as the train drifted past the food line and the scent of the stew wafted up to him.

When was the last time he had managed to down a hot meal? He looked at the caldrons longingly. One of the women turned to look up at him, and he felt as if his heart would skip a beat. It was Olivia, Julius's daughter. Now just what the hell was she doing here? Their gaze held for a second.

He had not seen her in weeks, not since the day she and her father had joined him for a tour of the aerosteamer works—on the day word had come that the Merki were moving at last. She had barely been out of his nighttime thoughts since. She smiled at him, and then he truly felt his heart skip a beat.

She remembers me! The train drifted on, and he was tempted to jump off. He looked over at Andre, who had seen the exchange and was smiling.

"Friend of yours?" the engineer asked.

"I guess she is," Chuck said shyly.

"A real beauty, that one," and the old man chuckled in a way that Chuck didn't much care for.

Chuck gave the man a cold stare, and the engineer, clearing his throat, looked away.

The locomotive continued on, rolling past the back of the station, which was piled to near roof level with rough-cut crossties and shiny rails. Several refugee families had arranged some of the ties into temporary shelters, and they looked up forlornly as the engine drifted by.

The mud-brick-and-limestone walls of old Hispania were now to the left, on a low rise of ground a couple of hundred yards away. Three years before, the small city had been the westernmost outpost of Roum territory, a provincial town on the edge of the Great Forest, a sleepy outpost where the wealthy families of Roum would come to escape the summer heat and to take sulfur baths, near where the powder works and a small mine produced the now precious quicksilver to supply the army's fulminate of mercury for percussion caps. Their villas were mostly south of the town, down in the half-moon-shaped valley below, where the soil was rich and some of the best wine grapes in all of Roum were cultivated.

The war had changed all that. He had always found it fascinating how simple factors of geography, geology, and random chance could take a town or village and in time of war make it the nexus point of the conflict. It had started when the rail line first crossed here into Roum territory and it was decided that this would be the location of a rail maintenance yard. That had brought in a thousand workers. A new town had sprung up overnight outside the walls of the city, the rail yard, engine shed, forges, warehouses, and workers' huts surrounded by an earthen wall. This was the first place that Rus and Roum culture had truly intermingled. Rus architecture was evident in the new town of log homes, adorned with the usual wood carvings and brightly colored doors, shutters, and roofs. The rapid expansion of the quicksilver mine, processing plant, and mill for turning out percussion caps had created another overnight town on the north side of the city, most of the workers in this new industry the newly freed Roum.

Twenty miles to the north, up in the forest, was the powder mill, located near the sulfur springs, and just east of it the aerosteamer works, both of them built in the forest to hide them from Merki airships. Another new town had gone up around these factories overnight, twelve hundred workers and their families living in the forests. And two miles east of the aerosteamer factory was yet another project, one that only Chuck and a small number of his confederates were fully aware of.

The language spoken in Hispania was now something of a strange polyglot of old Rus, English technical terminology, and the curious vulgar Latin of Roum. Gates, the newspaper editor, had even published an article in his weekly illustrated about how the languages might eventually blend into the common speech of commerce, the railroads, and diplomacy. Andrew had given Gates's newspaper a high priority for evacuation, believing it to be essential for morale purposes. Gates already had his press up and publishing in an office in the old part of Hispania.

The naval war of the previous year and the mad rush to relieve Roum had made this town the central supply depot of the army during that campaign, and from it the rebuilding of the destroyed rail lines had been directed after the defeat of the traitorous Cromwell. More warehouses, more cabins had gone up. Then the spur line was run north, into the forest to the new powder mill and aerosteamer yard, and the sawmills for turning out prefabricated parts for bridges and for crossties and now the lumber to build yet more factories and warehouses. More sidings had gone in, and yet more laborers, mainly former Roum slaves, had come to learn their new skills and to live here.

Now if only Bill Webster and his capitalist friends had been allowed to invest in real estate here, he thought with a smile, they'd have made a killing. But in this emergency, real estate dealings be damned, the land had simply been confiscated from the senators who had rebelled against Marcus.

And now the new emergency. Some of the factories—the cannon works, the iron, steel, bronze, and zinc foundries, the lead-processing plant, and the rail works—were being shipped to Roum, where ore and coke supplies were still available, and were easily moved to the capital city by ship from farther down the Roum coast. The rifle and musket works, the wheelwright and gun carriage shops, and the wire works for telegraph lines were going up here in Hispania. Ore and fuel supplies necessitated setting up the cannon works in Roum. Supplies of wood for weapon stocks, the location of lumber for housing and factories, and the fact that it was a major rail terminal argued for locating most of the other factories in Hispania. The one great drawback was power for the factories. If there had been enough time they could have dammed off the Sangros and Tiber, but that was out of the question. The only alternative was to cannibalize the rail engines yet again.

My precious engines, he thought sadly. They had been made to ride the rails, not to be stripped down and hooked into bellows, forges, trip-hammers, and lathes. It was a precarious balancing act—they needed every engine they had for the evacuation and for the coming battles, yet they needed new weapons as well. More than one of the locomotives had started out on the rails, then been converted to an ironclad engine, then back to rail, and now had become a power plant for a factory. John Mina had decided to keep thirty locomotives for the rail line, use another twenty-eight for the factories, and leave the remaining six, all the old engines from the first narrow-gauge line, as a reserve to be shifted either way as needed. The fifteen others they had made on this world were now either in the ironclads or on the bottom of the sea, and one, taken by the traitor Hinsen, was somewhere far to the south, in enemy hands.

He looked affectionately around the cab. Even in the rush of emergency building, the Rus had taken the time to add little affectionate details. The wooden handle to the whistle was carved in the rough likeness of a bear's head, and the engineer's side of the cab had a primitive icon of Kevin Malady set into the woodwork. Malady had become something like a patron saint of the railroad men.

Chuck smiled as he looked at the picture. Malady had been one of the old veterans of the 35th, a railroad man before the war and the first engineer of the line when the old Maine, Fort Lincoln, and Suzdal Railroad had opened with the first narrow-gauge line, even before the Tugars had come. On the day the Tugars had broken into the city he had smashed the safety valves and driven his engine straight into the enemy host. He and Hawthorne were the first to win the Congressional Medal of Honor. And now he was a saint. It was hard to imagine hard-swearing, hard-fighting Malady as a saint wearing a halo, but somehow his toughness suited these men who ran the rail lines. He raised his cup of tea in a quiet salute to the memory of an old friend, gone now like so many others.

The throttle was carved in the image of a dragon, and the door to the firebox had the sign of Perm, the Rus divinity, cast into the iron. The Rus had taken to the Yankee machines, forced perhaps at first by their even greater dread of the hordes, but ever so gradually they were changing their appearance, altering them step by step into something fitting into their own folk beliefs and style of art. He found that to be comforting.

The train lurched through another switch, moving slowly past a long line of Roum peasants, laden with shovels and picks, who were heading down into the valley south of town to work on fortifications. Still not quite used to the engine, they backed away as it approached, looking at it suspiciously.

"Think they'll ever get the fortifications ready along the river?" the engineer asked, looking at them with a superior disdain, a haughtiness that Ferguson knew all locomotive men had for the mere mortals who would never know the power of controlling the mysteries of steam.

"They haven't seen the war the way we have," the fireman chimed in.

"They know what's at stake," Ferguson said, trying to defend the Roum even though he knew the truth of what the fireman was saying. True desperation can be a wonderful spur to work, and he at times wondered if the Roum realized just how horrifying the Merki advance was.

"If they get here to the Sangros," the engineer said, "then it's over."

"Do you think we're going to lose?" Ferguson asked.

The old engineer looked over at him.

"I saw the way Saint Malady died." He nodded toward the icon. "That's how I plan to go when the time comes."

"Looking for a medal and sainthood?" Ferguson asked.

"No, I just want to take some of the bastards with me the way he did, and I'll be damned if they'll ever get their hands on this engine."

Ferguson nodded approvingly, leaning back out of the cab to watch as the Roum workers drifted past. Can we even hold the Sangros? he wondered.

Kal and many of the officers in the army had at first hesitated to put the final defense line here, along a front of nearly forty miles, from the ocean up into the forest, but Andrew had cinched the deal with the simple statement that if the Sangros line was lost the war was over anyhow. Roum was indefensible—Merki artillery on the hills above the town would batter its walls down in a day, though even now earthworks were going up in a great arc around the city. Besides, Roum held over one hundred and fifty thousand, and with the refugees swarming in it would most likely get closer to four hundred thousand by midsummer. Roum could never withstand a siege the way Suzdal had against the Tugars. But then the Tugars had had no artillery and the Merki did—even Suzdal would have been battered down with guns on the hills east of town. If the Sangros line fell, the Merki would hit Roum full-force and starve it out in a matter of days.

Hispania was the place of the last stand. Beyond Hispania the land of the Roum opened out southward down the east shore of the inland sea into the great open steppes. The long, narrow corridor of Rus, bordered on the south by the sea and the north by the forest, was the only terrain where an infantry army, relying on a single railroad for mobility, could hope to present a secured front to the horse-mounted Merki horde. The simple fact of geography, an ocean to the south, the woods to the north, had given them the hope to stand. Beyond the Sangros the army would be outflanked wherever it attempted to fight. Though the rail line did go another fifty miles to Roum and twenty miles beyond toward the Brindusia oil field, Hispania was the end of the line for retreat.

And with that thought in mind, Hispania was daily growing beyond imagining. In a fortnight, thirty thousand had settled in here. As the train continued on up the siding, Ferguson crossed the cab to the other side and looked back at the west and south. Along the low bluffs by the rail bridge the work crews were already laboring on the first line of entrenchments and earthen forts that would run along the forty-mile front from the ocean all the way into the forest. The first twenty miles were not much of a worry—the broad river delta was a tangle of wetlands and marshes—but strongpoints had to be constructed nevertheless.

North of the city, just above a low series of rapids, the river on both sides was bordered by high steep banks all the way into the forest and beyond. Defending this stretch would be fairly easy, but still required strongpoints and manpower. To leave any stretch of the river unprotected would be to invite a breakthrough.

The tactical problem started four miles south of Hispania, from where and on up to just south of the town the low sandy bluffs of the river were higher on the west side of the river. The riverbed was nearly five hundred feet across, and in the summer the Sangros could be crossed at nearly any point along this stretch without getting your knees wet except when a heavy rain triggered a flash flood.

To the east of this point a broad semicircle of flat land stretched back from the river for several miles, bounded finally on three sides by a low ridgeline of limestone hills.

The debate over defending this position had been a tough one. Merki artillery dug in on the west bank would make a killing zone of the east side, but defending the west bank was far too risky. A sudden storm could cut off the army, its back to the river and no place to run, and compounding the problem was the simple fact that a line of hills a half mile farther west was higher than the low ridge running along the river. It was decided to dig in on the east side, and the thought made Ferguson nervous. The riverbed would be a murder zone, they could kill the Merki by the tens of thousands, but this was the end of the line; if the Merki ever gained the east bank, it was open country beyond, and the last thing anyone wanted was an open-field engagement with the Merki—it would make the bloody day of Antietam pale in comparison. He somehow knew that it was here that the war would finally be decided, and the thought left him cold, as if he were gazing at his own place of burial.

The labor crew continued on heading southward. It was only a small beginning, a thousand men, Roum laborers under the direction of a dozen Suzdalian fortification engineers commanded by a former corporal of the 35th Maine.

The engineer pulled down on the cord, the high whistle shrieking sharp and clear, and he tapped out the beginning of a Rus folk song, obscene to be sure, which told of a boyar's daughter and the peasants of his estate, who to a man were all quite happy and contented—until their wives finally found out. Chuck looked over at the engineer and smiled.

"That song takes an hour to sing, for God's sake—you'll drain the steam lines dry if you play it all."

"You know, the song is true." The engineer grinned. "That lass initiated me into the mysteries of love."

"Go on."

"No, really, two hundred verses would barely do her justice."

"Wish I'd met her," Chuck said ruefully, shaking his head while the engineer laughed.

"Well, from the way that Roum girl was looking at you, I daresay you might find out some mysteries of your own soon enough, and I say from the looks of you it's about time."

"She barely knows me," Chuck said, embarrassed that the engineer might possibly guess just how truly virginal he was.

"Well, she obviously wants to know you a lot better, or I'm blind to such things."

"You're half blind already, Andre. I don't know why Mina allows you to run this engine."

The engineer gave Chuck a half-serious, half-playful poke to the shoulder, and then, leaning back out of the cab, he watched as the yardmaster motioned him to bring the engine to a stop. With a final blast of the whistle, he tapped out the end of the first verse of the song, and the train shuddered to a halt.

Chuck, patting the engineer on the shoulder, stepped past him and started to climb out of the cab, and then, pausing, he looked back.

"Stay with the engine. I'm cutting new route orders for you. You'll be moving again within the hour."

"I still say that General Mina will have your head over this. The schedule is chaos as it is without you going and changing it."

"Mina's over three hundred miles to the west, and what he doesn't know will never hurt him."

Chuck paused, as if suddenly remembering something, then reached into his tunic, pulled out a battered tin flask, and tossed it back to the engineer.

"Now don't go getting drunk on the job."

"Bribery, is it?"

"What else?" Chuck said with a grin.

The engineer, shaking his head, uncorked the flask and took a long pull, then handed the container over to his fireman.

"And another quart of it when we're done," Chuck said.

Andre, doing a quick calculation of just how much a quart of vodka was worth in these times, sighed.

"You were the one that trained me on these steaming monsters. I guess I owe you that."

"You do," Chuck said with a grin, and he jumped down from the cab and looked around.

The boxcars behind him were already open, men from the rifle factory, along with their women and children, spilling out, shouting, groaning with the pleasure of at last being able to stretch, and most of them looking frantically for the nearest latrine. The officers were already out, shouting orders, getting the men to fall into formation, their families behind them. Roum yard workers, with their feeble attempts at Rus, were shouting out directions, pointing to where the soup kitchens and the latrines were. Officers were shouting out orders, and labor crews were preparing to start unloading the string of flatcars. Though all seemed chaos, the evacuation work was finally starting to show some semblance of an organized plan. A factory area had already been staked out for the rifle works, open sheds had been constructed, foundations had been set for the various tools, and several thousand Rus refugees with axes had thrown up cabins and barracks. Emil had sent a team in within days of the beginning of the evacuation and laid out the sanitation and a rough aqueduct of terra-cotta pipes snaking down from a spring northeast of town to provide pure drinking water for the cisterns and bathhouses. By evening the men of this factory and their families would be settled in, and the following morning they could start in on getting their factory up and running again. All, that is, except two companies of fifty, with a precious flatcar of lathes and their tools.

Walking down the length of the train, Chuck approached the commander of the factory, who as a lieutenant colonel also commanded the same men, if they should be called into combat, as the 16th Suzdal of First Corps.

The two exchanged salutes, and without ceremony Chuck handed him an order. The officer, a former peasant who had risen through the ranks, struggled with the writing.

"It simply says that I'm detaching Companies A and B, along with one of the turning lathes, for other duty."

"But . . ."

"The orders are secret, Petya, so please see that they're done and let's not discuss this."

The officer looked at him closely, and finally, with a weary nod, he turned away to give the orders. Chuck called over one of the yardmasters, told him which cars were to be detached, and then quickly explained that the engine was to be routed over to pick up a string of other cars which he had been quietly stealing.

Leaving the perplexed yardmaster, he exhaled deeply. Finding an empty boxcar on an adjacent train, he climbed up through the open door and sat down in the shade. He wiped the perspiration from his face, even though the day was surprisingly cool. Subterfuge had never been one of his stronger suits. He had seen how Vincent Hawthorne had been changed by all of this, and he remembered, with a soft chuckle, how the general, who was three years younger than himself, had managed to blackmail him out of enough supplies for an entire division.

How the hell had he ever gotten himself into this? Over the last month and a half, he had been quietly pirating bits here, parts there, and hundreds of skilled men from the trains that had passed through. Never really enough to be missed from any one place, what with all the confusion of ripping up every factory in Rus and moving it five hundred miles east. But if anyone ever started to put the web together, it would quickly fall right back on top of him.

Hell of a life, he thought as he leaned back, wiping his brow. I have to steal from the very system I helped to invent. What will they do to me, though, if I'm caught? That was hard to imagine. He held far too much respect for Andrew to want to face his wrath if he was hauled up before him to confess his sins. But could they fire him?

Unlikely. It'd be like the war department back home firing Hermann Haupt or telling Ericsson or Spencer to go to hell. But then again they did tell all three of those men at one time or another to drop dead. If he was found out now, it might destroy everything. He tried not to think about it.

"Would you like some soup?"

Startled, he looked up, struggling for a moment to

translate in his mind the Roum dialect, which bore only a passing resemblance to the Latin he had learned in school. Olivia stood before him, and struggle as he might, it was impossible not to stare at her as if she were an apparition. Her dress of white linen, wrapped about her in typical Roum fashion, was cinched tight at the waist, and though the day was cool, standing over the boiling caldrons of soup had soaked her in sweat, which caused the linen to cling provocatively to every delightful curve of her voluptuous body. The view was, for Ferguson, simply startling, as if the girl were somehow naked. He had a mental flash that underneath this flimsy garment she was indeed naked. The thought stirred him, and he felt embarrassed as he looked into her eyes, as if she could read his every thought.

"Aren't you hungry?"

"Ah, yeah," and he realized that he had been staring far too long, and far too obviously. His face reddening, he quickly jumped back down to the ground and nervously accepted the wooden bowl of soup and hunk of fresh bread that she was holding.

"Sit down and eat."

Without waiting for an invitation to join him, Olivia pulled herself up into the open boxcar and motioned for him to join her. He handed her the bowl of soup and climbed up to sit by her side, then took the soup back. Tilting the bowl back, he sipped the broth, and instantly he felt his stomach tighten. It had been days since he had enjoyed a hot meal.

"Go on. I know you must be starving," she said, motioning for him to cast good manners aside.

He let the near-scalding liquid run down his throat. With a sigh he lowered the bowl, dipped the bread in, and scooped up the small hunks of meat and potato like paste, pausing only to make appreciative sounds of delight, while all the time she looked at him smiling.

"I was worried for you," she finally said.

Again he felt his heart thump over. They had met only the one time, and he had thought that she would have forgotten him by now.

"You remembered me?" he asked, not sure of his Latin.

"Of course, Chuck Urgesim."

"I remembered you."

A hint of color came to her cheeks.

Damn languages, Chuck thought, unsure of what to say next. But when it came to talking with women he was always at a loss anyway. He'd never met one before who could understand the machines which were the source of his delight, let alone appear to have even a passing interest in them after five minutes of his trying to explain. After all, women with an interest in engineering were an unknown phenomena as far as he was concerned.

"I like the things you build," she said, this time in Rus, saying each word slowly. "They are wonderful. They help to free people like my father from labor. They fight the Tugar, the Merki. And you make them from your thoughts."

She looked at him, unsure if she had said the words correctly, but the childlike grin that lit his features gave her answer enough, and she laughed softly at his dumbfounded response.

He let his eyes drop, unsure of himself, and he noticed that her nipples were straining through the sheer linen dress that clung to her sweat-streaked body.

"Oh my God," and he was startled and humiliated that he had actually spoken out loud, knowing that she was aware of the reason for his exclamation.

Quickly he slipped down from his perch in the open boxcar, stumbling slightly as he hit the ground. He looked back at her, and she was laughing softly, though he could see that she was somewhat embarrassed as well, crossing her arms over her breasts.

"Let's walk," he said quietly.

Smiling demurely, she nodded an agreement and slipped off her perch, falling in alongside him. He turned away from the railyard crossing over several lines of track. Everything about them was a sea of confusion. Refugees were wandering about, most of them aimlessly, having been dropped at Hispania and now waiting forlornly for the one worn-out train that ran back and forth to Roum to take them on the last leg of their journey to relative safety.

A labor battalion of Roum came past, returning from the morning shift of digging entrenchments, the men covered in mud, weary, stumbling. Stepping over the track, Ferguson went up to a low knoll on the south side of the line. Stakes had been set, marking out where a heavily fortified blockhouse was to be constructed, the position providing flanking cover for the bastion going up near the bridge.

He settled down, unslinging a blanket roll from his shoulder and spreading it out. Sitting down on the blanket, she looked up at him, and he nervously joined her.

"How long do you have here?" she asked.

He looked back at the rail yard and saw that his engine had already been detached and was moving forward, while a tiny yard engine was shuttling the cars onto the side tracks, putting together his little secret venture for the run up north into the woods. He pulled out his pocket watch to check the time.

"Not more than fifteen minutes or so."

"Fifteen minutes. You Yankees are so precise in your time."

Ferguson smiled, stifling the urge to launch into a little lecture on the need for accurate time measurement for an industrial society to function correctly. He somehow knew it would bore her.

"I've wondered whatever happened to you," she said, looking over at him boldly.

"Me?" He felt his voice squeak slightly.

She smiled and nodded.

Why would this woman ever wonder about him? Girls were something he always found it impossible to deal with, and he had long ago given up any hope of ever meeting one who would find him interesting. He tried to lean back casually. The drawing instruments and the old battered slide rule in his haversack poked him in the ribs, and he carefully shifted the canvas sack around. The slide rule was a cherished item, a miracle for this world, which Bullfinch had owned when he was still a lieutenant back on the old *Ogunquit* and had presented to Ferguson back before the First Tugar War. Ferguson had used it as template and now several dozen of them were in the hands of young Rus engineers, but this was the original, and the thought of the girl left him for a second as he absently checked to make sure the cherished instrument was all right.

She noticed him rummaging through the haversack.

"What's hidden in there?" she asked with a smile.

Almost nervously, he brought it out.

She looked at it curiously.

"What is it?"

Unable to help himself, he started to tell her about it, taking her through the step of adding two and four. When she saw the result, she looked up at him in amazement.

"Yankee sorcery?" But there was no fear in her voice, only delight.

He laughed and in broken Latin stumbled for the words to explain logarithmic functions. After several minutes of heroic effort, he gave up. She leaned over the instrument, her long black hair dangling in her face, and with an occasional swing of her head she tossed the hair out of the way, a faint scent of a jasminelike perfume drifting over him. He felt his heart thumping hard as he watched her move the slide, a grin of delight brightening her face.

She looked up at him.

"You Yankees—did you invent this too?"

She looked at him admiringly, and he almost wanted to steal Pascal's thunder. He shook his head no, but the look of admiration did not decrease.

"This is how the Merki will be defeated," she said. "Yankee thinking in this, in everything you've created."

"I'm glad you're so optimistic," he whispered.

She looked at him with concern.

"You do not think we will win?"

He shrugged. He wasn't even sure himself now. When he was focused on his newest project he felt that as in the last two wars his machines would come through. Now? He looked around. There was the smell of defeat, of stunned disbelief, a grim determination to be sure to die game, to take as many of them as possible when the time came. There was no surrender in this war. Yet he felt as if the Rus had resigned themselves, now that their country was lost. They had lost their country and they would lose their lives in the end, but they'd cut the hearts out of the Merki as well. A death grip, with both sides losing in the end. Well, if that was the case, he'd add to their toll. But as he looked over at Olivia he felt such a desire to live again, to maybe even not die a virgin.

There was the sharp toot of a whistle, the beginning of the second stanza of Andre's beloved obscene ballad about the boyar's daughter. Sighing, he looked back at the rail yard. The engineer was leaning out of the cab, looking at him, waving.

"I've got to go," he whispered.

"Already? I thought you would be here in Hispania for a while."

"I have to go up the line."

"To your secret place?"

"You mean the aerosteamer sheds?"

"No, the secret place beyond there."

"How did you know about that?" he asked sharply. She smiled.

"I am, after all, the daughter of the plebeian proconsul," she replied.

"Your father knows?"

"There have been rumors about a new factory going up in the woods. Flashes of light climbing into the sky at night."

Chuck felt nervous.

Sensing it, she shook her head.

"Oh, it is a secret. Father found out because our neighbor's nephew Fabian was working on the building and cut his leg and was sent back home to recover."

"Don't talk to anyone about it," Chuck snapped, making a mental note that from now on once someone went there to work he stayed no matter what.

She smiled reassuringly, and his nervousness disappeared; he knew she'd keep quiet.

They stood up, and she gathered up his blanket, rolling it back up into a horse collar, tying the ends together, and handing it up to him. He slung it over his shoulder and looked at her appraisingly. She would keep the secret. After all, she had grown up in the house of Marcus, her father a slave to the family. Slaves who talked too much usually had unpleasant ends in such situations. The thought of her in Marcus's house triggered another memory. There had been the rumor about her and Hawthorne. Hawthorne. Old friend, but now so distant, driven by the war, consumed perhaps more than anyone else who had survived from the 35th. He was tempted to ask. After all, a proper girl from Vassalboro, Maine, would not bathe naked with anyone, most likely not even with her own husband. There had been other rumors as well. He forced them out of his mind. That shouldn't matter now. None of that should matter. Chances were they'd all be dead in a couple of months anyhow.

Surprised at his own audacity, he suddenly leaned down, rested his hands on her shoulders, and kissed her lightly on the lips. Her eyes opened wide with surprise and delight and then half closed. Her mouth parted, and his chaste and proper kiss of a gentleman took on an explosive heated passion. A bit shocked, he drew back slightly.

Is this what kissing is all about? he wondered in surprise. She nestled against his shoulder, and in the distance he heard laughter. Looking up, he saw the locomotive crew waving, a group of Rus peasants smiling. The world suddenly felt very happy indeed, and he felt no embarrassment as he smiled back.

"You've got to go," she whispered.

He nodded, kissing her on the forehead, and she looked up at him, her eyes wide, almost innocent with wonder.

"I liked you when I first met you. You are different. One who thinks and dreams. I like that."

He put his arm around her shoulder, and together they started back to the train.

"When can I see you again?" she asked.

This was all so surprising. A Maine girl, first off, would never have allowed herself to be kissed like that, especially in front of everyone in broad daylight. It'd be months of proper conversation and chaperoning to even get this far. And then for her to ask when she could see him again? Never.

And the hell with it, he thought, a foolish grin lighting his features, which seemed to be reflected in the scores of people watching, as if their moment of pleasure had brightened everyone's day. This wasn't proper, and damned if he'd stop it now.

"Are you staying here in Hispania?" he asked.

"I'm staying with my uncle and my cousins, helping with feeding your people. Ask for the house of Lucius Gracchus, the former steward of the summer home of Marcus the proconsul. We live next to where Marcus's home was in town. Would you visit me when next you come here?"

He had a sudden flood of rather wicked thoughts and pushed them side. For a brief instant he was even tempted to ask her to come up to the factory with the lame offer that she could help out somehow. No. That was absolutely not proper at all.

"I'd be delighted," he choked out, his voice cracking slightly.

She put her arm around his waist and hugged him while they walked.

Crossing the main track, they weaved through the crowds at the edge of the station and were back into the railyard, waiting for a moment while the diminutive switching engine chugged past, straining as it pulled half a dozen boxcars, loaded down with precious cases of musket rounds destined for the army at Kev.

That train was supposed to be the one Chuck was now borrowing for the rest of the day. He forced the thought away. The switching engine and its load passed, and they at last came up to his train, eight cars behind it, two hundred workers and their families piled on board, sitting atop boxcars and hunkered down among the cases of tools on the flatcars.

The yardmaster came up to Chuck and saluted.

"I'm not signing the order for this, sir," the man announced.

"No one's signing anything," Chuck replied, forcing a smile. "We'll have the cars back here by two in the morning and the train can head back up to Kev. Just send this telegram."

He let go of Olivia, pulled an order pad from his haversack, and jotted the note. The yardmaster peered over his shoulder and then at the locomotive behind him.

"Cracked cylinder indeed," the man sniffed, and then turned about and walked away. Chuck almost wanted to laugh. Minor functionaries on any world, he realized, were always obsessed with the proper form and paperwork and went insane when someone broke the rules.

"Ready to go?" Andre asked, leaning out of his cab and staring appraisingly at Olivia.

Chuck nodded sadly. He looked down at her, and again that strange thump of the heart hit him.

"Next chance, I'll come see you," he said woodenly, cursing himself for not thinking of some wonderfully melodramatic parting line worthy of Scott or that French writer Hugo. Shyly he squeezed her hand and then climbed into the cab, Andre shaking his head. The fireman and his family were smiling, the grandmother clucking appreciatively.

Andre looked forward. The switch master was waving that the line was clear.

With a blast of his whistle, Andre pulled the throttle back. A shudder ran through the cab as the wheels spun and then engaged, and the train started forward.

Chuck looked down as she walked alongside the cab, then, as they passed through the switch and turned onto the northern line she fell behind and disappeared from view.

Chuck exhaled noisily, and his companions started to laugh.

"Ah, a railroad man should have a woman in every tank town," Andre announced. "Like Serge," and he nodded toward the fireman.

"I do not!" Serge announced defensively, his sister-in-law looking over at the man with suspicion as he quickly ducked down and pulled open the firebox door, mumbling a curse while he raked the coals out.

Chuck wanted to make some sort of retort. This

one was different. Hell, this one was the only one who'd ever shown any real interest in him. But instead he nodded in agreement, as if Olivia were just one of a dozen between here and Suzdal.

Andre smiled at him in a fatherly fashion.

"Enjoy life while it is spring, for winter comes without warning," he said.

Chuck, feeling a lump in his throat, looked away. He had managed to forget. For how long? A half hour with her at most, and that half hour had for a brief moment changed everything.

The train, now on the northern spur that ran up into the forest, started to gain speed. The city of Hispania to their left, the new city growing up around the old, swarmed with activity. A rhythmic plume of smoke was rising up from a long row of sheds, sparks swirling up from a roughly made chimney. Most likely the first section of rifle works. Good. Thirty-two hundred rifles were needed to replace lost equipment with the army, and fifteen thousand more were still needed for the troops Hawthorne was training.

All along the tracks was a bustle of activity, sheds, barracks, even a hangar for an aerosteamer. He looked at it all with pride, the pride only he out of all the people on this world could feel. He had reinvented for this world a fair part of what they were now making. He looked back out of the cab at the eight cars behind him. He'd invent a fair bit more if time was allowed.

He settled back against the side of the cab as the train raced northward, and as he shifted the blanket hung over his shoulder he caught a faint scent of jasmine.

It was good to be alive. Even here, with all that was coming, it was good to be alive.

Chapter 3

Cresting the top of the White Hills, the train turned southward, starting a long coasting run down the west slope. Vincent Hawthorne, military adviser to Proconsul Marcus and commander of two corps in training back in Roum, stepped out onto the platform behind his command car. Inside, his staff were packing up their gear, downing a last cup of tea fresh from the galley, looking nervously at their commander.

Dimitri, chief of staff, who had been with Vincent from his first days as a company commander, came out to join him. Vincent looked over his shoulder at the old Rus officer and said nothing.

He pulled the brim of his hardee hat down low over his eyes to shade them from the late-afternoon sun, which hung red in the afternoon sky. Along the side of the track, entrenchments were in place, tangles of abatis out forward, the forested slopes of the hills stripped bare for the fortifications. Sentries were deployed in a high watchtower looking west. But the rolling fields of Rus were empty. He could sense that somehow—that from here all the way back to Suzdal, two hundred miles away, the land was now completely empty, except for the recon patrols, and the detachments of engineers and guerrillas who were systematically preparing the once-friendly countryside for the Merki advance.

Absently he stroked his thin goatee, which still felt a bit strange. He had grown it with the intent of looking like Phil Sheridan, mustache, goatee, hardee hat, high riding boots, another diminutive hard-driving general for war on this strange distant world. Every army needed a Sheridan, someone who could fight without remorse. It was a role Vincent Hawthorne, former Quaker from the Oak Grove School of Vassalboro, Maine, was more than happy to fill.

Vassalboro, Maine. He rarely thought about it now. A different life, a different age. How innocent it had all been then. But youth was innocent, a truth he now fully knew at the age of twenty-three. A breeze stirred up from the west, carrying with it the scent of fresh green fields shimmering in the heat of a late, spring day, the hay ready for its first cutting. Mingled with it was the fresh pine smell of trees newly cut, the logs still oozing resin now laid out as breastworks.

Smells of home, of Maine in late May. School would be out now. He wondered what had ever become of his classmates and friends. Bonnie, lovely Bonnie, married now no doubt, most likely to George Cutler, who had clung to his Quaker upbringing and denounced Vincent for running off to war. Well, George most likely was alive and had won Bonnie in the process. He had a flash memory of Tim Greene, his neighbor and first friend, a good Methodist who had no moral qualms about fighting. No, Tim's qualms had not stopped him from joining up in '61, and he had been killed at Malvern Hill. His older brother Charlie had died of typhoid after Second Manassas. And Jacob Estes, who lived next to the Oak Grove School, had died with the 20th at Gettysburg. They most likely had put up a monument by now on the small village green down by China Lake with all their names upon it. The boys of Vassalboro gone off to see the elephant and be men and dying in the process.

Well, I'm not dead yet, he thought coldly, but Vassalboro will never know that. He pushed the memories away. They held within them too dark a contrast between what he had been and what he now was.

"Strange to see home again."

Vincent looked over his shoulder at Dimitri, who came up to stand beside him.

Vincent said nothing.

"Rus is the peasant and the peasant is Rus," Dimitri said, making the sign of the cross with a small amulet that hung about his neck. He kissed it before tucking it back into his tunic.

"Well, it's their's now," Vincent finally said. "Within a week they'll be coming straight in at us," and he nodded toward the peaceful fields which marched off to the west to disappear in a distant blue haze.

The train whistle sounded high and clear, the speed starting to drop off as they finished the descent toward Kev Station, on what had once been the easternmost boundary of Rus. A regiment was out in the field practicing an advance by line of companies. Vincent watched them appraisingly.

"Good troops," he said quietly.

"First brigade, first division, Second Corps," Dimitri chimed in, nodding to where the brigade flag fluttered in the breeze.

Vincent nodded. The men were veterans, moving with a loose ground-covering stride. They couldn't march in step worth a damn, but that didn't matter, he realized. It was guts, fighting guts, that mattered most. He saw the regiment commander turn his mount to watch as the train passed, the man snapping off a friendly salute to Vincent, which the young general returned.

"Mike Homula, you old bastard," Vincent said, a thin smile creasing his features. Mike had been a sergeant back in the old 35th when Vincent had still been a lowly private. But Vincent knew the man was a good soldier who harbored no resentment over Vincent's mercurial rise to top command.

"Your men are looking good," Vincent shouted. "Join me for a drink tonight."

Mike waved a good-natured thanks and turned back to his command. A stream of oaths filled the air, though they really weren't needed, since the regiment was going through its evolutions with a perfection that even the 35th would have envied.

"Our boys will look that good soon enough," Dimitri said, as if guessing what Vincent's mind was about to latch on to next.

Vincent, already dwelling on that very thought, said nothing. Since last fall he had been responsible for sixty regiments, thirty thousand men in two entirely new corps forming in Roum. As a result he had grown accustomed to all the nightmares associated with creating a new army, and in that he had learned an even deeper respect for Colonel Keane, who had first shaped the Army of the Rus Republic out of nothing but raw peasants. He was now doing the same, and hating every minute of it. Diplomacy in dealing with Marcus had been essential to start with. He had mastered the maddening art of logistics, requisitioning, and ordnance in getting his men outfitted, a task still only half completed. He suspected that Andrew had assigned him to the task in part to train him as well.

He was aware enough of his own ambitions to realize that, especially now that Hans Schuder was gone. If he could create and bring two fighting corps on line, he could do the same for an entire army. Though only five foot three and not much more than a hundred pounds, he had mastered the art of making men twice his size and age tremble at his mere approach. His reputation as perhaps the leading killer of Tugars, commander of the resistance against the Cartha attack on Roum, and hero of the naval battle of St. Gregory had helped to create the aura about him. Would it pay off again?

"And the evil eye shall wither," Dimitri said quietly, still looking out across the fields.

"What?"

"Emerson. I heard Homula read him at the theater one evening back before the naval war. Quite impressive. 'That the evil eye shall wither before the power of love.' "

Love. Emerson, yes, he remembered Emerson, Thoreau, the transcendentalists. He had attended some readings of their works at the Universalist Church back home, something his parents never knew. What would Emerson say about love, about the universality of all living things, when a Merki charge was bearing down upon him, their standards of polished human skulls glinting in the morning light? There was no place for Emerson on this world. He looked over at Dimitri, his perpetual conscience, self-appointed to look after his inner soul. He had been tempted to transfer the man more than once, but he was too good a chief of staff, and besides, he realized, there was part of him that almost wanted the tormenting.

A shudder ran through the train as it went into the final curve toward Kev Station. The city was now clearly in view. All civilians had been cleared out, the last trainload of them going east to Roum only this morning. Andrew's thirty days had indeed bought them that. They had evacuated Rus. All that was left now was the army, and Kev reflected it. The entrenchments along the White Hills curved down, linking into the north and south walls of the city, which was to be held by two regiments from First Corps.

Buildings had been torn down to create firebreaks, sections of the east wall torn open to allow easy access into the rear lines. The fields east of the city were covered with tents, an entire corps still encamped here, close to a water supply. The precious hoard of water in the cisterns above the city was to be used only when the Merki finally arrived.

Around the south gate was a bustle of activity in what had once been the station and was now military headquarters for the army. The army had grown, nearly five corps now active, though after this first part of the campaign the numbers would barely equal four. Staff swarmed about the area, and Vincent smiled at the perpetual raising and lowering of arms in salute as the hierarchy of command moved about.

He turned to look back at Dimitri, who knew why, and stepped up in a fatherly fashion to brush a bit of lint off Vincent's dark blue jacket.

"You look fine," Dimitri said, patting him lightly on the shoulder.

The whistle sounded out a long blast, the engineer refraining from playing a tune, since John Mina was most likely nearby and would not hesitate to climb into the cab and raise holy hell about the waste of steam. He was a lonely crusader of efficiency, this one objection about playing train whistles a near obsession.

The train drifted into the station, bell tolling, steam hissing out, brakes squealing, and they shuddered to a stop.

A small detachment was drawn up and came to attention, presenting arms. The door to the car behind him opened and his staff pushed their way out, the young men eagerly elbowing each other in a scramble for precedent to be first behind their general. Vincent looked back over his shoulder at them, his hard gaze stopping all of them.

A band struck up, bass drum thumping. Several trumpets, one of them very off-key, sounded Ruffles and Flourishes and then went straight into Hail to the Chief. Vincent stiffened slightly as he saw his father-in-law come out of a huge pavilion tent behind the station. Vincent climbed down from the train, the company of Rus infantry coming to present arms. Stepping onto the station platform, Vincent turned slightly to salute the flag of the Rus Republic and then moved down the line of men. His father-in-law approached with a quick stride, left hand outstretched.

The Lincoln image still held sway with the man—high stovepipe hat, chin whiskers, rumpled black coat, and the same dark sad eyes which revealed the truth beneath the happy smile. The two major differences, of course, were that Kal was nearly a foot shorter than his hero and his right sleeve, empty, was pinned up to the shoulder.

"My boy, so good to see you again," Kal exclaimed, grasping Vincent's hand and then pulling him into an affectionate embrace, kissing him loudly on each cheek. Vincent had given up long ago attempting to convert Kal to any semblance of presidential or military protocol.

"How's Tanya, the children?"

"They send their love," Vincent said quietly.

Kal looked into Vincent's eyes. Tanya's last letter had told about Vincent's distance, his near-total withdrawal from his family, and between the lines the old peasant had been able to read out the details, the empty bed night after night, the drinking, the snaps of rage, even the silence and lack of love to the children. Now was not the time.

Kal took Vincent by the shoulder and started back toward the pavilion. He looked over at the line of infantry, still at attention.

"Boris Revanovich! How's the arm?" Kal said, breaking away from Vincent and coming up to stand in front of a towering Rus soldier with a beard that reached down nearly to the man's waist. The bearlike soldier broke into a grin.

"Healed, praise Saint Olga, to whom my wife prayed every night."

"Let's see you move it, then," Kal said, not hesitating to grab the man's musket.

The soldier moved his arm up and down. There was a stiffness to it which he almost managed to hide.

Kal looked back at Vincent.

"These are all old friends," he said, as if introducing the line of privates to the major general. "Their regiment's Suzdalian, the old 8th. I've known them for years—we used to get together at Boris's tavern when I'd sneak out from my boyar's palace for a drink."

Vincent said nothing, finally responding by the slightest incline of his head in acknowledgment.

"Good, very good," Kal said quietly, looking back at Boris and returning his musket. "My love and prayers to your wife. When we take Suzdal back, the first drink at your tavern is on me."

The soldier smiled good-naturedly. "An honor, sire."

"Damn it all," Kal snapped with mock anger. "I'm nothing but a peasant like you, the mouse that happens to be president, and not a damned boyar, and don't you forget that. So don't insult me with that sire talk." He wagged his finger in the man's face.

Vincent waited, trying to hide his impatience at Kal's familiarity, even though he knew the man was most likely a friend from long ago, and that besides it was something even old Abe would do and the hell with protocol.

The men laughed, some of them lowering their muskets as if ready to break ranks and join in a general gab session with Kal, who seemed more than happy to oblige.

Vincent cleared his throat sharply, looking at the men, and they snapped back to attention, eyes straight ahead. Kal looked back at Vincent and nodded.

"My son-in-law here is reminding me that we've got another meeting. I'll try to find you men later and we'll talk some more about the old days at the tavern and what was her name . . ."

"Zvetlana," one of the men whispered, and the line broke into appreciative chuckles.

Kal smiled and looked at Vincent.

"Never say that name around my wife," he said with a conspiratorial wink, and the men laughed even louder.

"All right, my general, we're off," Kal said, and taking Vincent by the arm, he continued down the line, nodding at the men, who were now openly smiling.

Reaching the entry into the vast tent, Kal finally let go of Vincent's arm.

"I've got to go over and see Gates," the president said with a sigh, as if he was silently wishing that he could take the rest of the afternoon off, go back to his peasant friends, and wander off for a drink. "He wants to try this new thing he and Emil created that makes pictures without painting or drawing."

"A daguerreotype?"

"I don't know what its called. He's already made some pictures of the men here. You sure it won't steal your soul?"

Vincent smiled and shook his head. "It's safe."

Kal nodded as if still not assured. "We'll talk later, son." He hugged Vincent, looking into his eyes as if probing for some lost essence, and then left him.

Vincent looked about. The tent, he suddenly realized, had belonged once to Muzta Qar Qarth, and had been retrieved from the flood at the end of the war. It was more than a hundred feet across and was supported in the center by a pole as thick as a ship's mast. The sides were rolled up to let the breeze in. It was packed with the entire higher command of the Army of the Republic along with a sprinkling of Roum officers who were with a division of Fourth Corps and had seen good service in the withdrawal from the Potomac. At the sight of Vincent, the Roum officers started toward the line of men who were following him, eager to see their comrades who were on Vincent's staff. To one side he saw Marcus and Julius, who had arrived the day before for a private meeting with Andrew and Kal. Marcus, seeing Vincent, nodded a friendly greeting, which Vincent knew was genuine. The two had become far closer in the last several months, somehow recognizing a kinship of suffering that had helped to shape them into men impervious to pain.

Vincent drifted through the crowd, which was heavily spiced with the faded and often patched blue uniforms that denoted old veterans of the 35th Maine and 44th New York. He nodded an almost friendly greeting to Andrew Barry, who so long ago had been his sergeant in Company A and was now a corps commander. Twenty-six of them were now generals, and over sixty commanded regiments as lieutenant colonels. By a curious custom, since Andrew refused to promote himself, the rank of colonel was now held by only one man on this world. A fair percentage of the rest of the men from the old Union Army were in staff positions, technical or administrative jobs, either civilian, like Gates as newspaperman and Webster as secretary of the treasury, or military, like Ferguson as chief of the ordnance development department.

And of the six hundred and thirty two who had come through on the *Ogunquit,* nearly two hundred and thirty were dead, forty more were permanently disabled and retired, twenty were insane from the shock of all that had happened, and sixteen more were suicides. Thirty-one others, the sailors from the *Ogunquit,* commanded by Cromwell, were somewhere in Cartha under the traitor Hinsen or dead. Half of us gone, Vincent thought—Malady, Kindred, Houston, Dunlevy, the two Sadler brothers, and of course Hans Schuder. In actual battle casualties of killed, wounded, and missing the regiment and battery had sustained more than one hundred percent losses, some of the men having been wounded two or three times, many of them adding on to injuries endured against the rebels. We're using ourselves up, our bodies wearing down, he thought, looking around the room, seeing more than one empty sleeve, scarred face, eye patch, or slow stiff walk.

"Have a drink, me bucko."

Vincent looked up to see the flowing red mutton-chops and mustache of Pat O'Donald looming up before him.

"I thought this was an official staff meeting, which means no drinking," Vincent said as Pat looked around with a conspiratorial gaze while pulling a flask out of his breast pocket.

"Laddie, the old Army of the Potomac was the hardest-drinking army in history—hell, we didn't start to win until that bastard of a drunk took over. We're just carrying on military tradition, we are, especially with these Rus so willing to join in."

Vincent had heard rumors about the transformation of Pat since the death of Hans, how the man had gone for weeks without a single tear, nor even a nip. It was almost comforting to see him lapse back into his old form, at least for today, and he felt a quiet satisfaction as well that Pat now viewed him as a social equal in the club of killers.

Taking the flask, he ignored Dimitri's cold stare and downed a hard gulp, feeling the pleasant warmth spread out as the vodka did its work, no longer choking and burning him as it once had.

Pat took the flask back, took another swig, then corked it and returned it to his pocket.

"When this cruel war's over I'm going to see to it that we get some proper whiskey made up again. They've got barley on this bloody world, and I've even heard that where them Maya folks are back to the west they've got corn as well. We'll run a rail line out that way, teach 'em how to make stills, and get some trade going."

"When this cruel war's over your drinking days are done," Emil Weiss said, coming up to Pat and pulling the flask from his pocket. "I didn't patch that hole in your stomach up to . . ."

"I know, I know, damn ya " Pat said, and the two fell into squabbling over possession of the flask.

Vincent drifted away and stood in silence near the center of the yurt, his staff standing respectfully behind him. The commander of Sixth and Seventh Corps absently fingered his goatee, hat pulled low over his eyes. No one approached him.

Andrew Lawrence Keane stood in silence as well near the far side of the yurt, watching Vincent. Sheridan to my Grant, Andrew thought. Grant the butcher, who could lose ten thousand in one futile charge at Cold Harbor. Sheridan, who could remorselessly ride up the Shenandoah Valley destroying everything. The younger model of Andrew, but Andrew's heart had somehow been burned out of him. Something had died when he had shot the Merki hanging on the cross in the forum of Roum, as if he had shot the God he had once so fervently believed in and had filled his soul with emptiness.

He knew the emptiness—it had tried to creep into him more than once—but Hans or Kathleen had always pulled him back from the edge. And Hans was gone. He smiled sadly. No, he was not really gone; somehow he could almost sense Hans still alive inside of him, in the same way that a father always lives inside the soul of his son even after he is gone.

And Kathleen, she was always there as well, her wonderful lilt of a brogue coming out in moments of anger, and in those wonderful moments of passion too. When he felt his soul emptying, she put the touch of life back into him, a phenomenon he had believed would never come to him, not after what his fiancée had done to him back before the war. Kathleen had reached even deeper, and it was for her and for their daughter more than everything else that he continued to fight. He felt the burden of an entire nation, and of all of humankind on this planet, resting upon his shoulders. As surely as he lived, or died, the fate of the Rus, the Roum, and yes, the Cartha and all the others was somehow bound up with him in a strange mystical cord that pulsed with life and blood, with passions and dreams of freedom.

But it was their two faces that dwelled within him, his hopes and dreams for their survival that moved his heart the deepest. He had thought often of that and found it to be a powerful thought. So many years ago he had joined an army to fight for an abstraction, a word called union, and a concept of freedom for a race of people of which he knew not a single one by name. He would have willingly died for that; he almost had at Gettysburg.

Now the stakes were far more than Gettysburg and he was the one who would decide the hows and wheres of the fighting. This was no honorable fight as he had known on earth, with rules and even a deadly yet at times almost friendly respect between the two sides. This was brutality of war at its raw edge, a war of massacre, torture, assassination, a primal fight for survival by both sides, for he knew that just as he was fighting for the continuation of his race, so ultimately were the Merki fighting for their survival.

He looked about the room at all his young men, and more than a few old ones as well. When eyes locked for a second there was respect, awe, and from his old comrades of the 35th a deep affection that only soldiers who have served so long together can truly understand. Yet what moved him to continue the fight more than anything else was what he had seen only minutes before as he had slipped out of the small home in the city which served as his private dwelling. Kathleen had dozed off, exhausted after being called out in the middle of the night to try to save a boy brought in with a gut wound from a dropped musket. She had saved him, repairing the damage, and had stayed in the hospital till the afternoon, seeing after her other patients and then going the rounds with the score of doctors she was responsible for training.

She had fallen asleep with Maddie curled up beside her for her afternoon nap. The sunlight had streaked in low, filling the bedroom with a soft golden glow that always seemed to have a special warmth to it in the late days of spring. Their soft rhythmic breathing was the only sound in the room, the rumble and turmoil of war somehow hushed. He had felt tears come to his eyes as he had watched them sleeping, the sleep of innocence and of exhausted compassion. If need be he would die to save that, to save that for everyone, to save it for his own daughter so that someday, years from now, she might know such gentle peace as well.

He looked back at Vincent, who stood alone, and he felt a lingering sadness, remembering the young boy who had cried when he first confessed that he had killed a man. War burns the soul, but for this one the scars had fused into a cracked and twisted mass of pain.

"Everyone's here now."

Pat was by his side.

"How'd Vincent seem to you?"

"He'll be a killing devil when the mischief starts," Pat replied.

Andrew nodded to Bob Fletcher, who had been in charge of food supplies and now doubled as chief of staff with Hans gone. Fletcher went up to the low dais at the back end of the yurt, and as he stepped up behind the podium the conversation in the tent started to drop away.

"All right, dammit," Fletcher growled in his barely understandable Rus, "let's get started."

Appreciative laughter echoed in the tent, and the crowd of several hundred officers moved to the rough-hewn benches set up in a semicircle around the podium and the rough canvas map stretched out behind it.

The Roum officers moved to the back section of the yurt, where a translator stood ready to repeat what was being said. Andrew moved swiftly up to the podium, the call for attention sounding out sharply, and the men fell silent, standing up stiffly. He motioned with his one hand for Father Casmar to come up and join him.

The prelate of the church stepped up to the dais, and all in the room, Rus, Yankee, and even Roum, lowered their heads. Smiling in his usual affable way, the priest blessed them, then patted Andrew on the shoulder and withdrew without any fanfare.

Coming from a very Yankee New England, where suspicion of popery was something of a past time, the men of the 35th had taken to the prelate of the Church of Rus with a surprising and genuine affection. Not once had he ever attempted to proselytize, and he had gladly participated in the dedication of the various churches and small chapels that the men had erected back in Suzdal. Quite a few had gradually drifted into the Rus Church, especially the Catholics of the heavily Irish 44th New York, seeing in Perm just another name for God, and it was obvious just who Kesus was. The memory of early Russian Orthodoxy, with a good smattering of Slavic paganism, had survived in the thousand years since the Rus had first arrived on this world. Father Casmar had fully accepted Saint Patrick as a saint, and a green icon of the protector of Ireland had soon appeared on the church walls along with a stained-glass window of a shamrock to replace a window in the cathedral blown out in a bombing raid.

"Gentlemen, we've got a lot of ground to cover in the next day, so I suggest we get straight into it."

The tent was silent except for the high distant

thumping, the sound of an aerosteamer making its way westward on a reconnaissance flight up to Suzdal.

"Tomorrow will mark the end of thirty days since the death of Jubadi, Qar Qarth of the Merki. I thought it best that we try to gather together now, since I doubt if we will have a chance to do so again in such a relaxed fashion until this war is finished."

The men stirred. They all knew that the strange truce, which had given them a precious month, was about to end, but it was still hard to hear it so plainly spoken. Within a matter of days they would again be fighting for their lives.

"I just want to take these few moments to go over our plan of action in general terms so that all of us can see what will happen. Later you'll meet with your separate corps commanders to review things in detail. I know you do not want to face what I'm presenting now, but there is no other way."

He paused for a moment to look over at Kal. His old friend had stood shocked when he first told him of what he planned to do, and he was still sickened by it.

"I know all of us had hoped to hold them here in front of Kev, and perhaps we can, but I doubt it."

"But to lose all of Rus?"

A brigade commander stood up, looking up angrily at Andrew. His defiance caused a stir through the meeting.

"It's my land too," Andrew replied, his voice controlled, yet conveying that nothing would now change his mind. "My child was born in this land, Suzdal was my city, the soil of Rus gave all of us life. But I have no desire to have my scorched bones buried in it."

He hesitated for a brief instant.

"At least not until I am a very old man."

A soft chuckle echoed, easing the tension but not breaking it.

"Tomorrow the Merki will bury their Qar Qarth.

They can move fifty or more miles a day starting the following morning, which means in as few as four days they will be here."

He pointed back to the first map, lines in red drawn in to mark the probable advance routes of the Merki columns. From here all the way back to the approaches to Vazima, every road was laden with traps, the wells were filled with rocks, the bridges were burned, the river fords were sprinkled with submerged stakes, trees were felled to block roads going through forests. Campfires at night were enlivened with laughter over some of the tricks that had been laid out. Barely a poisonous snake could now be found in the wild in all of Rus after word had spread about one angry peasant who had caught several of them and put them inside a barrel that looked like it might contain food. His trick was now imitated in nearly every barn throughout the country. Beehives had been rigged to fall over or burst open, and wasp nests had been placed under overturned buckets next to wells that looked like they still might have water.

The thirty days had given them the chance to go back and do the damage, and also to retrieve quite a few thousand tons of food that had been abandoned in the initial evacuation. Seed stocks had even been retrieved as well and shipped to warehouses in Roum or moved up into the northern woods and hidden away for if and when they ever returned. The last of the peasants who had been moving east on foot had been sent on to Roum. Even now, crews were working to tear up the track starting east of Vazima, working backward toward Roum. At a hundred tons to the mile, several trainloads a day were now heading back east, the precious metal heading to the cannon and rifle works or stockpiles to be used for emergency repairs.

They had pulled it off. And it was still not enough.

"What we've done, surely it will slow them down," the brigadier replied.

Andrew looked over to Bob Fletcher, who stood to one side of the dais. He came up to join Andrew.

"You know that victualing the army is my job," Bob said, speaking slowly to choose his Rus words carefully. "We can surmise certain things about their forces from our own experiences."

He stepped back to the map and with upraised hand pointed across the length of Rus.

"Our land between the sea and the forest, from the Neiper to here, is something over thirty thousand square miles, just about the same size as Maine.

"For the last thirty days, the Merki have been moving their people up the roadbed of our military railroad, and up the old Tugar road, as you used to call it, west of the Neiper. Those bastards have been forced to funnel several million of their people and at least a million and a half horses and maybe upward of half a million head of other animals up those two paths. From what Bullfinch's ironclad reconnaissance up the Neiper has told us, they're still at it and most likely will be for another month.

"They've got to eat, and we have decided not to cooperate." He snapped out the last words, cold and angry, and there was a bristle of defiance in the room. Andrew looked at the men with pride. Five years ago they had been terrified peasants who would have lowered their heads and gone into the slaughter pits, would have offered their open barns, the years of food stockpiled for the horde's arrival.

Now they were soldiers.

"They've picked the best time to campaign, and in some ways the delay of a month has helped them in the short term. The grass here in Rus is at its richest; an acre of prime pasture can support several dozen horses for a single day's cropping.

"When the Merki advance, they'll have over a million horses with them. I estimate for right now they'll need a hundred square miles of land per day for their horses, a thousand square miles per week, that's not counting the need for water or for the food of their own army. We figure that if need be they'll start to eat their remounts to keep going."

He paused and looked back up at the map.

"In other words, for right now, their army should be able to cross Rus on a front forty miles wide, one umen per mile of front, and be able to move at nearly full speed."

"So they'll hit us with full force, then," Rick Schneid, commander of the Second Corps asked, shifting the cigar he had been half smoking and half chewing.

Andrew nodded.

"So why the hell have we been tearing up our own country?" the Rus brigade commander asked.

Fletcher smiled.

"It's what comes behind the advance. Oh, they'll move fast, all right, but I daresay that around Suzdal it's getting damned crowded and forage is short. It must be a logistical nightmare moving those people through a hundred miles of forest at most likely not more than ten to fifteen miles to the day. That entire horde will be moving behind the army, funneling through fords in the rivers, and it will be spread out wide and there'll be no willing humans to give them their food as they advance. It'll start to get tough. Those who are moving along the northern edge of the forest or down along the sea will have other problems."

He looked over at Andrew.

"Bullfinch's people will mount harassing raids. If they see a chance, they'll land some detachments, kill some, and pull back out. We've left a scattering of volunteers in the forests. They'll sweep out at night to raid and pull back in at dawn. The harassing will force them to contract in toward the center, giving them less forage."

It also meant, he realized, that he had given orders to kill Merki noncombatants. That had been a tough one, which to his surprise Kathleen had pushed for with the cold statement "They're on our land."

The land is still rich enough now to support them," Fletcher said. "However, they'll be tightening their belts a bit and going slow. The prime grazing lands used by the army will have been cropped over, and there are no stockpiles for the rest."

"Yet the army will still be here within the week," Schneid said.

Andrew nodded.

"If we tried to, we might be able to hold them here as we talked about nearly a month ago. If we could stop them for two weeks, better yet a month, they'd be in trouble, forced to disperse a good part of their horses and all remounts just to keep them alive."

He hesitated.

"However, I'm not expecting us to do that anymore."

There was a stirring in the room.

"We've got four corps here for a front of forty miles," someone from the back of the tent stated. "Hell, we tried to hold twice that length of the Potomac with only three."

"And we lost the Potomac," Andrew replied, "along with over ten thousand men, fifty-four guns, and over a million rounds of small-arms ammunition. The truth is that we have little more than three corps here after casualties over the last seventy days, and at best we took out maybe less than ten percent of their numbers."

He hesitated.

"I'm not making the same mistake twice. You men and those you command are too precious to be wasted in a futile stand here."

"We've fortified the hills out there for a month," a

young brigadier said, pointing toward the White Hills, which were visible behind Andrew through the open rear flap of the tent.

Andrew nodded.

"Was that for nothing, then?" the officer continued. "The hands of my men have been bleeding since last fall with all the digging we've been doing, first on the Potomac, then the Neiper, and now here."

"And we're going to keep on digging," Andrew replied. "If digging will save lives I'll have all of you dig right down to the pit of hell.

"The Merki expect this to be our place of last stand. Their aerosteamers have penetrated this far five times over the last month, and they've seen the work we've done. They're going to come on hard and expect to wrap up this campaign in a fortnight."

He hesitated for a moment. The men had been gearing for a showdown fight, a grim Alamo-like stand on the edge of their territory. He had been arguing this point with Kal and the senators for the last month. He had to admit that he had been lying to them from the first day that he had conceived of this mass evacuation and the assassination of Jubadi. Kev would not be the final fallback position—he had from the beginning felt that it would be impossible to hold. He could sense as well that the Merki now believed that they could rush forward for the knockout blow. He would leave them only thin air to strike at.

"Tonight, army artillery reserve and corps artillery reserve for all five corps will be evacuated back to Hispania. Tomorrow night and the night after, all available trains will evacuate Third Corps and First Corps back to Hispania, where you will start to dig in at once. At the end of four days the only formations left here will be a brigade from Pat's corps and the newly formed mounted light cavalry units."

He waited for a moment for the angry confusion to die down.

"That'll leave just over two thousand men and a couple of batteries of the four-pound guns to cover the entire White Hills front," Schneid said.

Andrew nodded.

"It's a question of mobility. It's always been mobility," Andrew replied. "We've got thirty-eight trains, and from the work they've been doing we'll be lucky to have thirty engines up and running by the end of the week. If we meet the Merki here and they break the line, we'll be able to evacuate only two corps at most. That'll mean thirty thousand men get left behind with all equipment, to be surrounded and wiped out by horse-mounted Merki warriors. It'll be the end of any hope of winning."

"Winning?" the angry brigadier replied. "Hell, you're telling us to abandon what little of our country we have left. I'm going to die, we all are going to die, we knew that two months ago, and I want to die on my own soil, the land of Rus."

Andrew felt a flicker of anger at the brigadier's defiance but let it pass. This might be the army, but it was the army of a republic, and he was telling these men that they had lost their country and were going into exile.

He stepped off the dais and went up to the brigadier, who looked nervous at his commander's approach.

"Mikhail of Murom, isn't it?"

The man nodded.

"Barry's corps, bloody second division," the man replied.

"I know you. You've been in the army from the beginning, haven't you."

The tent was silent, the Roum translator in the back speaking in a hushed whisper.

"I started as a private in Hawthorne's company, served on your staff during the Tugar siege, was promoted to lieutenant colonel after St. Gregory in command of the 1st Murom, and to brigadier with a Medal of Merit for holding the Ford on the Neiper."

The man rattled off his record with pride.

"And you were a peasant before the wars, before the republic?"

The man nodded, looking about at his comrades, who, like him, had risen the hard way, through skill, intelligence, and more than a shade of luck.

Knowing it was melodramatic, Andrew reached down and scooped up a handful of dust from the tent floor and stood back up. He held his hand out and let the dust trickle out between his fingers.

"This is nothing," he shouted.

He flung the rest of the dust down and then stepped forward and put his hand on the man's shoulder.

"And you, you are everything."

The brigadier blinked nervously.

Andrew looked away from him.

"You men here, you are everything, you are the hope of Rus, the only chance for a future we shall ever have. It is your blood, your hearts, your minds, and you strong right arms that will win this war. The soil, the land, it will be here now and forever. It cares not. It is unfeeling. It is the land. It will wait for us and we shall have it back!"

The men stood silent, gathering in around him to hear his words.

"An army can fight only as long as it lives. You, my friend," and he pointed back to Mikhail. "You think that this war is about the land. That is often how some think of war—a moving from place to place, victory counted by who holds what land, what town. I tell you that is not the way this war now is. It is about armies. Their goal is not to conquer the land, their goal is to destroy this army, just as our goal is to destroy theirs by whatever means possible.

"I need your flesh and blood to stay alive, and I have only thirty-eight trains to do it with. When they break the White Hills line—and there is no doubting they will do it—I will not have one man more here than I can evacuate in a single night. That means that nearly all our strength will already be far to the east.

"Our fight here will not be to the death because we are not yet ready and they are too strong."

He turned away, went back up to the map, and pointed to the vast stretch of open steppe between Kev and Hispania.

"We will give them this place if they come on strongly. We will fall back to the Penobscot, the Kennebec and then finally back to the Sangros. All the time falling back, destroying what they can use. Perm willing, if the grass of the steppe dries we'll burn it. We'll leave them nothing but ashes."

He looked back over to Bob Fletcher.

"What the colonel's getting at," Fletcher explained, "is that the farther they come after us the tougher it'll get. We'll pull out by rail but they'll be following on horse, a million horses to feed. The area east of the Penobscot for nearly eighty miles is damn near a desert, and a month from now there'll be precious little water if the rain holds off. The ground between the Kennebec and the Sangros is high prairie grass—at best eight or nine horses per acre per day can graze there, maybe even less, especially in the heat of summer. What the colonel here and I are figuring on is that we can let the land help us, slow them down, wear them out, make them pull their belts in tight. If we hold the Sangros line, within a matter of days they'll have to start picketing their horses thirty or forty miles to the rear to keep them alive. That'll cut their mobility down, which has always been their biggest advantage over us."

"And sooner or later we'll have to stand," Mikhail said, his words sounding now more like a question than defiance.

Andrew stepped back up to him and put his hand on the man's shoulder.

"Yes, in the end we'll stand. But they will have

advanced across five hundred miles of barrenness to reach us and we will have fallen back all the way to Hispania."

He looked over to the center of the pavilion where Vincent stood.

"And two fresh corps under General Hawthorne will be waiting there to join us, armed with the new weapons that even now are being produced again in the factories we took all the way from Suzdal to Hispania and Roum. There'll be a hundred additional field pieces, millions more rounds of small-arms ammunition. We'll have an army of near seven corps, over one hundred thousand men, rather than half the survivors of a massacre who retreated pell-mell with the Merki on their heels.

"We here will be together then, all of us, to make that final stand."

He looked around the tent.

"I cannot promise you victory, but I can promise you a near-run thing, and a battle unlike any this world has ever seen, the Merki hungry and desperate, and we as strong as we shall ever be. And when it is done, if we are victorious we will take this land back again rather than have our burned and cracked bones scattered across it. That is what I offer you; that is why we will not stand here."

Michael hesitated, looking straight at Mikhail.

He lowered his head.

"I am yours to command, Colonel Keane."

A growl of approval rose up from the men.

"We few, we happy few, we band of brothers."

Andrew looked over to Gregory, the young Rus student of Shakespeare, and now chief of staff for what was left of Third Corps. Gregory's eyes shone brightly with emotion.

Andrew patted Mikhail on the shoulder and went back to the podium. He had given the hard message, and they would follow. He looked over at Kal, who begrudgingly nodded his approval, though Andrew knew that his old friend was filled with anguish to hear that this time they were leaving Rus behind, most likely forever.

"John, would you go over the plan of withdrawal?" Andrew asked.

John Mina came up to stand beside him.

Andrew looked about once more at those who were so eager to follow him and then raised his gaze to the battle standards hanging from the canvas ceiling above him. The shot-torn standards of four of the corps were above him, clustered around each corps flag the standards and guidons of division and brigade commands. The standard of Third Corps was new, that of its first and second divisions missing. He pushed the thought away as his gaze shifted to the flag of the Army of the Republics, a golden eagle emblazoned on a navy-blue field, a gold star above each shoulder, flanked on either side by the faded stars and stripes and state regimental flags of the 35th Maine and 44th New York Light Artillery. It was as if all the ghosts now hovered above them.

He looked back at the flesh and blood in the room, most of them all so young, a young army made from scratch, a commander considered old if he was forty, as I now am, Andrew realized.

He looked at the men and wordlessly raised his hand in a salute, those before him coming to attention and saluting in reply. Without another word he turned and left the tent.

Though the sides of the tent had been open, it had still felt too stuffy, and he was glad to get back out into the open air. In the background he could hear John Mina going into the details of the withdrawal—train schedules, rendezvous points, emergency fall-backs. He walked away, starting across the rail yard, barely acknowledging the salutes of the sentries who had been posted in a perimeter around the tent.

Crossing over the main rail line, he started up the slope of the White Hills, skirting wide around a brigade encampment area, not willing to face all the rituals that a supreme commander would have to go through to get from one end of the camp to the other. From the corner of his eye he saw a young Roum captain standing next to a sentry who had summoned the officer. The two looked relieved that Andrew had gone in the opposite direction. He smiled to himself, remembering a similar moment shortly after Grant had taken command. Grant had gone on an unannounced early-evening tour, turning left to visit their sister regiment, the 80th New York. He had laughed to hear the mad scramble, while thanking God it had not been his own unit so rousted out. He was in no mood to subject others to that type of torture.

He continued up the slope, weaving through a line of abatis, stepping carefully around trap pits, still marked with stakes, which would be pulled up when the Merki finally came. The lines of entrenchments and breastworks were empty, the men in camps preparing their dinners, the scent of frying fatback wafting on the breeze, mingled with wood smoke and the smell of brewing sassafras tea.

The smell triggered pleasant memories, the memories of over a thousand nights camped in the field, on the march, or in winter quarters. Cooking fires were winking up from the encampments, with the stilling of the early-evening breeze the smoke curling straight up into the dark blue sky. To the west the sun was setting, a thin crescent of a moon dropping down behind it, the other moon already gone, not to appear until the hour before dawn.

Finding a stump of a tree, he settled down against it and looked out over the fields. The army was spread out along the hills, camps arranged, those lucky enough to have tents pitching them in neat company rows, the other units making due with pine bough lean-tos. Distant laughter carried in the still air, sounding sharp and clear, songs floating, an unusual minor-key ballad of the Roum, and an old familiar song in Rus. The English words drifted in his thoughts as he followed along: "Be it ever so humble, there's no place like home," he hummed along quietly.

It suddenly reminded him of a night like this, the week before Chancellorsville. The two armies, north and south, were encamped, facing each other on the Rappahannock River. It had started out simple enough, a group of rebs singing a tune, some Union sentries on the other side of the river joining in. Pretty soon thousands of soldiers from the two sides had drifted down to the riverbank, leaving their rifles behind in an impromptu truce, serenading each other in turn, a rebel "Dixie" to a union "Battle Hymn." Back and forth they had sung through evening, the sun going down, the stars coming out, Orion on its last days of spring hanging low in the western sky, chasing the twilight.

They were no longer enemies, they were away from home, boys of a common faith, once of a common country, caught in a drama of flags and drums and blood, who for this night had harkened back to a village green or a church picnic, singing the old songs together again.

And then the tattoo had sounded, the call to return to quarters before the final whispering of taps. The two sides started to break up, and then from the southern shore a clear high tenor had started, singing in the first line. In an instant, in the thousands they had joined together, voices from both sides of the river joining together.

"Be it ever so humble . . ."

Hardly a voice finished the song, silent tears choking the voices off, men lowering their heads, weeping for home, for lost friends, for peace. In the darkness the song drifted into silence and they turned away from each other to return to their camps. A week later, thirty thousand of them were dead or wounded in the woods of Chancellorsville.

He found his eyes clouded from the memory of that moment, the most poignant of the war. He heard a rustling. Startled, and a bit ashamed, he looked up, quickly wiping his eyes as Kal came up out of the gathering shadows.

"Just remembering," he said quietly.

Kal, smiling, nodded in understanding and sat down beside him.

"Peaceful evening," Kal said, leaning back against the stump, taking off his hat and wiping his brow. His shoulder touched against Andrew's, and the two sat in silence for several minutes looking out over the encampments, the fields, the purple sky of sunset.

"I can see how a soldier can come to love these moments," Kal said. "It's so peaceful now, the work of day finished, the boys singing, food cooking."

He looked about the valley twinkling with firelight.

"Its a good moment. Hard to believe somehow."

"Why?"

"Oh . . ." The old peasant sighed. "Difficult to explain. You can feel it on the wind, their young pride, their eagerness to do well, their belief in all of this. I remember us so different, when I was their age. We were slaves, laboring in the fields, the boyars and the church keeping us in fear, the dreaded whisper of the approaching Tugars. I remember when they first came."

He paused for a moment.

"I lost my first love, Anastasia. She was taken for their moon festival.

"I loved her," and his voice tightened. "You know, that was one of the reasons I so wanted to fight when you first came to us and I saw the chance. I feared my Tanya would be taken the same way."

Andrew nodded, thinking of his own daughter.

"We fight for ourselves when young, then we fight for our children," he said quietly.

"The young. That's what they are, an army of boys."

"My army back home was the same," Andrew said. "Boys who were men at eighteen."

He leaned back and looked up at the first stars of evening. " 'The fiery trial through which we pass will light us down, in honor or dishonor, to the last generation.' "

Kal looked over at him and smiled. "Lincoln. I remember Vincent telling me that, back near the beginning when he was recovering from his escape from Novrod and was in my cabin."

"I'm worried about that boy," Andrew said, unable to say more, to admit the guilt he felt for so using Vincent, making him into a superlative general and destroying him at the same time.

"So am I." Kal sighed. "I don't think the marriage with my daughter will last if he stays that way. She still loves him, always will, but she cannot live with a soul of ice who drinks himself into oblivion night after night."

"You're speaking as if we have a future," Andrew said, forcing a smile and looking over at his old friend.

"I forget myself sometimes," Kal replied. "I dream that this war is finished, that we've won, that life goes on."

"Hard to imagine somehow. I've been at it for eight years. Before we came here, through the tunnel of light, I figured in another six months my old war would be finished. The Confederacy was on its last legs."

"And you'd have gone home to your Maine?"

Andrew sighed. Since coming here he had imagined that path. Perhaps Kathleen and he would have come together even back on earth. He would have returned to Bowdoin with her, picked up college teaching again, raised a family on his professor's salary, and quietly slipped into middle age, saber hanging over the mantel, hair becoming gray, telling his children of his war, marching a bit stiffly in Fourth of July parades in Brunswick, Maine, and growing old in peace.

But would he ever have been happy? He remembered a friend of his from the 20th Massachusetts who had finally quit the army after one wound too many to body and soul. How one night he had so completely summed it all up. "We have shared the incommunicable experience of war," he had said. "In our youths our hearts were touched with fire."

There had been nearly five more years of it now. It was as much his life as breathing, eating, and, God forgive the comparison, even making love with Kathleen in the stillness before dawn.

"In a way you do love it all, don't you, Andrew?"

Andrew could only nod his head.

"I hate it," Kal whispered. "That's the difference. I'm sick to death of army camps, of looking at friends, their sons, standing stiffly in line, trying to look so brave. I almost wish I could just be a peasant again, singing some asinine ballad for my lord Ivor, the old drunken bully. The Tugars would be gone now for three years. Life would have gone on. That's the difference between soldiers and peasants. I look at these boys and know that you've made them into something else. They'll never be peasants again, and somehow that makes me sad. They've learned how to kill."

"And Tanya might be nothing but blackened bones."

Kal looked over angrily at Andrew.

"She will be nevertheless."

"Do you honestly believe that?"

Kal lowered his head.

"I try not to," he whispered. "Two months ago, the morning after we heard about Hans, I told you that we'll live or die by your decisions."

"I remember," Andrew whispered, ashamed in a

way that he had so thoroughly lost heart in everything on that shocking morning of defeat. He was still tormented by doubts, but in the last thirty days he had mastered his nerves again, knowing he had to if he was going to breathe any defiance back into an army, an entire race, that had been so thoroughly shaken by the first round of defeats and the loss of their country.

"We've lost our land," Kal said, and his voice was thick with pain. "To me, to the peasant, that is everything, his very soul. The boyars owned it all, but it was we who worked it, who brought life out of it. Not even the Tugars or the Merki can do that. They come and go, the name of the boyars changes from generation to generation, but the peasant is eternal. As long as he is on his land." He leaned back, looking up into the night sky.

"Half of all the Rus are dead now. Most of my friends are dead, and the rest are in the army, ready to die in another five days when the Merki finally get here."

"They'll not die in five days," Andrew said sharply.

"They'll die inside when they leave here forever."

"Damn you, Kal, do you want to lose?"

Kal looked over at him.

"Didn't you hear what I was saying down there? This land is nothing—Suzdal, all of it. All that counts now is two things. The factories, to make more weapons—and for the moment they're safe to the east," and he nodded toward the flickering fires. "And the army.

"That is what Vuka now has to defeat. He can occupy this entire damn world, but as long as the army exists and the tools for it to fight with are made, we still have a hope of winning."

"At what cost?"

"You made your choice back in the beginning," Andrew said coldly, his voice almost accusing. "On the night we were voting to decide whether to stay in Rus or to flee before the Tugars came, you started the peasant revolt in Suzdal."

Kal shifted uneasily beneath Andrew's gaze.

"My men voted then—they voted to come to your rescue and overthrow the boyars. You forced our hand. More than two hundred of those men who rushed to Suzdal that night are dead now, and most of the rest are scarred inside and out by what's happened since.

"But by God you are free. And better to die free than to live like the cattle you were."

He had chosen his word deliberately, and it stung. He could see Kal flinch at the word that no one now used, so loathsome were its connotations.

Low to the west, a circle of kerosene lamps flickered to life, marking the landing field for the aerosteamer that was coming back in to land, the evening patrol finished. The two watched intently as the shadowy bulk of the flying machine circled in and its ground crew secured its nose to the mast and then struggled with its bulk to tow it back into its hangar. From behind them a train whistle sounded in the distance, low and mournful, the engine coming through the gap in the White Hills, a thin plume of sparks marking its passage.

The night sounds were starting, crickets chirping, an owl hooting, a ghostly flutter of wings, while the silent flicking of fireflies blinked across the hillside, matching the campfires which illuminated the hills for miles around.

"When this cruel war is over . . ."

The voices echoed, mingling with other songs.

"Oh Perm, hear us now at eventide . . ."

"Bring the old bugle, boys, we'll sing another song . . ."

"There was a boyar's daughter, a lass of golden hair . . ."

"Amazing grace, how sweet the sound . . ."

The voices mingled together, the dozens of songs drifting, joining together into one harmony of living at the edge of war's destruction.

Kal stood up, hat in hand, listening to the voices which floated about them. Overhead the Great Wheel stood high in the sky, filling the heavens with light. The ground about them glowed with campfires, diffused now by the beginning of a soft milky ground fog that seemed to rise ghostlike from the earth.

Andrew stood up to join him, soaking in the life around him, feeling it in his heart, in his soul.

He knew what would happen tomorrow as he looked westward, imagining the nightmare two hundred miles away. Tomorrow they would bury the Qar Qarth, the one he had killed himself as surely as if he had pulled the trigger. He knew the horror of what would happen there, and he could feel the terror of the hundred thousand or more who tonight would be looking at this same sky, knowing that this would be the last night they would ever see such a sight.

That thought had come to him more than once, the cold sense that tomorrow he most likely would be dead, and that the world would continue on without him.

Tomorrow. God forgive me what happens tomorrow, he thought. He knew that he would not sleep tonight thinking about it, their fear reaching across all these miles to touch his heart.

"Perm help them," Kal whispered, and Andrew knew that Kal had been thinking the same thing.

"And help us after tomorrow," Andrew replied. "Let their deaths at least mean something for the future."

"Small comfort for the dying."

Andrew found he could not reply.

He tried to push the nightmare away, the massacre that the Merki would perform on their prisoners to water the grave of Jubadi. He looked back to his army, to his men, and tried to draw comfort from them, their innocence, their life.

A haunting tune drifted to him. Another old song from before, carried to this world, words changed to fit here . . . "Shenandoah."

He blinked back the tears as he listened.

> "Oh gentle Neiper, I long to see you.
> Roll away, you rolling river . . ."

The song leapt from campfire to campfire, the other songs drifting away, thousands of voicing joining into one.

> "Oh gentle Neiper, I long to see you . . .
> Away, I'm bound away,"

The night on the Rappahannock, and then a week later . . .

He lowered his head.

"Let's go back, my friend," Andrew whispered.

"Kesus help us," Kal sighed, putting his hat back on and looking up at Andrew. "I need your strength, Andrew."

"And I, Mr. President, need yours," Andrew said in reply.

He put his arm around Kal's shoulder, and together the two went slowly back down the hill.

Chapter 4

Tamuka, shield-bearer of the Qar Qarth, opened his eyes. The thin crescent of the morning moon hung low in the eastern sky, which was ablaze with the blood-red light of dawn. His breath of the *ka* came back to its slow steady rhythm, the near-deathlike breathing of meditation, which reached into the spirit of the *tu,* giving way to the quickening pace of life.

He felt an uneasy stirring about him. Though all was supposed to be silence, such a thing was impossible. Every hill was crowded with the multitudes who had sat through the night of vigil, and now with the final moments before dawn, there was a stirring— the creaking of leather armor, the cracking of joints, the sighing of the impatient, the sound of millions who lived, who had sat in silence for the dead. There was the other sound as well, the mournful cries of the cattle, which could not be stilled, their sobs cutting the night air like a sharpened blade—but then they were only cattle, and thus of no account, though their behavior lacked any semblance of dignity.

The cattle. Early in the evening, just after the setting of the sun, while the moon of receding twilight had yet hung in the sky, his *ka* had told him that the other was there, that Keane was somehow aware of him, of what was taking place. He had reached to Keane, his spirit sense seeking this one out, and with an inner sense of vision he could almost see him, standing upon a distant hill, looking back to the west.

His hatred had flared out for a moment, his thoughts driving a dagger of fear into the cattle's heart. War could be fought not just on the battlefield, but in the heart as well.

A single horn sounded, a deep-throated narga. Tamuka let his gaze shift for an instant to the high tower that had been constructed for this one single purpose. It stood on the hills to the north, the voice of the narga carrying through the light fog hanging in the valleys. Several seconds later he saw the thin sliver of light break the horizon, reflecting dimly in the waters of the lake stretching off to the east.

Other nargas sounded, their voices swelling, echoing across the fields, mingling with the sighs as hundreds of thousands came to their feet.

The chant started. It had no real words; it was just a deep plaintive call, which he suspected perhaps eons ago did have words, but through the endless generations the words had been lost and only the sounds, a bone-chilling growling, had remained.

The warriors rose, covering the fields and hills for miles with their dark forms. The sun slowly broke the horizon, shining dully on the burnished shields and helmets of the assembled.

Tamuka stood with them, the growl rising, growing stronger, chilling his blood with its ancient calling until it would have rivaled even the thunder of the skies, the howling of the wind.

"It is time."

The voice of Sarg was distant, as if calling from another world. Tamuka nodded, allowing his gaze to return fully to this time, this place.

He looked to his left.

Vuka. He felt nothing at the moment. The Qar Qarth wavered slightly, his features drawn, pained. Sarg reached out to touch him, and the Qar Qarth flinched.

"I'm all right," he whispered.

Tamuka ignored him, looking instead to his companion to his right.

Hulagar, shield-bearer to the dead Qar Qarth, was silent, a distant light in his eyes, as if in this final night the memories had swirled into his soul, and even now were bearing him away.

"Beautiful sight," Hulagar whispered, a thin smile lighting his features. His eyes darted, looking out upon the horde, which still faced to the east, its cry thundering about them.

"A beautiful sight, a world that was wondrous."

Hulagar sighed and turned to face Tamuka.

"Let's begin," Hulagar said, his voice almost cheerful.

Sarg nodded solemnly and turned away, going back into the yurt, the others following. The interior was dim, except for the single lamp that hung above the dais. The washers of the dead stood about the body, heads lowered, their task only now completed, the last incantation having been written upon the funeral shroud that encased the mortal remains of Jubadi with the sounding of the first narga of the last day of mourning.

Sarg approached the dais, Tamuka, Vuka, and Hulagar behind him. The silent ones, the guardians, stepped aside to let them pass.

One of the washers turned and bowed low.

"We return our Qar Qarth to his people for the final time. We return his mortal remains. His spirit is ready for the endless ride of the ancestors who soar over us."

The washers, with heads lowered, withdrew from the yurt.

Sarg turned to Vuka and nodded.

The new Qar Qarth, walking unsteadily, mounted the dais and knelt down before the remains of his father. The tent was silent, though outside the crying of the horde still thundered.

Tamuka watched him intently, wondering if now, at

this moment, some sense of all that he had to do had somehow been realized at last. He doubted it. All Vuka could see was the power, the glory, nothing beyond that, nothing of the struggle, of the cunning that would be needed, nothing of all the changes that would have to be wrought if there was to be any hope of surviving in this world.

Vuka had spoken of simply riding through the cattle, of slaughtering those who resisted, of scattering the rest, of taking their machines of war and then riding on to face again the old enemy the Bantag.

Madness.

He knew that within his soul the Qar Qarth was now truly afraid of the cattle. Had they not struck down his father from almost beyond sight? The report of the guns on the cattle ships that stood upon the river now made him flinch and look about fearfully. It was a war he now feared. If war could be fought in ways other than upon the battlefield, the Yankee cattle Keane had already defeated Vuka—in fact, he knew that this Keane most likely had planned for it. It was a strange transformation in Vuka, who had at one time been able to ride fearlessly, almost too impetuously, against the Bantag. But now he was terrified of being struck down by something as lowly as an animal, a mere cattle.

Vuka at last stirred, coming back to his feet. He stood unsteady for a moment, swaying. Sarg came up to him, reaching out. Vuka looked around the yurt, the yurt that after the purification would be his. He steadied himself, then stepped down and came back to Tamuka's side.

Sarg nodded a signal to the commander of the silent ones, who clapped his hand once. The guards turned, and a dozen of them gathered on either side of the dais. Long poles were inserted through rings set into the wooden platform. The commander clapped a second time. The guards stood up, hoisting the platform onto their shoulders.

They turned, holding the body of Jubadi high, while two other guards reached up to the lamp with a long pole, carefully unhooked it, and brought it down, placing it inside a glass carrying case so that no errant breeze might extinguish it during the procession.

Tamuka stepped back, letting the bearers of the lamp and of the funeral platform of Jubadi move pass. At the entrance to the yurt an even broader platform than the one Jubadi rested upon was brought in and laid upon the ground. The dozen guards carrying Jubadi stepped up upon it.

Eighty guards flanked it on all four sides. Again there was a single clap of command, and this platform was raised up to rest upon the guards' shoulders, standing atop it the dozen silent ones who bore upon their shoulders the body of Jubadi Qar Qarth. Nearly twenty feet high, the two-tiered funeral stage now stood waiting at the entrance to the yurt, the front flap pulled back to let them pass.

Tamuka had a flash of memory, remembering the moon feast the night before the beginning of the campaign, when, half drunk, Jubadi had been carried out of the yurt upon a raised shield, held high by his Qarths and umen commanders.

A great narga sounded before the yurt. Its single call was joined in an instant by a hundred more nargas surrounding the yurt. Their brazen call pierced the air, counterpointed by the rolling of the great drums, which picked up upon the low steady beat of the death drum that had rolled continuously for the last thirty days.

It was a wild cacophony of noise—the rising screams of the horde, the crashing of swords on shields, the great drums, the nargas. With a slow measured step, the eighty bearers stepped forward, bearing Jubadi into the light of early dawn. Though it was hard to imagine it possible, Tamuka felt as if the sound had taken on physical form, a wild primal release after the thirty days of deathly silence.

Walking with Hulagar and Vuka, Tamuka followed the body of Jubadi into the light, the sun hanging directly before them, blood-red, the light fog of dawn reflecting its sullen light. The Qarths of the tribes that were united as Merki stepped forward to flank the procession, joined in turn by the commanders of the umens, shamans, and the remaining silent ones who would not follow Jubadi at the end of this day. The sounders of the nargas lifted up their horns, assistants carrying the bells upon their shoulders, drummers joining them, the great kettledrums slung from their necks, moving to fall in behind the chief mourners.

Clearing the tent, the procession turned to the west, moving in an arc around the south side of the tent. The plains were dark with the horde, stretching back all the way to the walls of the cursed cattle city. He looked at it with hatred. He had wanted it to be the pyre of Jubadi, but had been overruled by Sarg and Vuka, who had declared the place accursed and to be left alone. He forced the sight of it out of his mind.

From the top of the hill, nearly all of the horde could see the procession, and as if moved by a single hand they surged forward, voices raised in lamentation, pushing to draw closer, surging inward. A full umen was drawn up shoulder to shoulder with spears lowered, keeping the path cleared, and so great was the crush that at times the lines threatened to break, and hundreds died, either flinging themselves upon the spears in sacrifice or being pushed upon them from the surging crowd.

Ever so slowly, the procession made its way down the hill, pausing for long minutes when the narrow path momentarily closed because of the surging mob. The bottom of the hill was reached, and Tamuka noticed that the ground was slippery with blood from where dozens had fallen and been crushed, or speared.

Foolish waste, he thought coldly. Better to die in battle than like this.

Gradually the procession started back up the next hill, the bearers on top of the platform leaning forward slightly to keep the body of Jubadi steady. The top of the next hill was flat, as if shaved off by a blade. Ten thousand cattle had labored upon the barrow of Jubadi, shearing the top of the hill off, digging into its heart. They had finished their work only the night before.

The platform reached the top of the hill and stopped. The crowd surged in again, and for a moment Tamuka felt a flicker of panic as the warriors lining either side of the narrow path were nearly crushed up against each other. The din was stunning. He saw Vuka blanch as guards were crushed up against him, and then the crush eased back again and with hurried step the group gained the top of the hill.

He took a deep breath and looked back. Behind them the narrow valley was filled, the path washed under by the press which struggled to get closer. But the hilltop was unreachable, for another umen had been positioned around it, its ranks six deep on three sides, and a stockade stood chest-high to keep the press back. The fourth side, to the south, was where the others waited, but that did not matter, for a high fence had been built to contain that place.

Tamuka turned his attention back to the barrow. The top of the hill, over a hundred and fifty feet across, had been razed flat. In the center a hole had been sunk, forty feet across and half as deep, in the middle of which was the pyre of stacked wood, laid out to accept the funeral platform. From the four corners of the hole, trenches half a dozen feet across had been sliced in at an angle gently rising from the floor of the burial pit up to ground level at the very edge

of the hill. Earthen steps had been set into the east
side of barrow for access to the bottom of the pit. The
entire subterranean pit was paved, floor and walls,
with stones, cunningly set, tightly fitted, and polished
to a mirrorlike sheen.

There was a bark of command, and the eighty bearing the great platform lowered their burden to the
ground and stepped back. Tamuka spared a glance at
Hulagar, and he felt his heart tighten. His old comrade, seeing his look, smiled and in an almost fatherly
fashion reached out and touched him on the shoulder.

Two shamans came up out of the hole, mounting
the earthen steps carved into the east side, bearing
two poles between which fluttered the black funeral
banner of Jubadi.

Tamuka looked at it uneasily, remembering the moment thirty days before when an identical banner had
floated before the walls of Suzdal.

As the banner emerged out of the grave, the nargas
sounded a high single note. Almost miraculously, all
sound died away, the multitude of the horde falling
silent, silent except for the wails of the hundred and
fifty thousand cattle who waited in the pen to the
south of the hill.

The shamans walked once around the open grave,
holding the banner high, and then came to stand before Jubadi's bier. Sarg nodded, and the two went
slowly back down the steps. The Qarths and umen
commanders, who had gathered around the body, now
stepped back, their farewells complete. The dozen
guards carrying the bier started down the steps, followed by two more bearing the single lamp, the only
flame that had flickered for thirty days of mourning.
Behind them walked Hulagar, Vuka, Sarg, and Tamuka.

As Tamuka stepped into the grave, the screams of
the cattle were blocked by the cool damp stones paving the walls and floor of the grave. Reaching the
bottom, Tamuka waited by the steps while the guards

stepped forward and placed the funeral bier atop the high wooden pyre that filled most of the pit nearly chest-high with seasoned wood. There was a moment of silence, as if all were unsure what next was to be done, a final hesitation before the end.

Sarg finally stepped up to the pyre and reached up to place his hand upon Jubadi's shroud-encased forehead.

"Go now, my Qar Qarth, go now, Jubadi, to the realm of our forefathers. Go now to ride the everlasting ride of the unending heavens. Look down upon us in thy nightly ride. Give strength to thy son Vuka and to all thy people, who will one day join you, where the steppes of heaven reach into eternity. Go now, Jubadi of the Merki, to join those who move between the stars."

Sarg lowered his head, pressing it against Jubadi's, his shoulders convulsing as he wept bitter tears.

"Farewell, my friend," Sarg whispered and then drew away.

The shaman nodded to Vuka, who stepped forward, Tamuka by his side.

Approaching the body, Tamuka noticed the faint smell of corruption, barely masked by the herbs and sweet woods which the body had been packed in. Vuka stood unsteadily beside him. Together they reached out, placing their hands where Jubadi's heart had once beaten.

"By the blood of my father, I now shall rule as Qar Qarth," Vuka whispered, "and by my blood shall rule he that comes after me."

Tamuka could feel the fever in Vuka's trembling, swollen hand. He almost felt a moment of pity for Vuka, whose arm was burning with infection, infection that had spread from the ceremonial cut he had received the morning after Jubadi's death. A cut that Tamuka, as shield-bearer, had bound with a cloth from his battle kit.

"As did Hulagar watch over you, I, Tamuka, shall be shield-bearer to the Qar Qarth Vuka," he whispered.

He paused for a brief instant.

"Guided always by the need of our people, and by the spirit of my *tu*."

Vuka looked over at him, not even aware that what he had spoken was not part of the ritual.

Tamuka nodded and withdrew his hand, and the two stepped back.

Tamuka turned to face Hulagar, who smiled sadly.

"So must this life end," Hulagar said with a gentle sigh. Reaching over, he unslung the bronze shield which rested upon his right shoulder, the ceremonial aegis of his office.

He hefted it up high, holding it aloft for a moment, and then lowered it, flicking off a mote of dust with his left hand, gazing at its burnished surface.

He held it out to Tamuka.

"Use it better than I did," Hulagar said, a sudden note of pain in his voice.

Tamuka took the emblem of office.

"Shield-bearer of the Qar Qarth Vuka, farewell."

Tamuka felt his throat tighten.

Slinging the shield over his right shoulder, Tamuka quietly started to draw his sword out of its scabbard. Hulagar looked down and extended his hand to stop him.

"No. You need not do that. I prefer the older custom today."

Tamuka looked at him, horrified.

"But . . ."

"No," Hulagar said, smiling again. "I failed my old friend, and he died. I think as a mild atonement I'll take the traditional path."

Sarg looked over at him and reluctantly nodded his approval, and Tamuka knew that it was useless to argue. He let the sword slip back into its scabbard, and in his heart he almost felt a relief, for this had been the one moment he had quietly dreaded for years—if Jubadi should die before Hulagar, then as the new shield-bearer it would be his task to behead his friend in the funeral pit of the Qar Qarth.

"Stay with me for a brief moment," Hulagar said.

The old shield-bearer bowed low to Vuka.

"Rule with an iron hand, but above all else, rule with truthfulness and justice, as your father did."

Without waiting for a reply from the Qar Qarth, Hulagar turned and walked up to the pyre to stand beside the body of his friend, and Tamuka joined him.

Hulagar looked over at Tamuka.

"I loved him," he said, reaching out to touch the shroud-wrapped body. "I loved him as a brother, as a father, as a friend."

"You did not fail him," Tamuka said. "Tonight you will ride together again. The eternal steppes of heaven wait for the both of you."

"Do you really think so?"

Taken aback, Tamuka hesitated and then gently reached out, resting his hand on Hulagar's shoulder.

"Of course," he said, forcing a smile even as tears clouded his eyes. "But you'll be young again, back as in the old days that you told me of. I remember your story of how you killed your first horse to save him. That horse will be there as well, eager to bear you again, Jubadi waiting as well. And the two of you will ride, laughing, uncaring, beside your fathers, and their fathers before them. You will drive your enemies, hearing their lamentations, and then rest by the campfires, eating, laughing, chanting the songs. This here of this world is but a pale shadow of what will be, my friend."

Hulagar sighed, looking into Tamuka's eyes.

"I know what you did," he whispered sadly. "And last night, as I walked one more time in the spirit of my *tu* I looked into your heart, and I know what you plan to do. And that, my friend, is what grieves me the most."

Tamuka was silent.

"Vuka is not fit to be Qar Qarth," Hulagar continued. "If there were another heir I would now counsel you to gather together the council of our clan and propose that he be killed. But there is no other heir, and thus he must be Qar Qarth until he has sired a son."

"His strength is weak," Tamuka whispered. "It is countless the number of concubines he has lain with, and there has been no issue. It was almost the same with his father, who in thirty years bore but three sons," and Tamuka, nodding toward the body before them, inwardly shocked that he would now say such a thing before Jubadi, fearing that his spirit would hear these words.

"There have been ways around that," Hulagar replied. "We both know that. But until such a quiet arrangement has been made, Vuka must be Qar Qarth."

Tamuka was silent. If need be, it would be his task to lie secretly with one of Vuka's concubines to produce a son. He found the thought of Vuka's then claiming the child as his own to be repulsive. For a brief instant he looked back at Vuka, wondering for the first time if Hulagar might not have been the father after all. Impossible—such shallowness could not come from such nobility of blood. But then what did that say of the blood of Jubadi?

"I know what is in your heart, the truth of what you now consider doing, what might even now be happening with Vuka," Hulagar said, his voice cold, "and that has broken my spirit as much as this," and he nodded toward the corpse.

"It was I who wished you to be my replacement." He hesitated. "And now I regret it, but it is too late to act."

Tamuka felt no anger, only pain at his mentor's words.

"I suspect even this death," Hulagar said.

Tamuka found that he could not look into Hulagar's eyes and slowly let his gaze drop.

"As it is in this world, so in the next," Tamuka finally replied, his voice full of pain and bitterness. "Pray in the afterworld that there is not a day when cattle spirits come even into the realm of our ancestors to make sport of them as they now do here."

"What will be will be," Hulagar said sadly. "Perhaps I lived in the last generation that knew the joy of the endless ride across the broad steppes that encircle this world. If it is at an end, then it is at an end, and the fates have decreed it to be such."

The two stood in silence for a moment.

"Bid me farewell," Hulagar finally said.

Tamuka looked back up, and his friend forced a sad distant smile.

"I go to be with my friend," Hulagar said, "and for you, Tamuka Shield Bearer, when it is your day to lie down next to the pyre, let us hope that in the end you kept your trust as a shield-bearer, and then I shall greet you in friendship as well."

Hulagar leaned forward and embraced Tamuka around the shoulders. Tamuka felt his strength dropping away, and tears clouded his eyes.

"Let us hope that you will greet me in an everlasting heaven free of cattle. I would sacrifice even our friendship to save that for you," Tamuka whispered, his voice so soft that not even Hulagar could hear him.

Hulagar, releasing his grip, stepped back, moved to the side of the pyre, and climbed up to sit at the feet of his Qar Qarth.

Tamuka, bowing low, backed away to join Sarg, his tears splashing on the paving stones.

The shaman turned and nodded. A dozen guards

came down into the grave by means of one of the four sloping side trenches that formed paved ramps back up to the surface. Two of them led Jubadi's mount, which balked and fought at its reins as it was pulled down the trench and brought to stand by Jubadi's pyre. A guard came up beside the beast and with a backhand slash cut its throat. The horse collapsed to the ground, its blood spilling across the stones. The dozen guards now approached the silent guardians who had carried Jubadi, quickly lashed them to upright posts set in the ground around the pyre, and then cut their throats as well. Silent unto death, they sagged forward and died.

Sarg now nodded to Vuka, and the two guards bearing the lamp came up to him. Taking the lamp, he stepped forward to where the funeral banner stood by Jubadi's head.

"Go now, spirit of my father, go now to paradise."

Vuka touched the lamp along the bottom of the banner. A curl of flame licked up along the black border.

Tamuka, eyes still upon Hulagar, saw the fire ignite and felt again a flash of memory, Jubadi doing the same before Suzdal.

Crouching low, Vuka touched the lamp into the kindling at the bottom of the pyre. Splinters of wood ignited, and within seconds their crackling echoed against the stone walls of the burial vault. Vuka inverted the lamp, letting the oil run out and spill into the fire, and then dropped it, stepped back, and without a backward glance started up the steps, the guards and Sarg following.

Tamuka hesitated for a moment, looking at Hulagar, who, with a low keening voice, was singing his death chant. Bowing low, Tamuka turned away and went back up the steps.

By the time he reached the top the kindling was fully ablaze, crackling and snapping, a coil of white smoke rising up. The fire spread, fanning out, curling the gold cloth of the bier; the banner at Jubadi's head was a blazing torch. Through the rising shimmers of heat he saw Hulagar, his death chant now difficult to hear, drowned out by the screams of the cattle and the growing cries of the horde, which upon seeing the first coil of smoke knew that the spirit of Jubadi was at last ascending to the everlasting sky.

Sarg turned away from the pyre and placed both hands upon Vuka's shoulders.

"Vuka, son of Jubadi, assume now the power of thy office. When the banner of peace again floats over the golden yurt, then you shall be fully invested as Qar Qarth before the council of all the clans of the Merki horde."

A shaman stepped forward, bearing Jubadi's sword. Wincing with pain, Vuka reached out and took the blade and held it up. Tamuka, stepping behind Vuka, unslung his bronze shield and held it up as well, protecting Vuka's right side.

A roar of approval ascended from the multitude. Lowering his sword, Vuka then turned back to face the pyre. Tamuka looked down into the pit and quickly closed his eyes. The flames were leaping high around the body, and huddled in the middle of them, curling into a tight ball, he saw his friend.

Tamuka wept unashamed.

The coil of smoke rose heavenward, bearing the twin spirits of Qar Qarth and shield-bearer, *ka* and *tu* united. A shower of sparks snapped upward as the pyre finally collapsed in upon itself, the bodies consumed at last, the scent of burned flesh hanging heavy in the air, cloaking the hilltop in a dark gray wreath.

At last he could bear to look again, but there was no longer anything to see, only the shimmers of white heat and the blackened bodies of the silent ones on the edge of the fire, but to him they mattered not.

Sarg, watching intently, judged at last that Jubadi

had been consumed and held his hand up as a signal. The nargas sounded again, and now the wailing of the cattle, which had quieted at the sight of the smoke and towering flames, grew loud again, a high bleating cry that filled Tamuka with a cold sense of joy.

At the far end of the holding pen, several hundred yards away, half a thousand warriors lifted up the wooden fence that blocked in one side and started to move it ever so slowly forward, while other warriors pushed spear points through loopholes carved into the long wooden wall.

Near the top of the hill a solid line of warriors half a dozen lines deep blocked off the open side of the pen, which reached almost to the top of the hill. The interior of the pen was divided into over a hundred narrow chutes, each one boarded up to a height of nearly ten feet, thus blocking the cattle into long thin lines, which prevented them from stampeding as one great crowd. Most of the warriors in the line held spears, pointed straight out; others, however, were armed merely with ropes or whips. The herd of cattle surging back and forth within the chutes was gradually pushed forward. They were stripped naked, their hands already bound behind their backs to prevent any last feeble resistance.

There had been a breakout of several thousand cattle four days before. Many of them had escaped into the woods and nearly ten thousand more had been killed before the rest were subdued. It had been an unpleasant waste, which Sarg had railed over, condemning the commander in charge to death for his mistake.

The new commander had designed the pen to avoid another such mishap, and he stood to one side, watching anxiously.

The first of the cattle were finally driven to the top of the hill. Warriors reached out, grabbing their victims, and within minutes after the first horn had

sounded, hundreds were being dragged up to the funeral pit and the trenches cut into the four corners,
the entire pit shimmering with a near-blinding heat.

The butchers were waiting. Without fanfare the first
ax rose and fell. A cattle head tumbled into the grave,
a butcher holding the body up, the shower of blood
cascading out from the still-twitching body, its blood
hissing to steam on the stones below. The hair of the
cattle head now resting in the pit burst into flames.
The butcher stepped back, moved to the north side of
the grave, and tossed the body down the steep slope
of the hill, blood still squirting out of it in spasmodic
jerks. The body had barely stopped rolling before
someone raced out, picked it up, and, holding it aloft
with a triumphal shout, bore it into the surging crowd.

Another head fell in, and another, and within seconds it became a steady hail, mingled with showers of
blood that hissed and steamed.

A mad insane press worked at the edge of the
grave, cattle being dragged up to the lip, some struggling, most shrieking, others walking numbly as if already dead. Blades flashed; bodies collapsed, were
dragged away still streaming blood, and were tossed
down the hill, where the crowd pushed and jostled.
From the four access trenches that led into the pit,
streams of blood started to race into the grave, boiling
and hissing, heads rolling down the incline, piling up
in a knot, then moving again, pushed in by the mass
of heads from behind, the skin and hair wrinkling,
coiling into plumes of smoke and fire.

Tamuka watched with cold satisfaction as the severed heads started to pile up, rolling about on the hot
stones, sizzling in their own blood, the air now filled
with the stench of burned hair and frying blood.

Sarg, watching intently, finally nodded, and a shaman stepped forward bearing a long pole, atop which
was a tightly woven bundle of sticks soaked in oil. The
shaman lowered the pole into the flames and then

drew it back up, held it aloft, and handed it back to Vuka.

A wild shout of exultation arose from the crowd. Vuka handed the torch to a heavily built warrior, who turned and started back down the hill. As if from nowhere, hundreds of torches suddenly appeared, the people reaching up to touch the sacred flame, which from this single source would reignite all the fires of the entire horde.

The fire seemed to leap down the side of the hill; soon thousands and then tens of thousands of burning torches were waving. There was a distant booming, and Tamuka turned to look, where on the far hills a long line of guns was arrayed, their gunners touching off their pieces.

Cattle shrieks rent the air, the frenzy of killing taking hold, the butchers not even waiting to get their victims to the edge of the pit or the access trenches, axes and scimitars rising and falling. Others were not cut at all, but rather were hurled bodily into the flames, so that they ran about the inside of the pit, screaming, writhing in agony on the hot coals, tripping on the heads that carpeted the stones, splashing in the boiling blood that in places was now ankle-deep.

From executions taking place away from the pit, a steady shower of heads arched through the air to land in the pit, mingled now with arms, legs, the scent of blood triggering a frenzy. A mad howling echoed across the fields as those lucky enough to get a body pushed through the madness to bring their treasure back to their yurts for the ceremonial feast, while others not yet so lucky fought and struggled, scores of them dying in the mad stampede.

A wall of guards surrounded Vuka, who swayed, on the point of collapse. Tamuka looked about, his eyes growing wide with rage and joy. A shrieking cattle, only half grown, which had somehow eluded its butcher came crawling past Tamuka. With a shout of joy Tamuka picked it up by its hair, severed the head from its body, and threw the head to where he believed Hulagar's body lay. Consumed now with passion, he did not even bother to save the body. Raising it up, he drank the blood still flowing from the severed neck, and then he hurled the body into the pit.

The crush around the grave was growing. A butcher, losing his balance when a male cattle lunged at him, tumbled into the pit, the cattle leaping after him. The two floundered around in the rising sea of boiling blood and piles of heads, screaming in rage at each other. Somehow the cattle got his hands free, grabbed the butcher's sword, and smashed his skull in. In an instant the cattle was transfixed by half a dozen spears, fell, and disappeared into the churning chaos.

The sun rose higher, the blood and cattle heads in the grave rising as well, the last of the flames winking out at last. Tamuka looked heavenward. The sun was reaching its zenith, and he wiped the sweat from his eyes. The air reeked of slaughter. The pens were still half full, and the slaughtering was now going on even inside the pens. The ground leading up to the grave was nearly impassable from the choke of bodies, and the stones paving the side of the hill were as slippery as ice from the scarlet river washing the side of the hill.

Tamuka turned around to see that Vuka was gone, long since escorted back to what was now his yurt. Sarg too was gone. He alone was left. He looked up at the heavens as if somehow hoping to see his friend's spirit.

Instead there was something else—a cloud machine. He cursed with a shrill voice, waving his blade to the sky. Laughing at what the cattle above were now witnessing. Turning, he waded into the slaughter.

*   *   *

"Merciful Kesus," Feyodor whispered, crossing himself as he gazed down at the madness below.

Jack Petracci, sick with rage, lowered his field glasses as if to blot out the image, but he knew that not until the final moment of his life could he ever erase from his nightmare thoughts what he was now seeing.

Yankee Clipper II shifted slightly with the breeze, and with a light touch Jack edged the nose of the ship around, pushing the elevator forward slightly to drop down a bit lower.

An eddy of wind washed around him, an updraft, and an instant later Jack leaned forward, vomiting from the stench rising up from below. He gasped for breath, drawing a slight moment of satisfaction from the knowledge that he was throwing up on the Merki, a thousand feet below. He leaned back, trying to suck in clean air, but the smell was all around him now, and he had a mad urge to tear his clothes off, fearing that somehow the stink would seep into his body, never to be washed out. Behind him he could hear Feyodor blubbering, alternating between weeping, praying, and cursing.

"Shut the fucking hell up," Jack roared, wanting to somehow lash out at anyone, anything, so overwhelming was the madness around him.

He could see the insane frenzy. The entire horde was packed in a vast circle around the hill, the multitude swaying, pushing, screaming, their voices thundering even above the steady whine of the propeller behind his back.

If only we had a thousand aerosteamers, he thought, a thousand, each of them loaded down with weapons, we could slaughter them wholesale, wipe the world clean of their murderous filth. He had a flash fantasy of a bomb, a bomb so powerful that it would scorch the earth clean of them in one blinding flash, a holy fire of purification.

He felt a cracking whine.

A bullet.

"The bastards can fight again," Feyodor shouted. "Take us back up!"

"Not yet."

He reached between his legs, pulling up the box that Emil and Gates had prepared for him. Leaning forward, he set the box into a frame built into the front of the pilot's basket. He locked the box in place and tilted it forward, sighting along a simple notch sight.

"Hold her steady!" Jack shouted.

"Another bastard just shot at us!"

Jack ignored him. Leaning forward, he uncapped the lens in the front of the box.

"Hold still, you damn bastards."

He counted to ten and then capped it shut.

One photograph down, two to go.

He unsnapped the camera from the frame, lowered it into the basket by his feet, and pulled up the second one, setting it up to photograph the slaughter pit.

It was Andrew who had first suggested the idea when Emil and Gates, the day before the staff meeting, had brought out their little miracle, the first cameras to be produced in Rus. The two of them had remembered the formula for Talbot's method of dry photography. Gates had made the box, and Emil, with his small side business in spectacles, had fashioned the lens. It was Andrew, however, who had thought of this other purpose, as a means of reconnaissance, and beyond that as a historical record.

"If ever we win this war and those barbarians are destroyed, I want it to be remembered what they did. Otherwise some damn fool might someday not believe it, or feel sorry somehow, the way you hear some idiots talking about the Aztecs," he had snapped when Jack had raised an objection to the weight involved.

Now Jack understood as he sighted the camera and uncapped the lens. He knew much of it would be blurred, the frenzied struggle of the Cartha prisoners and pets, but the pit, now over half full of skulls, might just be discernible if the image was magnified somehow.

He counted to fifteen and capped the lens. He unlatched the camera and started to move the third one into place.

"Company's coming!" Feyodor shouted.

Jack looked up to see half a dozen Merki aerosteamers rising up from the hills near Fort Lincoln, coming up from the south, moving fast on the gradually building westerly breeze. The ship surged again for a moment, rising on another upsweeping bubble of air, the stench of slaughter so thick that he started to gag again.

A loud hum hissed past, and from a wood-crested hill half a mile away he saw the puff of smoke of an artillery piece. The round missed, and he hoped that when it plunged to earth it would smash into the swarm below.

There was a sprinkling of smoke puffs eddying up from below, individual Merki firing their muskets straight up. He could see several small holes in the bag up forward. They weren't enough to cause a problem, but a six- or nine-pound artillery round might make getting back to Kev, two hundred miles to the east, an iffy thing, even with a growing tail wind. Fuel had been hidden away for him fifty miles east of Vazima, which they would need coming back, but it would be the loss of hydrogen that would make all the difference. The ship was near to overload as is, with the weight of the three cameras, weapons, and kerosene.

The bastards must have built sheds down somewhere near Fort Lincoln, moving their base up from the far side of the Shenandoah hills. If I only had the edge on altitude, he thought, we could venture a run south to try to scout it out, see if close enough to the river or the sea it might be worth trying to mount a raiding party from Bullfinch's marines. Not today—too much has already been done to us today, he thought coldly, just by witnessing the madness below.

He steadied the camera, locking it into its frame, and tilted it, pointing it straight down at the frenzy. He uncapped the lens, counted this time to twenty, and then recapped.

"Let's get the hell out of here!" Feyodor shouted. "They might have stripped their ships for speed— we don't know what they've done in the last thirty days."

"They're not that goddam smart," Jack shouted, not believing what he was saying. His rage was ready to explode. The hysterical screams of the men, women, and children below were like a pulsing thunder. He looked, horrified, at the hill drenched in red, the naked headless bodies, tens of thousands of them being dragged off in every direction. The air was filled with the smoke of thousands of fires, Merki dancing about the flames, and over each fire a body, or parts of a body, turned on a spit. Many of them were looking up, some shaking their fists, others beckoning for the ship to come down, others waving human arms, limbs, torsos, in mocking defiance.

Jack unslung the Sharps carbine by his side, and leaning out of the basket he started to shoot into the crowd. On the third shot he saw a bullet strike its mark. The crowd below swayed, drawing back from the hit. But the frenzy of killing around the pit continued.

Raising his aim slightly, he started to shoot into the butchering area, unable to miss. He saw a flash of light, a reflection of the noonday sun striking on something below—a circular bronze shield.

Resting the carbine on the side of the basket, he drew a careful bead and fired. The shield turned.

"You bastards!"

He could not even hear his own voice, was not even aware that he had been chanting the same phrase over and over in hysteria.

A crack snapped through the basket and splinters of wicker flew into his face, the musket ball cutting into the balloon straight overhead.

The near miss brought him to his senses, and again he heard Feyodor.

"Turn us! Turn us now!"

Jack looked up, squinting, suddenly aware the entire world seemed to have taken on a blood-red haze, as if he were staring down a long tunnel. His heart was racing, his mouth dry and sour with vomit, his breath heaving.

Shaking, he looked around, as if coming out of a dream. The Merki aerosteamers were spreading out, coming up on the empty city of Suzdal. He pushed the rudder hard over, and he heard Feyodor sigh with relief as the ship started to turn.

"Pour on the fire and close the balloon exhaust vent," Jack shouted, and Feyodor opened the fuel line full wide while Jack pulled the throttle all the way back. As *Yankee Clipper II* went through its ponderous wide turn, he looked back down at the slaughter pen, still filled with tens of thousands, many of them looking up, reaching up with beseeching hands, as if he were a god who could somehow swoop down and sweep them to safety.

Tears streaming down his face, he fixed his gaze straight ahead, and pointing the ship eastward he started to race back toward Kev, and safety.

The dark wall of a shadow raced out across the fields, the sun disappearing behind the high anvil-shaped clouds that were marching out of the south-west, their black-green bases wreathed with forks of lightning.

Tamuka turned to face the storm. The late-after-noon sun was gone, and the temperature was falling rapidly as the first cold gusts of wind swirled up. It was a good omen, that the fire of heaven was touching down to the world of mortals, drawing into its heart the spirit of Jubadi, and of Hulagar.

He flexed his right hand again. It was still numb, and the bruise on his knuckles was sore and swollen. The shield had taken the glancing blow of the bullet fired from the cloud machine; the bullet had scored its burnished surface, the impact snapping through him. He had silently raged at the perfidy of such an act, a sacrilege, and beyond that the damage to the shield of his office, which Hulagar had carried for over a circling, and polished each night with loving dili-gence. It was now marred, a long furrow denting the outer side. There was not even a cattle smith who could work it back to perfection—that one's head was most likely in the pit by now. The thought had trou-bled him. They had killed all their pets, all the Cartha prisoners, except for a small handful which had been moved far to the rear on the other side of the river, those who could forge guns and tend to the cloud fliers and those few with skills too valuable to waste, or owned by individuals with enough power to gain them exception. Only one cattle who was here today would live to see the end of it, and that was for a reason. But the rest? In the past it had been simple enough—after the death of a Qar Qarth the next place where they wintered would provide all the replace-ments necessary. Vuka would do such a thing—he would not.

The slaughter was nearly finished. New butchers were now at work, replacing those who had taken over late in the morning from those who had started at dawn. The air was so thick with blood that he felt as if he would choke on its rich cloying scent.

The entire grave was now filled with cattle heads, well over a hundred thousand, so that the butchers were now throwing them atop the growing pile that spilled out over the sides. Blood flowed in rivulets down the hill; all were covered with it, bright red from head to foot. The vast frenzy had worn down, for more than a hundred thousand cattle bodies were now turning on spits, being consumed in a surfeit of gorging. The countryside for miles around was cloaked in the smoke of thousands of fires, the smoke now curling away eastward, driven on the winds of the approaching storm, eastward to where Keane waited.

Silently, Tamuka walked about the great mound of heads, taking grim satisfaction from the lifeless eyes, the tormented features, the blood-matted hair, old and young down to infants, men, women, fair-skinned from the land of the Norse, dark from the Constan and Cartha, black from the Zimba, flat-faced and narrow-eyed from the Chin and Nippo, from all the endless steppe upon which the Merki roamed.

The last of the victims were being dragged up, the pen emptying at last, the victims strangely silent, most likely numbed, he realized, their primitive souls already dead from fear. The last thousand were soon a hundred and a moment later only a score. Unsheathing his sword, he went up to them, watching as the last were dispatched until only two were left.

He had one of them, an old man, dragged before him.

"So you are the last cattle," Tamuka said, his voice harsh, mocking.

The old man, a Constan pet, looked at him unflinchingly.

"You will never kill all of us," the cattle hissed. "Kill ten million of us and still Keane will defeat you."

The old man pursed his lips and spat into Tamuka's face.

With a scream of rage, Tamuka's sword arched up and snapped down, cutting off the cattle's defiant laugh. The head rolled on the red-drenched pavement, its blood spraying him. Picking up the head, he threw it to the top of the mound, where it came to rest, the open eyes looking back at him.

Tamuka, breathing heavily, looked around at the butchers, who stood as if dazed, their breath ragged and sharp, blood dripping from their armor, the air now strangely still.

"Cut its heart and liver out. I want them for dinner," Tamuka snapped and walked away.

To one side he saw the single remaining cattle. This one had not been told that he would be spared—that was part of his plan for eventually breaking him. Now he was the only one left of the prisoners from the cattle army defeated in the first attack of the war. The man stood silent, features drawn, ashen, head still bandaged from the blow that had almost killed him. Tamuka could sense that this cattle was finally realizing that he would live to see the next day.

The man stood there, watching with wary eyes, his blue Yankee jacket splattered with blood. He reached into his pocket and pulled out a plug of the tobacco that the cattle took such disgusting delight in chewing and bit into it, his jaws working slowly.

"I'm letting you live for now," Tamuka said.

The Yankee said nothing, only chewing, spitting on the ground, watching him with a cold gaze.

"I'm dead already," he said, "so the hell with you."

Tamuka felt a flicker of rage and was tempted to beckon for the man to be thrown in with the others.

The Yankee smiled, his gray beard crinkling up.

"Go on and kill me if it'll make you feel better, I don't give a good goddam. Andrew will kick your ass to hell, and I'll be there to greet you."

Afraid that his rage would take over, that it would spoil his plan, Tamuka turned and stalked away, not seeing the tears of rage and sickened horror in Sergeant Major Hans Schuder's eyes.

It was getting dark. Low clouds raced across the sky overhead, and the steady rumble of thunder filled the air. Tamuka walked back to the east side of the hill, his boots squishing over the blood-soaked paving stones. The last of the people quietly moved away from the hill, dragging their meals. So great had been the slaughter that thousands of cattle bodies, the less appetizing choices, littered the sides of the hill in great mounds.

A waste of good meat. It'll spoil in the rain, he thought coldly, if not gutted and hung tonight.

He stood alone, oblivious to the small retinue of silent ones who now stood watchfully over him, a distinction he had not known before, but was now part of his life as shield-bearer to the Qar Qarth.

He reached into his kit bag, pulled out a strip of cloth, wiped his blade clean, and resheathed it.

"Vuka calls for you,"

Tamuka turned to see Sarg, leaning heavily on his staff, standing behind him, his thin body silhouetted by the great mound of heads.

Tamuka nodded and said nothing.

"The fever grows worse again," Sarg said, his voice filled with concern.

"It will break."

"I'm not sure. The smell of the arm . . . it smells of death."

"We ride tomorrow," Tamuka said. "Twenty-two umens in the first wave. As Qar Qarth, he must go with them. We have delayed thirty days, and each day makes them stronger. We cannot give them one day more."

"I know that," Sarg said. "A palanquin can carry him, but it would be best if he stayed in his yurt."

"I've seen Jubadi hurt far worse and still go into a battle," Tamuka replied coldly. "His son should do no less."

"You as shield-bearer should be the one counseling that the army wait until the Qar Qarth can ride," Sarg said.

Tamuka looked back at him and nodded.

"Shaman, there is a war to be fought. We cannot retreat back through the forest. We must sweep forward and get food. Otherwise the entire horde will begin to starve. This is not the open steppe of the south, or our own lands. This is Tugar realm, and the Tugar horde was but a third our size. It could support them, but it cannot support us unless we push beyond the Roum and move out into open grazing land. We are hemmed in here between the sea and the forest."

"You speak like a warrior filled with the spirit of his *ka,* and not the *tu* of the shield-bearer."

"It is my *tu* that speaks, for the good of the clans, from the power of my spirit walking that not even you, Sarg, can see with."

The shaman bristled slightly.

Tamuka stepped up to him, putting a soothing hand on his shoulder.

"I do not mean to insult you. I need your help if the Merki are to survive."

"And Vuka, is he not Merki?"

"I speak of all the Merki. Shaman, if you could but know where my *tu* has led me. I think in your heart you've agreed with my counsel."

"The cattle must be destroyed," Sarg finally agreed.

"We move tomorrow. That is the word of Vuka."

"Of Tamuka who moves to become Qar Qarth."

Tamuka fixed Sarg with his gaze, blinking only when a flash of lightning forked out of the clouds, striking the hills behind him, the thunder washing over them with a crackling roar.

"You dare to suggest such a thing?"

"It was you who dressed his wound, which now reeks of corruption," Sarg replied.

"Are you accusing me?"

"No one accuses you." Sarg drew closer. "If any dared to, there would be chaos, the Merki horde splintering into warring factions, as it was in the beginning before we became one. Not even I would voice such a challenge."

Tamuka nodded, watching Sarg closely.

"But if he should die without issue, you would rule until the council of Qarths selected a new line to rule. For two hundred circlings it has been his lineage that ruled us all, and Vuka is all that is left."

"Is he even one of the blood?" Tamuka whispered, his words almost drowned out by the thunder. He was barely able to say out loud what only Hulagar would truly have known.

Sarg remained silent.

"I have heard that the cattle now even know ways of tending wounds so that they do not ooze the green fluid that all our wounds have always shown."

"Should we fetch a Yankee shaman then to tend him?" Tamuka asked sarcastically.

"No. But it does indicate something to me of what is happening here."

Tamuka shook his head, shivering as a cold gust swirled around them. The first heavy drops of rain splattered about him, streaking the blood on his armor, stirring the congealing blood on the paving stones.

A crack of lightning snapped overhead, causing him to flinch, blinding him momentarily. Blinking, he lowered his gaze, looking back at Sarg and the great pyramid of skulls behind him, which glowed with an unearthly blue light from the sheets of lightning that raged in the heavens above.

"Tomorrow we ride," Tamuka hissed, and turning, he walked back to the yurt of the Qar Qarth.

Chapter 5

It was almost too easy, and the fact made him nervous.

Hamilcar Baca, his way blocked by the cheering throngs, pushed slowly through the main square of Cartha, his guards swarmed under by the mad crush. There was a time when the mere attempt of a commoner to come up and touch him would have resulted in the man's death, or at the least the loss of his hand. Too much had changed to even consider that now. Today was a day of liberation, the sound of fighting still reverberating in the suburbs of the city as the Merki umen which had occupied Cartha retreated out into the open steppe.

The attack had gone as planned. After leaving Suzdal with the ironclad ship, he had returned to the settlements of his former army now living on the coastal territory of the Rus. Using every galley in their possession, they had traveled southward, leaving their families behind. It was a precarious situation. Many of the men had moved their families north, throwing their lot in with the Rus, and now the families were left behind again, to wait for a return. There had been no move, at least, from Andrew to try to take the galleys back, and though he now hated the Yankees more than ever, at least they had behaved honorably on that account, though if they had not there would have been a fight. Many of the people left behind were now caught in the retreat to Roum.

With the ironclad ship in the lead and nearly seventy galleys bearing close to fourteen thousand men, he had moved down the east coast of the Inland Sea and then cut straight back in on Cartha, landing on the docks in the hour before dawn. He had taken heavy casualties at first, and nearly a dozen of the galleys had been shattered by Merki artillery. The tide finally turned, however, when the populace rose up in support. The slaughter in the great square had been fearful, but the Merki had broken. If there had been more than one umen guarding the city, however, it would have been far different.

The question was, though, now that he had the city, what he would do with it. Already he could see that nearly half the people were gone, dead to the Merki occupation. The countryside beyond was occupied, and the minimal food supplies had been taken by the Merki to support the campaign in the north. His country had been raped by the Merki, thanks to the rebellion of the Rus and the Roum. His people had died by the tens of thousands laboring in the mines and in the factories to build the machines. Rather than an occupation of one winter, the horde had stayed now for over two and taken everything of value. If one umen had stayed in the city to guard the factories, there had to be several others still to the south keeping watch on the Bantag, and they would come straight back here.

He had none of the new weapons—the Yankees had made sure that all such things were in the hands of their own. Now that he had started a rebellion, just what the hell was he going to do with it?

Masking his fears, he slowly pressed through the square, taking the greetings of his people, all of them gaunt, hollow-eyed, reduced to near starvation.

The Merki would be back, and in his heart he knew there would be precious little he could do to stop them.

*   *   *

"They're coming in!"

The trooper reined up beside Pat, horse lathered, the boy's face flushed with excitement.

Pat merely nodded. He did not need the messenger to tell him what was already so evident. From horizon to horizon he could see the swirls of dust, on distant hills the flash of shields and sabers. Overhead two aerosteamers hovered, one nearly a mile up, the other less than six hundred feet high, trailing a line of telegraph wire hooked into the roof of the command car, the key inside chattering out the latest count.

Twenty-two umens confirmed so far in the first wave, he saw in the latest report.

Forty miles out past Vazima, a hundred and thirty from Suzdal in three days, coming on damn fast. At least their artillery was bogging down, trapped on the roads, where movement was at times nearly at a crawl, thanks to the infernal machines, smashed bridges, and entanglements. It'd be seven or eight days before they'd have their guns up to Kev. He looked back up at the machine and saw Jack Petracci leaning far forward, telescope balanced on the front of the basket, scanning the terrain to the north.

The machines were paying off, allowing a dawn-to-dusk watch, allowing as well the chance for harassing raids against the enemy advance without fear of envelopment by a fast-moving column. Unlike the last campaign, in which the Merki had complete control of the sky, this one at least had some semblance of balance. Though the Merki now had more aerosteamers, at last count sixteen to five, their near-limitless range was offset by the slightly greater speed and climbing ability of Jack's fleet, the latest ship having a slightly more powerful engine than the first models. Never again could the Merki advance behind a total screen of security and surprise. There had been several aerosteamer skirmishes as well, but Jack and his four other crews, following strict orders from Andrew, combined with a desire not to crash before an advancing host, had avoided close contact and merely exchanged shots at long range.

A troop of cavalry came over the next ridge, the homes in the village behind it crackling with fire, columns of smoke swirling heavenward. Raising his field glasses, he watched intently. The two four-pounders kicked back, the cavalry troop waiting beside the gun section, some of the men firing off a ragged volley. The gunners limbered their pieces up and lashed the teams into a gallop, coming down the hill.

"Seven Merki aerosteamers coming up from the southwest again."

Pat nodded, sensing the nervousness of his staff. Late yesterday a steamer had swung down almost to ground level and dropped off two Merki, who tore up a section of track before they were hunted down, giving them a couple of tense moments while the line was repaired, a full umen swinging up from the south to try to cut them off.

The two-gun section, retreating from the next slope forward, hit the short bridge at a hard gallop, the hooves of their mounts thundering on the planking, the cavalry troop following, several of the riders turning, reloading their carbines. From over the crest of the hill, which had been empty only seconds before, hundreds of Merki riders appeared, a shower of arrows arcing over their heads, falling short of the bridge.

The troopers fired, one of the Merki going down in a tangled heap, and then turned to gallop across the bridge. One of them stopped, dismounted, and kicked a barrel onto the bridge, while another took a flaming brand from a fire which had been built by the side of the bridge and threw it at the barrel. The flame barely took, licking across the planks. Beside it the railroad bridge was already down, a smoldering ruin.

The Merki, seeing the still-intact bridge, kicked their mounts into a charge, sweeping down the road. Pat stood quiet, watching intently, his staff talking nervously to each other, some of them unholstering their revolvers, the two companies of infantry on the train's flatcars dismounting and starting to spread out. The deep guttural shouts of the enemy carried on the wind.

The flames on the bridge flickered low, a thin curl of dark smoke swirling up. The first Merki hit the bridge, galloping hard across, flame scattering from the horse's hooves, the rider struggling to keep his mount moving forward. Then another. A fast-moving column, over a score of riders, charged down the road, following a horsetail standard, hundreds more cutting down across the fields behind them. The column hit the bridge, ignoring the low smoldering fire, lashing their horses through it and on to the other side of the stream, their leader standing tall in his stirrups, scimitar flashing over his head. The leader reined in for a moment, motioning for several of his riders to dismount to fight the fire, and then with a wave of his scimitar pointed up the hill.

"Come on, you bastard," Pat hissed. "Come and get it."

The leader, spurring his mount, went into a charge, the score of riders behind him with bows raised following their leader and the horsetail standard.

Hundreds of Merki converged on the bridge, struggling to get across, horses neighing as their riders forced them through the low flames and dark swirling smoke.

The thirty-yard-long bridge was packed with Merki.

Pat turned and nodded to a grinning Suzdalian engineer. The boy took the battery to a telegraph key and connected the leads.

The bridge disappeared in a flash of fire from the fifty-pound charge, two thirty-gallon barrels of benzene strapped to the gunpowder igniting into an inferno that soared up with the explosion, splashing out in every direction in a brilliant red-and-yellow fireball.

The triumphant shouts of the Merki were replaced in an instant by high piercing shrieks. Horses and riders, covered in flame, plunged into the river, which was awash with fire. The charging column, unable to slow, continued to push onto the burning bridge, Merki at the front of the column falling into the flames, horses plunging madly, foaming the flaming water.

"Burn, you bastards, burn!" Pat roared, jumping up and down excitedly. The staff officers around him cheered, slapping each other on the back.

The Suzdalian cavalry troop turned, the gunners swinging about, unlimbering their pieces, and within seconds sending a spray of canister into the packed column struggling to back up on the far side of the bridge. The troopers started back down the hill, steadying their mounts for a moment, firing into those trapped on the east side of the bridge. The lead column of Merki, a hundred yards up the slope, reined in and clustered around a standard, firing arrows at the troopers as they closed in. A trooper with drawn revolver started into a gallop, a bugler beside him sounding the charge. High human cries sounded and the cavalry swept back down the slope, crashing into the Merki, pistol shots reverberating.

"Damn, they weren't suppose to close. They're getting carried away," Pat snapped peevishly. The Merki were swarmed under, the standard dropping, and then coming back up again in the hands of a Suzdalian cavalryman. A volley of arrows snapped out from the far side of the stream, several of the cavalry falling under the blow. The remaining troopers, grabbing hold of the reins of the now riderless Merki horses, turned and started back up the slope, which was littered with the dead. The four-pounders continued to fire in support, unable to miss in the crush of Merki and horses jammed together on the far bank.

Directly behind Pat, the two rear-mounted guns in the armored car snapped off, the twelve-pound case shot screaming into the valley, one of them detonating over the bridge, spraying the far side with shrapnel, the other round burying itself in the riverbank, igniting in a geyser of flame and mud. A narga sounded from the top of the opposite hill, and the Merki at the destroyed bridge started to pull back, dragging their wounded with them. The bank of the river, alight with the flames of the bridge, was dark with bodies.

The cluster of men around Pat shouted their defiance.

"Cutting the telegraph line!"

Pat looked over at the operator leaning out of the command car and then up at the aerosteamer. The copper line was disconnected from the roof of the command car by a Rus boy and started to snake upward, reeled in by Feyodor aboard *Yankee Clipper II*, which turned back to the east, propeller humming, nose pointed up, struggling to gain altitude. The other airship, *China Cloud*, more than a mile up, kept its position, ready to swoop if one of the Merki ships coming up from the southwest should make a mistake or get into trouble.

"Time to pack up," Pat said.

"Damn, we could hold the bastards here for the rest of the day," a Roum officer, assigned as an observer, announced triumphantly in broken Rus, pointing at the still-burning bridge and the dozens of Merki corpses that littered the banks.

"Bloody-nose 'em, that's what Andrew wanted—then pull back and bloody 'em again. From now on, when they find a bridge they'll tiptoe across it, assholes knotted tight."

"Last report was two umens have crossed the stream at a ford five miles north of here," the telegrapher shouted, leaning out of the command car.

Pat looked back at the Roum officer, who nodded an agreement for the withdrawal order.

The first of the cavalry troopers came up to the top of the hill, waving a Merki battle standard triumphantly. The standard was adorned with twelve horsetails dyed blue, and affixed to the top of it were a dozen human skulls.

Pat looked up at it coldly.

"Bloody bastards."

He looked back at the Merki lining the ridge on the other hill, their angry voices and what sounded like anguished cries carrying on the gentle afternoon breeze.

A regimental flag—we've taken one of their flags and the bastards are upset, he thought. Let 'em howl.

"Lash it to the armored car, but for God's sake take them skulls off it first," he snarled.

The grinning trooper, blood flowing from a scalp wound, turned and went over to the train.

Dennis Showalter, the brigadier general commanding the newly created 1st and 2nd Mounted Infantry of the Republics, came up to Pat's side and saluted, a grin lighting his powder-blackened features.

Pat motioned for him to dismount, and the lanky cavalryman tucked his Sharps carbine into its scabbard and slid down from his Clydesdale-size horse.

"Good show down there," Pat said quietly.

"We got at least fifty of the bastards."

"Fine, fine," Pat replied quietly. "That means we've only got something like three hundred and ninety-nine thousand and some odd figure left to go."

"We took one of their standards—that really set them off."

"And how many did you lose taking it?"

"Four dead, three wounded, plus two more got cut off on the other side of the hill. I hope for their sakes they saved the last round for themselves," Dennis said, his voice suddenly quiet.

"Not a fair trade."

"The boys' blood was up," Dennis said defensively.

"You mean your blood was up. I don't need some Jeb Stewart or Ashby galloping around out there looking for glory," Pat snarled. "It looks great in the *Illustrated Weekly,* but it kills men. You aren't going to stop those bastards by yourself. You're to hurt them, slow them down, make 'em nervous, and not lose any more men than you have to. You could have gunned those bastards down from a distance. Hell, your entire troop is carrying those precious new Sharps carbines. Learn how to use them. Fight with your goddam brain, not your guts. Do you understand me?"

Dennis nodded dejectedly.

"You've got boys who can only half ride, and you've got eight hundred precious horses, horses we can't spare but have to. And a hundred of the new Sharps carbines, the only ones on this entire world. Use them carefully."

Pat looked at Dennis appraisingly. He had been a gunnery sergeant with the old 44th. A good man, who knew horses and used to moan about not having joined a light horse artillery unit. Now he was getting his chance. It was just that he needed to learn some caution. That was the problem with cavalrymen. They needed guts and daring, but they had to be careful or they'd get their asses in a crack, and out here, there wouldn't be any infantry to pull them out the way both he and Andrew's old 35th had come to Buford's aid at Gettysburg.

Mina had thrown a fit when Andrew insisted that a light cavalry brigade of two regiments was to be formed, a fit made worse when it came to light that before Ferguson had shut down the Sharps carbine project he had already secretly turned out a hundred of the weapons against John's orders to focus production on infantry muzzle-loaders. Only the accidental discovery of them by one of John's staff people had brought their production to light. Pat smiled at the memory of it, John coming to Andrew looking for Ferguson's head and Andrew turning it around as the clinching argument for the cavalry unit. The weapons were .58 caliber, unlike Hans's precious .52 caliber weapon, which had been used as a template, in order to standardize the ammunition with the Springfields.

All of John's arguments were undoubtedly right, especially when it came to the simple fact that less than twenty percent of the field batteries had full complements of horses and remounts, but Andrew had insisted, and the eight hundred horses were transferred and the regiments formed from volunteers. A fair number of mounted men at arms from the old days of the boyars and from the Roum legion were still around to act as instructors, officers, and noncoms, and were overjoyed to be back in the saddle again. As always there were more than enough impetuous Rus and Roum boys ready to sign, eager for glory and the chance to save themselves from footsore marching. Most of them had managed to find hardee hats, which, following Dennis's romantic lead, were adorned with what passed for plumes and crossed sabers of brass on the front. From Roum some precious blue cloth had even been found and many of the men were now wearing navy-blue jackets trimmed with gold and reinforced sky-blue trousers. Pat looked at the troopers as they trotted up the hill, moving behind their swallowtailed flag, and felt a lump in his throat. Except for the plowhorse mounts, they seemed straight out of the glory days of the Army of the Potomac. The unit was working on another level as well, not formed as regiments from one community but rather combined out of all the Rus and Roum, the first combined command, like the regular army units from back home. It was a good unifying point, even including a handful of Cartha who had decided to stay on even though Hamilcar had pulled out of the war.

Though less than a month old, the two regiments were already bonded by a strong esprit, the men full of swagger, touting their precious Sharps carbines, revolvers, or sawed-off muskets converted into shotguns, hats pushed back from sweat-streaked faces, the men joking after the heart-thumping withdrawal into the trap at the bridge.

Though Pat wouldn't admit it to Dennis now, the skirmish had been masterful, the Merki lured straight into the trap with the fake attempt to burn the bridge and the beautiful bait of a command train. If the roles had been reversed, he'd have charged for their damn standard as well.

Goddammit, I've changed, Pat realized, tempted to offer Dennis a drink, tempted to near insanity to take one as well. But not now, not while there was fighting, especially this type of operation, dodging back before the Merki advance, slowing them down ever so slightly, even if only by a day. It was practice for what was coming.

"We captured twenty-two mounts," Dennis said, his voice a bit hopeful as if looking for approval.

Pat finally smiled, slapped him on the shoulder.

"Get six of your boys to move them to the rear. It'll make Mina happy to get a few horses back. I'll take the wounded"—he hesitated for a second—"and your dead as well on the train. We don't leave our dead for those animals. Get them aboard."

Pat looked back at the host on the far slope, which was gaining strength at each passing second. Riders were already moving toward the distant flanks, probing down toward the river. A flurry of shots echoed, and a mile or more away he could see a squadron of troopers pulling back from the ford to the south, several hundred Merki swarming down to the stream. In the distance the Merki aerosteamers were now clearly in view, moving up to try to cut him off once again.

"It's like trying to spit against a hurricane. Prick

'em like you set up here, then get the hell out. Do you understand me? Now be careful."

Dennis grinned and with a bit of a dramatic flourish he saluted while his horse reared up. Spurring his mount, he set off, his troopers falling in behind him. Pat watched, feeling a wave of jealousy for the young general, commander of the first human cavalry on this planet. It was a hell of a good day for some mischief, and he wished he could ride along for the fun.

With a wave of his hand he motioned the staff to get aboard the train. The engineer, leaning out of the cab, waved the clear signal, and with a spinning of wheels the engine started forward, pushing an armored car in front of it, pulling the staff car, a couple of flatcars loaded with infantry and emergency repair equipment, and another armored car hooked behind.

Pat climbed aboard, noticing the still-warm bodies of the four dead troopers spread out on the flatcar, blankets covering their features. There used to be an old joke that no one had ever seen a dead cavalryman. This war would certainly prove that one wrong, he thought darkly as went into his car, wishing more than ever for a solid drink.

"Cattle scum," Tamuka hissed, looking down at Garg, former second in command of the umen of the blue horse, now first in command, his superior dead on the other side of the stream.

Garg, features contorted with rage, said nothing, fingers knotted around the hilt of his scimitar so tightly that the veins on the back of his hand stood out.

A puff of smoke shot upward from the distance, and the high shriek of the train whistle rolled across the countryside as if shouting out a defiant taunt.

Two umen commanders dead in the first three days, one of them a clan chief bitten by a viper inside what he had thought was a bucket filled with water, which in fact had a false bottom, the snake falling on him when he lifted it up for a drink. And now the cattle were fighting from horseback.

He looked back at the palanquin that only now was cresting over the next hill, the curtains on it drawn shut.

"He's starting to feel better."

Tamuka looked over at Sarg, who had finally caught up, thanks to this latest delay.

Tamuka said nothing.

"The fever is dropping, and he even asked for some broth." Sarg looked over at the dead cavalryman that one of the warriors had slung over the rump of his horse.

The warrior, hearing Sarg, immediately bowed low from his saddle, motioning that the fresh food was a willing gift for the Qar Qarth. Dangling from a belt slung over the cattle's shoulder was a gun. Tamuka edged his mount up to the warrior, leaned over, and tugged at the gun, nearly pulling the body off the rear of the horse. Grabbing hold of the body, he un-snapped the gun from its holding clip and let the body fall at Sarg's feet.

"For our Qar Qarth," he said.

He looked down at the gun, turning it over to examine it closely.

"Everything is moving too slow," Tamuka snapped, looking up at a knot of clan chieftains and commanders of five umens. He could see resentment in the eyes of some of them. Many of them were of the age of Jubadi, had ridden with him in battle for more than a circling. Now, with Vuka ill, and no heir of age to command in his place, he as shield-bearer was in control—and they did not like it.

"The cattle have dark tricks," growled Norgua, commander of the third umen of the black horse. "I've lost fourscore to their tricks, two of them commanders of a thousand."

"Are you advising caution before cattle?" Tamuka asked.

"It is hard to see your kin, your young ones, die," Norgua replied. "Especially when it is against sorcery, snakes, stinging insects, traps of cattle."

"They want us to be afraid," Tamuka said, his voice even, but edged with the slightest contempt. "Listen to you—you voice fear of the filth of this world, soulless cattle."

Norgua lowered his head.

"Is Norgua afraid of cattle?"

Tamuka looked over at Pauka, one of the youngest umen commanders, hiding his own smile of approval.

Norgua growled darkly, hand going to sword hilt.

"They are cattle possessed," Pauka snapped angrily, looking at the other umen and clan commanders for support. "Slaughter them all, gorge on their flesh, I say. The words of Tamuka are truth. Kill them now before they make even greater weapons to destroy us. Even the great Jubadi saw that, and that is why he rode north to defeat them."

"If we can trap them at this place they call Kev, destroy them there, the rest will fall without a fight. They are loath to leave their land, so they will try to stand there. We must rush to them before they change their mind and strike with all our strength."

"But our cannons," Norgua replied angrily. "It will be six, maybe seven days before they arrive."

"The Vushka Hush turned the Yankee line without cannons and defeated them," Pauka responded, looking with admiration at Gubta, the new commander of the Hush.

"Six thousand of the Vushka Hush are dead or crippled, Shield-Bearer Tamuka," Caug, commander of the spotted horse clan, interjected, "my own son of my first concubine one of them."

"And I want revenge for thy son," Tamuka replied, his voice edged with anger.

"You are but temporary of command," Norgua said, looking defiantly at Tamuka. "You heard Sarg— in days the new Qar Qarth will be well again, and then we shall see what he says of this war."

"Are you afraid to fight cattle?" Tamuka replied.

Norgua looked at him darkly.

"There is no glory, no honor, in this chase. Besides, this is Tugar land. What of our own, what of the Bantag? While we chase through this forsaken place, the Bantag feast on our own cattle. There is even rumor that the Cartha have an iron ship and plan to take their city back. What then? I followed Jubadi because he was my Qar Qarth. I follow Vuka because he is now my Qar Qarth."

"And I am only a shield-bearer," Tamuka said without irony.

Norgua, without reply turned away and with a bark of command turned and started down the hill.

"By tomorrow at sunset we'll be before Kev."

Tamuka looked over his shoulder at Muzta beside the Tugar, the bearer of the great scroll map, who was pointing out their position to a group of warriors who had gathered around.

Tamuka sensed a near taunting in Muzta's voice.

"Find a ford, get across the river," he snapped, looking over at his umen commanders. Turning his mount, he trotted back toward the burning village. Dismounting, he relieved himself, and then leaned against his horse, watching the thatch-roofed buildings disintegrate, the empty barns roaring as their log sides and split-shingle roofs were consumed by fire.

Looking down at the cattle gun that he was still holding, he played with the mechanism for a moment until the breech dropped open. Pushing the trigger guard open and shut, he realized that this was like the gun found with the Yankee Schuder, a gun that could be loaded from the breech, faster, more deadly, ideal for men fighting from horseback.

He felt a cold chill. Could the animals have made these in the last thirty days, perhaps outfitting their entire army with them? He doubted that, but the mere thought of it made him nervous. Again they had made something new, always making something new. Couldn't his own fools see that? Norgua, wanting to quit the fight, to run away from something too strange to be understood, not seeing that if they did not kill all of them now, in five years, or ten, the Yankees would come unto the steppes of the south and hunt them down as sport.

A throbbing hum sounded above the crackling roar of the fire, and he looked up to see the line of cloud fliers advancing overhead, their undersides painted with the dark eyes of the hunting hawk. Far above them, like a small line, lingered one of the Yankee cloud fliers, staying out of range. Absently he worked the breech mechanism of the Sharps, watching as the machines lumbered on eastward.

"New type of gun."

Tamuka looked up at Muzta Qar Qarth, who edged his mount up beside him.

Tamuka held the gun up, and Muzta took it and looked at it with open curiosity, holding the weapon up to look down the bore and then fumbling with the breech mechanism.

"They don't have to push the black powder and bullet down the barrel, they just slide it in from the back," Muzta said, looking at the weapon admiringly. "Good crafting here."

Tamuka nodded glumly.

"Always good crafting."

"Too bad you killed all your pets three days ago— maybe some of them could have made a few."

"We're finished with pets. We'll learn how ourselves."

Muzta laughed softly. "You speak as if you were the Qar Qarth."

"Norgua is a fool. I mean to see this campaign to the end."

"Of course you do, and it'll cost you a hundred thousand dead."

"Then if that is the cost, that is the cost," Tamuka snarled. "But then we'll be done with them once and for all."

Muzta leaned over his mount, pulled up his water bag, took a long drink, and offered it over to Tamuka, who shook his head.

"I don't doubt that you'll do it," Muzta said. "In a way I can see your point, unlike the others. Norgua is a fool, still mourning Jubadi and not seeing the truth that the old Qar Qarth had only half grasped and you fully grasped."

A bit surprised, Tamuka nodded a thanks.

"When they can make such as these," Muzta said, handing the Sharps carbine back, "they are far too dangerous. For that matter, their mere thinking that they can kill those of the hordes was dangerous enough. We never thought that cattle could conceive of such things. I lost eighteen umens learning that fact.

"I fear, though, that you are fighting the future. You might win, if you fight as you told Jubadi to, and now plan to do. Perhaps you will destroy them." He hesitated. "But there'll always be others."

"There were the Yor and the Sartag," Tamuka replied. "Not even cattle. We have the legends as do you. And our ancestors fought and defeated them when they came through the tunnel of light."

"But they were only hundreds, and they did not have time to make new weapons. The same was true with the cattle in the wooden ships of fifteen circlings back who appeared near where the Yankees did. We found them within a year and killed nearly all of them."

Tamuka nodded, suddenly angry at the memory of their descendants, led by the cattle called Jamie. They had stolen the iron rail machine and disappeared back into the southern sea last year after the war of the iron ships. He had barely thought of them, wondering if they too were now making new machines.

"I almost agree with you," Muzta said. "I suspect that even many of the younger umen commanders feel the same. But asking warriors to die hunting cattle, without hope of honor, is hard."

"Their hatred will drive them forward," Tamuka replied coldly.

"It certainly is driving you forward," Muzta said with a smile.

"Don't you hate them after what they did to you, to your horde?"

"Of course I do," Muzta replied. "It's just that I have no intention of dying in the process."

"Tomorrow we'll be at Kev. There they will be waiting, there we shall finish them, and then we shall ride on to Roum unopposed. We'll leave this land a waste, killing every cattle, gorging until the grease runs from our mouths."

Muzta said nothing. With a smile he nodded, turned his horse, and trotted back to where his staff waited.

Tamuka looked at him with barely concealed contempt.

"And I'll fight them to the last Tugar," he whispered.

His heart full, Andrew Lawrence Keane sat atop the hill, looking off to the west. It was late in the afternoon of a beautiful spring day, the type of day back home that would have sorely tempted nim to let his classes out early so that he could go for a walk in the pine forest next to the campus. The air was warm, filled with the rich scent of early summer, slightly hazy, lazy, the type of day to lie beneath a tree and read a good book until sleep lulled you away, your dog curled up by your side. No dogs on this world. He missed their company.

He ran his finger inside his open shirt collar, grimacing slightly from the dirty sweat-soaked feel. Almost absently he picked up a piece of hardtack smeared with a sour-smelling cheese and chewed on it, washing the dry cracker down with a swill of cold tea from his battered tin cup. Pat, Emil, Kal, and Gregory sat around him, field glasses or telescopes raised, silently watching the show.

From north to south the Merki were advancing, arrayed in their checkerboard formation, ten blocks of a thousand to each umen, each block a hundred riders across and ten deep, five regiments to a mile of front, skirmishers in loose order ranging far ahead. The last of Showalter's cavalry was pulling back in through the outer line of fortifications, occasionally reining in to trade a flurry of shots at long range, the carbines thumping in the heavy air.

Kathleen sat by his side, a fact which bothered him. She should have gone east with Maddie days ago, but had somehow arranged that her hospital unit would be the last to pull out. She denounced his protest as favoritism, an argument which filled him with guilt, for in this situation he would have been more than willing to pull rank on her and send her packing east. At least the baby was safe, going back to Roum with Kal's wife, Ludmilla, to stay with Tanya and her children in the city. Though he would admit it to no one, he had made Ludmilla promise that if they lost she was to take her grandchildren and Maddie and head into the Great Forest to hide. It wasn't fair, his singling out his own child and the president's grandchildren thusly, but dammit, after all these years of service he wanted some small part of his life to have an advantage if he failed and the war was lost. For the sake of the children, Ludmilla had readily agreed, showing him that the bonds of blood and mothering cared little for republican sentiment.

"I can see how you can become addicted to this," Kathleen whispered, nodding toward the vast array of the Merki horde, which moved across the open fields, deployed out across the broad valley below, four hundred thousand warriors on a front of forty miles. "As terrible as an army with banners," she said, looking over at Emil, who nodded an agreement.

"Only problem is, this army has a most unpleasant way of finishing a fight," Emil replied.

The crack of an artillery piece sounded behind them, causing Kathleen to start. Andrew looked back at the four-pounder mounted atop an armor car. The crew were swinging the yoke-mounted gun back down to reload. From the north the two Merki aerosteamers at which the piece had been firing continued to close in. He held his breath for a moment as tiny black dots detached from the bottom of the ships, growing larger with the second. They landed to the south of the rail line, a hundred yards away. Two of the bombs were duds, and the other four exploded harmlessly.

The antisteamer gun fired again while the ships turned to race back to the west.

There had been a clash of air fleets earlier in the day, Jack venturing all five of his ships against three Merki. One of each side had fallen in flames, a fact which caused Andrew to mark Petracci down for a sound chewing-out. Nine aerosteamers had been built in the last two months. Three had been lost in combat and one in a storm, and another had exploded on its first test flight. Such losses could not be tolerated if all their strength was to be marshaled for what was to come. The wreckage of the two ships burned to the south, the area quarantined by Emil's orders; the doctor suspected there might be some form of arsenic poisoning from the Merki engine. Last year one of the engines had burst open after a crash; those who approached it had vomited blood, and their hair had fallen out before they died, the classic symptoms of ingesting the heavy metal. The few men in the area gave the burning wreckage a wide berth.

The Merki airships had penetrated over the lines often enough by now to gather the assessment that the army had pulled out, all except for this last line of trains. If the Merki were hoping to end it here, they were mistaken.

The withdrawal had gone without a hitch, three and a half corps moved back to the Penobscot in four days, only one brigade of Fourth Corps left now in front of Kev, the men already loaded. All that would be left behind were Showalter's cavalry and a regiment of volunteers hiding up in the north woods, volunteers taken from all the ranks and formed into the first of five guerrilla regiments which would deploy into the forest all the way from Vazima to the Sangros. Another brigade, detached from Schneid's corps, was now serving as a marine force under Bullfinch out at sea. As the Merki continued their advance they would soon discover a series of nasty surprises to their flanks and especially to the rear. It was another aspect of this new type of war which Andrew found distasteful, but which he knew would have to be pursued. There was no such thing as a noncombatant any longer. Factory workers were now perhaps even more important than the men at the front. The Merki had made this a total war; it had been nothing less from the start.

He looked down at the latest issue of *Gates's Illustrated Weekly,* the entire front page a woodcut of the one photograph that had successfully been taken by Petracci. Emblazed across the top in Cyrillic and the bottom in Latin was the new rally cry—"We Shall Avenge."

The image was horrifying, as he had hoped it would be, a reminder to all of their ultimate fate if they should fail. He knew what the guerrillas would do after the army passed. Orders had been given that Merki children were to be spared—he could not allow this war to sink to that final level of genocide—but everyone else was now a fair target. The Merki women and the old were to be killed, their yurts burned, horses slaughtered or captured. It was a violation of how the hordes had fought war against each other, a convention between them that he had scrupulously observed himself back on earth. He looked over at Kathleen, knowing what would happen if the Merki should take her. Let them now face the same, he thought darkly, sickened by what this had all become, but knowing that there was no other way. If it forced but a single umen to stay to the rear, it might make the difference, and in total war there was no other consideration but final victory at whatever cost or action. It was a long way from the Christian civility of his last war, as were assassination, aerosteamers, and even the burning of the dead to keep their bodies from the hands of the Merki.

Andrew sipped at the cold tea, watching the enemy lines, their outriders slowing to a stop before the walls of Kev. Kal, his features drawn and pale, stood up and turned to go back to the train. He hesitated and then leaned over and scooped up a handful of dirt, put it in his pocket, and then continued on.

"He can't bear to watch this final piece fall," Kathleen sighed, looking back at the president, who with hunched shoulders climbed aboard the train.

"Let's get out of here," Andrew said, coming back up to his feet.

Wrapped in silence, Tamuka rode through the darkened streets of Kev in the hour before dawn, the silent ones looking nervously at the shuttered windows of the houses that crowded in upon them in the narrow alleyways.

Empty, again empty. He had not truly believed the cloud fliers' reports—surely they had to be mistaken; some semblance of a fight would have to be offered here.

But there was nothing. Five days of riding only to find this, rather than the climactic battle.

"They can't run forever," Tamuka snarled, looking over at Sarg in the twilight.

"They're doing a good job of it," the shaman replied coldly. "And now the other concerns."

"You know what it will mean if we give them even more time."

"That is why I came and told you, Shield-Bearer," Sarg said, his voice barely a whisper.

"I did not believe in what Jubadi wished at first. But now I see. These cattle are demons, fleeing the very land given on to them out of our hands. Only a madness, a possession, could have moved them so. I now see what a delay of a year might mean."

"Or twenty years, as I suspect," Tamuka replied.

"That is why I told you."

Tamuka nodded, saying nothing. With the report of cattle again fleeing east had also come the belled rider of the Qar Qarth from out of the south. The cattle of Cartha had rebelled, taking their city back, several thousand dying with the withdrawal of the umen. With the two umens still posted to the south now facing a rebellion, it was not hard to imagine that such a sign of weakness might cause the Bantag to try to seize the place for themselves. It had been agreed that they could share in what the factories there produced, but only after the Rus and Roum had been destroyed. Now it was quite possible that the Bantag would move and the Merki horde would then be cut off, holding nothing but empty land.

Nothing was now going right. The blood of his riders had at least been stirred to seek this vengeance against the Rus, but they were gone, vanished, and it had cast a pall over the encampments, which had believed that by tomorrow night there would again be a feast of cattle flesh and then the easy pickings of the rest of them after the army had been destroyed.

Thirty-five days ago they were beaten, their army demoralized, their families fleeing. Now the country was empty. Reaching the main square of the city, he paused for a moment and then turned to go back out the main gate. On the open gates he again gazed at the strangely crafted picture.

"We Shall Avenge" were the words written across it, or so he had been told. Dismounting, he looked over at Sarg.

"The two of us are to remain alone," Tamuka said, his voice soft, betraying no emotion.

Sarg nodded, saying nothing, motioning for the silent ones to withdraw.

Bowing low to the fires of purification which flickered at either side of the entryway into the yurt of the Qar Qarth, Tamuka went in.

Vuka Qar Qarth stirred from his bed and looked up.

"I said I was to be alone," he whispered.

Tamuka bowed low and approached him.

"Sarg has told me about your fever dream and what you now wish."

Vuka looked up cautiously at his shield-bearer. "My fever is gone, the infection has drained," he said, holding his right arm up weakly.

"You are still ill."

Vuka nodded slowly. "I know why."

"And that is?" Tamuka replied.

"You."

Tamuka did not move.

"Sarg made the ceremonial cut, and then you bound it with a dressing from your battle kit. Sarg has treated it since. The cloth, the blade, or his poultices were unclean. The two of you wanted the infection to kill me."

He smiled coldly at the shield-bearer.

"Nonsense. Now what of this dream?" Tamuka asked.

Vuka looked away, suddenly nervous, as if he had said too much. "My father spoke to me tonight."

Tamuka felt a chill ripple down his back, the hairs at the nape of his neck standing up. It could only mean that Jubadi did not rest well, that his spirit was troubled, or that in the spirit world he had learned something of such importance that he had risked the perilous journey back to the land of the living to give warning.

"He said that the cattle war must end. That we must retake Cartha, elsewise the Bantag will seize it, learn the Yankee secrets, and turn them against us, with my people trapped here between two fires."

Tamuka said nothing, as if frozen.

"I have heard the reports," Vuka said, "though you have tried to keep them from me. The Yankees, the Rus, have fled to Roum. The crossing of the lands between the two realms is difficult even for the smaller horde of the Tugars. Without the loot of the Rus the march will be hard, and then still there is a battle to fight, while the Bantag will grow fat in the rich lands of the south. My father has spoken with the spirits and sees the truth that you, Shield-Bearer, do not."

"The Yankees will still be waiting, growing stronger. One hard campaign now will finish them forever. Your father knew that, and so do I. If we delay another year, they will still be here, stronger than before. We must strangle them in the cradle before they can walk. If we ride away and in the next circling your son comes to face them, he will face a giant."

There was almost a note of pleading in Tamuka's voice, and he cursed himself for this show of weakness.

Vuka snorted with disdain. "They will fight against themselves, or another plague will take them, or we will find some poison as it is said the Yor once used, a mere breath killing him who breathes it. I am now Qar Qarth, and I will not sacrifice my people the way Muzta did his. The Bantag laugh at our folly. We could barely match them before. And what would this campaign cost us? Already the Vushka Hush is a shadow, two more umens shattered, hundreds more dead in this last march. I hear that the cooking pots of our women, the old ones, will soon be empty in this cursed land."

He raised himself up.

"No more. Tomorrow I call a meeting of the clans. Tomorrow we ride back to Cartha, where there will still be food, if we get there before the Bantag. I shall leave four umens behind to ravage this land from end to end, and when winter comes the Rus will starve. Do you honestly think that with this land destroyed, their cities flattened, their buildings shattered, they will survive? The Roum will cast them out, they will fight among themselves, they will die and rot."

He looked up coldly at Tamuka.

"I am so sick of their flesh I wish them all to rot, and not one more of my warriors shall die by their cursed ways. Many now say that the cattle here are mad, possessed by demons. I will not see my horde destroyed fighting their madness. Some call for revenge for my father. Let the cattle starve in a ravaged land, that is vengeance, and it will cost not one more life of our horde.

"Today I shall declare my decisions and begin a withdrawal out of this cursed land. Once across the boundary river, I shall order the white banner unfurled, and then I shall become Qar Qarth through full ceremony."

He smiled coldly.

"And end for you the ambition I know you harbor in your soul."

He hesitated for a moment.

"Tamuka, you are no longer my shield-bearer. I shall select another, one I can trust."

Tamuka stood as if frozen to the ground.

"You lie," Tamuka hissed. "It was not your father in a dream, for when your father came into the land of his ancestors, there also he met Mupa, the brother that you murdered, who told him the truth, who told him of the filth of your black soul. If your father returned to your dreams, it was to spit upon you."

Startled, Vuka could not even reply. His face was contorted with rage.

"As he will spit upon you now!"

Tamuka leaped forward, landing on top of Vuka, driving his knee into the Qar Qarth's chest, snapping the wind out of him. Reaching up, Vuka tried to claw at his face, grimacing from the pain in his injured arm and the weight bearing down upon him. Tamuka wrapped his hands around Vuka's throat, bearing down with his knees, pinning Vuka's arms tight against the bed. If Vuka could have screamed from the pain he would have done so, but it was now impossible to breath.

It was almost too simple, Tamuka found. He had strangled the life out of cattle that had fought harder. The illness had taken its toll. It should have killed Vuka as he had planned, but this would now do.

He pressed his thumbs in tight around Vuka's throat. Vuka's eyes seemed as if they would burst from their sockets, looking straight up at him in rage, and then growing disbelief. He felt the strength slip from the Qar Qarth's arms, the kicking legs stilling into spasmodic jerks. He bore down upon him. The eyes were still wide, mouth open, tongue protruding, cheeks running with saliva.

Vuka's eyes held upon him, and he felt a sudden urge to look away, but he could not. For a moment he felt as if he were being drawn into them, his soul being pulled into the abyss along with Vuka's.

The neck muscles suddenly went slack, relaxing beneath his grip, and he eased back ever so slightly, fearful that if he bore down hard he might snap the Qar Qarth's neck. Yet he continued to hold on. He felt the body beneath him relax as if it had turned already to emptiness and dust.

"He's dead."

With a startled cry, Tamuka looked up to see Sarg standing in the entryway to the yurt.

Tamuka fell back, becoming tangled in the silken sheets. Frantically he pulled himself clear of the body and stood up.

Sarg stepped past him, put his hand to Vuka's chest, and then looked back up at Tamuka.

"It appears that our Qar Qarth has died from a fit," the shaman said quietly, moving to position the body neatly upon the sleeping pallet, closing the protruding eyes, and then pulling a sheet up to cover the face.

Hands trembling, Tamuka went over to a small side table, grabbed hold of a goblet of fermented horse's milk, and raised it up.

"I wouldn't do that if I were you," Sarg said.

Tamuka stopped and looked at the goblet.

"I only came to you when he declared that henceforth he would eat nothing that I had touched," the old shaman said quietly.

Tamuka threw the goblet to the ground. "So you only agreed to this because you feared he would replace you as he was about to replace me?"

The shaman smiled. "I suspected the death of his brother, and he feared any who suspected that."

"The war, then—you didn't care?"

"Actually, I think he was right."

"And for your own power you would have murdered him?" Tamuka snarled. "Only the council of the white clan of all those who are shield-bearers can decide to remove a Qar Qarth."

"I don't see a council meeting here," Sarg sniffed, "so who is calling whom murderer? And don't look so startled, my friend—it is not the first time a Qar Qarth died by having a fit."

"You disgust me," Tamuka snapped. "I acted to save our people, to save this world from the cattle."

"Oh, but of course," Sarg replied with mock sincerity.

The shaman turned to look back at the covered body.

"Since he had not gone through the full investiture of the Qar Qarth, we can dispense with the usual thirty days of ritual," Sarg said, as if the issue were of no real concern to him. "The three days' mourning for a Qarth will be sufficient. Then you can have your war again."

"And since there is no issue from him . . ." Tamuka said, his breath coming hard.

"Until the white banner of peace is unfurled and this war is finished, there is no time for a gathering of council. That is the tradition of our ancestors. It is the same rule that prevented him from gaining full title as Qar Qarth until this war was ended. There is no time in war for such lengthy things. Therefore, you as shield-bearer will act as Qar Qarth."

With a near-mocking bow, Sarg lowered his head.

"I bow before the Qar Qarth Tamuka."

Aware that the bronze shield was still slung to his back, Tamuka loosened its leather strap. He held it for a brief moment, looking at his reflection, distorted by the mar of the rifle bullet that had struck it during the burial of Jubadi.

Hulagar. He felt a cold chill, as if the spirit of Hulagar somehow floated above him, having seen all, and worse, having seen into his heart of hearts as well.

He flung the shield to the ground at Sarg's feet.

"And you will remain shaman of the Merki," Tamuka said coldly. "Now go and announce the lamented death of Vuka. Announce as well that council of war shall be held at dawn. In three days we continue the campaign."

He closed his eyes for a moment, as if to purge the memory of Vuka's gaze and with it the ghost of Hulagar watching and seeing all.

Without a backward glance at the corpse, he strode out of the tent and into the early light of dawn.

Chapter 6

It was hard to control the shaking of his hands. It wasn't the test, that he was sure of, at least as sure as was possible. He looked over his shoulder, and the mere sight of her set his heart to turning over again.

"Olivia, why don't you go back to the dugout until this is over?" Chuck asked, still not sure if his Latin was coming out quite right.

She smiled and shook her head.

"You're out here, all your staff is out here. I think I'll stay."

The Roum personnel on his staff could not hide their grins of amusement at her calm defiance and the visible discomfort of their chief.

"After all, last time I did save you from getting chopped up by that engine of yours."

His face red, he turned away, ashamed at the reminder that her quick thinking and a fast tackle had saved him from being decapitated when the first airship engine had decided to take off from its testing bench.

"All right, then," he mumbled.

Looking back at the waiting team of workers, he grumbled out a quick curse and walked away, knowing that she was walking behind him, the scent of her perfume drifting with the early-evening breeze.

He walked up to the side of his latest project and looked at it admiringly, as always excited by the first rolling out of one of his newest creations. Several dozen pipes were strapped together into an oaken frame, a dozen pipes to each layer, each pipe nearly six feet long and four inches in diameter.

"Let's set it at fifteen hundred yards," Chuck announced, and a Rus worker, who only weeks before had been laboring in the musket factory, climbed up on the flatbed wagon. Working a simple crank with wooden gears, he jacked the front end of the mass of pipes skyward, stopping when a crude pointer indicated the correct range. The array was now pointing menacingly at a long spread of white canvas set up nearly a mile downrange at the far end of the clearing.

"Signal 'get ready,' " Chuck said quietly.

A young Roum boy raised a red flag and waved it. Antlike figures at the far end of the field waved a flag in return and disappeared from view into a heavily fortified dugout.

Chuck looked around nervously. Several months of hard work were tied into this moment, and five hundred workers back at the factory were ready to start mass production on this project if everything tested out correctly.

"All right, gentlemen," Chuck said, his voice barely a whisper, "I suggest we step back now."

The crew retreated into a narrow trench a dozen yards behind and to one side of the wagon. Chuck went up to the side of the wagon, took a thin coil of rope, and tied it to a musket trigger. The barrel of the weapon was gone. In its place, three thin copper tubes, each one containing a quick-fire fuse, ran from the nipple, each tube running behind the back end of the pipes. A quick fuse hooked into the rocket inside of each tube was in turn connected to the copper pipe fuse line.

Chuck cocked the musket and gingerly placed a percussion cap on the nipple. Slowly walking backward, he payed out the rope, careful not to put any pressure on the trigger. He slipped into the trench and gently pulled the rope taut.

He hesitated and looked over at Olivia, then handed the rope over.

"Pull it hard," he said.

Not quite sure of what she was doing, Olivia took hold of the rope, shut her eyes, and yanked.

The clear snap of the percussion cap cut the evening air. For a second Chuck thought that something had gone wrong. And then all hell broke loose.

Fire belched from the back end of the three pipes closest to the trigger, the next three igniting half a second later, followed by the next three and the rest after them. There was no explosive report in the first seconds, only a boiling cloud of smoke and fire. A high, piercing shriek suddenly filled the air as if a pack of demons had set to howling. And then he saw them, arcing out through the smoke, the first rocket going downrange, spinning on its axis, flying straight, other rockets, blurring upward, chasing after the first, all of them shrieking. One of the rockets emerged from its launch tube at an angle, climbing straight upward, and another seemed to tumble from its tube, detonating with a thunderclap a dozen yards downrange. But the rest continued straight on, trailing fire and smoke, reaching apogee as the propellant burned out and then slowly arcing over back toward the ground.

Ferguson and his companions leaped from the trench, choking on the smoke, cheering wildly. Running through the billowing cloud, Chuck pulled his field glasses from their case and, pushing his spectacles up on his forehead, focused on the target. The first rocket slammed into the ground two hundred yards short, the time fuse and percussion fuse both failing. The next one detonated in the air fifty yards farther on. Then the volley slammed down in a bracket a hundred yards to either side of the target, detonating in the air or exploding on the ground, thirty rounds, fifteen hundred musket balls spraying outward. The distant hillside disappeared in a pall of white smoke and geysering earth. Long seconds later, the distant reports echoed across the field, causing a renewed cheer and backslapping.

Losing all inhibitions, Chuck turned to Olivia, picked her up, and squeezed her tightly, spinning her around, suddenly very aware of her round body pressed against his. He wanted to kiss her again, but, embarrassed, he lowered her to the ground, his cheeks reddening as she laughed and kissed him on the cheek.

As the smoke cleared, the observation crew on the far hill emerged from their dugout and ran up to the target, one of them waving the red flag to point out where a rocket had actually gone through the target, the impact on the far side shredding it to ribbons.

"Reload!" Chuck shouted, pulling out his watch to time the action.

The Rus battery crew turned and ran back to the trench. Pulling out a heavy wooden box, they unloaded a dozen more rockets, each one fashioned from a pressed cylinder of tin four inches in diameter and nearly two feet in length.

"Ten-second fuses," Chuck shouted.

The loaders and their assistants inserted the appropriate fuses into the noses of the rockets. The rockets were built in two parts, the powder propellant in the rear, separated by wadding from an explosive nose cone, which held a central bursting charge surrounded by fifty musket balls packed in sawdust and beeswax. The cardboard-and-wax fuses were preset to different times and color-coded, as were the artillery fuses, for quick identification in the heat of battle; they were inserted just before firing. The innovation in this area, which Chuck was inordinately proud of, was the backup of a heavy percussion-cap head, which would detonate the charge if it should strike the ground before the time fuse ignited.

The handlers, each armed with a quill, checked the four vents at the aft end of the rocket. Each vent was set to blow some of the exhaust out at an angle to the long axis, thus giving the weapon its spin. Next they checked the small clipped vent for the shrieking whistle, an idea Chuck had seized upon primarily out of his love for whistling firecrackers as a boy, which he sensed might have something of an effect on morale.

Half a dozen boys with sponge staffs ran up to the launcher as the range setter cranked it back down to the horizontal. The boys ran the swabs through the open pipes to kill any lingering sparks.

The loaders now came up, pushed the rockets into the tubes from the rear, and pulled out the wooden plugs which closed off the back ends of the rockets.

"Arm!"

Now came the toughest part, and Chuck stepped back to watch the battery lieutenant and the corporal assisting him. The lieutenant, carrying a long thin case, over six feet in length, came out of the trench and placed it behind the rocket launcher. Opening it, the two removed the copper fuse line, a dozen quick fuses emerging from it at six-inch intervals. Coming up behind the launcher, they laid the fuse line into a lead-lined tray set behind the launch pipes, clamping one end into the musket nipple, the other end to a support bracket. Going down the line, the lieutenant now inserted a fuse into the back end of each rocket. Watching him, Chuck realized that this was the slow part and that another person would have to be assigned to speed the operation up.

Reaching the end of the copper tube, the lieutenant stood back up.

"Fused and ready."

"Range fifteen hundred yards!"

The sergeant standing at the elevation control cranked the weapon back up, and Chuck looked down at his watch.

"Three minutes ten seconds," he said, trying to sound disappointed but secretly excited. The weapon was not designed to replace the close-in rapid-fire support of artillery, but rather to serve as area bombardment. He wasn't sure if they'd even have enough rockets for a second volley, but it was best to plan for these things now.

He nodded to the Rus boy holding the red flag, and the banner was held aloft, the men at the far end of the field scurrying back to their shelter.

The crew went back into their trench while Chuck hooked the trigger line back up and, paying it out, climbed in after them. He would have preferred a second full volley test, but a dozen rounds used up nearly three hundred pounds of powder, and besides, the next dozen rounds to be fired were all that were left on the entire planet.

He drew back on the lanyard, looked over at Olivia, who smiled encouragement, and gave it a sharp yank.

Again there was the second delay and the first rocket snapped off, the others crackling to life at half-second intervals. The fifth went veering off at nearly a right angle to the battery, arcing up toward the woods that surrounded the clearing. The next-to-last round, however, detonated inside the launch tube. Shrapnel sprayed out both ends, the tube burst open, the firing tube next to it tumbled up into the air, and the rocket ignited out of it, coming straight back down half a dozen yards behind the trench and spraying shrapnel in every direction.

His ears ringing from the explosion, Chuck looked over at the rest of the crew, whose eyes were wide with fear and astonishment. Feeble grins broke out at the close call.

"Your crazy inventions are going to kill you," Olivia announced, her voice slightly shaky as she solicitously brushed a sprinkling of dirt off his uniform. The smoke clearing, Chuck climbed out of the trench and walked up to the launcher. It was a total wreck, the firing tubes perforated by the .75 caliber iron balls used as shrapnel, the frame twisted, a dozen tubes littering the field, the remaining two dozen bent at nearly every angle but straight ahead.

Far downrange, the remaining nine rockets had already impacted, and as Chuck raised his field glasses to check, the crew on the opposite side of the clearing jumped up and down excitedly, not yet aware that the test had ended in the total destruction of the battery.

He felt a curious mix of emotions. The actual firing had delivered almost ninety percent of the rockets into a target a couple of acres in area, an effect that would be devastating. It had also sent half a dozen rockets off at random directions and totally destroyed the one multiple launcher in existence. He knew that this new weapon should be employed only in this manner. Firing a single rocket at a time by individual crews was simply too dangerous, and the effect was far too random. It had to be done all at once by massed batteries for the shock effect. The test, however, validated all the complaints that Mina had laid against the system, and it could also be charged that Ferguson had stolen hundreds of workers and wasted a month of their time to build a factory for a weapon that really didn't even work right.

He had hoped that it would go flawlessly, so that he could break the secrecy, take it down for Andrew to examine, and then go on without all this subterfuge. That was obviously impossible, he thought as he looked at the wreckage.

He looked over at Olivia.

"Goddammit, I know this thing will work, but we just don't have the time to fool around and wait."

He had been in isolation at the factory for more than a week, and it was Olivia who had brought him the news of the fall of Kev and the pullback into the steppes between Rus and Roum. With a hard enough push the Merki could very well be before Hispania in two weeks.

He looked back at the battery crew, who stood around sheepishly, as if they had somehow been responsible for the disaster, and back out at the men downrange, who were still running around excitedly, marking out impact points and examining pieces of the rockets to see how they had burst. Through his field glasses he could even see the tears in the canvas target.

He lowered his glasses and looked back at Theodor, the factory foreman, whose twin brother was serving as engineer aboard Petracci's airship.

"Round-the-clock production starts immediately," he said quietly.

"But it still isn't working right," one of the men replied, pointing at the still-smoking wreckage.

"We don't have any more time," Chuck replied. "You heard the order. Now let's get to it."

The men looked at him with surprise, some of them excited that he was forging ahead, more than a few of them, however, looking at Chuck as if he had taken leave of his senses.

Theodor, whom he had transferred from the aerosteamer factory to manage this new project, came to join him as the others turned away and started the long hike back to the factory a couple of miles away.

"Some powder must have leaked through the wadding between the propulsion and the explosive charge."

Chuck nodded absently.

"A full tin shield, soldered in place and separating the chambers, would prevent that."

"It'd mean each piece would have to be hand-soldered, and we'd have to make a stamp press to turn out the shields. We already talked about that and figured it'd take too much time," Chuck replied, his voice weary.

Theodor nodded.

"You know, if we start mass production it's going to eat up everything we've hidden away within ten days. After that it'll be fifteen tons of powder and over seventy-five thousand shrapnel balls a week. We can't hide that for long—they're crying for ammunition like mad down in Hispania."

Chuck sighed. He had hoped to come clean on his little subterfuge, it was impossible now. John would shut him down without a second's hesitation.

"With luck it'll take 'em a week to find out, maybe even two, and several more days to track it all down. By then we'll have what I want."

"You can't win this war all by yourself," Theodor replied.

Chuck smiled, taking off his glasses to wipe them on his dirty linen shirt.

"I was right about the railroads, the aerosteamers, the Whitworth rifle, even the damned Sharps, and you saw what happened when they found out about that project. They're not going to stop this one."

"We all are on the same side," Theodor replied softly.

Chuck laughed softly.

"There was a fellow named Ripley back in the war I fought in back on earth. In charge of ordnance, the same as John now is. Our entire army could have had breechloaders by the fall of 1862, we could have had rocket batteries, even automatic guns, if it hadn't been for that narrow-minded pencil pusher. Sometimes I swear they had the same mother."

"I don't know about this Ripley, but somehow I think you've just insulted General Mina."

Chuck smiled sadly.

"No insult was really intended. I can see John's side of it. We're short of everything, especially time. Its just that he doesn't have the imagination to see what our projects can do."

"Projects?" Theodor said cautiously. "I thought even you were going to give up on the other one."

"Hell, the thing's made. We just have to work a couple of kinks out of it."

Theodor looked back at the ruined rocket launcher. "It makes this look like a damn success."

"Don't worry about it," Chuck snapped.

"Worry? Me worry? I just don't want to see my commander led away in chains for stealing five hundred workers, thirty tons of powder, and Kesus knows what else that you haven't confessed to me yet."

"Get a team of horses up here to haul the wagon back to the factory," Chuck said, and without waiting for a reply he turned and walked away.

"Chuck?"

Startled, he looked up to see that Olivia was still waiting for him, and was suddenly embarrassed to realize that he had, at least for the moment, completely forgotten about her.

"You're upset," she said, coming up to stand in front of him.

It took him a moment to shift from Rus back to her Latin.

"Sorry."

"Let's walk. It's a beautiful evening."

She fell in alongside of him, slipping her hand around his arm, guiding him away from the path back to the rocket factory.

The tiny meadow in the middle of the forest was now nearly thigh-high with spring grass and wildflowers, a fact which he suddenly became aware of when she paused for a moment to scoop up an orchidlike bloom, its color an iridescent violet. Laughing, she slipped it into her hair.

The evening air was pleasant after the scorching heat of day, the cumulus clouds of afternoon now breaking apart into high twisted strands, glowing pink from the light of the setting sun. The birds of the

forest were settling in for the night, their last songs of
the day echoing through the woods. Hundreds of tiny
hummingbird-size swallows, their wings a brilliant orange, fluttered and darted over the meadow, sweeping
up the insects that were coming out in the evening
coolness. Occasionally one of the birds would dart before the couple and hover for a second, as if sizing
them up, and then dart away. Olivia watched them
and smiled.

"I never saw such birds before in Roum. It's beautiful here in the forest."

"They're certainly not from earth," Chuck replied,
watching their darting flight, which reminded him of
barn swallows. It was such a curious place. The trees
were almost like those of home, as were many of the
flowers, but then other things had found their place
here from other worlds—birds, the hated field adder,
antelope, the freshwater whales, and of course the
hordes. He had heard about Darwin, for debates
about his writings were already stormy back at his old
college, and he wondered what the man would say
about this planet.

They reached the edge of the clearing, and Chuck
started to turn as if to head them back along the forest
edge to the factory complex.

With a soft laugh, she held his arm and led him into
the forest, the high pines above them blocking out the
open sky, the early twilight of the field replaced in an
instant by a soft gathering darkness.

He felt his heart start to race as she led him farther
into the woods.

"The train for Hispania leaves the aerosteamer yard
in an hour," Chuck said nervously. "I have to catch
it and be back in Hispania tonight, and you do as
well."

"I'm staying," she whispered.

"What?"

"I got a pass to come up here—I had to go to Roum

and see my father and Marcus to get it. Do you know how much trouble I went through to see you? And now you want to send me back."

She laughed, shaking her head as if in mock anger, her long black hair swishing about her waist, the scent of lavender washing over Chuck.

"But where will you stay? The barracks are jammed to overflowing as is."

"In your cabin."

Chuck was unable to reply and took a step backward.

She looked up at him, her smile barely visible.

She reached up to her shoulder, unclasped the single strap of her tunic, and let it slip down to her waist.

"Oh my God," Chuck whispered.

Still smiling, she pulled the dress down over her hips and let it slip to the ground. Wordlessly she looked up at him.

"Olivia, I've got to catch a train," he whispered.

Stepping forward, she took his hand and placed it over her breast. Unable to stop himself, he cupped the breast, feeling as if his heart were about to burst. This was a moment he had dreamed of for years, but had never known. No Maine girl would have allowed this, at least the Maine girls he knew, until the preacher had done a powerful bit of praying over them and made things very permanent.

"Kiss them," she whispered even as she placed her hands around his neck and lovingly pulled him down. He let his lips brush against her nipple, and then in a rising panic he stood straight up again, his glasses smeared from pressing against her.

"I've got to catch that train," he gasped.

She laughed softly and wrapped him in an embrace. "You're trembling."

"Of course I'm trembling," he gasped.

"I love you, Chuck. I've wanted you since we first met."

"I love you too," he whispered, thrilled to finally be saying it without fear of being laughed at.

"Then it's all right. We both know there might not be much time left before they come. Let's have what we can of each other until then."

That was a certain ticket to hell. He had heard way too many sermons on that subject not to know that she was talking Ten Commandments–type violations. But the logic she was presenting, reinforced by the feel of her naked body against his, was too much to stand against.

"But the train . . ." he said feebly.

She looked up at him, still smiling.

"You're a virgin, aren't you?"

Embarrassed beyond words, he could only nod his head.

"Then don't worry." She laughed softly. "If you're a virgin, we can do this and still have plenty of time to catch your silly train."

"We've got orders!"

Vincent Hawthorne turned from chewing out a regimental commander and looked at the courier galloping across the drill field, waving his hat like a madman. The courier reined up hard and leaped off his mount, offering the piece of paper to Vincent.

Vincent looked at the young Rus telegrapher coldly.

"Soldier, the orders are directed to me, and not to be shouted to the entire army," Vincent snapped. The boy's excitement was instantly replaced by fear. "If you ever dare to do this again, I'll have you emptying slop buckets for the sick ward till the day you die."

Without waiting for a reply, he turned away, unfolding the orders, ignoring his staff, who were anxious for the details but now too intimidated to join him.

He smiled finally and looked back at his men.

"From Colonel Keane," Vincent said quietly. "Sixth

and Seventh Corps as of today are officially attached to the Army of the Republics. In four days we are to march to Hispania and take our position in the line." He turned and walked away.

The word of the orders spread like fire across the fields, the men cheering in their naivety, eager to be released from the incessant dawn-to-desk drilling. Vincent ignored them, looking back toward the city, noticing that Marcus was coming out of the main gate to join him, the soldiers to either side of the road stopping their celebration and coming to attention to salute.

Marcus reined up beside Vincent and dismounted to join him.

"I just got the word as well," Marcus said.

"We're still four thousand muskets short, only a third of the men are armed with the newer Springfields, and we're only at three-quarter strength for artillery," Vincent replied coldly. "These boys will get chewed to hell in a stand-up fight."

"They're good men," Marcus said quietly, looking across the field. "The division of our troops fighting with your Fourth Corps did splendidly, as have the men of Fifth Corps holding the southern border against the Merki raiders. These will too, after all you trained them."

Vincent nodded a curt thanks for the compliment.

"I heard you want one of the two corps for your own command," Vincent said, coming straight to the point of what had been bothering him since he had received word of the decision the previous evening.

"I want to be where the final battle will be fought," Marcus replied.

"You have ten thousand men to the south preventing the two umens of the Merki from raiding, you have the militia here in Roum, Brindusia, Capri, Metapontium. I think that is responsibility enough."

"One of my lieutenants can take care of that. We

both know that the main battle will be fought at Hispania. If that falls, everything else falls as well."

"I know the style of fighting better than you," Vincent replied, his voice cold. "I was responsible for
training these two corps."

"And now you want to lead both of them in battle."

"Precisely."

"You might know the drill," Marcus replied soothingly, "but remember I was proconsul of these men
before they ever heard of you, or for that matter the
Merki. That counts for a lot. I've been out here on
the drill field with them, when I was not in the south,
or meeting with Andrew. I can handle Seventh Corps
when the time comes."

Vincent looked over sharply at Marcus.

"Lincoln had the same problem for years with political generals," Vincent said, his voice deceptively
quiet.

Marcus bristled, sensing that he had been insulted
in a way that he had never experienced before. The
Roum turned and walked away, hands clenched behind his back. The staffs of both commanders, as if
sensing an explosion, drew farther away. Marcus finally turned back, his features red.

"Just what the hell is wrong with you?"

"I want to win and not see it thrown away."

"The gods damn you," Marcus roared.

Vincent drew himself up, standing rigid, his features
hard.

"One mistake," Vincent hissed, "one goddam mistake, and six months of training, thirty thousand men,
the entire war might be lost."

"And you won't make any mistakes, while I will?"
Marcus snapped.

"I see it that way."

"Well, I don't. You're nothing but a mad pup. You
saw a little too much killing, got a bit too much blood

on your delicate hands, and now you're soulless. Now you think you're the son of Mars incarnate."

"I came up through the ranks the hard way," Vincent replied.

"And I didn't, is that it?"

"Some could say that."

"I was leading these people before you were even born," Marcus snapped. "You think you've seen too much death? When I was ten and saw the Tugars come for the first time, I watched as my closest friend was dragged into a moon feast, my father as proconsul powerless to do anything. When I was thirty and proconsul I watched three hundred thousand of my people die. At fifty I was prepared to see it happen again until your people smashed the Tugars. I know as well that if we lose at Hispania every last one of my people will die. So don't play the hardened warrior with me. It makes you look ridiculous in my eyes."

Vincent felt a sudden rage with himself. His jaw muscles were twitching, his hands shaking with anger, and he couldn't control it.

"My Suzdalian regiment died to protect you when your own Senate and army turned on you last year," Vincent said, his voice near to breaking from anger.

"And I acknowledge that debt," Marcus replied, his features suddenly softening into a smile. "But son, you're pressing yourself too hard, taking too much of the responsibility. It'll kill you. You've already killed yourself inside. Now you think you can stand and watch your corps fight, killing ten thousand of them to win a battle, without flinching. Well, I don't want to be around when that day comes for you."

"I'm not your son."

"All right, then, dammit, general, god, whatever you want to call yourself now."

Marcus drew closer and started to put his hand on Vincent's shoulder, but thinking better of it he clumsily stopped himself.

"But I'm telling you this as a friend," he continued, his voice now soft. "We live in the same house. I can hear your children laughing, and it warms my heart. I now have no family but them," and he looked away for a moment.

"I can also hear your wife crying, the fights when you drink in a vain attempt to sleep. I remember you different, before the Cartha attacked. I knew the darkness that haunted you, but you could still laugh, still smile. I listened for hours to your dreams of how the world should be and came to believe some of it. It was you far more than Kal or Andrew that taught me to trust your people. It was you far more than your armies that taught me that we could fight and beat the hordes. You were honest to a fault. I cannot forget the times you told me the secrets of how my own people might better compete against the Rus and Yankees when it came to these new ways of making things and wealth. That was an honesty some would call madness, but I came to see as from the heart of a worthy soul. You said just now that you are not my son. You know that my own son died from the pox just before your healers came to teach us inoculation."

He stopped for a moment as if unsure of his own control.

"You became that son, your children my grandchildren. That is how I'm trying to speak to you now."

Vincent felt the distant tug of a stirring, and with it a blackness. There was a flash memory of the dying Merki hanging on the cross, and swirling into it all the other nightmares, the Neiper choked with the bodies he put there, nameless soldiers dying in his arms, the horror of the Tugars charging through the pass, the first man he killed, lying crumpled on the pavement in Novrod. How, oh God, how did this happen to me? he wondered.

He felt his hands trembling, the all-powerful need for another drink stealing over him. And Emerson had dared to talk about the universality of all living things, he thought coldly, had said that evil shall wither before the power of love. Let the bastards who had taught him those lies of youth come to this place. He felt a self-loathing, a sudden urge to vomit, and now it wasn't two in the morning, the daze of an alcoholic's dream sweeping over him. It was noon, in the field, his army around him in the sunlight—the army which he had forged to be his striking hand, the destroyer of worlds.

The trembling faded. His features throughout had not changed, except perhaps for the eyes, which attempted to focus on Marcus.

"Seventh Corps is yours," Vincent Hawthorne whispered, "but God help you if you kill them without taking down the Merki with you."

He turned and walked away, not even seeing the troubled look and returning anger in Marcus's eyes.

Tamuka Qar Qarth sat in silence, watching the conflagration, and was well pleased.

"A fitting pyre for the son of Jubadi," Sarg said, nodding his head with approval.

The inferno of Kev shimmered before them, the heat so intense that his horse nickered, attempting to shy away even though the walls were more than an arrow flight's distance.

The ceremony had been simple enough. The fact that Vuka had not been officially confirmed as Qar Qarth was argued by Sarg as a legitimate reason to observe but three days of mourning without loss of fire. Vuka's body had been placed upon a bier in the center of the town square. A full umen of mounted archers then surrounded the city and sent volley after volley of flaming arrows into the town. Cannons had arrived just before dawn and added their thunder to the firing of the city. The first coils of smoke started within minutes, and now the entire city was being consumed. Tamuka found the sight of the destruction to be strangely exciting, the flames leaping hundreds of feet into the air, the column of smoke soaring for thousands. So he would do to all cities ever built by the filth of cattle.

He was tempted now to send the order back to ravage the other towns of the Rus, especially Suzdal, but he hesitated; such places would still be required in the near future to house and feed the cattle that might be needed to make yet further war on the Bantag, once this campaign was finished. The burning of this place called Kev would be sufficient for now. When he was done with using those whom he suffered to live, he could wall them up in the towns and burn them alive for his amusement.

The three days had been most curious. The death of Vuka had elicited none of the genuine lamenting that had marked Jubadi's passing. Sarg's pronouncement of who the new Qar Qarth was to be, however, was far more difficult. Roaka, Qarth of the red horse clans, was now a problem to be reckoned with and had openly called for ending the war and turning back to the south to deal with the Bantag.

Roaka as well had questioned Sarg's description of the fit which had taken Vuka's life. Tamuka looked back at the array of clan and umen leaders drawn up behind him. They were not happy, that was all too obvious. They were deep into a strange land, they had lost their leader of over a full circling, the heir holding his title for less than two moons. And now, for the first time in more than fifty circlings, a shield-bearer ruled them.

He smiled inwardly. Jubadi's brothers had all died before having issue. There were several second cousins who could claim the saddle and sword of the Qar Qarth, but that would not be until the white banner

of peace fluttered above the golden yurt. That had
always been the custom, a decision made by long-
forgotten ancestors when the hordes were first forming
and it was realized that a fight for succession in time
of war could excite rivalry or even cause a permanent
splitting.

But none of them had ever reckoned on a shield-
bearer who had discovered his *ka,* his warrior spirit,
and was willing to exercise it. That he knew would be
his strength in convincing the younger umen commanders, the warriors bent on vengeance, to follow
him. It would work as well in the time afterward. It
might be years before the white banner flew again.

He turned his mount and rode slowly up to where
the leaders of the Merki horde awaited him. He
looked over at Sarg, who dismounted and approached
the group.

"As shaman of the great horde of the Merki, I now
proclaim that with the passing of the spirit of Vuka,
Tamuka Shield-Bearer is Qar Qarth."

The gathering looked one to the other, some with
nods of approval, others feigning disinterest, and
those around Roaka with disdain.

"Not since the death of Zorgah in the circling when
the great fire fell from heaven and the earth shook
and his son Baktu was not yet born has this occurred.
But it is the way as decreed by our ancestors, and so
must it be now, until there is peace and the great may
gather for a season of snow to decide who of the white
clan shall lead us next."

Sarg looked at the group with a cold challenge in
his eyes.

"Is there any who now disputes this and is willing
to show his blood?"

Tamuka waited, as if not interested in the proceedings.

Roaka stirred and looked at his followers.

"I am not eager for a blood feud to break between

us, and hence issue no challenge," the aging Qarth said, nudging his horse out of the group.

Sarg looked back at Tamuka.

"You are free to speak. You were a trusted friend of Jubadi's from his youth," Tamuka said, sounding gracious and almost deferential.

Roaka, taken aback by Tamuka's reply, nodded a thanks.

"This war now serves us no purpose," Roaka said. "There is no honor, no glory, no calling of our lineage to face those of equal worth. We waste our time in the worthless lands of the Tugars, which might be fit for those of such a class, but is not sufficient for us of the Merki."

Several of the group looked over with mocking gazes at Muzta Qar Qarth, who sat astride his horse to one side, observing the proceedings.

"Even by the estimates of Jubadi, perhaps upward of thirty thousand of our best warriors will die in this campaign to stamp out these rebellious cattle. I say to the dark regions with them all—the world is wide enough, and there are still the Bantag to the south. I rode without protest because it was Jubadi who wished it. Now Jubadi is dead and the smoke of Vuka goes to meet him."

"If we allow cattle to kill even our Qar Qarth and punish them not for this greatest of sins, we shall be mocked by the Bantag, and our ancestors will turn their faces from us," Tamuka replied sharply, and he smiled inwardly at the nods of approval and barks of agreement from the umen commanders.

"This is a war of revenge," snarled Gubta, the new commander of the Vushka Hush. "We buried one in three of my umen, the commander, my elder brother, among them. And one in three is crippled or still sore from injuries. I will not rest till I drink blood from the skull of Keane and piss upon his blackened bones. If any attempt to stop me from this fate, I shall ride alone into the east, until my sword is wet with their blood and I am struck down. But I shall know in so doing that my fathers will sing my praise and curse those who do not ride with me."

Gubta now drew out his short blade and slashed his arm, holding it aloft as sign of blood oath.

The barks of approval grew louder, many of the warriors drawing out swords, brandishing them, making ritual cuts upon their arms, thus swearing a blood oath upon the words of Gubta to see the deed accomplished or to die in the attempting. Tamuka, seeing the moment, drew out his own blade and slashed his forearm, edging his mount forward until he was alongside Gubta. The commander of the Vushka Hush, his eyes bright with emotion from the honor now offered, leaned forward and sucked the blood from Tamuka's arm.

The shouts of approval grew louder.

"I swear to lead you not as shield-bearer, but as a warrior guided by his *ka*. I seek revenge for Jubadi, and for the Vushka Hush, and I pledge destruction of Keane and all cattle who dare to raise their heads up from the dirt, which is their origin and fate. This I swear upon my blood. This I swear as well, to give to Gubta my brotherhood in his oath of blood."

Leaning over, he grabbed hold of Gubta's arm and sucked blood from it. For a brief instant their eyes locked, an understanding between them already known. It had not been difficult for Sarg, in the hours before dawn, to go to Gubta and speak of the death of his brother and the need for revenge, which a retreat would prevent. Gubta had not the intelligence to see the plan within the plan and by the coming of dawn was weeping tears of rage at the thought that his brother might even now be languishing in the afterworld, taunted because he had not been avenged by his kin. It had all been so easy, though Gubta would never know just how he had been used to sway the others.

For with all Merki the swearing of blood oath, the sight of the red running down another's arm, the chanting of oaths of vengeance, was certain to elicit a frenzied response. Without honor, without bonds of helping in war and vengeance, there was nothing to the joy of living.

It was all so easy. All it truly required of Tamuka was understanding of the traditions and the ways to use them to his own advantage.

Gubta drew back from Tamuka, unsheathed his scimitar, stood in his stirrups, and brandished the blade overhead, roaring his battle cry.

Tamuka looked back at Roaka, who sat patiently, observing the ritual with indifference.

"Strange that a shield-bearer would drink a blood oath. I thought you were ruled by your *tu* and thus incapable of such emotion."

"I am now Qar Qarth."

"You have yet to receive the sword of the Qar Qarth, for I am not finished with what I have to say."

"Then speak."

"I doubt the death of Vuka."

The group fell silent, Roaka daring to voice what more than one of them secretly thought.

Tamuka sighed and looked back at the inferno that even now was consuming the body of the one he had sworn to defend.

"Will you swear blood oath to the truth of his death?"

An angry ripple of comments swept the group.

"You know he murdered his own brother, who would now be Qar Qarth."

All were silent, stunned by Tamuka's words.

"There is no proof of that," Roaka snarled angrily.

"I know it," Tamuka replied, his voice barely a whisper, and looking away from Roaka he fixed each in the group in turn.

"For I had looked into his soul, guided by the spirit

of the *tu,* and saw the dark truth." His voice was distant, as if he were speaking from the spirit world, and his eyes were bright. More than one of the group averted their gaze, for the power of the shield-bearer to look into the hearts of others was known, and a thing to be feared—feared even more now that such a thing could be done by one who would be Qar Qarth.

"Vuka murdered Mupa on the night that the iron ship sank. I was there, as was Hulagar, and we both saw it in his soul."

"And did Jubadi know this thing?" Roaka asked.

"No."

"Why not?"

"Because Vuka was sole heir. If Jubadi had sired again, Hulagar would have told him. Vuka killed his brother and lied when he was asked how Mupa died."

"You dare say such a thing even when the smoke of Vuka's soul is about us?" Roaka asked.

"I do not dare say such a thing," Tamuka said, his voice growing hard and sharp, and he looked straight back at the pyre. "I shout such a denouncement."

The group was silent.

"It is he as well that lost us the first part of the war. It was he who demanded to ride into the cattle city of Roum when it was fairly taken, the cattle not yet aware of our hand in that thing. Upon seeing him they rioted. The youngest brother was taken and beaten to death by the stampede of cattle. The city was lost, and with it our plan to defeat them without ever having to ride north. He was not only a murderer, he was a fool. If there had been another heir I myself would have called for a council of my clan to decide his death as one unfit to rule over us."

He fell silent, waiting.

Roaka shifted uncomfortably. "Nevertheless, he was still rightful Qar Qarth. Will you now take blood oath that you had no hand in killing Vuka?"

Tamuka looked over angrily at Roaka, a shift of the

wind sweeping them all with the heat and smoke of the fire.

Tamuka yanked the short blade from his belt and cut his arm again.

"I swear blood oath," he snarled.

Roaka stared at him coldly.

"May Hulagar and all the ancestors see the blood and hear the words," he said coldly.

Tamuka looked past him to the raging fire and again felt the coldness, as if the eyes of Hulagar were still upon him.

With an angry snarl, Tamuka looked back at the others, most of them nodding, mumbling their disapproval of Roaka, the others silent, nervously watching the firestorm of the city.

"Are there any others to speak?" Sarg asked.

The group was silent.

Returning to his horse, Sarg pulled the sword of the Qar Qarth from its scabbard, than approached Tamuka, who dismounted.

"The sword of the Qar Qarth Tamuka," Sarg announced, holding the blade aloft, his thin gray-haired arm knotting with the effort. "To be held by Tamuka, giving unto him the power of Qar Qarth until the white banner floats in the wind in the time of snow."

Tamuka reached up and grabbed hold of the hilt, taking it from Sarg. As one the clan Qarths dismounted and approached him, each bowing in turn to kiss the tip of the blade. Roaka waited until last, and finally, without comment, he dismounted, walked up, and kissed the blade.

Tamuka returned to his horse and mounted, and as he did so the nargas sounded, the call being picked up. He kicked his mount into a gallop, making his way up the hill, holding the sword aloft. Crossing over the iron rails, he continued up the hill, weaving his way through the entanglements, clambering over the empty line of fortifications, and stopped atop the battlement, the valley for miles around now visible, the city in flames below him.

Across the plains, the umens were drawn up, the checkerboard blocks of ten thousand spread out before him. His spirit soared with delight, with the power and the joy. The brash cry of the nargas echoed across the fields, soon drowned by the clashing of swords on shields, the weapons glittering in the midmorning light.

"Tamuka, Tamuka, Tamuka Qar Qarth!"

Around him the others, now his subordinates, came to be at his side, even Roaka, head lowered, the roaring of four hundred thousand rising to the heavens.

"You know what is to be done now!" Tamuka shouted. "We ride east until, as Gubta demanded, we gather to drink blood from the skull of Keane, the cities of the cattle laid waste, the grease of their fat running from our mouths until our stomachs are ready to burst."

The Qarths and umen commanders shouted their approval.

He looked over at Roaka.

"I give to you now a special task."

Roaka looked up at him suspiciously.

"The three umens of your clan and your people are to return upon the path from which we came. You are then to ride south to Cartha and take it back, either from the cattle or from the Bantag."

Shocked, Roaka could not reply.

"I trust this to you."

Roaka, not sure whether to react with anger, could only nod his head.

Tamuka looked over at Sarg, who gave a subtle grin of approval. It removed Roaka from their camp, thus stilling any voice of dissent. It would safeguard their southern border. Three umens were not enough for him to go renegade with, and Roaka's own council of tribal Qarths would kill him if he attempted to break clan bonds and desert to the Bantag. If he failed in his mission, it would weaken his position as well. It reduced Tamuka's forces to thirty-five umens at full strength, but that was still more than sufficient.

Tamuka turned away from the crestfallen leader, sweeping the others with his gaze, the message clear.

He pointed his sword to the east.

"We ride!"

"Admiral Bullfinch."

Stirred from his thoughts, Bullfinch looked back at Elazar, envoy of the Cartha.

"I think they're burning Kev," Bullfinch said, and pointed to the distant plume of smoke that even from forty miles away filled the northern sky, a single black cloud in an otherwise clear blue heaven.

The Cartha said nothing.

"It was beautiful city, maybe even more beautiful than Suzdal. The Cathedral there is supposedly the oldest in all of Rus. They say it's where the Rus first appeared in this world a thousand years ago. I guess it's all gone now."

Elazar nodded sadly. "A strange history for all of us. We and the Roum, the Rus, you Yankees, the Constan and Maya, the Chin to the east, the ancient ones of the Nile far away to our south in the lands of the Bantag. All of us remembering something of our lost world.

"It means we should be brothers united against the hordes."

Bullfinch nodded in agreement. "But your Hamilcar broke ranks. Andrew offered him shelter even after he fought against us. We gave shelter to forty thousand of your people, many of them still here, treated fairly by us even now. Remember it was one of my ships that Hamilcar stole, along with most of our galleys, to return to Cartha."

"Which he took back from the Merki."

"He broke the treaty agreement with us nevertheless," Bullfinch snapped angrily.

Elazar extended his arms as if conceding the point. "Just tell me this. If all of what happened had been reversed, if it had been your people who were slaughtered in the ritual of burying a Qar Qarth, if it had been the people you were ruler of, would you not have felt rage?"

"I would still have remembered the higher goal, that only through being united may we win."

Elazar smiled. "Do you honestly believe your own words?"

Bullfinch could not reply, for in his heart he knew that he had been speaking as commander of the Navy of the Republics and not as himself. He had seen glimpses of the burial; he still could not block the screams from his darkest nightmares.

"As I already told you, I came here unsolicited," Elazar said. "My lord Hamilcar acted out of rage, believing if he did not move quickly all in Cartha would be slaughtered. Even as we speak, five umens of the Bantag which had stayed behind from the march of their clan move toward Cartha, eager to seize it in hope of finding weapons. It was easy for Hamilcar to take Cartha by surprise and drive out the one umen there. It is another thing altogether to face five umens ready for war. He has but the one ship, maybe twenty of the small cannons. The factory might make another twenty, perhaps several hundred of the weapons one can fire from the shoulder. But of powder, the place of making that is far outside the city and still in Merki hands."

"And you have the gall to come here and ask me to help." Bullfinch pointed at the patch covering his right eye. "I lost this eye to one of your cannons in last year's war against you. It's incredible that I now find you on the deck of this ship asking me for help."

"We were trapped into that war. It was either that

or be slaughtered by the Merki. We fought for survival the same as you."

"This is incredible. You fight us, then you desert us, and now you want me to help you again." Bullfinch shook his head in disbelief.

"Precisely. As I told you, Hamilcar has no idea I am asking this. If I had told him he would have forbade me. He believes I've come north to try to bring back the families of some our soldiers."

"I have my duty here, my own war to fight," Bullfinch snapped.

"And what have you accomplished since the Merki moved?"

Precious little, Bullfinch thought to himself. The first raid had been a moderate success, catching a caravan of yurts moving along the coastal road. The work had sickened him, slaughtering several hundred Merki women and old men, his own soldiers driven to such a frenzy of rage that many of the young had died as well. It was a type of war that turned his stomach. The lesson, though, had apparently been taken; the following day no Merki were moving within five miles of the coast, and he would not venture his forces outside the supporting range of the guns of his ironclad fleet. He had ten ironclad and thirty galleys. Two of the ironclads still lay off Suzdal, harassing the river road and the Ford, over which the Merki were still moving their people. His mere presence was forcing them to forage on a narrower front, but nothing more for the moment.

"What you ask is too much," Bullfinch said. "I'd have to have orders from Colonel Keane for what you want me to do."

"And where is Keane?"

"I don't know," Bullfinch replied. "I could send a ship up the Penobscot and get a telegram out to him if he's not there."

"Telegram?"

"The talking wire. From here it'd take three days each way, maybe more. For all I know, the Merki might even be hitting the Penobscot now, though that fire tells me the bastards are still a hundred miles back."

"Six days, maybe seven," Elazar said. "I'm telling you that the Bantag might very well be in Cartha by that time. Baal blessed me with a fair wind and strong rowers that I might come here first to look for you.

"If you hesitate now, all that is left of my people will die. Has not your war killed enough of them already?"

Bullfinch tried to look at the man, but all he could think about was the screams. He looked down at his hands, which held the crumpled issue of Gates's paper, brought out this morning by the message boat from Roum.

"You talk about the solidarity of all humans on this world against the horde. I'm begging you to honor that now, no matter what our past differences," Elazar said.

Bullfinch found he could not answer. He looked back at the smoke on the horizon.

"I only pray that your city of Kev was empty of women and children, because I can tell you," and Elazar's voice choked as he tried to blurt out his words, "when the smoke of Cartha drifts north it will be the pyre of half a million souls who never wanted this war and were destroyed by it nevertheless."

Chapter 7

"Get ready." Dennis Showalter's voice was a hoarse whisper, as if he were afraid that the Merki could hear him even over the thunder of the approaching hooves.

He looked down the skirmish line, the boys deployed out, lying in the grass, keeping back from the edge of the ridge. Lifting his head up over the lip of the hill, he trained his field glasses forward. He could see them clearly, individual features. It was horrible— leathery faces, helmets adorned with human bones, bows strung and resting on pommels, lacquered armor creaking as they rode forward watchfully, following the tracks that led like an arrow across the steppe back to where he was now hiding.

A full regiment of a thousand at least, he thought, spread across several miles of front. Behind them, several miles farther south, the checkerboard pattern of at least five full umens moved over the sun-soaked steppe, pennants flying, heading east toward the upper ford of the Penobscot, where several troops of his men were waiting to contest the crossing.

A barked command sounded, and the line of Merki skirmishers halted.

Damn.

A lone rider broke from the line, trotting up the rise straight at him, now less than two hundred yards away.

Bastards. He had hoped to bag the whole forward line.

Far out to either flank the Merki skirmish line continued to move northward toward the forest, the riders weaving their way through the open glades which marked the transition point from steppe to the beginning of the northern forest.

He looked up at the scorching sun. The heat was maddening. No rain now in ten days, and the grass going dry, rustling as he pressed himself down.

The rider was a hundred yards away, the rest of the line waiting.

He slid back down from the crest.

"They're not coming in. Get ready to mount and get the hell out of here. Mount when I fire. Pass the word down the line."

He edged back up to the top.

The lone scout was fifty yards out, pausing to look down at the ground, becoming more cautious.

He cocked his Sharps carbine and poked it through the grass, drawing a bead on the Merki's chest.

Behind him the men started to slide back down the hill to where the holders waited with their mounts, three men to the skirmish line, one horse holder in the rear.

A horse on the line nickered, rearing up.

The Merki froze and suddenly shouted, his speech grating, harsh.

Showalter squeezed the trigger.

The Merki crumpled, the impact of the bullet doubling him over.

Dennis turned and slid back down the hill, not waiting to see what the opposing skirmish line would do. The men were already mounting, and he ran to join them, throwing his carbine to his holder, climbing atop his mount, and taking the carbine back.

"Let's get the hell out of here!" He pointed north, raking his spurs into his mount. The horse kicked and then bolted, going through the long buildup from trot to canter to gallop.

A horn sounded behind them, a harsh shrill cry growing louder by the second.

The wave of Merki crested the hill. A shower of arrows arced into the morning sky, hovering and then plummeting down, most of the bolts falling fifty or more yards to the rear, a few reaching the retreating cavalry, one striking a horse, causing it to burst into a panic of speed.

A cry went up from the far end of the troop. Showalter looked to his right to see a trooper tumble to the ground and then come to his feet. He had fallen off, his horse continuing on. He felt a temptation to swerve from the line and gallop down to him, but a look over his shoulder told him it was already too late.

The Merki charge bore down, the riders nearly stirrup to stirrup. The fallen trooper pulled out his revolver, cocked it, and waited for the range to close.

"Goddammit, take a bastard with you," Showalter shouted.

The next rise was before him, and the line of eighty troopers crested over it, and the fallen boy was lost to view. They were now into a heavy scattering of single pines, the ground sloping straight up as it would now for miles into the high plateau of the forest. The men weaved their way in and out, ducking low to avoid the branches.

Arrows snicked through the forest, birds scattering up as the retreating men spurred their way into the woods. A solid stand was ahead, and with a shout he pointed toward it, the men closing in around him.

Behind the group the Merki continued the pursuit, their fresher mounts and years of skill giving them an edge. Slowly the range closed; arrows were now starting to wing in at nearly a flat trajectory. Another trooper tumbled from the saddle, slamming into a tree as he went down, already dead from the arrow in his back.

Dennis spurred his horse around the edge of the heavy stand and started to rein in.

The Merki were less than fifty yards away, their harsh cries echoing in the woods.

The crack of two field pieces thundered in the forest, the spray of canister dropping a dozen of the enemy. A ragged volley roared through the woods, and Dennis gave a shout of triumph.

They had led the Merki straight into half the regiment.

The gunners leaped to reload, swabbing the bores, ramming down double charges of canister, turning the guns to fire to either flank. The tiny four-pounders lifted into the air and recoiled.

From out of the smoke a few remaining Merki emerged, bows up, a gunner screaming, pinned to a tree, the Merki who killed him lifting out of the saddle from the blast of a sawed-off musket loaded with buckshot. Dennis drew his revolver, snapping off a full cylinder at a Merki who weaved his way through the battery, slashing with his sword, killing a gun sergeant. A gunner dismounted him with a blow from a sponge staff, the Merki falling off his horse, the gunner then remembering that he had a revolver and finishing the job by putting the gun in the fallen warrior's face and firing.

The other cannon fired again, this time into the smoke, no targets visible.

"Cease fire!" Dennis shouted. The bugler picked up the order and sounded the call.

The spattering of fire died away.

An occasional arrow still came from the other side, but they were drawing back—at least for the moment, until the flanking units came up to support.

"Bugler sound retreat! Let's get the hell out of here!"

Within a minute the gun section was limbered and started moving up the narrow trail into the forest, their two dead comrades lying in the battery wagon, four troops of cavalry moving to either side, spread out in loose order, the woods closing in around them, growing thicker the higher they climbed into the forest.

Dennis and the last troops waited to provide rear guard, armed as they were with the quick-firing carbines. There was an occasional crack of a rifle. The woods were eerie with smoke, and the piercing singsong keening of a wounded Merki.

Forward he could again hear the sound of hooves. So they were coming after him. He smiled.

Andrew had said to slow them down, tie them up. Well, he knew the woods and they didn't. His guide was a Rus hunter, who had lived in the forest all his life since fleeing from the Tugars over forty years before. He had not even known there was a war on until yesterday, and for that matter still thought that the old boyars were in charge of things. But at the mention that they were killing the horde, his eyes sparkled with delight. To Dennis's amazement there was an entire outlaw world in the forest, hundreds of people, nearly all of them Rus, but some Roum, even a few from farther west, Maya, Totec, and a fellow he thought must be from India or some such place. They had fled before the coming of the horde, most of them before the last arrival of the Tugars, but a significant number had been in the woods for generations, banned from the world to the south because they would not submit to the slaughter pits.

Quite a few disappeared farther north to wait things out, but enough of them, like the Rus hunter, wanted to help, eager for a good fight of vengeance.

If the Merki were dumb enough to follow, they'd get a taste of it, Dennis thought with a grin, and when they finally quit he'd come back out and hit them again. He had another battalion of cavalry waiting to do the same trick at the river ford, and nearly twenty-five hundred men, on foot and mounted, working in small bands from Kev all the way back to the ford of the Neiper.

An arrow shot past, striking the tree beside him. Raising his carbine, he cracked off a round at a distant shadow, barely visible through the smoke, then turned and galloped off. He started to laugh. He was fulfilling his fantasy to be a cavalryman and having the time of his life.

"Soldiers of Roum, I am proud of you this day."

Marcus Licinius Gracca gazed out upon the two corps drawn up before the gate of Roum, the men arrayed by column of battalions, their serried ranks filling the field upon which they had drilled so hard and for so many long months.

"Less than a year ago, by the will of the Senate you were slaves, and now you stand proud as free men."

A cheer rose up from the ranks, and Vincent Hawthorne looked upon the men, feeling a sense of pride that even as they cheered they still stood at attention. He looked over at Marcus, Almost amused at the man's placing all of the blame of slavery upon the Senate. But after all, what else could he do, and that dishonored assembly was a convenient enough target.

"Today you officially become part of the Army of the Republics, designated as Sixth and Seventh Corps."

The men nodded their approval, proud of the corps badges which only this morning Vincent had allowed them to affix to their caps, the Greek cross for the Sixth Corps, the crescent moon and star for the Seventh Corps, red for first division, white for second, and blue for third of each. The symbols of themselves meant nothing to the men, but word had been passed down to them about how in the legendary armies of the Union back in the old world the badges had been the symbols for the same units, though the most famed of all had been the simple red circle belonging to the 35th Maine.

"I know you will soon match the honors won by your brothers in the third division of the Fourth Corps."

He pointed back to the city walls, which were crammed with spectators.

"Remember that you are now the walls of Roum for this new type of war that we fight. Upon you rests the burden of defending your homes, your loved ones, your newfound freedom."

He looked over at Kal, who stood erect, face shadowed by his stovepipe hat.

"We fight as a united people, to help our comrades as they helped us last year. We fight for the freedom of all people who look to us to shatter the black tyranny of the cursed hordes. I am proud to march with you into battle."

He raised his hand in salute, and a thundering roar went up from the ranks.

Marcus turned to Kal, who stood beside him.

The president stepped up to the platform.

"Comrades, fellow citizens of our united republics," he said, and to Vincent's amazement, his Latin was nearly free of the broad Rus accent. "I, like all of you, was a peasant. But now I am free. I gave this arm to fight for that freedom," and he pointed to his empty right sleeve.

Vincent knew how embarrassing this must be for Kal, who thought that the waving of the bloody shirt was the lowest form of politicking. But it was the right move for these people, who didn't know him as his own did. There was a murmur of approval from the ranks.

"I don't know when this terrible war will finally end, or if it ever will. But I do know that you are free men, as am I, and for that I will continue to fight until the day I die."

He paused, looking out at the men, his features tired and sad.

"We might call God by different names, but He is still God to us all. Let's pray together, my friends, that there will come a day when we can put aside our weapons, raise our families, and live together in peace."

Kal, taking off his hat, made the sign of the cross, the Roum soldiery standing with heads bowed. A long quiet moment passed, and then he looked up again and smiled.

"When this is all over with, I plan to retire, and perhaps open a tavern."

The men in the ranks broke into smiles and started to chuckle.

"Now don't tell my wife I made this promise, but if you should ever come to Suzdal, all you have to do is tell me you're one of the boys with the Sixth or Seventh Corps and I'll stand you a couple of rounds for free. Good luck to you."

He lowered his head and stepped down, to a rousing cheer, even louder than the one for Marcus.

Vincent stood to one side, and Kal came up to him.

"Did I do all right with them?"

"Well enough," Vincent replied.

"Ah, you and your presidential dignity," Kal said. "Kesus allow that there'll be enough of these boys left to put a dent in my pocketbook someday."

"We should get going now," Vincent said. He had already delivered his comments—short and to the point: he expected them to do their duty. There had been no cheers for him, and he had not expected them; such things left him cold. But he could see their pride, their determination to prove themselves, and that was enough.

Kal nodded sadly, as if not yet ready to let go of him. Vincent smiled wanly. They had tried to talk last night, but it was impossible. If he loved any man on this world for his gentleness, it was his father-in-law. Yet at the same time he felt almost ashamed to be near him.

"Take care of yourself, Father," he said, feeling a slight catch in his voice. "And if . . ."

His words faltered, and he looked back at the men who stood waiting.

"It's all right, son, go on."

"If I shouldn't come back," he whispered, his voice starting to shake, "tell Tanya that it was never her fault. Tell her that I loved her. It's something that's gone wrong inside of me. I know she thinks I don't love her anymore. It's not that at all."

"It's just that you don't love yourself," Kal said softly.

Vincent looked at him, eyes suddenly smarting.

"I hate all that I now am," he whispered, "and God help me, if there is a God, I can't stop it now. I love this war and I hate myself for the loving of it."

"You'll find a way out. Perhaps Andrew understands it better than all of us. I know he's worried about you. Try talking to him."

Vincent shook his head.

"Not now. And besides, I'm not sure if I want to. I'm not sure if there's even the time."

He looked at Kal and tried to force a smile.

"Take care of her. And when this is over, if she should find someone else, let her know that it's all right, that I wanted her to be happy."

"Don't say goodbye like this."

"I think it is goodbye. I've had the feeling for weeks. Call it an atonement."

Kal found himself unable to speak. Reaching over with his one hand, he pulled Vincent tight to him, kissing him on both cheeks. When he finally let go he lowered his head, unable to look at Vincent, or at all the others.

Vincent stepped back, came to attention, and sa-

luted Kal, and then the flags of the two republics behind him. Leaving the stand, he mounted his horse.
Dimitri and his staff were waiting. The 7th Suzdal, its
ranks barely more than that of a company, stood to
the front, the rest of their comrades now serving as
officers for the two corps, or dead in the defense of
Roum. What few remained now served as corps headquarters detail. Their tattered flag fluttered in the
breeze. Vincent stopped to look at it—"Hawthorne's
Guard," emblazed in faded gold letters upon its
stained silken folds, an action the men had done themselves when he was reported missing after the first
defense of Suzdal. He looked over at Dimitri for a
moment, distant memories stirring. At the front of the
column were the corps banners, and the flags of the
two republics and of the army moving to join them.

Marcus edged his mount up beside Vincent's.

A trumpet call echoed and a thunder of drums
sounded. The first battalion wheeled out of line, went
into column of fours, and turned to the north and the
road to Hispania. As it approached the review stand,
the 7th Suzdal moved out in front and marched past.
Vincent drew his saber and saluted the colors as they
passed. The crowds lining the walls and crowding the
hills to the west cheered wildly.

The song started somewhere in the middle of the
mass formation, and within seconds the entire army
started to sing "The Battle Hymn of the Republic" in
Latin.

It sounded so strange to Vincent, as if it were some
absurd schoolyard exercise led by a warlike and de-
mented teacher of ancient languages. Yet it had a
power to it, as if an ideal engendered within the song
could somehow leap across the universe.

"It's worth dying for," Vincent whispered.

Marcus looked over at him.

Vincent, seeing his gaze, said nothing, and after the
colors passed he nudged his mount forward to fall in

with the column. As they passed the gate of the city he looked to his right and felt his heart go suddenly to ice.

Little Andrew had been down with a fever, and so they had said their sad, almost wooden goodbyes at home. But she had come anyhow.

How could he ever explain it all—that there was part of a lost boy within him that still loved her as passionately as they had loved before all of this had ever started? The worship of Mars, of vengeance, of being all so much the general had consumed him, leaving him barren inside, empty of any semblance of loving, or caring, other than for the training for and the consummation of killing. She had first borne the drinking with quiet patience, then scolding, then tears, and finally with silence, shielding his own children away from him.

He could never blame her for that, only himself.

Their gaze held for a brief instant, her raven-black hair covering her shoulders, her eyes still childlike, her youthful body sacrificed to three children but still young-looking and beckoning. Yet it was as if she were an image, a floating memory gone now to a fading picture in a book that was starting already to turn to dust.

Tentatively she raised her hand as if to wave.

"Go to her."

He looked away from her.

It was Marcus.

He turned his gaze forward and continued on, saying nothing.

She'll be better off when I'm dead—for that matter, I'll be better off as well. At least let me take enough of the bastards with me when the time comes, he thought sadly. And then silence, and a sleep without dreams.

The firefight flared to life along half a mile of front. Pat grinned with delight at the sight of the Merki tumbling from their saddles, pushing their mounts into the shallow river, riding hard, spray foaming up around them.

"Not a single bloody cannon on the opposite slope!" Pat shouted.

Robert Morgan, in charge of the brigade covering the river crossing, slammed his fist into his glove hand.

"Goddammit, we could hold 'em here for a week."

Pat shook his head. There were far too many fords along the Penobscot in its eighty-mile run out of the forest to the sea. All the Merki needed to do was take one of them, push an umen across, and cut the rail line farther up, and anyone along the river line would be cut off. It was only here on the rail line that they could quickly retreat. An aerosteamer was keeping a watchful eye on the fords farther north, and Showalter, he hoped, was engaging them up at the forest. The bridge across the river was already a smoking ruin, fired before dawn.

A twelve-pound shot whistled overhead, and he instinctively ducked. The round reached the far bank of the river, bursting beyond a file of Merki cavalry with no effect. He looked back at the armored car, a quarter mile to the rear.

"Damn amateurs—how could they miss?" he growled impatiently.

Shading his eyes, he looked westward at the setting sun, which silhouetted the vast lines of Merki moving relentlessly eastward. Four days to cross a hundred miles to the Androsocggin. They were coming on slowly, deliberately. According to the aerosteamer, their artillery was fifty miles behind them. Eighty miles from here to the Kennebec and then a hundred and twenty more to the Sangros and the main line.

They could do it in a week, ten days. He looked back eastward. But this was the hard part of the crossing, with barely any running water for the next eighty miles, the grass already drying in the scorching heat of early summer. Please God don't let it rain for a month, he thought.

A thundering cry went up from the opposite bank, and he looked up to watch a heavy line of Merki cavalry coming down the slope, the first line in midstream turning to get out of the way. The charge waded in, muddy water splashing up, riders leaning forward, another line behind them cresting the bank, bows raised. A dark shadow of arrows winged over the river, bracketing the entrenchments and breastworks hastily prepared by Morgan's men.

The cries of wounded now joined the uproar. The Merki charge pressed in, and the firing on the line died away. Pat looked over at Robert, who grinned wickedly.

The first of the riders gained the east bank, another volley of arrows passing over them. From out of the entrenchments the entire line stood up and fired a volley at point-blank range. The Merki charge disintegrated. Yet another volley of arrows came in, dozens of men dropping, yet they continued to stand and fire, the river littered with corpses.

"You've got good men," Pat said appreciatively.

"Bloody Fourth Corps. We learned that trick holding the fords—let 'em get to point-blank range. Half my boys still got old smoothbores, so they load 'em up with a ball and half a dozen buckshot. That's how the New Jersey boys chewed up Pickett's charge—got 'em at ten yards."

A deep-throated horn sounded from the opposite bank, and the Merki firing support turned their mounts and retreated back over the hills. The few survivors who had gained the east shore died fighting, pressing into the trenches, disappearing under a swarm of bayonet thrusts and clubbed muskets.

On the next line of hills, Pat saw a knot of standards. He knew that there must be their chief, Vuka they called him. Through his field glasses he could barely distinguish them. He saw one raise a long tube, a telescope, and point it in his direction. Unable to resist the urge, he lowered his glasses and made a rude gesture, a universal sign of contempt.

"We hold until night, then pack 'em up on the trains and fall back to the Kennebec," Pat announced. "And then bloody 'em again."

Tamuka scanned the group of cattle.

Was that Keane? he wondered. No, this one had both arms, obvious by the curious gesture, which Tamuka knew was undoubtedly directed toward himself. A red-haired cattle. It must be the second in command. He thought about the prisoner, who even now was under guard to the rear. That one would take a long time to convert into a pet. Twice already he had tried to kill himself, the second time nearly succeeding with a thin strip of cattlehide rope. No, he wanted to save that one—he might be useful once he was sufficiently broken.

"So, Qar Qarth Tamuka, they are still game for a fight."

Tamuka looked over at Muzta and said nothing.

"After this river, according to my chart reader, the grass is short and water scarce all the way to the next great river."

"The Merki are used to deserts," Gubta of the Vushka Hush snapped peevishly.

"But there the Merki ride with four umens covering the same area through which thirty-six and my own two must now ride. I remember this region. We did the crossing a month earlier than now, when the grass was still sweet with spring, the few brooks still flowing with water."

"You have to cross it with us," Tamuka replied.

"It will be interesting to watch nevertheless."

Tamuka looked over at his commanders of five umens.

"All warriors are to make sure their water bags are full. Water for the horses first until the next river. We will not wait here for the cannons to catch up. They can follow. At least their wagons can be loaded with water skins."

He looked back toward the opposite side of the river. Shagta would be almost full in the sky tonight. It was tempting to order an assault across at night, but he thought better of it. Let the horses crop until midday tomorrow, then cross and ride for half the night. Sarg would have to find some appropriate excuse, the same as when they crossed the sand deserts near the cattle lands of the Ubi. He was tempted to push the attack right now, even without cannons and the cloud fliers, which were still based back at Suzdal while a new base was prepared at Kev. Once the next river was reached they would tear up the wooden part of the iron track lines and build new sheds closer to where the fighting would be.

All these damn cattle weapons simply made war slower, the cannons moving not much faster than the yurts, the cloud fliers forever needing new sheds built to protect them and put them in convenient range of the fighting. He almost wished that somehow they had the machines to move on iron rails. Far off to the north he saw a tiny sliver of white in the sky, a Yankee cloud flier. They knew where he was, but for the moment he wasn't sure of anything regarding what the cattle were doing.

He looked down at the river, at dozens of his warriors floating down to sea upon its slowly moving current.

"Next river we cross, Tugar, I think it is time that your warriors lead the way," Tamuka snapped, and turning his mount he rode away.

Andrew thought about the message from Bullfinch, angrily stuffed into his pants pocket.

Damn him, running off like a knight errant in violation of orders. Too much was happening too quickly now, and he didn't like it when a part of his plan was thrown off by a young officer who should have known better than to simply take his fleet out of the war. Especially now.

He could sense their coming, as if they were an unstoppable force of nature, like a hurricane or tornado just beyond the horizon. It must be some hidden sense, a change in the weather, impending battle; you could feel it gathering its forces, just before rushing in to destroy. The road to Gettysburg had felt like this, and so too the Wilderness and the march to Cold Harbor. Hans could feel it as well, and looked to the horizon like a prairie farmer fearful of a summer storm. He'd shake his head, mutter to himself, and finally look up at him with that curious tilt to his head, as if he somehow had to look at things sideways in order to see them straight.

"A hell of a fight buildin' up ahead," he'd mumble—and he'd damn near always be right.

"A hell of a battle coming," Andrew Keane said, his voice a drawn-out sigh.

"Perhaps then it'll be finished with," Kathleen said, sitting down to rest, "and then we can go back home."

"Home? Suzdal, Maine?"

"Suzdal. Of course I mean Suzdal."

"Don't you ever miss the other place?"

She looked up at him and smiled.

"At first. Of course I did. The war there, at least it was different. I never thought there could be a worse type of war, but we certainly found it here. But in spite of that, this is home."

A worse kind of war. He looked down at her, barely visible in the evening shadows. She never spoke of her fiancé, and he couldn't even recall his name now. Didn't want to. Dead at First Bull Run and she goes off to be a nurse. It was hard to imagine she might have loved someone else once. Unpleasant thought. But he had loved others. He remembered Mary, and how he finally and so brutally had found out the truth. Kathleen never asked; it was just as well.

They had both lost and gained. If he should fall this time, he wondered what she would do. Fall. Funny the euphemisms of war. Fall. Far better that way, almost clean in its imagery, like a sudden going into the earth. Not gut-shot, or bayoneted and clubbed to death or blown apart by canister. A simple lying down into peace, like the leaves of autumn drifting to the ground.

"If I don't come out of this one, I want you to live," he said, the words almost blurted out.

Startled, she looked up at him, and there was a sudden trickle of a tear, as if she had almost been thinking the same thoughts.

"Find Maddie. I've already arranged for Ludmilla to take Maddie and Vincent's children to a hiding place north of Brindusia if things go wrong. For her sake, please."

She nodded, unable to speak.

A worse kind of war. God, it made the old one look pleasant in comparison. Still had rules. You would share your last drop of water with a wounded reb, bandage him up, and write a letter to his kin telling them that he was all right. Here we cut the throats of the wounded and shoot our own rather than leave them behind. The memory of the blurred photograph haunted him. he looked down at Kathleen. He'd do the same with her to spare her that type of end.

And she calls this place home.

Yet it was home, Maine starting to blur into fuzziness. Five years here, eight years since he'd last seen Brunswick. No, this was home.

He looked around. The shadows of evening concealed the presence of war, the lines of entrenchments and breastworks, the mad bustle at Hispania, the city of lean-tos and tents housing over a hundred thousand soldiers, factory workers, families, refugees, even the prostitutes who'd come up from Roum to work the army camps.

The campfires lit the hills, a glow that stretched on for miles, a distant rumbling of talking, laughing, singing, praying, the sad crying of those so far from home, or afraid of dying.

A flight of ducks kicked up noisily from the river and headed north for the forest.

The wind, still blowing hot, drifted in from the steppe, bringing with it the scent of dry grass, blowing the smells of the camp away. One of the reasons he liked this particular place—the air was fresh, clean.

He sat down beside her, almost shyly putting his arm around her waist, she doing the same to him, leaning her head against his shoulder.

"Peaceful now," she whispered.

He said nothing. Nothing needed to be said.

"If I could steal you away from all this. Find a hidden place, just the two of us, far away . . ."

Her words trailed off into silence.

Would he go? He knew that's what she was wishing for. And give this up? When he was a boy he had dreamed of great and heroic things, reading Scott and later Arrian and Shakespeare's *Henry V,* imagining himself with the knights of Arthur, marching with Alexander, standing with the few at Agincourt. He still almost believed it now, despite the horror, the filth, the pain. Even after Gettysburg, his left arm gone, his brother dead, even then he almost still believed in it all. Here, right now, he had the chance to somehow change an entire world. He had never wanted it; fate had put it in front of him. He could hate what he had to do, but he could never turn away, trade it for something else. He had seen a people become free; he could see an entire world be free, and a fair part of it would be his dreams and idealisms of youth come to life in such an alien world.

A bugle sounded in the distance. Tattoo, in fifteen minutes taps. A world where the day was an hour and a half shorter, going into summer, night not settling until nine, first light of dawn at four, what he felt should be five-thirty. Tomorrow another round of it. Still thousands of shoulder weapons short, millions of musket rounds short of what he wanted, the strange disappearance of gunpowder making it worse. Emil and his ranting about fresh water, shortage of nurses and doctors, the hospital area not yet finished for what might be fifteen thousand or more causalities just in the first day.

What if they broke through? He tried to push that thought aside. The nurses were to shoot the men who couldn't be evacuated in time. But then again, we'll all die if they do break through here, there's no retreating now, that's settled, he thought.

Tomorrow so much more to do.

Bob Fletcher was coming in on the Roum train tomorrow with the latest food reports, improving with the early harvest of vegetables coming up from the south of Roum, enough to give the men a better ration to prevent scurvy. Then Kal and the senators, their problems, then back to John Mina and Emil at the end of the day to inspect the fortifications.

He sighed.

She raised her head and looked at him.

"Your thoughts are a million miles away from me, aren't they?"

He smiled shyly.

"No, of course not."

"Liar," and she smiled and leaned her head back on his shoulder.

"Signal the fleet, cast off towed ships once the harbor wall is cleared."

The multicolored pennants shot up the stubby mast behind him. He looked aft. The eight ironclad ships were strung out for several miles, moving slow, each of them towing two galleys crammed with troops.

The race was almost over. Straight ahead the Cartha galley moved steadily forward, acting as pilot ship as they rounded the mole. The walls were crammed with tens of thousands, who stood in silence.

"I daresay they're still not sure whose side we're on at the moment," Bullfinch said, looking over at his ensign.

"I think it's the other way around," the ensign replied. "Whose side are they on?"

"Their own, for the moment, and I can't blame the bastards."

"Well, they'd better give us one hell of a lot of wood, sir, or we're stranded here. The bulkheads are empty."

Bullfinch said nothing, displaying an outward calm. Inside he was a nervous wreck. He had jumped without orders, taking eight out of his ten ships five hundred miles south on what might be a fool's errand. Worse yet, the darker voice inside of him now started to wonder if the whole thing was an elaborate trap to take the fleet. A couple of minutes more would tell.

As they rounded the harbor mole he felt the ship start to surge ahead, the two galleys astern casting off. Straight ahead he saw the *Antietam* and trained his field glasses on it. The ship was riding fairly high. Not much fuel aboard. A thin puff of steam came from its smokestack. A plume of exhaust came up and the ship started to leave its dock, slowly gaining speed.

"If he wants to fight, just remember she's got some cracked ribs to the port side of the forward gunport," the ensign said.

Bullfinch did not reply.

Below deck he had his two guns loaded with double shot, gunports closed, but the crews standing ready.

"Quarter speed."

His ship started to slow. Looking aft again, he saw the galleys crammed with men waiting outside the harbor, the second ironclad just starting to round the outer point.

A pennant snapped out from atop *Antietam*, a white flag.

He started to breathe a bit easier. The galley with Elazar swung up alongside the ship, lines snaking out, tying alongside.

"Bring us to port side of her," Bullfinch announced, the pilot turning the wheel over, calling below for all engines to stop.

Bullfinch watched the performance with feigned disinterest. The men were learning their craft well after months of constant drill. His ship slowly dropped off speed, the simple equation of her mass and momentum sending her forward for another couple of hundred yards, the bow wake flattening out. They came to a stop amidships to *Antietam*, half a dozen feet separating the two.

Bullfinch stood exposed upon the upper works.

The gunport of *Antietam* opened, and Hamilcar, looking almost like a surprised tavernkeeper sticking his head out from a shuttered window, gazed out at him. He withdrew his head and Elazar appeared, climbing through the gunport a moment later. Hamilcar followed.

Bullfinch climbed down from atop the gunhouse.

He was tempted to make a quip, "Fancy seeing you again," or something about coming to take his ship back, but knew the joke might very well backfire.

Hamilcar, his features uncertain, turned to Elazar, and the two started to talk excitedly in Carthan as if Bullfinch weren't there.

After a moment, Hamilcar looked back at Bullfinch.

"I didn't ask for your damned help," he snapped in broken Rus.

"Well, you've got it. Can I come over to talk?"

Hamilcar, looking thoroughly confused, said nothing.

Without waiting for a response, Bullfinch leaped the narrow distance between the two ships, almost losing his footing on the other side so that Elazar had to reach out to steady him.

Without waiting for a comment from Hamilcar, he turned first to the flag of Cartha and saluted, and then saluted Hamilcar in turn.

The Cartha's features softened ever so slightly.

"I didn't ask for this," Hamilcar said again, this time in his own tongue, Elazar quickly translating.

"I know you didn't, sir. But your friend here came and explained that maybe half a dozen umens of the Bantag might be moving against you to take this city. I've brought a full brigade of marine troops and eight ironclads to help. I think a few modern weapons might be enough to hold the bastards off until our own problems get settled and then we can bring down some more support."

"Your own problems settled?" Hamilcar sniffed. "You're all dead and you know it."

"Maybe so," Bullfinch replied coldly. "But the offer still stands."

"By whose orders, yours or Keane's?"

Bullfinch stiffened at the anger in Hamilcar's voice when he spat out Keane's name.

"I acted as admiral of the Rus and Roum fleets. I'm sure Colonel Keane will back it up."

"I doubt it."

Angry, Bullfinch suddenly felt that it was simply best to leave now and the hell with them.

Bullfinch looked at Elazar, who, caught in a crossfire of his own creating, stood pale with shock.

"Translate this straight," Bullfinch snapped. "I

don't want any niceties thrown in, I want it word for word."

Elazar nodded, now nervous.

"Tell that fat bastard that I came five hundred miles to help, and get the word 'bastard' in the translation."

Elazar started to speak nervously, his voice low. Hamilcar's features started to redden.

"Tell him he's a prideful ass. He's lost hundreds of thousands of his people—well, goddammit, so have we. We didn't want this war but now we've got it. I lost my eye and damn near got killed fighting against you people last year, but I've put that aside, because the real enemy is out there," and he pointed west as if the open steppe were directly before them.

"Now if he wants our help, fine. I've got twenty-five hundred men, four hundred thousand rounds of ammunition, and the guns on the ironclads. A sharp demonstration might bluff the Bantag into staying the hell out of here. And if he doesn't agree to that, well, then . . ."

He hesitated.

". . . then he can kiss my royal ass, because I'm going back to Rus to fight."

He turned around, preparing to jump back to his ship, which was slowly starting to drift farther away.

The laugh came low, a deep full-bellied chuckle.

"Fine, very good."

Bullfinch looked back, breathing hard. It had come from a sharp rage and had nothing at all to do with any kind of maneuvering.

Hamilcar extended his hand.

Behind Hamilcar he saw a crowd of shocked Cartha sailors, who were even more stunned by Hamilcar's laughter.

"I need your help," Hamilcar said. "But more important, I know you to be a fair man and truthful, a good warrior who defeated me and yet greeted me later with honor."

He hesitated, his features growing serious.

"I will not lie now in turn. I still blame Keane for what happened to my people, and that I cannot forgive. I think you came here on your own, to atone for that. From you I accept that offer, but from Keane, or the Rus, it is still the same in my heart.

"Six umens of the Bantag approach. There is no hope of standing against them alone. The Merki stripped everything—most of the factories were burned when we took the city back. Except for the men I brought with me, my people are armed with sharpened sticks, clubs. A shower of fire arrows and they'll burn us out. I hate to stand here now like this. I need your help."

"That's why I came here to start with," Bullfinch replied sharply.

Hamilcar relaxed, a smile lighting his features.

Elazar, his eyes clouded with tears, came up to Bullfinch and, grabbing hold of him, kissed him on both cheeks.

"Thank you."

"Did you translate what I said?" Bullfinch asked.

"Almost," Elazar replied with a smile.

Pulling away from the front of the column, Vincent turned his horse to the left and rode westward up the long gentle slope, leaving the road behind. The ground was hard, baked under the heat of the noonday sun. For nearly a quarter mile he rode, barely noticing that Dimitri trailed behind him.

Cresting the low rise of the ridge, Vincent reined his mount in and stood up in his stirrups, his legs stiff after hours of riding. He turned and looked back.

Far out across the open plain southward the column extended. Ten miles of road, filled with the two corps, muskets glinting in the sunlight. The butternut-colored uniforms, blanket rolls, and slouch caps made them look like Confederate infantry. Regimental flags were uncased; every two hundred yards another flag, sixty regiments of infantry. He felt his heart swell at the sight of them. His men, his corps, his army.

Across the plain ahead to the north, dotted with the villas of now long-departed nobles, was the rest of the army, camped in the fields and vineyards. Straight ahead and to the northwest he could see Hispania sitting on a low rise of ground four miles off, plumes of smoke from the factories and works rising into the evening air. To his left, several miles away, were the low banks of the Sangros, the higher west bank already looking threatening. The river was low, sandbars jutting up from the sluggish water. The flat east side of the river plain was spread out before him, a broad open bow that would be hard to defend. Curving out from the low ridge upon which Hispania rested, the gentle sloping ridge curved southeast, then south. He surveyed the line, as it finally started to turn southwesterly, moving back toward where he now was. A small knoll, a villa atop it surrounded by trees, was a hundred yards ahead. He looked over his shoulder to the southwest, where the ridge continued on toward the river, meeting it where again the east bank stood far higher than the west, all the way down to the sea.

Already he could see all so clearly how this would be the deciding place. South of here, the higher east bank dominated the crossing, making it a killing zone. But across this four-mile-wide plain, the Merki could get in. It was like half a bowl cut by the Sangros, and as he looked he realized that there must have been a time when the river had curved up along this low ridge, only to finally cut back farther to the west.

The ground down below was rich farmland, vineyards dotting the plain all the way up to the slope upon which wealthy nobles had built their summer homes to catch the cooling breeze when it came down from the forest to the north. A half-dozen square miles of basin land. It must have produced a lot of wine, he realized. Most of the vineyards were in ruins. A heavy line of entrenchments cut straight across the valley all the way up to Hispania, set back several hundred yards from the river. The ground between the entrenchments and the Sangros was torn apart by trap holes and entanglements. The fortifications were well laid out, he could see that, but he could also see that if the Merki were willing to take the losses they could most likely storm the line.

Interior lines for the bastards if they gain the valley, but we'll have the higher ground, he thought, looking back again to the fallback position of the low hills. Four miles of front if we try to hold the low land, over six miles if we're forced back to the hill. A corps per mile of front and one in reserve. Less, he suddenly realized. Third Corps was a skeleton, barely more than division strength. At least another corps would need to picket the river line northward far into the woods, even though the east bank up in that direction was a sharp ridge fifty feet or more higher than the west bank. Leave it unguarded and the bastards will flank us the way they did on the Potomac, he thought. Another division would have to picket farther south down to where the river turned into a broad marshy flood plain cut by a deep channel in the middle. Four corps forward and one in reserve for six miles.

And the Merki would have at least three hundred and fifty thousand. Six-to-one odds. Worse than Bobbie Lee faced at Petersburg, far worse. He surveyed the ground and the bow-shaped ridge, which was slashed along its crest by entrenchments. He imagined that from an aerosteamer it looked exactly like a bow and string, or a pie cut in half.

Nudging his mount into a slow trot, he turned and started up the slope to his right, moving toward a knoll that projected up from the ridge, offering an extra thirty feet of height.

Along the crest of the low ridge a long ugly slash marked the line of entrenchments, abatis and brush entanglements already in place, Rus soldiers still busy digging, coming to attention at his approach.

He gained the entrenched line from the rear. Inside the trench, men were working with picks.

"It's not very deep."

The men, seeing him, came to attention and saluted, standing less than waist-deep in the line. He heard his name whispered, the soldiers looking at him with friendly respect.

"Not like home," a sergeant said, wiping the sweat from his brow. "Not the good earth of Rus, where you can dig all day and still be in topsoil, or even the earth down in the valley below us."

Dimitri, coming up behind Vincent, reined in and looked down at the men.

"Vasiliy Borisovich, blessing upon you," Dimitri said, getting off his mount to go up and shake the sergeant's hand. "Hard work, is it?"

"I was just telling the general here. Go down two feet and you're into limestone."

"Well, keep digging," Vincent said and continued on, heading for the knoll where a small villa stood, the crest surrounded on three sides by shallow gun pits for a grand battery of artillery.

Reaching the building, he dismounted, leading his horse over to a trough set next to a well. Lowering the bucket, he pulled up some cold water and poured it into the trough. Unclipping a tin cup from his saddle pack, he poured himself a drink and downed it. The water was cold, mineral-hard. From behind the villa in a shaded veranda a group of soldiers looked over at him cautiously. He was tempted to chew them out for shirking as they came to attention and saluted. He saluted in turn and then walked around to the other side.

A commanding spot here, he realized. A good place

for a massed battery. They might outnumber us six to one, but they'll have to come up this slope facing nearly four hundred guns. The emplacements, pits for thirty pieces, offered scant protection, barely thigh-deep, the soil piled up a foot higher around the position. No overhead protection; if the Merki closed to two hundred yards, even two hundred and fifty, their plunging bow fire would be deadly. This wasn't good at all.

He looked north, his gaze following the crestline. The entrenchments were laid out well enough, a sharp upcropping of bare rock surrounded by two batteries of the precious rifled three-inch cannons, already set in place, breastworks of logs built in front of them a mile to the north. Between that position and here it would be a splendid crossfire, a tailor-made killing ground.

Dimitri, breaking off his conversation, came up to join him.

"The sergeant's right—back in Rus we'd have a triple line of trenches six feet deep here."

Vincent nodded in agreement. Around Hispania the soil was deeper, and entrenchments there were even covered with log head protection and roofing to protect from plunging arrow fire. But along this ridge it was bare rock or thinly covered.

"I thought they have more lumber breastworks in place by now," Dimitri said.

"Wood for shelters, charcoal for powder, fuel for the trains—it's not at our back door like in Suzdal, it's twenty miles north. This is going to be a stand-up fight that I don't care for."

An obviously nervous lieutenant came out of the villa, hurriedly buttoning his tunic. From inside Vincent heard a woman's voice, which was quickly hushed.

"Having fun, lieutenant?" Vincent asked coldly.

The young Rus officer turned red, unable to reply.

"What regiment?"

"Third Vazima, sir."

"Is this your assigned position?"

"No sir, we were just sent up here to work. Nobody's got permanent line positions yet. The higher-ups . . ." He fumbled. "Excuse me, sir. the generals are waiting to see if they come in here, or try the flank again. At least that's what I heard."

"So what the hell are you doing here?" Vincent looked back at the villa.

"We're supposed to dig gun emplacements and work on the trenches."

"Then Perm damn you, get out there, take your men with you, and do it."

The lieutenant saluted nervously, shouted a command, and was off at a run, several of the men piling out of the villa after him, joined by the group from the back of the building.

Vincent shook his head angrily. "I should get his name and have him kicked back to private. Damn him."

Dimitri laughed softly. "Arcn't soldiers always the same?"

Vincent looked over at the old man.

"If it's his hide that gets stuck here when the Merki charge, he'll wish he'd been digging rather than fornicating."

Dimitri smiled. "Perhaps the memory might give him courage."

Vincent ignored the reply.

A high whistle cut into his thoughts, and he looked back to the reverse slope. A train, moving slowly, was coming up from Roum, moving parallel to the road, the troops waving at the engineer, who tooted out the first bar of a Roum drinking song, the men cheering in reply.

Vincent felt the stirring again. On the road south a column of shining muskets swayed rhythmically as the men marched. The train continued on, following the track which ran a hundred yards to the rear of the ridge, laid out parallel to the ridge as it curved its way through its bowlike curve, north then northwestward and then finally west into Hispania. Crews were still busy on the near side of the main track, laying in a second line alongside the first, which would help speed tactical movement when the battle was joined. Barely concealed behind a low fold of ground off to the southwest he could see a turntable and switchyard going up so that trains could be quickly shifted around at the end of the spur line.

The song started to ripple down the line, the men barking it out, its cadence perfect for marching. Up ahead he could see the white tunics of Rus soldiers moving down toward the road, eager to greet the reinforcements. Such a show was good for morale, Vincent realized.

He turned his mount away from the crest and started back to rejoin the column. His army was about to march before the veterans of Rus. Waving for his corps guidon, he broke into a gallop, moving to rejoin the head of the column. As he rode along the line of troops, the men, feeling in good spirits, gave him a friendly cheer, something they had not done since the early days of their training. They were feeling proud, still innocent and eager, something he had forgotten a long time ago.

At the head of thirty thousand men, Vincent Hawthorne, the Quaker from Vassalboro, Maine, suddenly felt a cold eager joy. They were ready for battle. He was now ready for the killing to begin.

Chapter 8

It was midnight, the Great Wheel of heaven straight overhead, Shagta drifting low in the western sky, Borgta chasing after it. The day had been hot, and tomorrow would be the same, perhaps worse. He licked his dried, cracked lips. Water was running scarce. Hundreds of horses were dropping. Though he and all those of the hordes loathed to do it, they had been consigned to the cooking pots.

There would be no time this morning for the greeting of the sun. The ride would be straight out and hard, timed to arrive at the river at the hour before dawn.

With luck the killing would be good.

All around him through the darkness, he could sense his riders advancing, heads lowered, weary, an occasional mumbled song or chant drifting in the stillness, the warriors nervous to be riding at night when the steppe was ruled by the ancestor spirits.

From his left came the jingling of a message rider. He looked over and saw the colored lantern bobbing, suspended over the rider's head by a pole strapped to his back. He came straight up to Tamuka, guided by the three yellow lanterns carried by the message flag bearer who marked the position of the Qar Qarth.

The rider came up out of the darkness and swung alongside Tamuka, breathing hard, the smell of horse sweat strong in the air.

"My Qar Qarth, Gubta of the Vushka Hush reports."

"Go on."

"Forward scouts saw a column of cattle horse riders moving southward at sunset, on the far side of the next river. Four hundred, it is believed. A forward scout reported their continuing to move south after the first quarter of night had passed."

Tamuka smiled. It was a chance to trap a tidbit, to wipe out some of those who dared to ride the horse.

"Tell Gubta to force the river by the hour before dawn," Tamuka barked, his sharp teeth glinting in the lantern light. "Close the left wing of the horn upon them. I will be upon the right."

"I am to tell Gubta to cross in the hour before dawn, to close the left wing, you will be upon the right."

Tamuka nodded, and the courier turned and galloped back to the north, the bells of his harness ringing.

A small prize, Tamuka thought, not even half of a thousand, but at least enough to feed two umens for a day, and a chance for a minor victory to change the mood of his warriors.

A dull flicker of red light flared up on the far horizon, and he reined in. There was a moment of superstitious dread, it looked like the beginning of a heavenly fire, when sheets of red and green light, the Curtain of Bugglaah, filled the night sky. If it was so, there was no way the army would continue to move, for all would go to ground, hiding their eyes from the heavens until dawn drove the manifestation of the goddess of death back behind her curtain.

He looked over at Sarg, dimly visible in the starlight. The shaman was watching the glow intently.

"The animals," Sarg hissed. 'Cowardly scum."

Tamuka, understanding at last, snarled a curse and urged his mount forward at a gallop, shouting for the vast line of umens to move forward.

*   *   *

It somehow reminded Jack Petracci of a painting he had once seen of the Apocalypse. From several miles south of the forest halfway down to the bridge over the Kennebec, the wall of fire moved relentlessly forward to the northeast, driven by the gentle early-morning breeze, the flames marching forward, the pall of smoke rising to the heavens, darkening the morning sky.

Pulling back full on the elevator stick, he brought the nose of *Yankee Clipper II,* up to nearly a forty-five-degree angle as he strove to put himself higher. He knew that at several thousand feet the chance of an errant spark hitting the hydrogen-filled balloon was remote, but there was no sense in taking any chances.

The flight out had been slow to conserve fuel, ground speed barely twenty miles an hour. Taking off at midnight had been pleasant, the stars to navigate by, the entire world spread out before him. As he crossed out and over the Sangros the campfires to the south had flickered down, the foundry at Hispania showing clear from the plumes of sparks. The ride had been smooth, the breeze steady, barely a ripple or bump, unlike afternoon flying, when more often than not the upsurges of hot air made him decidedly green.

He looked to his right and saw *Flying Cloud II,* half a dozen miles off, edging up toward the forest. To his left, *China Star* was nearly ten miles to the south. The Merki were expected to hit the river by midday, and it was time to count the bastards again.

Yesterday he had flown up to the forest to drop a message for Showalter, ordering him to burn the steppe to the front and rear of the horde. With luck the bastards would be caught and fried.

The first wisps of smoke drifted past them, carrying a smell that reminded him of autumn back home, and then he was into it, the world going in an instant to a choking dirty brown.

Coughing, he pulled his bandanna up over his face,

his eyes tearing beneath his goggles. The ship bucked and heaved, and behind him he heard Feyodor cursing. His stomach felt as if it were dropping away as the ship surged up on the roiling column of hot air and smoke. For long minutes he waited, coughing, gasping for breath, and then the world lightened, the dark blue of early dawn showing through the smoke, and he was out in the clear. Far ahead he could see the second line of fire, a distant smudge on the horizon, more than fifty miles off.

He looked down at the ground, a mile or more below. The flames were directly beneath him, the line of fire stretching for miles, the steppe beyond it blackened. It was a scene of magnificent destruction. A long column of horsemen was nearly directly below, half a regiment at the least, a battalion, their yellow flag showing up in stark relief against the blackened steppe.

To his right, *Flying Cloud II* emerged from the wall of smoke and at almost the same moment started to turn toward Jack, the long thin sausage shape shifting into a circle of white.

What the hell is he breaking station for? Jack wondered.

He looked back to the north, to the edge of the forest. He pulled up his field glasses and checked.

"Going down now, and give me full throttle!" Jack shouted, slamming the elevator stick full forward, while at the same time grabbing hold of the cord that would open the top of the hot-air bag in the center of the ship, spilling out the additional lift from the engine exhaust.

"Merki aerosteamers," Feyodor shouted, tapping Jack on the shoulder and pointing off to the southwest. Jack looked up and saw five of them, moving low over the steppe six or seven miles away, coming on fast with the tail wind behind them.

"We've got to get down first!" he shouted, and

pointed the nose of his ship down toward the front of the column.

Dennis Showalter stood up in his stirrups, his eyes stinging from the eddy of smoke that swirled about him. He knew dawn was approaching, but it was impossible to tell for sure. For miles southward the wall of smoke and fire moved relentlessly to the northeast.

It was a good night's work, a spectacular show. Petracci had dropped the message only yesterday morning for him to move half his regiment through the woods to get ahead of the Merki, then swing over to the east bank of the Kennebec and set the dry grass of the steppe afire. The other battalion was to move back to the west and set a second blaze far to the rear. It had taken a hard day along a forest trail to get ahead of the Merki and across the Kennebec. They had gone south till nearly midnight and then set the first blaze and turned back to the north, firing the steppe as they rode. A troop had been detached to continue riding south through the night to Kennebec Station, while he had turned back north, the battalion riding a steady pace back toward their forest sanctuary, the men setting the grass afire as they passed.

He reined in for a moment and lifted his canteen. The muddy Kennebec water was cool, refreshing, washing the dry smoke from his throat. To his right the blaze was half a mile off. The steppe straight ahead was still clear, but before dawn was an hour past the wall of fire would go all the way to the forest.

It'll burn all the way to the Sangros, and the bastards' horses will starve, he thought with a grin. South of the rail line, infantry was most likely setting more fires. He remembered reading how it was an old Indian trick. Well, it was a damn good one.

Being a cavalryman was one of life's finer joys, he thought with a grin, nodding cheerfully at the weary troopers who rode past, their faces blackened, eyes red-rimmed, tired from nearly twenty-four hours of straight riding but happy with the arson they'd just done.

He heard a shout go up and turned to look toward the rear of the column. The men were pointing straight up, some still with that bit of superstitious fear, the others waving and laughing. Several of the horses, seeing the aerosteamer dropping down like some great primordial flier, complete to the eyes painted at the bow, started to buck in panic. One trooper was thrown off his mount, the horse running away.

"Guidon!"

Dennis turned and started to gallop off at a right angle to the column, hoping that the pilot would see him and follow. The ship turned, swinging out in a wide ponderous circle.

Gaining a low rise several hundred yards to the west, Dennis reared in and dismounted, throwing his horse's reins to the flag bearer, who drew back.

The ship came in low, flattening out its dive, the wicker cabin barely skimming the ground. Behind the ship a plume of ashes rose up, occasional sparks fanning to life and swirling in the wash of the propeller. The thumping of the propeller dropped down to a low whooshing hum.

The nose of the ship passed straight over Dennis's head, and he looked up at the huge ship with awe. This was the closest he had ever been to an aerosteamer, and he felt a sudden flicker of envy. Being a cavalryman was grand work, but piloting an aerosteamer must be godlike. But at the same time he knew something was wrong. He had heard how the ship would go up in a fireball if it ever caught fire. Something had to be up for the pilot to come this low and risk a spark catching hold of the silk bag.

The ship edged forward, nose straight into the wind. The pilot leaned out of the wicker basket hung amidships and wildly gesture for Dennis to come up. As he approached the ship, the pilot pushed his goggles up on his forehead

"Petracci, you crazy bastard, how's the fire look from up there?"

"Merki are closing in," Jack shouted.

"Ah, the bastards must still be ten miles short of the river. We'll be into the forest long before they get here."

"They're already forded the Kennebec north of you and are swinging around to cut you off."

Dennis felt a cold chill knot into his stomach.

"How about to the south?"

"The same—across the river and nearly up to the fire, three, maybe four miles off!"

Jack held up his hands and gestured like two horns closing in on each other.

"Ride northeast, hug the fire, and try to lose them in the smoke, or find a hole and get through. Move it!"

Jack leaned out of the cab and extended his hand.

"Take care. I've got to get back up—Merki aerosteamers are moving in. I'll stay above you. Follow my lead and I'll try to guide you out!"

Dennis reached up and shook Jack's hand.

Petracci looked down at him, filled with a horrible guilt. There was nothing more he could do. He felt Dennis's fingers slip out of his.

"Full throttle, Feyodor," Jack shouted and pulled back hard on the elevator. The nose of the aerosteamer started to lift, the propeller howling, and he started back up, the tail of the ship nearly hitting the ground, so that Dennis had to jump back to get out of the way. The ship turned, pointing its nose northward, the wind now striking it on its forward port side and causing it to fly in a northeasterly direction.

Jack ran back to his mount and leaped into the saddle.

"Bugler! Sound forward at the gallop!"

The weary boy, who was still looking up gap-mouthed at the aerosteamer, looked over in confusion at Dennis.

"Do it!"

The high clarion call rolled across the blackened steppe. Dennis leaned forward and went into a gallop, riding straight across the head of the column, waving his hat and pointing to the northeast. Spurring his mount, he started up the long slope, the guidon bearer and bugler falling in beside him. The front of the column turned to follow. He crested the low ridge and looked back. The column extended out, the front of it moving fast, the rear just beginning to move.

Far off to the south, he suddenly saw them, a dark block moving up over a distant crest four or five miles away, riding almost to the edge of the fire.

Showalter started down the long slope, reached the bottom of a broad valley, and then started back up again. Halfway up he looked back. The rear of his column was just coming over the top, some of the horses barely moving at a trot, the slower mounts falling back, all formation lost.

He dug his spurs in, feeling almost guilty, knowing that his mount was doing all that it could. The slope started to shallow out, and at last he crested it. He reined in hard, waving the guidon bearer to continue forward.

From what he judged to be four miles or more off to the north he saw them—a long line of Merki, moving southeast, swinging down toward the edge of the fire. Turning, he looked back. The other column was moving down into the valley, and beyond them a vast checkerboard array was cresting the hill which the advance guard had occupied only minutes before.

A full umen, he realized.

He looked back up at the aerosteamer, which was now hovering, drifting easterly. He spurred his mount again, the horse giving a cry of pain. Dennis turned the column straight toward the east and started toward it. The edge of the conflagration was straight ahead, the open steppe to the north. But far out across the steppe he saw a thin line of Merki picket riders closing the ring in. After several minutes he could see that he was clearly boxed, the fire to the east, the Merki angling in to either side, edging closer. Behind him no one needed now to be told; the men were riding hard, those with the best horses surging up around him, the weaker falling to the rear.

A rider alongside him suddenly lost control of his mount, the horse stopping, rearing up, having stepped on a burning ember. Plumes of ash rose up around them, clouds of ash marking the Merki riders as well.

The hard minutes passed, the horses weakening, the column slowing. The ground smoked, patches of flame still flared. They gained the next ridge. A long line of Merki was spreading out on the next hill, two miles off, with each passing second the line extending farther to the southeast. He reined in hard. He looked eastward. They were at the edge of the fire. He could try to get in front of it, go into the smoke. His mounts were exhausted—there was no possible way they could stay ahead of it all the way back to the Sangros a hundred and twenty miles away. If they stopped and tried to build a firebreak, once it cleared the Merki would be over them and his back would be to the fire again.

They had to cut a way through to the forest, which stood out on the northern skyline, illuminated now by the low rays of the rising sun, the distant hills dark blue, inviting, offering safety.

"Bugler sound halt!"

The call carried down the line, the riders drawing up to Dennis, wide-eyed, confused.

He looked back over his shoulder. The other horn

of the Merki envelopment was still three or four miles off.

"Battalion form front!"

The troops were jumbled, confused. He should have changed formations while still moving, but it would have been impossible; the men simply were not trained for it.

Troopers reined in, breaking from ragged column into an equally ragged line, the men fighting to control their mounts. He looked back again. Some of the men were still hundreds of yards to the rear. He couldn't wait.

Dennis stood up in his stirrups.

"We're going to charge straight through the bastards!"

The men looked at him wide-eyed, their eyes filled with a sudden mad excitement.

He drew his saber out of its scabbard.

"Action to the front, forward at the trot. Follow me!"

"No, Perm damn you, no!" Feyodor screamed. "Go into the smoke, the smoke!"

"He thinks he can cut his way through," Jack groaned, slamming his fist against the side of the cab.

He was tempted to drop back down again to shout a warning, but a look over his right shoulder told him it was impossible. Five Merki ships were already across the Kennebec, still above him. Prudence told him he should turn and run for home. He couldn't, not now.

The massive airbag above him blocked his view straight up, but he knew that *Flying Cloud II* must be directly above him, providing cover. Elevator still all the way back, he continued to climb, turning his ship around, knowing that Dennis and his battalion were beyond his help.

Gubta grinned sardonically.

"Let them come!"

Around him the battle chant started, stirring his blood: "Vushka, Vushka, Vushka."

He knew what battle sense told him he should do. But he wanted blood on his sword, for vengeance.

He stood up tall, waving his scimitar, the red flag bearer spurring his mount out in front of the single line, waving it overhead and then pointing it straight down.

"Vushka!"

The Merki line charged.

"Charge!"

Dennis pointed his saber forward, spurring his mount, the exhausted animal offering one final spurt of energy. Around him, men with swords drew them, others unholstered their revolvers; many, still unsteady in a saddle, hung on tightly to their reins with both hands.

A hundred yards ahead, the line of Merki came thundering down, growing larger by the second.

It was incredible, he realized, too amazed by the sight of the charge, too carried away by thc mad insane rush to feel fear. The lines closed in, Merki leaning forward, screaming hoarsely, scimitars flashing.

A rider came straight at him, and for a brief instant he thought they'd collide. Screaming, he crouched low over his horse's neck, sword up. The Merki filled the world before him, blade flashing. Dennis ducked low, blade cutting over his head. He felt a bone-numbing jar that almost pulled his sword from his hand, and heard a howl of pain.

A wild insanity of noise exploded, men, Merki, horses screaming in panic, joy, pain. Mounts rearing up, a staccato burst of revolver shots snapping off. Dennis turned his mount. The two lines had gone completely through each other. To either flank he saw lines of Merki starting to swing in. But miraculously, straight ahead was clear. The Merki line they had charged through continued on, slowing, as if starting to turn, the ground between the two separating lines littered with dozens of bodies, most of them his own men.

"Over the hill!" Dennis screamed. "Keep moving!"

He pointed his saber forward, suddenly aware for the first time that blood was dripping off it, not sure if it was Merki, horse, or perhaps even his own.

He urged his mount on, the guidon bearer swinging in beside him, bugler still blowing the charge. The men, seeing the way ahead clear, continued on up the slope.

Dennis looked back over his shoulder.

They weren't pursuing, weren't turning back. A deep-throated horn sounded, and a Merki standing tall in his stirrups was waving a red flag straight overhead. From the corner of his eye, Dennis saw another Merki flag bearer a quarter mile to the right flank, atop the ridge, waving a flag as well.

The top of the crest was nearly straight ahead, and he raced toward it, dropping down into a low, nearly circular depression, and then back up a short steep rise to the top of the hill, his horse nearly losing its footing as it went up over the short steep embankment.

Cresting the hill, he felt his heart skip over. Dennis Showalter realized with a cold sharp clarity that today he was going to die.

A hundred yards away, at the bottom of the next valley, a solid wall of several thousand Merki was deployed.

A dark cloud rose up from their ranks, soaring upward. Even before the wall of four-foot shafts came hurtling down he could clearly hear their whispered approach, growing louder. It appeared as if a forest of young saplings sprouted up all along the crest of the hill. Horses screamed, rearing up, riders tumbling, shouting, screaming. The charge disintegrated.

Another wall of arrows rose up, hurtling in, the crest of the hill a mad confusion.

Die game, dammit.

"Dismount!" Dennis screamed.

The bugler looked over at him in terror.

"Goddammit, boy we're going to die here. At least let's try to shoot some of the bastards first! Dismount!"

The final call sounded. Many of his men were already down on the ground, dead, wounded.

Jack tossed his sword away and leaped down from his mount, pulling his Sharps out of its scabbard. He looked at his horse for a second, filled with a sudden pain. He'd be damned if they'd ever ride her again. Unholstering his revolver, he shot the horse in the head. The animal collapsed.

"Shoot your horses, use them for cover!"

Around him was mad confusion. Another pistol shot sounded, the guidon bearer killing his mount, the animal kicking backward, nearly collapsing on top of Dennis. More shots rang out, animals going down, men lying down behind the still-quivering horses. There was the click of rifle breeches opening, and the first heavy crack of a carbine cut the air.

Some of the men, mad with panic, turned and tried to ride off back to the east.

"Damn you, stand and die!" Dennis screamed. The rush of men thundered past, followed by riderless horses and a number of men on foot.

Back down the slope, a section of Merki broke from the line which was deploying out into a solid circle encompassing the beleaguered cavalrymen. Dennis could hear their sharp barking shouts of laughter as they rode to intercept the fleeing men, cutting out in front and then closing the net. Pistol shots rang out, the Merki staying back, firing arrows while at a full gallop, men pitching from the horses. The few who had tried to escape on foot turned and started back up the slope. None made it. The Merki swarmed in on the half a hundred men who had tried to flee, scimitars flashing.

The curtain of arrows continued to thunder down. No one was still mounted. The top of the hill was littered with the dark forms of dead horses and the blue-clad bodies of what were now mostly the dead or dying cavalry men.

Another volley came in, and Dennis ducked down low against the belly of his horse and came back up. Several arrows were now buried in the animal's flank. He raised his carbine and fired, unable to miss, so thick were the Merki at the bottom of the hill.

He stood up, crouching low, and started to move down the line, pulling a section of men in to cover the south side, positioning his men in a circle in the small depression near the crest of the hill. The Merki broke off from volleys, firing independently. A continual rain of arrows came in, the line which had charged them and the flanking units now adding their weight, shafts screaming in from every direction.

Dennis looked back to the south. A heavy line of Merki was charging down the opposite slope, the other horn of the closing trap, not much more than a mile away.

Carbine fire crackled along the line. The men armed with shotguns raised their weapons high to fire, reloading with round ball to increase the range.

He felt a stunning blow that nearly turned him half around. An arrow had gone clean through his shoulder. He straightened and continued on, feeling lightheaded, his knees weak, as if he were about to faint.

He looked up and suddenly realized there was another battle going on overhead, five Merki aerosteamers swinging about, the smaller steamers of his own side wheeling about, circling.

I should have been a flier, he thought wistfully.

He could see that the fire of his own side was weakening. For every man still fighting, two or three to either side were dead or wounded.

God forgive me for what I have to do now, he thought, feeling his voice go tight.

"Shoot the wounded," he shouted. "For God's sake don't let anyone get taken alive by those bastards. Save the last round for yourselves."

The men looked up at him.

Dennis hesitated. A Rus trooper lay before him, an arrow sticking out of his chest, another pinning his leg to the ground.

"Forgive me," Dennis whispered, and to his horror the man made the sign of the cross, forced a smile, and then closed his eyes.

Dennis pointed his revolver at the man's forehead and fired.

He looked back up at his men, who were finally stirred to action.

Revolver shots started to snap. His eyes clouded with tears when he saw two boys, whom he knew were brothers, embrace, the older of the two shooting the younger even while he held him. The boy didn't hesitate, putting the gun to his own head and firing.

Dennis suddenly found himself looking straight up at the sky, an aerosteamer filling his vision, flame pouring out of it. Ours? theirs? I'm lying down, he realized. Why?

He tried to sit up, the feathered tip of an arrow now blocking his view, a flame of agony causing him to try to double up, the arrow quivering as his movement caused it to cut deeper into his chest.

He screamed, tasting blood.

Pistol shots still echoed. A boy was praying, another singing defiantly, others crying, shouting.

He rolled onto his side and came back up onto his knees, screaming in agony.

Beside him the guidon bearer was dead, flagstaff planted into the ground, yellow banner fluttering in

the morning breeze. The bugler lay spread-eagled on
the ground, his features almost serene, as if asleep. A
Rus trooper was kneeling beside them, on his knees,
praying, making the sign of the cross, and then with
shaking hand putting a revolver to his temple. Dennis
looked away.

The ground started to thunder, shake, and he
looked back up.

A solid wall of Merki closed in, coming up the
slope, swords flashing, their harsh barking laughter
filling his world.

He tried to struggle to his feet, to face it.

There was a final flurry, a few shots, a man standing
up with carbine raised, screaming his defiance, a
trooper kneeling beside him trying to aim a pistol at
the charge, blood-soaked hands shaking.

Dennis Showalter raised his revolver and pointed at
the charging line, squeezing off a final round. The
Merki filled his world, a high standard adorned with
human skulls his entire universe.

He turned his revolver, putting it to his temple.

Suppose it's empty, he thought. He squeezed the
trigger.

Fortunately the gun was still loaded.

Jack tore his concentration away from his own fight
to look back down. The solid wall of Merki came up
the slope, a few puffs of smoke from pistol or rifle
shots flashing out, the ground below covered with
blue-clad bodies and dead horses. The charge pressed
in, sweeping over the crest, swords flashing, the
massed Merki covering the earth, Showalter's command disappearing from view.

A snapping jar cracked through his ship, splinters
and torn fabric blowing out the port side twenty feet
ahead. He looked back to starboard, where he saw
the Merki aerosteamer passing him in the opposite
direction. Feyodor aimed his swivel gun and fired. The

spray of canister slammed into the Merki ship directly above the pilot, who ducked down low while his companion started to reload.

There was a flash of fire, and Jack turned to look back to the left.

An enemy aerosteamer was coming down, flame roaring out of it with an infernolike intensity, the Merki pilot leaping out, wrapped in fire, plummeting down.

"That's it, burn!" Jack screamed.

The airship continued down, the Merki on the ground scattering as the ship crashed on the crest of the hill less than a hundred yards from where Showalter's command had died. A number of Merki, unable to get out of the way, were caught in the conflagration.

"It's *Flying Cloud*!" Feyodor screamed, and for an instant Jack thought that his companion was shouting an acknowledgment of the kill.

Jack looked back and to his horror saw *Flying Cloud* coming down, nose pointed straight at the ground, the entire aft end of the ship exploding with flames. For a brief instant he saw the pilot, Sergei, his hand raised to Jack in a defiant salute.

The ship continued down, flame pouring out in a long blue tongue more than a hundred yards in length. The forward half of the ship impacted in the valley where Showalter had gone into his final charge. A massive fireball erupted heavenward, mushrooming out, the wicker framework of the ship glowing hotly like a skeleton of some great beast now made of fire, collapsing in upon itself.

He couldn't mourn, not now, not for Dennis, Sergei, any of them in this madness. Hands still on the controls, he looked back to the other side. The enemy ship was ponderously turning, the gunner working to reload. Forward to the southeast he could see two of the ships going for height. He had lost track of *China Star* and wasn't even sure if she was in the fight. The other ship might still be above him. A quick look forward told him they were leaking gas, Fortunately it hadn't been a straight-down shot from above or they'd never get back to base.

It was time to get out.

He hit the rudder hard, the ship slowly turning broadside to the wind, and then turning to the northeast, wind at their back. If he couldn't get back he wanted to go down in the forest, where at least they'd have a chance.

"We're getting the hell out of here!" Jack shouted.

He felt another shudder but couldn't tell where the hit was. The nose of his ship was at nearly a fortyfive degree climb. Leaning out of the cab, he looked up and saw the Merki ship off to his right, ready to block his escape toward home. He continued his turn, now heading straight north, aiming for the forest.

The gun behind him thumped, Feyodor trying a long-distance shot at their last target. Seconds later he heard a return shot scream past, missing.

Jack looked back down as the scene of the massacre drifted astern. The two aerosteamers were burning fiercely. He saw the blue-clad bodies of the men already being carried off. He turned away, trying to blot the image out, to concentrate on his own survival.

Tamuka looked up at the battle raging overhead and back at the raging fires of the two cloud fliers.

The loss of another ship had dulled the sense of triumph which had swept into his soul, causing him to lead the final charge personally. Around the burning ship, injured warriors were being pulled back, and already he could see that he had lost more there than in the destruction of the cattle horse riders, the airship crashing down upon a block of a warriors who were riding up to share in the final triumph.

"A good fight," Gubta shouted, edging his way through the press, bloodied sword still in hand.

The commander of the Vushka, as was his right, pointed out a body to claim for his own, and a warrior on foot threw it up over the rump of Gubta's horse.

"Make sure everything is taken," Tamuka ordered. "Every one of their guns, the ammunition, everything."

He looked at the hundreds of dead horses, raging at the slaughter, which was beyond his comprehension—to kill one's own mount was beneath the honor of a warrior. Horses were the booty of battle, the taking of the horse by the victor a payment by the vanquished for the release of his soul into the next world.

He looked back to the east, at the wall of smoke moving away from him. A rider had already come in to report that similar fires were burning far to the rear. Unthinkable! The grass of the steppe was sacred. To burn it, even in battle, was the act of a race of cowards. Only the god Yulta, when he hurled the bolts of flame from the heavens, could burn the grass.

Perhaps Sarg was right after all, the cattle were possessed by evil demons, for surely only evil would conduct war in such a way. It might be a full circling of moons before the grass would be long enough for the horses to feed.

He couldn't wait; he had to press on.

He looked around at the warriors around him, the silent ones. Their features were grim. Throughout the long night's ride, when it had become clear what the cattle were doing, the rage had been building.

Good. Let his people see even more clearly the evil of these cattle. Let it fuel their hatred to kill them all. Keane had thought to deny his horses food, yet every action only made the hatred worse, compounding now even onto the rage over the death of Jubadi. He could see it in the frenzy around him, the butchering of the dead a venting of frustration, the warriors shouting, hacking the bodies apart, holding pieces aloft, not even bothering to cook the meat but tearing into it, eating it raw, so filled were they with battle lust.

"Send out the messengers," Tamuka said. "Tell the umens to continue the advance until darkness. If they can get ahead of the fire they should try to cut the grass and tear up the ground to prevent its spread.

"Shaman, you'd better persuade the gods to bring rain for us," Tamuka snapped, turning to face Sarg as if the priest were now personally responsible for controlling the weather and would face the consequences if he failed.

He looked back at the still-burning cloud flier, remembering the stories of how aboard one of the ships all who rode upon it had lost their hair, vomited blood, and died, until the ship had gone up to raid and disappeared over Rus lands. He felt a superstitious dread of the things, powered as they were by strange devices taken from the barrows of ancestors from even before the beginning of the endless ride about the world. Sarg and Jubadi had agreed to the creating of them, when the traitor cattle Hinsen had told of the secret of making the air that caused such things to float. He wished such things had never been created, but now that they were here he would use them, use anything to finish the cattle.

"Let's leave this place," he snarled. Before continuing, he pointed out the body of Dennis and claimed it as his own.

The train slowed as it reached the Sangros, edging onto the bridge, the steady rumble of the track changing to a hollow sound which Pat always found to be disquieting.

He leaned over the platform and looked down at the riverbed below. Everything was obscured in a dark brown haze, and the air was smoky, thick with the smell of the burning steppe. A distant booming echoed almost like artillery. He looked back up at the sky, the darkness moving in.

Goddammit. They had waited until the last minute to burn the grass, until the heat of the previous three weeks had dried it to tinder. The wind had shifted to the south by midmorning, unusual for this time of year, bringing with it moisture from the sea, and the thunderheads had been building.

Pat was enough of an old soldier to believe that battles shook rain loose from the heavens. Perhaps prairie fires did the same, either that or there was a curse on them.

The train continued on, the men on the flatcars behind him standing up, leaning over to watch. Below, the Sangros moved sluggishly, the river down, broad flats of sandbars dotting it. The hollow rumble gave way to the reassuring sound of solid ground underneath the train. On either side of the track, log-and-earth bastions flanked the line, anchor points for the earthworks running up north along the river. A quarter mile to the rear a second line of fortifications was tied into the walls of Hispania, laid out in a great circle to completely encompass the old city, along with the new town and factories on the east side of town.

Bell tolling and with the engineer playing the beginning of "Marching Through Georgia," the train turned onto a side track, Hispania Station drifting by on the right.

Pat looked at it with interest. It was far different from what he had last seen three weeks ago, when everything was still a mad chaos of refugees. The only presence now was military. Heavy earthworks, thrown up seven and eight feet high, were on the south side of the main line, following the track as it ran eastward along the low ridge. Another line of earthworks, again anchored to the bastion on the south side of the tracks, went due south, dropping down into the low valley, turning back slightly from the riverbank, and cutting straight through the vineyards down in the valley, villas now fortified into strongpoints along the line. Far off to the south, four miles away, he saw the line of entrenchments rise up to meet the southern point on the ridge that curved like a bow around the valley.

Canvas sacks filled with sand were piled up against the walls of Hispania Station. On parallel sidings, strings of boxcars and flatcars were drawn up. There wasn't as much use for the railroad now as before, now that the withdrawal was complete. A dozen trains a day were all that were running down to Roum and back and up north into the forest, hauling lumber, saltpeter, rations, and all the other items of supply for the army. He was aboard the last train in from the west.

Standing in the doorway of what had once been the station and was now headquarters stood Andrew, Emil at his side.

Pat climbed down from his command car and leaped off onto the platform. He looked back at the weary soldiers on the flatcar.

"A good job, me hearties. You're off duty till day after tomorrow."

He looked back at Andrew and then turned again to the men as the flatcar drifted past, raising his hand to cover the side of his mouth as if keeping Andrew from hearing.

"Now go find some vodka, and your wives or sweethearts, maybe even both."

The men smiled, several of them laughing, and Pat turned away, went up to Andrew, and saluted.

Andrew, smiling, grabbed his hand.

"Glad you're back safely."

"We almost got caught," Pat said, stepping inside the headquarters, pulling up a chair, and collapsing wearily into it, putting his dust-covered boots up on another chair.

"Bastards came on hard during the night, got across the river to the north and south of Kennebec Station and started to close in. Had a running fight from the train right through the fire."

"Casualties?"

"Lost fifty men on the two trains." He hesitated. "We also had to leave a company behind at the crossing that was setting fires to the south of the track."

Andrew nodded.

"Showalter and half his regiment were killed this morning," Emil said.

Pat looked over at the doctor, unable to reply.

"Got caught out on the prairie, surrounded, wiped out to a man."

"He was a good gunner," Pat sighed. "I told him to stay with the artillery, but he was out after glory. I guess he found it."

"The troop he was supposed to send south—did they hook up with you?"

"Never saw them," Pat said.

Andrew nodded sadly, sitting down across from Pat.

"We lost two acrosteamers as well," Emil said, pouring out a drink from his flask and passing it over to Pat. "*Flying Cloud* and *China Star*. We had three new ships come on line, the last we'll be making, and then we lose two in a day. We're back down to six ships again. They killed only one of the Merki ships."

"Petracci all right?"

"That's how we found out about Showalter. His ship limped in shot full of holes, just clearing the trees. He saw the whole thing, came down by train to report. He's pretty shook up by it all."

Pat looked over and saw Petracci in the corner of the room, sitting numbly, hands clasped around a mug. Pat nodded to the pilot, who smiled wanly, as if barely noticing that anyone was there.

"I wouldn't want to have his job," Pat whispered.

"Pilots sure don't live long," Emil said in

agreement. "Half of them dead and we've been flying less than three months. Jack cooked up a plan several days ago to get back at them. I think they're all crazy if they try it."

"The fire?" Andrew asked, interrupting Emil, not wanting the aerosteamer pilot to hear what Emil was whispering a bit too loudly.

"Burning like hell itself," Pat said, forcing his thoughts away from the forlorn figure in the corner. "All the way from Kennebec Station north. The boys who got cut off south were setting 'em as well. A grand and terrible sight it was."

"I've got people setting more ten miles west of here."

"We saw it coming in."

A peal of thunder rattled through the room, and Pat looked out through the open door. The first heavy splats of rain were hitting the ground.

"Should have done it yesterday," Pat said.

Andrew nodded in sad agreement. He had not expected the Merki to do a fifty-mile overnight dash to the river. It had cost him over half a thousand men. This commander was behaving differently, not like the way Yuri had told him Vuka would behave. He had expected a slower approach, a night march being outside the norm for the hordes. Qubata had nearly destroyed him using the same tactic during the Tugar War, and Jubadi might have done it, but Vuka was supposed to be far more superstitious. He had wanted to let them see the fires, to shake their morale; instead it appeared to have spurred them on.

The rain started to come down harder, a gust of cold wind swirling the dank smell of wet smoke into the room.

Damn.

The storm might be local—perhaps out on the steppe it was still clear. He doubted it, though. It looked like a line front closing in, the end of three hot dry weeks. Perhaps it could bring the river back up, giving him more time. It'd have to be a hell of a rain.

"Do you think we burned half the steppe between here and the Kennebec?" Andrew asked.

"Likely," Pat replied, savoring the sharp jolt of vodka that Emil had offered, the first liquor he had allowed himself in weeks.

"Dennis covered twenty-five miles south of the forest. He was supposed to send a troop down to us, another twenty miles, and I had boys on foot going north to meet them. If they got things going before the Merki crossed, that's fifty miles to the north of the track, and the thirty miles down to the sea was fairly well covered. It was twenty miles deep when we pulled out before dawn. I bet thirty miles or more, maybe forty if this rain holds off."

He smiled.

"Driving the train through it was a hell of a thrill, the Merki chasing us the whole way. Another ten minutes and the bastards would have been on the track in front of us and cut it. As it was, the rails had sagged in a couple of places where the ties had caught fire and burned. A near thing."

Andrew sat back with a sigh. Maybe a quarter, a third at best, of the steppe burned, though he had others out forward burning and pulling back. He looked over at Bob Fletcher.

"What do you think?"

"It's about eight thousand square miles of open prairie from the Kennebec to the Sangros. That's over five million acres."

Pat looked over at Bob, wondering how long it had taken him to figure out such numbers.

"Let's say we burned a third of it. That'll cut it down to three and a third million acres."

"Still a lot of ground," Emil said.

"Not really. They've got forty umens, with remounts, and the artillery. That comes out to over a million horses. This ain't like the steppe near Rus—high grass, rich soil, good farmland. It's sort of like a short prairie grass. You might get ten horses of grazing per acre in a day on it."

"Thirty days' worth, then," Emil said.

"Yeah, but that's a hell of a problem. We're burning a lot of it right now, near up to the river. Even if they camp right up on the river and keep bunched up, within a day they'll need a hundred thousand acres, over a hundred and fifty square miles of land. Since its fifty miles here north to south from the sea to the forest, on the second day they'll have to picket their horses three miles back. The prairie widens out a hell of a lot up to a hundred miles farther back, and they'll run into a nightmare. Large sections of it are burning right now. Within a week they'll have to keep most of their mounts twenty, fifty, maybe even a hundred miles back, or the horses will starve.

"This damn rain will help the grass come back, especially in the burned-over sections—seems that fire helps the damn stuff grow somehow. But it'll be several weeks before they can graze the same ground again, maybe a month, and in the middle of the summer they'll be lucky to get five horses to the acre. I figure they need something like three to four million acres overall to keep them supplied through the summer. They'll be spreading out horses from here to back beyond the Kennebec."

"And that's burning too," Pat said with a grin, not quite following the math behind it all, but as an artilleryman understanding well enough the constant problem of keeping horses in the field supplied with fodder. Most of the trains, he remembered, that had supplied the Army of the Potomac had been loaded not with rations or ammunition, but with plain old hay for the tens of thousands of army horses, and the Merki had a million of them.

"Their own food?"

"Well, there are no willing peasants storing the stuff up or ready to offer themselves," Bob said. "I figure eight hundred of those big horses a day should do it, maybe twelve hundred if the animals start losing weight."

"They're not going to like that a bit," Andrew said, remembering how Yuri had told him that the eating of horseflesh was considered an unclean act.

"Almost as much a logistical nightmare as ours, but we still have the railroad behind us," Bob said. "Otherwise our bringing this many men together would be impossible for more than a couple of days."

"They'll send most of their mounts to the rear," Andrew said quietly, looking at the ceiling as if listening to the heavy rain now rattling against the tile roof. "I'd keep maybe four umens and my artillery mounted for the breakthrough. The rest will have to fight on foot."

"It'll hurt their damn pride," Emil said.

"It'll keep them more local as well, forcing them straight in here as we planned. They won't be able to shift their entire army fifty miles in a day up north. We'll have the rails to move along the front, they won't. Vuka knows he can't waste time here—he'll have to punch through in a hurry to get to the prairie beyond us."

"They'll still have the equal of over twenty corps of warriors on foot," Pat said quietly, and Andrew looked over at him and nodded, as if the voice of reality had cut back to the heart of the issue.

Pat looked down at the map spread out upon the table.

"You're going to try to hold the straight line across the valley?"

Andrew nodded.

"Their artillery on the opposite bank will dominate the entire line."

"The entrenchments there are solid. If we pull back to the high ground the only advantage we'll have is high ground. The hills are solid rock—most places the best we could do was dig shallow rifle pits. We're hauling wood down now to try to strengthen it up more. A battle on the hills will be a stand-up fight, like Gettysburg; in the valley it's Petersburg all over again. The main point is, its only four miles from Hispania to the southern ridge on a straight line. If we lose the valley it'll be more than six miles of front." As he spoke, Andrew traced the curving line with his finger.

"And at Petersburg, before we went off on this little adventure, we were getting close to breaking Lee," Pat interjected.

Andrew looked over at his friend. "I know that," he snapped, and Pat held up his hand as if in offer of apology.

My hundred thousand to their three hundred and fifty to four hundred thousand, or worse actually. Andrew thought. I'll still have to picket the entire river front and have patrols up into the forest. At best I'll have seventy-five thousand here. They can force me to spread out while they concentrate. If they gain the valley they can mass and then charge anywhere along the entire line, their interior to my exterior.

He had run through the calculations daily for the last two months, ever since the day on the Neiper when he had had to face the fact that Rus would fall.

All of it was pointed to this final encounter, the buying of time, the calculating and recalculating. A hundred thousand more men and he would have laughed at the Merki, but he didn't have them. Every Rus who could carry arms was doing so. As soon as the Merki started the action, the factories would close down in Hispania, the men forming up as ten regiments distributed throughout the first three corps. The Roum were manpower, but training and arming them was far too slow. If he had another two months he could get another corps thrown together, but a corps needed at least two hundred rounds of ammunition in reserve per man if it was to be worth anything. A hard day's fighting and they could go through half of that. There was no sense in fielding more men if they ran out after one day of fighting. And that was assuming he could even get another fifteen thousand rifles or smoothbore muskets turned out. Production would just barely arm the rest of Marcus's corps before this battle started. He had all that he was going to get in manpower. He would have to spend it carefully, kill Merki at six or seven to one, if he was to win.

Pat yawned and leaned back in his chair. The steady rain outside was soothing.

Andrew looked around the room. His staff were huddled in the back going over charts and maps, the telegraph key silent, the station quiet, as if it were nothing more than a sleepy backwater post. He got up from his chair and walked over to the doorway, leaning against the frame. Outside the wind drove the rain down, eddies and swirls of it racing across the switching yard, men huddling inside boxcars, taking a break from work.

The air was heavy with the damp sodden smell of smoke, almost unpleasant, slightly reminiscent of a rainy autumn day.

Five hundred men dead today. He'd miss Showalter. He had wanted to be another Jeb Stewart. He had his wish; Jeb dead at Yellow Tavern, and Showalter dead on the Kennebec. They wouldn't even get a decent grave. He pushed the rest of the thought aside.

Over by the telegrapher's booth the station clock ticked away the seconds, pendulum swinging slowly back and forth, marking off the eternal passage. Bringing closer the inevitable.

If they rode hard, advanced scouts might make it

here by tomorrow night, the rest of them within another day, two at the outside.

A snap of lightning flickered overhead, thunder booming, the rain redoubling.

He reached over to a wall peg and grabbed hold of his poncho. He clumsily worked it over his head, again painfully aware of just how difficult so many things were when you had only one arm. Poncho on, he took his kepi hat and pulled it low over his eyes.

He looked back at Pat and Emil and smiled.

"I'm going home to Kathleen, taking the rest of the day off. It'll be the last for a while, I guess."

Emil nodded his agreement, and Andrew went out the door and into the swirling storm.

"How's he holding up?" Pat asked, motioning for Emil to pour another drink, which the doctor reluctantly did.

"As well as is to be expected. The death of Showalter and his boys hit him hard."

"It always hits hard when you're responsible," Pat said quietly.

"We're as ready as we'll ever be," Emil said, grabbing hold of an empty mug and pouring out the rest of the flask for himself.

Pat sighed, leaning back in his chair.

"I wish we had another six months to get ready. But I think, good doctor, that the game is up and Andrew knows it."

"We've been waiting for this for a year, running for nearly three months, ever since the Potomac. In a week, two weeks, it'll be over with, one way or the other."

"And you know which way that'll be."

"I'm not sure," Emil said, his voice low. "The boys know what's at stake," and he nodded toward the poster nailed to the wall, showing the infamous massacre at Suzdal. "We still might beat the bastards."

"Well, we gave 'em a run for it," Pat replied with

a low chuckle. "I wouldn't have missed it for the world, or even a ticket back to New York. Me, a corps commander, high and mighty like Hancock or John Reynolds, blessed be his memory, and a good fighter he was."

Pat looked into his mug and then drained the rest off.

"We'll give 'em a fight here to be sure, and when we're gone they'll wish the hell they'd never seen the likes of us."

"You honestly believe it's finished?"

"Who wouldn't?" Pat said with a laugh. "But what the hell, it'll be fun while it lasts, and in a week I expect to be in the best damn fight since Gettysburg."

Chapter 9

How much longer he could stand this pace he wasn't sure. But at the moment he honestly didn't care. After all, who needed sleep?

Chuck Ferguson leaned on his elbow and looked down at her. She had drifted off to sleep, the moonlight slanting in through the window of his cabin, her olive skin shining, now pale, glowing.

After the storm of yesterday evening the heat had returned. By the following afternoon even the forest was hot, sweltering, mosquitoes rising up and plaguing the work crews. The cabin was still warm, and in their mad insane lovemaking they had kicked the wool army blanket off the bed.

She was stretched out naked beside him, her full breasts rising and falling softly. He ran his hand lightly down her side, resting it for a moment on her rounded buttock. He felt the stirring again. Just looking at her was more than sufficient.

She sighed, moving, arching her back to snuggle up closer, taking his hand in her half-dreaming state and moving it back up to cup her breast.

He considered waking her up, to begin again.

He looked over at the clock. No.

He kissed her lightly on the nape of the neck and slid out of the bed, pulling on his faded blue wool army trousers and a loose-fitting Rus tunic. He wanted to check on the repairs and relaunching of *Yankee*

Clipper II. The crew had been working nonstop, the ground crews from the two lost ships helping out.

A mission was about to take off, *Yankee Clipper,* along with four of the five other remaining ships, going out on a desperate gamble. There wouldn't be any more of them built while the war lasted, for the supply of silk had been totally used up. If a balance wasn't made between the two sides, and damn quick, the Merki would rule the air, a situation that could be disastrous.

Pulling on his boots, he slipped out of the cabin, gently closing the door. Over at the sheds, on the far side of the clearing, the first of the ships was already out of its hangar, glowing in the moonlight. Chuck walked up to it, looking at it with awe. *"Star of the West"* was emblazoned upon its side in Cyrillic and Roman characters. Magnificent, but only the beginning.

He had taken to watching the flight of vultures that hovered above the clearing, and ducks down in the marshy ground near the Sangros. Something about the way their wings seemed to curve had set him to thinking. When this damn war was over he'd take the time to experiment a bit.

The two-man crew, looking hot in their heavy canvas coveralls, goggles pushed up on their foreheads, were walking around the ship, checking it one last time.

"Everything ready?" Chuck asked.

The pilot nodded, saying nothing. Chuck stepped back and left him alone. Chuck could well understand the man's fear and tension.

The ground crew looked equally concerned. It was a strange bond, the men loving their ships, watching anxiously as they lifted up, waiting nervously through the long hours until the return, raising their gaze to scan the sky, rushing to the watchtower when the lookout announced a ship coming in. After the landing they'd barely listen to the pilot excitedly pouring out a description of the action, looking instead at their ship, almost angry when the pilots brought back a shot-up vessel, as if a child of theirs had been recklessly put in harm's way. And when a ship didn't return they would continue to wait, sittiing alone outside the empty hangar, as if their giving up would somehow be a confirmation that hope was gone.

Chuck walked away and headed for *Yankee Clipper*'s shed. Red flags, which looked black in the moonlight, were posted around the hangar, warning that the ship was still being refilled with hydrogen, a small caloric engine air pump, outside the hangar, chattering away, sucking the gas out of the vats of zinc and sulfuric acid, feeding the gas by a canvas hose into the ship inside the hangar. Except for the explosion-proof miner's lamps the building was dark.

He knew that according to Andrew's rules he was not supposed to be anywhere near a hangar when a ship was being gassed up. He ignored the flag and the sentry and went in anyhow. Petracci stood to one side, Feyodor beside him, hands in their pockets, watching as the balloon slowly started to hover.

"How's it going?" Chuck asked.

"Closing the hose off now," Feyodor said.

"The patches?"

"I guess they're all right," Jack said, his voice flat and calm.

"Gas line's clear. Bringing her out!" The shout echoed from the back of the shed.

Chuck stepped back as the ground crew started to walk forward, the ship hovering above them, the detachable wheels under the ship barely touching the ground.

The nose emerged into the light of the twin moons, which shone dull and red on the eastern horizon. The cab rolled past and finally the tail of the ship, and the three walked out after it. The clatter of the pump was silent, the clearing ghostly. The other four ships were already outside, engines running. They moved into the center of the clearing past the red flags around the hangar, and the Rus ground chief moved up to the caloric engine mounted at the stern of the wicker basket. Striking a match, he lit the pilot. The crew waited as Feyodor joined the crew chief, the burner flashing to life as he opened up the fuel line, kerosene rushing in, igniting.

After several mintues, Feyodor pushed on the fly-wheel. The engine kicked half over, then the engine hesitated, went through a full cycle, and started into a steady run. Chuck noticed that the ship was rising up slightly, the hot exhaust from the engine filling the center bag, helping to provide additional lift along with the two gas bags set fore and aft inside the long sausage-shaped ship. The ground crew were leaning into the ropes.

Jack broke away from Chuck's side and took a final walk around the ship, looking up at it, standing back to examine the patches that had been stitched over the dozens of holes from the enemy canister rounds.

Chuck walked up and joined him.

"Thought it'd take three, four days to fix her," Jack said quietly.

"You had two additional crews from the lost ships on her." He silently cursed himself for mentioning the fact.

Jack nodded, his features tense.

"Scared?"

"Shitless," Jack whispered, looking over at Chuck and forcing a sad smile.

"How long do you think it'll take?"

"It's been calm since the front passed through. I hope there's no weather. With luck a tail wind will kick up on the way back. Maybe a day, maybe thirty hours."

"You could have taken the shorter run. Nobody would have thought less of you," Chuck said.

Jack shook his head. "I'm the senior pilot, it's my job," he said. "Hell, I'm the one that thought of the plan in the first place, goddam me."

"We've got full lift."

Jack nodded to the crew chief.

"Good luck," Chuck said, extending his hand.

"Bad luck to wish an aerosteamer pilot luck," Jack said, looking at Chuck as if he had committed a heinous crime.

He had noticed the rituals and jargon that were already developing among the small team of pilots, who died almost as quickly as they and their ships were launched. The crew of *China Star* had survived only their half-dozen training flights and one combat mission before going down, and *Flying Cloud*'s crew had survived barely ten days of flying. The unfortunate two in *Star of the East* had died on their first solo when the ship caught fire and exploded. Jack, with over sixty flights, three kills, and one crash, all in less than three months, was considered to be almost godlike in his invincibility.

"Time to go," Jack said quietly, and taking Chuck's hand he shook it, his grip loose, almost rubbery. He went up to the ship's basket and climbed in.

"Cast off all lines!"

The ground crew stepped back, releasing their holds. The ship slowly started to rise straight up, an easy launch in the dead calm of night. As the ship reached fifty feet, the propeller hummed to life and the ship started to move, nose pointing up, turning to the south. The second ship, *Star of the West*, cast off, rising up, and a moment later *China Wind* and *Republic* drifted up to join their comrades, engines humming to life, *Star of the West* turning to follow Jack, the other two turning north, followed by the last ship, *California Clipper*, its crew going out on their first battle flight. The thumping of the propellers died away, the air becoming still, the excitement of launch gone.

The ground crews stood silent, looking up into the night sky, and slowly wandered back to the hangars to wait.

Chuck turned and started back across the clearing to his cabin. Perhaps he could catch a brief nap before going up to the rocket factory. But then again . . .

Whistling softly, he followed the path up to his cabin, noticing that a lantern was shining within. She must be up, he thought. He heard low voices, one of them angry.

What the hell? He quickened his pace and pushed the door open.

Olivia sat on the bed, eyes wide, blanket pulled up to cover her body. John Mina sat at Chuck's desk, two officers behind him.

"What the hell are you doing here like this?" Chuck shouted.

"I should ask what the hell you're doing," John said.

"Goddammit, get out of my house."

"I wouldn't be so sure this is your house anymore."

Chuck ignored him, turning back to Olivia.

"Are you all right?"

"They just came walking in," she said, her voice shaking.

"We apologize for that, sir," one of the Rus officers said. "We came in here looking for you."

"Get out."

John stood up and looked at the couple.

"I'm sorry to have embarrassed the lady," he said, a note of sarcasm in the way he said "lady," and he stepped out of the cabin.

"Get dressed," Chuck said, and she grabbed his hand.

"That's Mina, isn't it?" she whispered.

Chuck nodded, suddenly feeling queasy and slightly

weak-kneed. John's barging in like this could only mean that he was already in a towering rage.

"Wait here."

Chuck stepped out of the cabin and closed the door behind him.

"I'm placing you under arrest," John snapped, turning on Chuck before he was even through the door.

"What the hell for?" he asked, angry with himself that his voice was shaky.

"Disobedience of a direct order, malfeasance, insubordination, embezzlement, and theft of government property, for starters. I'll think up half a dozen more charges on the train ride back to Hispania."

"John, be reasonable," Chuck said.

"General Mina to you, Lieutenant Colonel Ferguson."

"Goddammit, John we started out as privates together, so don't pull this petty rank business on me."

"Well, damn you, it stands now," John roared. "I've known something was wrong for weeks—workers listed as deserted, trains mysteriously pulled for repairs, powder by the ton unaccounted for. I come up here to look around and I find that!" He pointed up the path toward the hidden rocket factory.

"How much have you stolen?" he demanded, and he stepped closer, his nose almost touching Chuck's. "Ten tons, twenty? How about fifty?"

"Somewhere around there," Chuck whispered.

"Damn your hide. A ton of powder is eighty thousand rounds. We're short by millions."

"Even if you had it, the problem is casting rounds and wrapping them, not the powder."

"Don't argue with me, damn you. What about the workers? I need ten thousand more rifles, better yet forty thousand to replace all the smoothbores. I need everything. Everything, and here you're building your own little empire. Damn you! God damn you to hell!"

His words started to slur into an incoherent scream, the explosion of months of tension at last finding a release. One of the two aides stepped up to John's side as if to restrain him, taking hold of him by the shoulder. John pushed the man off, turning, his rage switching in an instant from Chuck.

"Calm down, sir," the man said quietly.

"And you go to hell too, all of you. I've had it, goddammit, I've had it with everything!

"I've been getting the blame for months, and it was you who was wrecking everything, you bastard. I ought to blow your brains out, and your whore's too while I'm at it."

He started to reach for the revolver in his holster, and one of the two aides was instantly at John's side, grabbing hold of his arm.

"Please, sir, he isn't worth it," and as he spoke he quickly pulled the revolver out of its holster and tossed it to the side of the cabin.

"God damn all of you!"

John turned and staggered off, his voice breaking into a convulsive sob, the one officer following him.

"You'd better come with us," the aide whispered, looking nervously back at John.

"He's mad," Chuck hissed, shaken by what he had just seen. He had believed for an instant that John was going to shoot him down. "The hell with you. I'm staying here. I've got work to do."

"Sir, you'd better come with us." The man's voice was low but insistent.

"He's mad."

"Sir, when he saw that factory of yours he threatened to blow your brains out. We won't let him, but if you don't come with us quietly . . ." He fell silent.

"God damn him, I'll kill the son of a bitch if he comes near me," Chuck snapped. "Who the hell is he to break into my home?"

Chuck turned to go back into his cabin to grab his revolver.

The captain reached out, grabbing Chuck by the arm.

"Sir, I'm telling you. According to General Mina, you're under arrest."

Chuck started to pull his arm back, but the man held on, his grip viselike.

"Please, sir, be reasonable. We'll go see the colonel. Let him straighten this out. Vasiliy over there," and he nodded to his companion, "he'll keep an eye on the general, and I'll watch out for you."

Chuck stood rigid, sensing that this man could disable him with a single blow.

"Please, sir, be a good gentleman about this. He'll calm down. He's had a terrible time of things. Before you know it, you'll both have a drink over this and laugh," and a note of peasant deference was clear in the man's voice, as if he were trying once again to argue sense with an obstinant boyar.

Chuck nodded. "Keep him away from me," he snapped, ashamed that he was forced to give in, struggling to appear in some semblance of control, knowing that Olivia was watching.

"I promise, sir."

Chuck looked back into the cabin and saw Olivia in the corner, out of sight of the officer, a short dagger in her hand.

"It's all right," he said in Latin. "Put that thing down."

"He wants to kill you."

Chuck smiled weakly. "Just a squabble between friends. I've got to go see Keane and straighten it out. I'll be back tomorrow evening."

Her shoulders started to shake, and she ran up to him, grabbing him around the waist as if ready to struggle for possession of him.

The Rus captain looked back nervously to where Vasiliy and John stood in the shadows, Mina still shouting and sobbing. "Please, sir, we don't want to set him off again."

Chuck kissed her lightly on the forehead and with his free arm started to push her back.

"I love you, and don't worry. The colonel will straighten this out. Go find Theodor and tell him what happened, that I've been arrested and taken to Colonel Keane. He'll know what to do.

"Come on let's get going," Chuck said to the captain.

"Thank you, sir." The relief in his voice was evident, and he fell in alongside Chuck.

John, still cursing loudly, followed, and all four disappeared into the dark, leaving Olivia standing alone by the door. Sobbing, she turned away and started to run to the rocket factory.

"All right, Feyodor, give me full power!"

Skimming low over the ocean, the ship turned north, heading into the mouth of the Neiper River. Jack pulled up slightly, passing directly over the lone ironclad at the river's mouth, its deck crowded with men who jumped up and down, waving, shouting.

The shadow of *Yankee Clipper II* raced over the mouth of the river, less than twenty feet below, flocks of ducks kicking up in every direction at the passage of the ship. He looked back. *China Wind* was a quarter mile behind him, just clearing the ironclad, the pilot pulling up too high.

"Stay low, stay low, damn you," Jack cursed.

It would have been better if he had gone alone. Eurik Vasilovich, the new pilot, was still too green, with only four battle flights; he bobbed up and down, surging ahead and falling back. Jack had tried to wave him off, to send him back, but Eurik had acted as if he didn't understand Jack's hand signals and had doggedly kept on.

Jack found that he was starting to shake. He was

not sure if it was fear or exhaustion after nearly fourteen hours of flying, which had taken him due south to the sea and then straight west along the coast. At dawn he had dropped down to right above the water, hugging the coast, hoping to avoid being seen. It felt horrible flying this low; he found he couldn't control the obsessive fear that an enemy ship was patrolling a mile or more up, ready to swoop down for the kill. His neck was stiff from constantly leaning over the side of the cab to look forward and up. But the sky was clear.

The other ships, with luck, would be almost back home by now, for their mission was only half the distance of his, just out to Kev and back. Just out to Kev. Damn, that was considered a record in itself. When the first ship had left the hangar to go to war, it had been towed by train across the three hundred miles. If he survived this, it would be over a thousand miles round trip. As it was, there was barely enough fuel for one way.

"How's fuel?" He looked over his shoulder.

Feyodor held up the last five-gallon tin can and with a shrug threw it over the side.

"The last can went into the tank. Five, maybe six gallons."

Jack nodded and turned to look forward.

The ground was hauntingly familiar. The Neiper made its curve to the west and then back north. As they rounded the bend in the river, he saw the weed-choked remains of Fort Lincoln, their first home in this new world. A mile farther up, on the west bank, he saw the scorched section of forest where his first kill had fallen.

A small group of Merki, women clad in silken robes, children running naked, stood on the bank of the river. It looked as if they were fishing. They started to shout and wave.

"They think we're one of them," Feyodor laughed, and leaning out of the cab, he waved back.

Realizing their mistake, the Merki started to shake their fists.

The river turned again, and then straight ahead the city of Suzdal came into view. Jack felt a knot in his throat, remembering the first time he had seen it, coming up the river aboard *Ogunquit,* the church bells ringing, thousands of Rus peasants lining the banks of the river. The place looked empty.

"Home," Feyodor said, his voice shaking, and he made the sign of the cross. "At least they haven't burned it."

"Get ready."

He hit the up elevator stick, pulling it back, closing off the heat exhaust port on the top of the ship. Running light, without the burden of over a hundred gallons of fuel, the ship, even with the exhaust port full open, had wanted to rise, forcing him to keep more and more down elevator.

The ship surged up, and he pushed the rudder full forward. The nose of the aerosteamer swung to the right, heading back east. They turned out of the riverbed, rising up over the east shore of the river, the south walls of Suzdal a mile to his left, the dome of the cathedral glinting in the noonday sun.

As he climbed, he saw the reservoir off his forward port quarter, the lake nearly empty, the smokestacks of the factories poking up out of the forest. Feyodor leaned out of his rear position, craning his head to look forward.

"Where the hell is it?"

"Somewhere south of the lake."

"Did we go too far north?"

"Couldn't have. I remember seeing them coming up from that direction."

He continued to climb.

Feyodor raised his field glasses, scanning the ground ahead.

"There it is!" He pointed forward and slightly to the south.

"Going back down," Jack shouted, pulling the exhaust vent full open and pushing the elevator stick forward. The ship responded slowly, picking up speed.

They skimmed over the hills east of town, Jack sparing a quick glance to the north, where the burial mound of Jubadi, shaped like a pyramid, rose up out of the fields. He knew what the pyramid was made of, and he quickly turned away.

The ship dived down reluctantly, because of its light load and the heat of the sun, which had warmed the hydrogen, causing it to expand. He was tempted to open the vent and bleed some of the gas off, but knew that come nightfall he was going to need it. He pushed the stick forward even farther and then eased back. The ship leveled out at treetop level, racing forward at full speed. The low rise continued. At the top of the crest stood a watchtower, and he aimed straight at it. The lone Merki raised his bow, fired, and then ducked as they skimmed over, the Merki crouching not a dozen feet below.

And on the reverse slope he saw what he had come for. Eight hangars were spread out in a long row at the opposite end of the field. The ground below was swarming with Merki, their harsh cries rising up in anger even as they ran to the buildings.

"Get ready!" Jack shouted, and he eased back slightly on the throttle.

A puff of smoke snapped off from the north side of the field, a shot screaming past, the gunner far too eager in his excitement. There was another puff. Jack ignored it, pressing on.

"First hangar on the left's empty," Feyodor shouted. "Two's empty, so is the third."

He hadn't expected to get all of them on the

ground. Eight hangars, three empty. There were ten
more at Kev, and he hoped that the other three ships
had burned the lot. With luck, maybe the three emp-
ties were already abandoned, the air fleet moving forward as new hangars went up.

On the far side of the field, he could see straight
in. A dark nose appeared out of the fourth, the same
with the other four.

"Five ships!"

He looked back.

Star of the West was nowhere in view. He couldn't
worry about it now.

He edged to the north, preparing to turn south
when he reached the hangars for a run straight down
the line.

The Merki ground crews were at the open doors,
pulling on ropes, struggling to drag their ships out.

"They're bringing the ships out. Get the harpoons
ready!"

Almost parallel to the line and a quarter mile north,
Jack turned the ship hard, diving down lower, lining
up for his pass.

"Get ready!"

Another shot screamed past. From a shed alongside
the northernmost hangar Merki started to run out,
bows raised, flame and smoke flickering from the tips.

"Jesus Christ!" It was a simple enough defense he
had never thought of.

He ignored them, pressing on. Feyodor, leaning
over the side of the cab, unsnapped an oil-soaked
board which was fastened to the side of the cab. With
a sharp jerk he raked a rough iron file across the top
of a fist-size friction-head match attached to the
board. It flare to life, and he let go, the board falling
a dozen feet before jerking to a stop, dangling by a
length of rope, which was tied to the end of a harpoon
that Feyodor now unclipped from the side of the cab.

Grabbing hold of the harpoon with both hands, Feyodor held it up. The flaming board swayed and bobbed below the cab, and Jack spared a quick anxious look back at the trail of smoke and fire.

A flaming arrow suddenly arched up from below. Another one snapped past, slamming into the propeller, and a third struck the bottom of the cab.

The shadow of *Yankee Clipper II* raced over the nose of the first enemy ship. Feyodor leaned out, held only by his safety belt.

"One fired!" he screamed and threw the harpoon down. It was nearly impossible to miss the enemy ship barely twenty feet below. The harpoon sliced into the Merki airship, punching a hole through the silken bag and disappearing. The flaming board followed, slamming lengthwise across the hole and jerking to a stop on the outside of the bag, burning brightly. Instantly a tongue of nearly invisible blue flame shot up, the hydrogen pouring out of the hole from the harpoon hitting the flaming board and igniting. The tail of *Yankee Clipper II* rose up on the wave of heat.

Jack pulled the nose up. The second ship was almost upon them. It was impossible to slow down. Feyodor struggled with the board of the second harpoon, striking it into flame, dropping it, and then grabbing hold of the harpoon. The third ship in the line was already directly beneath them. He was tempted to throw, but let it pass. The fourth ship in line was half out of its hangar.

Jack aimed for the midsection.

"Two fired!"

Jack looked down, following the harpoon as it sliced in, the flaming board catching the same as the first one. Beyond the fifth ship a knot of Merki, bows raised, were waiting. He pulled back hard on both the elevator and the rudder stick, and *Yankee Clipper II* arced up into a sweeping graceful turn to the east.

As they passed over the last hangar, Feyodor leaned out and struck the friction-match fuse atop a jug filled with benzene. The flare ignited and the jar tumbled down, striking the roof, liquid flame splattering.

Jack looked over his shoulder as they continued the turn. Two fireballs were igniting, the ships exploding, half out of their hangars. Flame was shooting straight up, and from out of each building a blue-and-yellow fireball exploded straight out parallel to the ground. The roof of a third hanger ripped open, flame soaring a hundred feet into the sky. Merki on the ground were running in every direction like a stirred-up nest of ants.

He watched in awe, stunned by the destruction.

"Star of the West," Feyodor shouted, and pointed back across the far side of the clearing.

The ship was slowly floating across the field on the light westerly breeze, nose pointed down, tail high, barely underway. Jack snapped his field glasses up to look.

"The damn bastard's out of fuel!" he screamed. "Idiot! Damn him, damn him!" He slumped back in his chair, stunned that Eurik had been so insane as to not break off and head back out to sea before running out.

The ship's propeller was still. With headway lost, the ship was out of control, the engine most likely running dry only a couple of minutes too soon.

He felt a sudden guilt for cursing two dead men. Chances were that, overeager to impress Jack, they had forged ahead, thinking they could attack and still get out and away.

On the far side of the field a swarm of Merki raced toward the ship as if to capture it as it came down. A thin trail of smoke shot up, and within seconds a steady stream.

Puffs of smoke burst from the cab, a defiant last blow, the trading of a ship and its crew for the final chance of a pistol shot killing a lone Merki.

A tongue of flame started to lick up the side of the

ship. The silken bag peeled away, fire exploding straight up into the heavens, and the ship slammed into the ground, fire bursting out its sides.

Jack pushed the rudder stick to the left and the elevator back forward.

"What the hell are you doing?"

"We've still got two harpoons. Get ready."

"You're crazy."

"You knew that when you signed on with me. Now get ready."

"I pulled your ass out of the last crash—I won't do it again."

"You've got that girl Svetlana and I don't, so it's even. Now shut up and get ready."

He brought the ship full around and started into a dive. It would be impossible to do a right-angle run again. The first and fourth ships were still burning fiercely, their hangars exploding into flame, and the hangar of the fifth ship was starting to flare as well. He lined up to run straight down the length of the second hangar. The ship was completely out of it, nose already starting to edge up.

On the back end of the building, a small knot of Merki were gathered, bows raised, arrows snaked up, fortunately none with flames. Several arrows struck the ship directly in front of Jack, the arrows disappearing.

He raced down along the roof, going slower than he wanted to into the headwind. Fifty yards to his right, the first hangar was exploding with fire, the heat glaring. A hundred yards to his left, the other building was awash with flames.

They cleared the edge of the hangar.

"Three fired! Let's get the hell out of here," Feyodor screamed.

Afraid of turning into the fires to either side, Jack pushed straight ahead into the headwind. A dull thumping whoosh sounded behind him, and he looked back to see the tail of their third target peel open, flame racing along the top spine of the ship, splitting the bag.

Merki were running across the field in front of him, bows raised, this time smoke coiling around them.

The fire arrows came up, another striking the basket. To his horror, one came straight up, slamming into the bag overhead.

He held his breath, expecting the end.

Nothing happened, the arrow having struck the hot-air section. He watched the bag for several seconds, afraid that the arrow might still be burning inside.

A sharp crack snapped behind Jack, startling him, and he looked down to see several Merki crumple up, caught by the blast of Feyodor's swivel gun. Straight ahead, the *Star of the West* continued to burn, the wicker framework collapsing into a heap.

With full back elevator and exhaust port closed, the ship angled straight up. He turned southward.

The field was chaos. The third ship flared, tent-size sections of burning silk soaring up from the heat. The hangars to either side crackled, dark smoke coiling up.

But two of the ships were still intact, and out of the confusion they started to rise up.

Jack was tempted to turn back in, and fight it out above the range of the ground. A dull thump shook the ship, and he looked back to the field, saw a puff of smoke snapping from a cannon.

"How much fuel?"

"Barely enough."

That decided it.

He pushed on to the south. Behind him, from out of the wreckage of the field, the two remaining ships rose, the flame of four dying aerosteamers and burning hangars filling the sky.

He crested back up over the hills, afraid to put on too much altitude for fear that it would be impossible to get back down when the engine finally died.

Straight ahead he saw the low hills that marked where the iron ore mine was. He shot over the abandoned site, great piles of slag littering the side of the mountain, the small first foundry nearly directly below. Atop the hill was the watchtower which had been built to keep an eye on the southern approaches, back when this land had still been theirs.

He felt heat, and looked down to see flame licking up between his feet. The bottom of the cab was on fire. He turned to look aft and saw a trail of smoke whisking out behind him, caught in the prop wash and swirling around in tight circles behind the ship.

"We're on fire!" Feyodor shouted.

"Shut up! I know it!"

He swerved slightly to avoid the lone Merki, not wanting to take any more chances. From this vantage point he saw how his approach in had worked, hugging the shore and staying low—the coast, blocked by the next series of hills, was not visible. He aimed for the hills, racing over the valley.

"How we doing?"

"Two ships up and after us, maybe two miles back. But Perm damn it, it's getting hot back here."

It was going to be tight.

He crested the hill, and before him, hugging the shore, the ironclad stood waiting.

"We'll have time for only one pass. Miss it and we're finished," Jack shouted. "So be sharp."

"You're the one at the controls," Feyodor shouted, "not me."

He leaned forward, judging the approach, swinging slightly to the left as they crossed the shoreline and then turning to point straight into the wind.

He lined up on the ironclad, pushing the nose down and yanking down hard on the exhaust vent, watching the green flag on the ship, which told him that they had received the fuel, and using it to judge any shifts in the wind.

"Quarter power."

Feyodor eased back on the throttle, and their forward speed died.

"You handle it."

As they slowed, the flame, which had been licking to the rear, started to come straight up. He lifted his feet, and smoke billowed up into the cab.

Jack leaned over the side, gauging the approach, easing back slowly, edging it up to meet an eddy of wind, then dropping it off again.

Jack nudged the nose of the ship down till it almost hit the water, wanting to touch down, but afraid that with the forward speed of the ship it would cause the nose to plow into the ocean. He had to hang on. He lifted the nose up slightly, drifting forward. The ship was anchored. There was no smoke from the stack, which had been taken down, the crew having dampened the fire. The green flag was dropped down, clearing the top of the ironclad.

The nose of *Yankee Clipper II* edged up over the stern of the ship, moving forward. Sailors standing on the deck of the ironclad tentatively reached up to grab the dangling ropes.

Several sailors came out of an open gunport carrying buckets. They ran to the side of the ship, leaned over, filled the buckets, and passed them up to men standing atop the gundeck.

"Grab hold, damn you!" Jack roared, and the men responded.

Feyodor edged the throttle back up. The aerosteamer moved forward down the length of the ironclad, the sailors adding their muscle, pulling on the ropes, more grabbing hold. Jack edged the elevator forward, and the cab hovered above the iron grating of the gundeck. A sailor came up alongside and threw a bucket of water straight in at Jack, soaking him. Steam and smoke swirled around. Another bucket splashed along the bottom, and then another, putting the fire out.

Sailors grabbed hold of the cab, steadying it, pulling it down to rest atop the ironclad. The ship's captain stood alongside, as awestruck as his men.

"Load us up quick!" Jack shouted, choking on the steam and smoke. "We've got two ships after us!"

"Where's the other one?"

"Dead."

The captain grabbed hold of the first can of kerosene and hoisted it up. Jack passed it back to Feyodor, who dropped it into one of the brackets to either side of his legs.

Jack looked down and saw that most of the bottom of the basket was scorched black, and several holes had been burned clean through. He grabbed a bucket of water and poured it down to make sure the fire was out. A sailor pulled on the side of the basket and stood back, holding up a four-foot-long Merki arrow, a scorched bundle of straw tied to the head.

Jack stood up to stretch, and one foot went through the bottom of the basket. He pulled it back up, steadying himself, suddenly realizing that he had a terrible need to relieve himself. He'd have to wait.

"The message galley came up with this load of kerosene yesterday. I thought the captain was insane when he told me what you were going to do."

"Well, dammit, I wouldn't have had to if your damn admiral hadn't gone gallivanting off to the south."

"Admiral Bullfinch was doing his duty," the captain shouted back defensively. "And you're crazy if you think we could have cut ten miles inland to that place. We'd have been wiped out."

"Well, I lost a good ship doing it."

"I'm sorry," the captain said. He pulled a flask out of his pocket, looked at it for a moment, and then, as if reaching a decision, passed it over. "Keep it."

Jack nodded his thanks.

"Aerosteamers!"

Down on the main deck a sailor was pointing to the north.

"How far?"

"A mile, maybe less."

"Hurry it up!" Jack shouted, grabbing a tin of kerosene from a waiting sailor and dropping it into his section of the cab. Reaching up, he pulled the exhaust vent closed; the load of fuel now firmly anchored the aerosteamer to the ironclad.

"How many, Feyodor?"

"Sixteen."

"I've got two," and he grabbed another one.

"Twenty! Let's go!"

"Cast us off!"

The captain stepped back from the cab.

"Cast away all lines!"

He came to attention and saluted.

"Good luck to you."

'Goddammit," Jack growled, forgetting to return the salute.

Feyodor, without waiting to be told, pushed the throttle full forward, the propeller humming up to a blur, while Jack pulled the elevator stick back to his stomach as he sat back down.

Yankee Clipper II started forward, the cab dragging across the deck.

Reaching the end of the gundeck, the cab started to slip down the sloped side of the ship, and in a moment of blind panic Jack looked aft, expecting to see the propeller slam into the deck.

The nose of the ship started to angle up, and the tip of the propeller nicked the deck, splinters howling, and then they were up, moving slow, their former buoyancy replaced now by a heavy sluggish action. They turned slowly over the water.

"Throw that damn gun overboard."

"Like hell! We're going to need it."

"If they're above us, we're dead. Throw the damn thing over."

Cursing, Feyodor grabbed the small one-inch cannon, pulled it up out of its mount, and tossed it into the sea. The ship rose up, responding, helped as well by the gathering heat inside the now tightly sealed hot-air bag.

"Where are they?"

"A shadow's moving over the ironclad."

Jack looked back to see the sailors. Some were standing, pointing straight up, others scattering, pushing to get into the gunports. The captain stood alone, revolver drawn, pointing it straight up and firing.

Swinging around to the east, putting the wind at their back, *Yankee Clipper II* raced off, two Merki ships above and only a hundred yards astern.

Reining in hard, Tamuka Qar Qarth came to the top of the rise, a shout of exultation escaping him. Turning, he looked back to the line of warriors riding up behind him and pointed forward.

"There they are!"

At last, dammit, at last, the long chase finished.

He leaped down from his mount, stretched, pulled the water bag from his saddle, and took a deep draft. Grabbing a small bucket clipped to his saddlebag, he poured the rest of the water into it and held the bucket up to his horse, which drank the water greedily.

His standard-bearer rode up beside him, followed seconds later by the silent ones, the message riders, and Sarg. The old shaman was swaying from exhaustion.

To the north he saw the long line of riders, stretching to the far horizon, coming up over the crest with a splendid precision. To the south, on the other side of the iron rail tracks, the view was the same. He had wanted it that way. A full umen, ten thousand riders,

to appear at once covering a front of five leagues, to
show the cattle the precision and control of the horde.

He let the bucket drop and pulled the far-seeing
glass out of his saddlebag. He uncapped the lens and
slowly swept the river line half a league away. The
silent ones moved cautiously forward, watching the
other side, ready to react if a single puff of smoke
snapped out.

Advanced scouts and maps drawn by the aerosteamer pilots had already told him how they were
deployed, and now he could see for himself.

He looked north, seeing the sharp-cut riverbank of
the eastern shore, bluffs rising up to fifty feet high,
the walls sheer, gradually dropping down. Straight
ahead was their small city, limestone walls shining dull
red from the afternoon sun. And then the long section
of flat bottomland, the ground rich, green, slashed
from north to south by earthworks, the low hills curving eastward, then marching back down to the river.
This side of the riverbank was higher than the other
only along this stretch. He looked to the south, noticing where the hills on the other side finally came back
down to meet the river and then continued south, disappearing in the afternoon haze.

"The chart reader of the Tugars said that it was
here that they cross the river," Sarg said. "This is the
first town of the Room. North of here the banks are
too steep, to the south are the hills, and on the east
side there is river bottom swamp and marsh down to
the sea."

Tamuka nodded. Leaning over, he scooped up a
handful of water that his horse had left in the bottom
of the bucket and wiped the dust from his face.

"Keane chose his ground well," Tamuka whispered,
turning to look back at the enemy line. At Kev he
could have attacked anywhere along a full day's ride
of front, the land west rich, laced with streams for
water to feed his army. Here the front would be nar-

row, no room to flank, water scarce. He would threaten, the north flank, with luck perhaps even succeed, but it would be here, and it would be bloody.

But at least it was here, a final decision. If they broke the line there was no place for the cattle to run except to the open steppe, where they would be ridden down.

He looked up at his chart master and snapped his finger. The scribe dismounted, uncased the parchment scroll, and rolled it out at Tamuka's feet. The Qar Qarth motioned for the clan Qarths and commanders of five who were riding with him to dismount. The warriors gathered around, Tamuka kneeling down by the chart and pointing.

"We are here. The last great river we crossed is this line here, two days of battle riding behind us, eight days of march by yurts."

He pointed to the blackened sections drawn in east of the Kennebec, then to several thousand square miles of ground burned fifty miles to the west of the river, and then finally to the half-dozen-mile line burned just west of the Sangros.

"This is the grass these animals burned." Several of the warriors growled angrily at the sacrilege.

"Except for those of the umen of the white horse and the Vushka Hush, we have left all remounts back behind the river."

The commanders nodded.

"There is not enough grass here. Thus I command that except for the Vushka, the umen of the white horse clan, and four umens of the gray, all umens are to ride up to their position here and dismount, sending their horses to the rear. A relay of twenty thousand horses of the blue clan will be used to transport heavy water skins up from the last great river, or whatever small streams we find to here, and then back until we've breached their line."

There was an angry growl of dissent from those who

had heard for the first time that they were to be on foot.

Tamuka looked up at the circle that stood above him.

"Merki do not fight on foot," Haga, senior Qarth of the black horse clan, snarled.

Tamuka stood up to face him.

"If we keep our horses here, in a week they will die," he said. "There is not enough food for them, or water. There is barely enough food and drink for our warriors—already we are eating the flesh of our mounts. Water at least will be eased once we secure a section of the river they now control."

"He speaks wisely," Gubta said.

"What care of it is yours? You will continue to ride."

"We fought on foot in the first battle that turned their line," Gubta said.

"And it crippled you."

"We won nevertheless, and ate cattle till we choked on the grease."

Haga, unable to reply to Gubta, looked back at Tamuka and said, "All the umens should be up by tomorrow. The following day let us ride—many will die, but we will cross the river and be into the fertile lands beyond, our horses fat again, our bellies distended from the feasting after victory."

Tamuka smiled as if in agreement. "And too many will die."

He pointed back to the river line. "This side of the riverbank here is higher than theirs. They have given it to us, and I will use it. Five days behind us come all our cannons—already I have sent twenty thousand of our remounts back to move them both day and night. Let us bring them up, and mount them wheel to wheel along the river. I will have them all fire as one, slaughtering the cattle, and only then shall we cross. Fewer of our warriors will die to these animals, and we shall laugh as we see them die by the machines they themselves created. I will not show the stupidity of a Tugar and rush my warriors into a battle not yet ready to be fought.

"I will send three mounted umens to the north, to probe into the woods, to force him to cover that side, and then the rest of us shall go straight in here," and he pointed to the plain south of Hispania.

Haga nodded slowly in agreement. "You speak wisely, Tamuka. You have combined the *ka* of your warrior to that of the *tu*, and it has given you a powerful wisdom."

"I have had the meat of one of the horse-riding cattle salted," Tamuka said. "I would be honored, Haga, if you would join me in the eating of its heart tonight."

Unable to reply to the honor, Haga bowed low.

"Let my warriors lead the first attack," the Qarth of the black horse clans said.

"The lead position shall be yours," and Tamuka smiled, hiding the terrible concern locked within, not revealing just how difficult he knew it was going to be, now that he was shorn of the ability to move his army quickly. Compounding it all was not just the fighting, but the simple question of keeping his mounts and warriors alive and fit until the battle was joined and finally won.

"I guess that's him," Andrew said, lowering his telescope and pointing to the knot of Merki on the distant hill a couple of miles from the far side of the river.

Andrew nodded to the Rus engineer standing at the corner of the bastion. The old man hesitated and then connected the wire to the telegraph battery.

Two-hundred-pound charges detonated at either end of the bridge, benzene barrels strapped to the powder igniting into fireballs. Slowly, as if not willing to die, the bridge started to sag down, and then with a rush it plummeted into the riverbed.

Andrew swung his telescope up to watch the group of warriors, one of them stepping forward several feet, hands coming to rest on his hips.

"That's it, you bastard," Andrew said, chuckling softly. "We've got all the powder in the world to waste."

Powder. It reminded him of what he had to decide, but not now.

"They came up damn fast," Pat said dejectedly, as if he had somehow failed in his delaying actions.

"Ten days from Kev to here, three hundred miles," Andrew replied, trying to sound unconcerned, "but they're strung out all to hell. It'll be five days, a week, before they're ready, and by then their belts are going to be damn tight."

He lowered the telescope, which he had been resting on the walls of the earthen bastion, and handed it over to Emil, who climbed up on the firing step to take a look. The bastion of the northern grand battery was dark, gloomy, roasting hot, the only air circulating through the firing ports, the overhead ceiling of logs and earth giving him a claustrophobic sense as if he were somehow in a tomb. In the darkness he could see his corps commanders, Barry of the First, Schneid of the Second, Mikhail Mikhailovich commanding the three-brigade division of what had once been the Third, Gregory as his chief of staff standing behind him. Pat, still up on the firing step, was second in command of the army and commander of both Fourth Corps and the artillery reserve, and then Vincent of the Sixth and Marcus of the Seventh, also commanding the Fifth, which was guarding the south of Roum and picketing the southern end of the Sangros River.

"It's only an advance line out there," Andrew said. The men looked through the firing ports, Marcus and Vincent leaning over to gaze through the open shutter door for a twelve-pound Napoleon. "We can expect the bulk of the army to be up by tomorrow."

"Think they'll attack?" Andy Barry asked, rubbing the stubble of his beard, the scar from a Tugar arrow furrowing the dark skin under his left eye.

"It's possible. That's what they've done in the past—launch a forward probe to fix our attention, and then go for the maneuver to the flank. I doubt they'll try south of here. We command the river channel, and they'd have to build boats to get through the swamps, and there isn't a stick of lumber except by the coast, where we'll keep an eye on things.

"I'm thinking it'll be north, and that's you, as we already discussed," Andrew said, nodding to Barry.

Andrew looked back down at the map, illuminated in the gloom by an overhead lantern. Two divisions out of three of Barry's First Corps were strung out along the river up into the forest, scouts ranging far to the west of the Sangros in the forest to watch for any flanking maneuvers through the woods. The third division was still working in the musket and Springfield rifle factories in Hispania; they would remain there until the fighting actually started and then would serve as a mobile reserve, waiting aboard five trains kept in the rail yard. The artillery works in Roum had already been shut down, the men transported back up to the front, their standing in the lines now more important than the few additional Napoleons or three-inch rifles they could still turn out. The powder and percussion cap works, it was decided, would continue to function even after the battle began.

"Rick, you'll hold from Hispania down a half mile into the valley."

Schneid nodded, looking up at Andrew with a grin. "If they hit here the river will be red."

"I hope they come straight at you," Andrew said, doubting that they would. Hispania, sitting up on the bluff, was a near-impregnable fortress.

It was in the center that he knew the show would start, and he traced out the line to be held by Pat's Fourth Corps, stretching directly across the center of the valley, with the heavy division that had been Third Corps deployed a half mile to their rear as reserve. On their left flank anchoring up to the grand battery of fifty guns positioned at the southern end of the bowl would be two divisions of Vincent's corps, one division in reserve, and behind them as strategic reserve was one division of Marcus's Seventh, the other two divisions holding the line farther south. He was worried about the two new corps, having debated throwing Marcus to the north to hold the flank, but had decided against it, wanting his best-trained veterans to protect that position. Both the Tugars and the Merki had preferred the turning of the flank anchored in the woods; this time there would be veterans dug in and waiting if they should try it again.

Marcus's reserve division was deployed at the switching yard built behind the grand battery. A second line of track had been built from Hispania, running parallel to the line going to Roum, which curved behind the hills, both rail lines tying into a just-completed switch yard and turntable. Using it, a mobile reserve could be moved in a matter of minutes and dropped off at any point along the six-mile rear line. Andrew realized with the building of it that it might be his only hope to counter the interior lines the Merki would occupy if they ever broke into the valley and forced him back to the surrounding hills. But if they wanted the valley they were going to have to pay for it, and he hoped that the decision might be made right there.

"The bastards are leaving," Emil said, nodding toward the distant ridge.

Andrew went back up to the firing step and took the telescope back. It was hard to see, the setting sun silhouetting the enemy commander in sharp relief.

The Merki stood with arms raised, as if using a

telescope as well, and then lowered it. Andrew felt a chill, as if a presence were trying to probe into his very thoughts. He remembered Yuri telling him that shield-bearers were capable of such things.

Where was the shield-bearer? He looked at the others. There was no bronze symbol of office, yet there was the skull-and-horsetail standard of the Qar Qarth.

Curious. Was that Vuka, or was this a trick, was the Qar Qarth elsewhere, maybe north at the forest? They had done the same thing on the Potomac, and it made him uneasy.

He watched closely. Those around the leader were obviously talking, pointing, a command council, a lowering of a head, one kneeling down for a moment, the other putting a hand on his shoulder, the kneeler standing back up.

Yet no shield-bearer, the one called Tamuka. Or was he on the other side of the ridge? The last of the riders mounted, turned, and disappeared over the other side of the slope. The one stood alone for a moment, then mounted. Andrew felt as if the Merki were somehow trying to look straight at him, to pierce into his soul. Foolish, but he sensed it nevertheless, and defiantly he stared straight back.

"I'm waiting for you, you fucking son of a bitch," Andrew whispered. Emil looked over at Andrew in surprise, having never heard Andrew use the foulest of soldier curses.

The rider raised his arm, scimitar flashing out, and he pointed the blade straight at Andrew, then turned and rode off, a circle of sentry riders following after him.

"What was that all about?" Emil whispered.

"I'm not sure," Andrew said, suddenly aware that his heart was racing.

Emil pulled out his pocket watch and looked at it, stopping first to move it back an hour and a half to readjust it from old earth time to the time on this world. "I've got a meeting with my staff. I've got to go."

"Everything ready?"

"Never be ready for what's coming," Emil said. "I want supplies for thirty thousand casualties, the doctors and nurses ready for them, and hospital trains to take the serious cases back to Roum. Hell, nearly three thousand of the boys in this army are on sick call as is, two hundred of them with typhoid, and there's typhoid in the city as well. And you ask me if I'm ready."

Andrew held up his hand and smiled.

"You know what I mean," he said, "and damn it all, I keep telling you if we take thirty thousand casualties they'll break through and it'll be over anyhow."

"Well, damn me, that's what I'm planning for. We had damn near that many at Gettysburg and we still won."

'And Lee lost around the same and lost," Pat said. "Remember I was there too."

"You didn't see the fighting the way we did," Emil replied.

"Didn't see the fighting? I was on Seminary Ridge and then Cemetery Hill the whole three days, fired over a thousand rounds, and you tell me we didn't see fighting?"

"We both saw enough at Gettysburg," Andrew said, holding up his hand for silence.

"I'm still planning for thirty thousand," Emil said and started out of the bastion.

"Tell Kathleen I'll be home around dark."

"She's on night shift in the hospital," Emil replied.

"Oh," and he struggled to control the disappointment in his voice.

"Don't worry, I'll order her home."

Andrew looked around in embarrassment at the round of suppressed chuckles.

"Rank does have its privilege," Pat announced with

a laugh, and he followed Emil out, eager to continue the well-worn argument of whether the 35th or 44th New York had been in the worst of it at Gettysburg, Antietam, Fredericksburg, or at whatever place they decided to argue about.

Made aware of the time by Emil, Andrew looked back at the group.

"Would you gentlemen excuse me," he said, and he followed the two out, moving off to one side to avoid being pulled in by Emil to back up a point.

Walking along the track that ran past the bastion, he paused to look back. The bridge was burning fiercely, oily smoke drifting straight up into the silent uncaring sky. He turned back and continued on, walking along the railroad ties. It triggered a flash memory of when he was still a boy. The first train into Maine had come through his town, the Irish work crews laying track, the old-fashioned Norris locomotive following behind the workers. He had scrambled up onto the track and then tried to walk from tie to tie, finding that they were set in such a way that his steps either had to be too long or too short. He had asked a rail layer why they were set that way and received what he guessed now must be the stock reply, that it was to keep damn fools like himself from walking on the track.

He smiled at the memory, noticing that as before the ties were set in such a way that it was impossible to walk upon them and keep a normal stride. He finally left the railbed and stepped onto the platform of the old train station, which was now serving as headquarters. Atop the building flew the flags of the two republics. Slightly lower was the flag of the Army of the Republics, and alongside it the faded and stained flags of the 35th Maine, one the blue state flag of Maine, the other the Stars and Stripes, upon its shot-torn folds emblazoned in gold letters the name of every action the regiment had fought in. He

stopped for a moment to look at them as they stirred
with the passing of a light breeze, drifting in hot from
the steppe. More than twenty actions in eight years.
It was 1869 back home. He smiled, imagining all his
old comrades back to civilian life by now, the war
undoubtably won. By now they'd most likely have a
statue up to the 35th someplace, grieving widows, parents, and orphans setting flowers before it on the
Fourth of July.

He did a quick calculation. Midsummer night here
on Valdennia had passed several days back; it was
getting near to the equivalent of July on this world.
July in Maine, best time of the year, he thought with
a sigh, but then except for mud season nearly every
month could be called a best month back home.
School would be out, a few students staying on; he'd
have the summer off to write, to go up to his summer
cottage near Waterville to fish and boat. The Fourth
of July. He could imagine Lincoln back home by now
in Illinois, practicing law again, the nation at peace.
He looked back to the west, where a thin line of
Merki pickets occupied the hills back beyond the
river, sitting astride their mounts, watching, waiting.

He sighed, knowing that he was stalling, and stepping up on to the platform, he acknowledged the salute of the sentry, dressed in the Union Army blue of
the 35th. He scanned the boy's face for a second. Not
one of the old ones from home, which would have
been an excuse to talk for another minute.

"Where you from, son?" The boy looked at him
quizzically. He asked the same question again in stumbling Latin.

"Ah, Capri."

Andrew nodded, smiled, not wanting to get into the
complexities of trying to speak in Latin, and went into
the headquarters, the boy beaming nervously, delighted that the legendary Keane had spoken to him.

He walked over to his office, which had once belonged to the stationmaster, and looked to the back door.

"You can show them in," he snapped. He went into his office, and with a dramatic flourish slammed the door shut behind him.

He went behind his desk, piled high with the usual paperwork, and he silently cursed his adjutant, who should have taken care of it. There was a knock on the door.

"Enter."

The door swung open, and John Mina stepped in, features drawn, pale, eyes hollow. Behind him Chuck entered the room, looking nervous, eyes lowered.

"I've talked to each of you alone," Andrew began, his voice cold. "I've also talked to the two other officers present, and several other witnesses."

John looked through Andrew as if he were somehow not there, his gaze fixed on the far wall.

"There will be no court-martial of Captain Ferguson."

John's gaze came back to focus, and he started to open his mouth.

"No comment from either of you, dammit."

They were silent.

"I should bust you from lieutenant colonel all the way back to private, Mr. Ferguson."

Andrew stood up and approached Chuck, coming up to within inches of his face.

"You're a loose cannon. Just because you're so goddam smart, you think you can run your own show whenever you disagree. Just how the hell am I to run an army with the likes of you?"

Chuck was silent.

"Answer me!"

"I knew I was right," Chuck whispered, shooting an angry glance over at John.

"And you were, and I emphasize were, a lieutenant colonel, and General Mina is still General Mina and your superior officer. Do I make myself clear?"

Chuck swallowed hard, saying nothing.

"Get out of my office and wait for me."

Chuck, hand shaking, saluted, and walked out.

Andrew went back and sat against the side of his desk.

"He should be in the guardhouse," said John Mina. "It's somewhere around forty tons of powder gone so far, five hundred workers wasted for a month, and that other monstrosity he's building, it's eating up brass like mad. God damn him, he should—"

"Calm down, John."

Andrew motioned for him to sit down. John hesitated and then stiffly walked over to the chair and slumped into it.

"Chuck and your two aides said you tried to pull a revolver on him, that you threatened, and I quote, 'to blow out his goddam brains and shoot his whore too.' "

John nodded and lowered his head.

"Strong language," Andrew said quietly.

"I blew my top. All these months I've been trying to keep things running, to sort out this insanity," and he vaguely waved his hand toward the window and the rail yard outside.

"I knew I was using you up, John," Andrew said soothingly. "I think you're a miracle worker, the best logistical chief I could ever have wanted. None of this would have been possible without your mind for organization. Without you, any hope I'd have for victory would be as worthless as a pile of horseshit."

"We could still use an extra five or six million rounds of ammunition, forty thousands rifles, an extra hundred field pieces."

"Shut up," Andrew said quietly.

John looked up at him.

"We just happen to have over eighty thousand smoothbore and rifled muskets, well over three hundred and fifty field pieces, ten ironclads, and eighteen million rounds of small-arms ammunition. I'm looking at what you created for us, not what you think we should have had. John, that's what's driving you insane—you think about what we should have had on your checklist. I'm telling you, I look at you and see all that we do have, and by God I thank heaven that you joined the old 35th. Otherwise I think we'd all be dead by now."

John lowered his head. His shoulders started to shake, and tears dropped to the wooden floor.

"I'm used up, I can't take it anymore, I just can't take it."

Andrew sat in silence, the only sound in the room the ticking of the clock and John's quiet sobbing. He felt a terrible wave of guilt. John was right, he had been used up, the same way Andrew had used up so many others, to buy a minute of time, to plug a hole in the line, to build an army from scratch. In a perverse sort of way, he almost envied John. The man had finally let go. He came so dangerously close, the morning Hans died, Andrew thought, defeat staring him in the face, the end of my rope, Kal pulling me back from the edge of final despair, Kathleen keeping me anchored if only for another day, a week. And then it would be finally over. But in a way John's job was finally done and he could let go of it all.

"I'm sorry, I'm so ashamed. If I could find my gun," John whispered, looking back up at Andrew, tears still streaming down his face. "I can't find my gun, you know. I want to end it, but I can't find my gun. I wish I was dead."

Andrew stepped up to John and squatted down in front of him.

"Don't. Never be ashamed. Never. You've done more than any man should be expected to do."

"And you?" John whispered.

Andrew tried to smile.

"I'm on the edge the same as you," he said softly.

John lowered his head, shaking.

Andrew got back up and slipped to the back door of his office, stepped out for a moment, and then came back in to sit on the edge of his desk. John continued to cry softly.

The door behind him finally opened, and Emil came in, breathless. He looked at John and then back at Andrew.

"John's not feeling well," Andrew said softly, and the man looked up at Andrew and then at Emil.

"Typhoid's been going around. You might have a touch of it, from the looks of you," Emil said, and John smiled weakly at the face-saving lie.

"John, please listen to me," Andrew said, and the broken man looked back up at him.

"There's all kinds of heroism in war, not just the type like Malady's or Jack Petracci's." He almost went on to mention Vincent but didn't. "I put you in the same book with those men."

John nodded.

"I'm putting you in the hospital."

"Not to Roum," John whispered. "I need to stay here. Don't send me to the rear."

Andrew shook his head and smiled.

"I wouldn't think of it. I still need you, I want you close by. But I'm ordering you into the hospital for a week or so. I'll look after your work. The toughest part is over with anyhow."

"That shortage of leather for cartridge boxes I was going to—"

Andrew put up his hand and made a gentle hushing noise.

"I'll see to it. You go get some rest. If I have any questions I'll drop in to see you. All right?"

John nodded and stood back up.

He tried to salute and started to shake again, eyes red with tears. Andrew stood up and clumsily embraced him, patting him on the back, then stood back, looking over at Emil.

To Andrew's surprise, John suddenly stood up straight, reached into his pocket, and pulled out a handkerchief to wipe his face.

"Let's go," he whispered, and walked out the back door.

Emil looked back at Andrew.

"I'll dose him with laudanum. It'll keep him quiet."

"Can you do anything?"

"You mean give him back to you ready to work? Like hell."

"I don't mean that," Andrew said wearily. "I just want him well."

"For now I just want him quiet, want to keep an eye on him so he won't hurt himself. When there's time . . ." He hesitated. "Later, I'll start talking to him, see what comes out."

Andrew nodded sadly.

"Take care of yourself, Andrew, or I'll be seeing you like this as well," Emil said and left the room. Andrew stepped over to the window and watched the two walk slowly back toward the hospital area, Emil putting his hand on John's shoulder as if to steady him, John walking stiffly, far too erect, as if struggling for a final moment of control until he was safely inside the hospital.

Andrew returned to his desk and pulled open a drawer. Picking up his old battered tin cup, he poured out a stiff dose of vodka and downed it, his eyes watering. He leaned back in his chair for a moment, looking at the clock. The room was deathly quiet, except for the ticking. The late-afternoon sun slanted in through the open window, which would be sandbagged over once the shooting started. Dust motes hung in the air, glowing red from the sunlight, drifting and swirling, and he watched them float.

Why the hell had Emil had to say that? He had seen

his worst fear played out before him, a final losing of all control, knowing Emil had not lied in telling him that he wasn't far behind.

There was no time for guilt, not now.

He sighed and put the bottle and cup away.

"Mr. Ferguson."

The door out into the waiting room swung open, and Chuck peeked in. "You call me, sir?"

Andrew nodded. "Come in, close the door, and have a seat."

Chuck slipped into the room and sat down.

"Is John all right?"

Andrew didn't reply.

"I'm sorry, sir. It was kind of hard not to hear."

"He's just tired, son. We're all tired."

"I'm sorry," Chuck sighed. "I mean, I know I went off half-cocked on the rockets and such. John kept saying no and telling you the same. I never wanted it to end like this."

"It's not your fault. It was everything, everything else. A lesser man would have broken months ago. Don't blame yourself."

"I can't help it. Now I feel like it's my fault."

"I know how you feel."

Chuck fell silent.

"What's going to happen now?" he finally asked nervously.

"You've got me over a barrel, Mr. Ferguson. That damned mind of yours gave us railroads, aerosteamers, trained mechanics to make all our tools, and God knows what else. John was right, you know—you should be court-martialed, thrown in the guardhouse, and forgotten about."

He paused.

"But damn you, I still need that mind of yours."

Chuck struggled to keep from smiling.

"But so help me God," Andrew snapped, his voice

rising, "if you ever go outside channels again, I'll personally see you hung from the nearest telegraph pole."

"Would you really, sir?" Chuck blurted out in astonishment.

Andrew leaned back, a bit ashamed of his own theatrics.

"No, I guess not. But I'll find some way to keep you in line. I'll post you to one side of wherever we are and have that daughter of Julius's sent to the far side of the Roum Republic."

Chuck's features became serious.

"I swear it won't happen again, sir."

"Right, then, we understand each other. Now go back to work."

Chuck breathed a noisy sigh of relief and stood back up.

"Use whatever supplies you've got left, but no more. Even after the fighting starts, first priority for powder goes to small arms and artillery rounds, especially canister. That other mad project of yours stops the moment the brass runs out. Understood? And from now on, any projects you might cook up come to me first."

"Yes sir."

"You do it in writing, and none of this horseshit of tricking me into signing blanket requisitions and then using them for something else."

"You found out about that too?"

Andrew wanted to tell him that he had been suspicious for weeks but decided not too. "It finally came out."

"I promise, sir. I'll toe the line."

"Fine. Now get the hell out of my office."

Chuck hurriedly saluted and fled the room.

Andrew watched as he ran out, forgetting to close the door, and stood up to close it himself.

He still wasn't sure if he had done the right thing. Nearly anyone else and he would have relieved him on the spot. But dammit, he needed the boy, the same way he needed Vincent, and Pat, and John as well. Each one different, a fine juggling act. An army needed an occasional Ferguson to keep things stirred up, the same way it needed a Mina to make sure it ran smoothly. Yet it also killed men, maybe not with a bullet, but killed their soul nevertheless.

He went back to his chair and settled down, looking at all the reports that had to be read, realizing that for the next few days he'd have to take John's job on as well, not even really sure where to begin, not ready to delegate it with the crisis now so close at hand.

The top telegram on the pile caught his eye, and he sat back and scanned it. More boys lost, the report sterile in black and white, but he had a flash image of what the final moment must have been like, falling from the sky, in flames. He reached into the drawer, pulled out the bottle, and poured another drink.

"There's the beacon."

Jack pushed the goggles up from his eyes and looked off the starboard side to where Feyodor was pointing. He waited, and then saw it, the lantern flashing brightly against the darkness of the forest.

"That's it."

He pushed the rudder forward, the ship swinging to the east, the moonlit river below drifting astern.

He had the elevator stick all the way back into his stomach, barely able to maintain height. The hydrogen bag overhead was no longer visible in the dark, but at sundown it had already been starting to look slack. How many holes were in the bag he couldn't even begin to guess. The two pursuing ships had each hit him several times. The long pursuit up the coast had gone on for most of the day, the Merki finally giving up when he had climbed well above what he guessed was nearly three miles or more, damn near freezing to death in the process, the winds aloft pushing him a hundred miles south out to sea.

The propeller was the next worry. Nicking the ironclad had cracked the blades. After they had thrown off the pursuit, Feyodor had disengaged the engine to check. A foot-long section on one blade had been sliced clean off, and the other three blades were cracked and bent. And then finally the engine itself was acting up, hissing and wheezing, the cylinder packing most likely long gone by now. He could have put down at Roum—the city was clearly visible at night—but to do so would undoubtedly have meant the end of the ship. Now he was wondering if they'd make it at all.

Directly below he saw the powder mill, the top of the building planted with trees to hide it from above, but visible now from the lantern light shining through the windows. He'd have to tell Chuck about that.

"We're getting too low."

"I've got the stick full in my gut as is. Give me more heat."

"The damn engine's red-hot now," Feyodor shouted.

"Well, shut up and hang on."

"What the hell do you think I've been doing? May all the saints curse you. I'll be damned if I'll ever fly with you again, you madman."

"Well, I wouldn't want you, you son of a bitch."

A circle of lanterns suddenly snapped to life, the ground crew unhooding them, marking out the center of the airfield.

"Throttle back to one quarter."

The rackety hum of the propeller died away, speed dropping, and the ship started to drop.

Damn. He pulled back harder on the elevator, afraid it would break off in his hands. With the speed cut back there was less lift on the elevator surface and the ship started to drop.

"Hang on."

"What the hell do you think I'm doing?"

The light of the nearest lanterns disappeared. It took him several seconds to realize why. They were dropping into the woods.

"Full power!"

The propeller hummed back up to life. A jarring blow went through the basket, the top of a pine tree snapping off directly under his feet, a branch slicing through, slashing his leg. The ship pitched forward, the basket dragging over the treetop, the propeller hitting it with a howl of splinters, and they were past it, over the field.

"Cut the engine and douse the fire!"

"Propeller's gone anyhow," Feyodor shouted.

The lanterns nearest to him were back in view, and suddenly they were moving, the ground crew picking them up and running to get out of the way, shouts now echoing up from the field below. It was impossible to see just how high they were. He hung on, bracing for the blow.

They hit the ground, Jack nearly pitching out of the basket, the overhead struts that held it to the balloon cracking.

The basket dragged along the ground, and with a shuddering groan the ship came to a stop, ground crew racing up, the support struts of the basket punching into the bag.

"Water on the engine! Kill it, kill it!" Feyodor shouted.

A hiss of steam washed over Jack as he simply let go and fell the last foot, head first, to the ground. More steam washed over him as buckets of water were thrown directly onto the engine, killing the fire, and along with it cracking the boiler and ruining it. He lay on the ground panting, afraid to move, terrified that an arrant wisp of hydrogen might hit a live spark in the engine, sending them all up in a fireball.

Hands reached out to grab him, pulling him back

up to his feet, leading him away from the ship. He looked around. He and Feyodor were surrounded by dozens of men, all of them shouting questions.

"We got three of the bastards," Feyodor announced. "Harpooned them coming out of the hangers."

A triumphal shout went up, men slapping him on the back, the crew chief eagerly pressing a bottle of vodka into Jack's hand. He took a long drink, and hugging Feyodor, he inverted the bottle over Feyodor's open mouth, the aerosteamer engineer finally choking and sputtering.

"He was better than Queequeg in *Moby-Dick*," Jack announced, not caring that the literary allusion would be totally lost, laughing with the sheer numbing relief that they were still alive, Feyodor already holding his hands up, moving them about, showing how Jack had piloted them down the line of hangers.

"How'd the others do?" Jack finally asked, and the group fell silent.

"They got nine of them."

"Well goddam, I knew Petrov would lead 'em in and get it done. Where the hell is that damn fool?"

"He didn't come back," the chief said. "He got four of them in the hangars. The last one blew up underneath him and got him too."

"What about Yuri?"

"*California Clipper* got three, and they put a flaming arrow into her. He got out alive from the wreck and the Merki captured him."

"Jesus help him," Jack whispered.

"And Ilya Basilovich?" Feyodor asked, his voice flat.

"The *Republic* got back. They got the other two, the last one fighting a mile up, then he was hit by canister. Sergei Gromica, the engineer, flew it back, but Ilya . . ."

The engineer hesitated.

"He died a couple of hours ago after they took off his leg."

Feyodor lowered his head and made the sign of the cross, the other men doing the same.

"Star of the West?"

It was the crew chief for the lost ship, standing at the edge of the crowd.

"Gone," Jack whispered, not wanting to say just how senseless the loss was, already deciding that he would lie and create a heroic end, crediting Eurik with a brilliant kill before going down in flames.

The crew chief of the lost ship lowered his head and walked away to break the news to the others who had waited throughout the long night.

Jack turned to look back at his ship in the moonlight.

"It's full of holes, the propeller's gone, and we'll need a new engine. Get it ready to go up by tomorrow. They've still got at least five ships left."

"Damn you, can't you ever come back in one piece?" the chief snapped. He hesitated and then patted Jack on the shoulder.

"We're proud of you. It worked. You got the bastards good and proper."

Jack nodded, unable to reply.

"All right, you heard the man, let's get to work," the chief said, and the crew walked off, leaving the two alone.

"I need some sleep," Feyodor sighed, lifting the half-empty bottle from Jack's hands and taking another long pull.

"Three ships gone, four pilots dead," Jack sighed. "I wish to hell I'd never thought of it."

"We had to try," Feyodor said. "It wasn't your fault, and besides, we evened things up."

"Yeah, sure."

"Try to get some sleep," Feyodor said. "You know we'll have to go back out again tomorrow."

"Thanks."

The engineer handed the bottle back, turned, and walked off into the darkness.

He stood alone. It was so strange, the silence after thirty hours of the howling engine. His knees felt like rubber, the ground tingling beneath his feet.

"You did well."

Jack looked up, recognizing the voice, and saw a shadowy form standing before him.

"Thanks, Chuck, but I lost four good pilots today."

"I heard."

Jack said nothing, leaning back to look at the stars overhead, the horizon to the east already streaked with the first light of approaching dawn.

"Come on home with me. Olivia's waiting up. She managed to find some real eggs, and a slab of salt pork. It'll do you good."

Jack turned, walking silently beside Chuck, following him across the clearing and back to the cabin, pausing for a moment to watch as the ground crew chopped the basket and engine off from under the ship, working in the dark for fear of a leak. He turned away and continued on, the light in the cabin window ahead suddenly warm and inviting.

"So what have you been up to while I was away?" Jack finally asked woodenly, as if the conversation might help to drive out the memories.

Chuck shook his head, unable to reply.

Chapter 10

Shagta was low on the horizon, crescent-horned. The Great Wheel moved westward, the stars so bright that he felt as if he could reach up to touch them.

Tamuka sat alone, head back, watching the heavens. He smiled. Could it be that once we truly walked between the stars, ruling the universe, entering the gates of light to emerge in distant places?

He sighed. If true, so much have we lost. He let his imagination race, dreaming, the people of the hordes leaping across the universe to far worlds, the universe at their feet. He remembered the chant of Tuka, brother of Gormash, god of fire, and how they had fought against the powers of the darkness. Gormash had died, his soul becoming the sun, which gave light to this world, and Tuka had left, mourning his brother, unable to bear the sight of his flaming soul, proclaiming that the map of the heavens should be brought before him, so that he could discover what worlds were left to conquer.

Worlds to conquer.

Tamuka stirred. Around him was a low but steady rumble. The first of the cannons had come up yesterday, and the last were arriving even now. Already his hosts were up, moving to their positions, the assault to begin after the chanting of the greeting to day, to Gormash. Far to the north the battle had already started, two umens fighting in the forest, gaining little, not even up in the forest, the cattle fighting well.

The thought bothered him, to think that animals could fight well. No sense of honor, of the ritual of war, of glory. It was a shame to waste the blood of the horde in such a way, for in years to come no one would chant his tales of glory and skill when describing a fight against mere cattle. It was a job of slaughtering and nothing more.

Yet through them I have gained my power as Qar Qarth, he realized. For without them Jubadi would still be alive, perhaps even Mupa as well, and I would still be shield-bearer to the Zan Qarth Vuka.

He looked back up to the heavens.

"Do you now understand why I did as I did?" he whispered, fearful again that Hulagar was stirring, looking down upon him.

He was afraid even to think the darker thoughts, the realization that when he had sent out the cattle Yuri with the supposed intent of killing Keane, there was yet another twist to the plot, a path he had dimly seen, that Yuri would serve Keane, and perhaps even return to kill Jubadi.

And he had.

And I killed Vuka and am now Qar Qarth.

They could never have seen all that I now understand, Tamuka thought, as if searching for some justification to ease the gnawing of guilt. This is a war unto death with the cattle, and here will be decided who will rule this world, whether it will be a world of cattle or of the hordes. He alone had seen that with such crystal clarity. Some of the others perceived it dimly, and thus fought; others sought but vengeance; others fought simply because it was a fight and that is what a warrior did. Yet few understood exactly where all of this could lead if the cattle lived.

There were other hordes, southward of the Bantag yet four, perhaps five more, supposedly even greater than the sixty umens of the Bantag. They rode oblivious to what was being decided here, asleep now in their yurts, dreaming of past glories, soon to rise to seek battle against their equals or to feast off cattle, or whatever creatures they ruled in their lands.

Yet here, in the next days, it would be decided. He held a dream beyond this, and he saw two paths to it. To slaughter the Yankees, the Roum, the Rus, to slaughter all of the cattle wherever he rode, was part of that dream, for now that they had risen up, they must not be allowed to live, to dream of some future time to rise and kill again. Hulagar had hoped that when the war was finished life could return to what it was, an endless circling of the world yet again, as it had been for over two hundred circlings before. But now he could sense another dream, a different one, and that was to take the machines, to learn their mastery, from them to build even greater machines, until one day the Merki ruled the entire world, all other hordes subservient and uniting under him. And from there to use the gates of light, to find their means of control, and to leap across the stars, retaking all that had once been—like Tuka, to spread forth the map of the heavens and rediscover what worlds there were to conquer.

. He thought of the ark, which even now resided in the yurt of Sarg, containing within it the great scrolls, written in the lost languages of the ancients, supposedly containing within them the true histories, marking where the gates appeared, the means of controlling them. It was said that the ancients used them deliberately at first to walk between worlds and to bring forth cattle and other beasts as slaves and that the art of them was now lost, that the gates opened and closed as if by their own will. The language of them was lost, but it could be relearned.

And as he thought of the ark he remembered the other thing that resided with it, the urn that contained the moldering heart of Jubadi, the dust of the hearts of all the Qar Qarths. Vuka's heart is not in it, he thought, but mine will be when I at last go to join my ancestors. Already he was forming that plot as well, to make sure that when the time came, the cousins of Jubadi who might pretend to the saddle of the Qar Qarth would be no more and a new lineage would be proclaimed.

A string of oaths broke the silence, and he looked to his right. A torch flickered, showing a line of wagons, cannons moving forward, whips cracking. The procession passed on, moving down the slope, heading to the rise on the bank of the river. Beside it a solid block of warriors marched, most likely the umens of the black horse, he thought, the first wave to go in.

He turned, looked back to the east, and closed his eyes again, letting his spirit soar.

You are not asleep, he realized, sensing the stirring, the lying awake, fear clutching at the heart. Good. Be afraid. I am coming for you. Your heart I shall carve out of your living body. Your brain is already devoured.

He smiled and let the vision form. Today it would begin.

He opened his eyes, not sure if he had been dreaming or if the vision had somehow been real. He knew, damn him, he was here, inside of me, cutting into me, he thought.

Shaken, Andrew sat up. The bedsheets were clammy with sweat. He stood and walked over to the window and looked out. Still night. He looked at the clock in the town forum. Almost two in the morning. The narrow street below was empty, but he could sense that few were sleeping tonight. He opened the window shutters and leaned out, thankful for the cooling breeze on his naked body. A soft crying echoed from the house across the alleyway, a woman's voice sobbing, a man talking soothingly. There was another sound from the next house, of pleasant and gentle lovemaking, and he could not help but listen for a moment, not embarrassed, touched, imagining the fear inside both as they clung to each other. A baby cried from up the street, and a moment later the cry was stilled by a soft lullaby in Rus.

"Come to bed."

He turned and looked back. Kathleen was sitting up, looking at him.

"Can't sleep."

She slipped out of the bed and came up, putting her arm around his waist, pressing up against him, resting her head on his shoulder. She listened with him, laughed softly.

"That's Gregory's room, isn't it?" she asked.

He smiled and nodded. Gregory's young bride had found a room in the city, a nearly impossible feat.

Again he had a flash image—the other, standing in the darkness, looking at him, waiting.

"You're shaking."

"Just chilled."

She went back to the bed and pulled a blanket off, came back up and put it over his shoulders moving around to hold him underneath the blanket.

"He's looking for me," Andrew whispered.

"Who?"

"Him. I'm not sure. It's as if he were inside my head, trying to probe my thoughts, to make me afraid of him. Yuri told me about him, the shield-bearer."

"Superstition."

"I'm not sure," Andrew whispered.

The sounds from Gregory's room died away, a gentle laugh replacing the passion, and then a moment later there were tears as well.

Andrew smiled sadly.

"All we wanted was to live in peace," he whispered. "Just to be left alone. Was that too much to ask for?"

"Maybe someday."

A door creaked open, and he looked out. Up the

street a man appeared, white tunic of a Rus, sword of an officer at his side, blanket roll over his shoulder. He stopped, and a woman came out, hugging him fiercely, a small child grabbing hold of his leg. He gently pulled himself away, and the child started to cry. He bent down, picked the child up, and hugged him, then gave the crying boy back to his mother, who held him tightly. The man walked down the street, passing under Andrew's window, not even knowing that he was being watched. He continued on, not looking back, yet Andrew could sense the man was in tears, now letting them fall where he felt no one would see him. The woman and child stood in the street, watching, both crying, and then disappeared back into the house.

"I hope he makes it," Kathleen said, her words choked.

How many won't? he thought. By the end of this day, how many will be left, and how many will be silent, unclosed eyes looking straight up to the heavens, waiting with luck for the burial, or for the pits of the Merki? He tried to imagine it over with, the unknown man he had just seen running back up the street to a waiting embrace; tried not to imagine the other.

"I have to get ready," Andrew whispered.

"Come back to bed."

He knew what she was thinking, what she wanted.

"I can't," he sighed, embarrassed suddenly, knowing that he couldn't make love, not now. It would have too much of a sense of finality to it, something he couldn't bear.

"No, not that," she whispered, and led him away from the window, lying down atop the sheets, gently pulling him down alongside.

"Just hold me," she whispered. "Please hold me."

She grabbed hold of him fiercely, and the tears

came, sobs bursting out, the sound muffled against his chest.

He put his single arm around her, holding her, kissing the top of her head, the smell of her hair pleasant, so familiar. Ashamed, he tried to hold back his own tears, which were wetting her hair.

"It's all right, love, it's all right," she whispered.

The crying drifted away into a gentle quiet, both remembering so much, all that they had been together. He realized that never had he felt such love for her as he did now, and that if he should die today, if it should all be lost, he at least had this moment. He felt the tears coming again, finding it impossible to imagine that it might be ending now, today, that when he rose up and went out the door, it was finished forever.

It all came down to the simplest of things, a child in your arms, lying awake in the early morning with your lover, a walk through the woods on a snowy day, a warm fire waiting at home. All of it so simple, yet so precious, living all so precious when it was on the edge of being lost. Funny, he mused, we never think about this while alive, the wonder of it all, only when it is lost, or going away into the night.

"If something should happen to me . . ." he whispered.

"Please, no, don't."

"Hush."

She started to cry again.

"If something should happen to me, I want you to know how much I love you, how much I'll always love you, even after I'm gone. I'll wait for you, I'll wait forever for you."

"Don't die, please don't die, I couldn't live without you."

"There'll always be Maddie."

She nodded.

He held her tight, pulling her in as if he could somehow press her soul into his own. In the distance a bell tolled twice.

"I've got to go," he whispered. "It's time."

She nodded, her tears soaking his chest, but wouldn't let go.

He waited another minute and then two, unwilling to leave, praying that if there was a way to stop all time it would be now, freezing them at the edge of the abyss, holding back the day to come forever.

She took a deep breath, sighed, and let go, looking back up into his face.

"I love you."

"I love you," he whispered and gently pulled away.

He stood up, not looking back at her, lit a candle, and started to dress. She slipped on a robe and came over to help him, buttoning his shirt, taking down his field jacket from its hanger, helping him to pull it on. She opened a dresser drawer and brought out his red sash, wrapped it around his waist, tying the ends together, and then helped to buckle on his sword belt and revolver.

He had never grown used to needing help with getting dressed, but this morning he was grateful for the sharing. She went to the dresser and came back with a small box and opened it. Inside was his Congressional Medal of Honor won at Gettysburg.

"Wear it today."

He nodded, knowing that for her it was some sort of talisman. She pinned the medal to his breast.

She picked up the candle and went to the door.

"Let me get breakfast for you." Her voice was hopeful, as if a few additional moments could thus be stolen.

"I'll grab something down at headquarters."

She nodded and went down the stairs, and he followed her, the tip of his sword scabbard banging on the steps behind him. She opened the door and put the candle on the side table. In the dim light her long flowing red hair seemed to shine, her pale skin and green eyes iridescent in the light.

They stood looking at each other, and he stepped forward, grabbing hold of her, lifting her off the ground, hugging, kissing her on the neck, the lips, and then ever so slowly let her slip to the ground.

She started to speak, and he put a finger to her lips.

"I love you," he whispered, and turning, he stepped out into the street, shoulders back, and started down to the city gate. He knew she was watching, crying, but he wouldn't look back.

Again there was a flash moment, the image formed, the Merki standing before him, scimitar drawn, the world about him in ruins and he the last to die after witnessing the final horror.

He struggled and pushed the thought away, focusing on the memory of her standing in the doorway, the taste of the last kiss still on his lips. He continued on, and from other doorways, one after another, other men emerged, saying their goodbyes, and started to fall in around him, moving to the city gate and the fate that waited on the other side.

"Bringer of life, bringer of day, sun of the heavens, we bow in greeting to thy presence."

As Sarg intoned the chant the cry was picked up, hundreds of thousands of the Merki thundered the words, the steppes reverberating with their cry, the serried ranks going down to their knees, bowing low, taking a ritual handful of dust and pressing it to their foreheads to remind them of what they came from and to what they would return. The great nargas of the Qar Qarth sounded, the brazen cry picked up by the nargas of the clan chiefs, the commanders of five umens, the umen commanders, and finally the commanders of a thousand.

Tamuka came back up to his feet, turning to bow to the west, to the last fleeing of night, the ride of the ancestors, and the hundreds of thousands of warriors followed his lead, armor creaking, accouterments rattling, scimitars flashing up in salute, hundreds of thousands of blades flickering in the first light of dawn.

The great cry died away, and they turned, facing back to the east, to where the cattle waited.

A mild breeze stirred from the steppe behind them, harbinger of a day of heat. From his vantage point he looked to the south. Along the ridge four umens were arrayed on foot, standing in rank in the checkerboard pattern, the regiment of a thousand a hundred across and ten deep, five regiments to the front rank, five to the rear, two umens to a league of front. Behind them on the reverse slope stood six more umens, and deployed behind them were ten more, and stretching in a great arc yet fourteen more on a front that ran from north to south for twenty miles. Far to the north in the forest were two umens on foot, the fighting there now in its second day. And behind them all were yet four more umens on horse, waiting to ride when the breakthrough had been achieved.

All was ready.

He turned to the pennant holder.

"Let it begin."

The red flag was raised from the ground and held aloft. Far forward, on the low bluff near the river, a single puff of smoke snapped out, long seconds later the dull thunderclap boom echoing back. And then from one end to the other, three hundred cannons of the Merki fired, the first round of the opening barrage.

"For that which we are about to receive . . ." Andrew whispered, as the first gun of the Tugar line fired. Suddenly the entire west bank of the river, eight hundred yards away, disappeared.

". . . we thank you kindly, Lord," and he ducked low as the first shot screamed overhead. A hail of artillery rounds passed over, plumes of dirt geysering up in front of the bastion, the earth-and-log walls of the fortress shaking from the impact, dirt flying up over the walls.

"Let her go!" an excited Rus artillery commander shouted, and stepping up to the three-inch rifle, which he had aimed with care, he grabbed hold of the lanyard and stepped back.

"Stand clear!"

He jerked the lanyard back, the gun kicking with a high piercing crack, the round screaming downrange. He peered through the smoke, field glasses raised, and saw the flash of light.

"By damn, right over 'em! Now pour it on!"

The other thirty guns of the northern grand battery, all of them Napoleons or one of the precious three-inch rifles, opened up, the four surviving guns of the old 44th New York firing a salvo that cracked out like a single shot.

Andrew watched the opening rounds slam into the Merki artillery line, hitting the rough earthworks they had thrown up to protect the battery. A Merki gun rose up, flipping over, a second later a caisson detonating, the thunderclap of the explosion washing back over the lines, men standing up down in the trenches and cheering defiantly. These would be the best shots we'll make, Andrew realized, the smoke from the first volley already obscuring the view.

He looked south. Along the four miles of entrenchments across the valley floor, half a dozen batteries opened up, their return fire capped by the grand battery to the far south, that position again a mix of Napoleons and three-inch pieces. Strict orders had already been issued that return fire was to be slow and measured, ammunition conserved and only used when a target was clearly visible. Counterbattery fire was of secondary importance when compared to the task of smashing the charges once they started.

He looked down at his watch, going through the ritual of turning the time back to match the station clock behind him. It was four-thirty in the morning.

Jack Petracci wheeled his ship around. The air smelled sulfurous; the intense barrage below had been going on for nearly two hours. He could see that the fire was slackening from his own side, some of the guns completely silent, others firing not more than once every two or three minutes. The Merki line continued to fire away, and as he looked back to the east he saw a caisson go up near the center of the line. He watched the explosion soar up and then come back down, several bodies tumbling.

Directly below, the Merki artillery line was impossible to observe, so thick was the smoke which now eddied down over the riverbed in great sheets like a spreading fog.

He leaned back in his cab and stretched. Except for the climactic battle below, the morning was actually uneventful, the air still, even though it was approaching midmorning. Yesterday three Merki ships had been up in an attempt to go over the line for a recon, but the sight of his own squadron of three had caused them to turn back. Maybe the fight was out of the bastards and he could have the air to himself. He looked off to the north. Far to the horizon he saw *China Seas*, a distant speck of white, hovering over the woods, observing if the Merki were attempting to shift north, the battle in the forest at a standstill along the banks of the river. A skirmish was brewing up a dozen miles north, the Merki already attempting to cross the river at a place where the eastern bank was low, but the river was chest-deep for a human and at least hip-deep for them. They'd be sitting ducks for the men of First Corps. Parties of Merki had been attempting to infiltrate for three days previous, several succeeding, one getting right up to the powder factory before being detected and destroyed. Now it was flaring up to a full-pitch battle at last.

"That red banner is fluttering again," Feyodor shouted, and pointed straight down to what they assumed had to be the Merki command post.

Jack leaned over to watch, noticing that other flags were now waving in front of the enemy ranks. Above the roar of the artillery he heard a low steady chanting, growing louder.

"I think they're gearing up for the charge."

The first line started forward at a walk, a three-mile-wide advance of Merki, forty thousand strong.

"Here it comes! Cut power and send the signal! Four umens coming straight in."

Feyodor cut loose the red pennant coiled up under the basket, the flag unrolling, Jack turning his ship to point straight back toward headquarters so that the flag was visible full on. Next he tied four green flags for the umens and one orange flag to signify the center of the line between two ropes, which were spread apart by wooden dowels so that the flags would not flutter astern but rather be clearly visible to the front. He lowered them down in front of the red flag so that they would show up clearly.

"All right, let's head for home," Jack shouted. "We need to top off the hydrogen—it's still leaking from those new patches."

Feyodor lowered a second flag of yellow, to signal they were returning to base, and then suddenly cut the power back.

Jack looked back anxiously, frightened at first that the new engine had seized up. Forward speed dropped, and Feyodor leaned over the side of the ship, looking straight down. He struck a friction-head match mounted into the neck of a ten-gallon jug of benzene, let it drop, and then started the power back up again.

Jack leaned over to watch as it plummeted a half mile down. For a second he thought it was going to hit the enemy command post straight on, but instead it impacted fifty or more yards away, at least catching several of the Merki standing to one side. They twisted and writhed on the ground, and Jack howled with delight.

He pointed the ship north and headed back in to the air station.

"We've got company," Feyodor shouted, and Jack looked astern to see three Merki ships coming up out of the west. He quickly judged the distance, fifteen miles or more. He had two harpoons and was tempted to swing back out for a fight. But already the elevator was too far back; there must be a major leak opening up. *China Sea* and *Republic* could run interference for right now. He shouted for Feyodor to open up the throttle full-bore as he turned north-northeast.

Pat looked over excitedly at the telegrapher hunched over his machine down in the command dugout.

The boy looked up.

"Report from headquarters. Aerosteamer reports Merki have begun advance, four umens coming our way."

Pat nodded, a sardonic grin lighting his face.

"Sound the alarm. Get the boys up and ready."

He ran up out of the bunker. The air was thick with smoke. An artillery round screamed overhead, plowing into a torn-up vineyard a hundred yards to the rear, vines and their frames hurtling up into the air.

If the barrage was designed for killing, it was doing precious little. He'd lost four guns and a caisson, maybe a couple of dozen infantry, but to think they could be shaken loose by a bombardment while hunkered down in the trenches was absurd. He looked up at a mortar round hissing down, striking the ground near where the last round had hit, the fuse failing.

He climbed up on the firing step and looked

through the firing slot, his staff standing around him anxiously, ducking low as another shot screamed past.

"The Merki couldn't hit the broad side of a barn," he laughed and turned back, remembering with a sudden superstitious dread that old Uncle John Sedgwick had said the same thing at Spotsylvania and was dead before the words were out of his mouth.

The view forward was nothing but smoke. At least the barrage was providing that.

The sound of the bombardment from the far side of the river died away. They must be crossing through the guns. Bugles sounded along the line, drums rolled, and men stepped up to the firing line, muskets poked through the firing slits, loaders standing down in the trench, ready to grab empty guns and pass up reloads. The excitement was electric. No more running withdrawals, abandoning positions; this was going to be a stand-up knock-down, and they were ready. An angry defiant cheering started, swelling, racing down the line, a high rising scream of rage that sent a corkscrew chill down his back.

Officers were walking the line, shouting, chanting the same refrains over and over.

"Wait for the order, wait for the order."

"Aim low, boys, aim low."

A spattering of rifle fire sounded forward in the smoke.

He turned his head, his good ear cocked toward the enemy line. He could hear them now, even above the yelling of his own men. A steadily rising chant, growing louder.

From out of the smoke a thin line of men appeared, running low, skirmishers coming in, weaving their way along the marked paths through the deadfalls and abatis.

"They're coming, millions of them, in the river!"

A man wiggled through the firing slit into the trench next to him, panting hard.

"Got one of the bastards," he said proudly between gasps.

The damn river was too low, calf-deep for most of them, easily passable along its rocky bottom. He wished he could have held it there, but the heights on the other side would have given the Merki a plunging fire that would have been killing.

The chanting was sounding louder, coming forward, a horn sounding, other horns picking up the brazen cry.

He found himself breathing hard. It sounded like an ocean rolling in, a wave of insanity, screaming, advancing at the run, the thunder of their approach filling the world.

The smoke curled, shadows within moving.

"Get ready!"

To his left he heard a roaring explosion, Vincent's divisions opening with a crackling volley. He pulled himself up out of the trench through a narrow sally port, his staff shouting at him angrily.

"Ah, shut the hell up," he roared, and raising his glasses, he looked to the south.

Coming up out of the riverbed and onto the flood plain of the valley was a solid wall of Merki, casualties going down by the hundreds from the artillery and rifle fire to the left, a thick curtain of smoke rising up from Vincent's trenches.

"That's it, Hawthorne!" Pat screamed. "Feed it to 'em, God damn their souls, feed it to 'em!"

"General O'Donald, for Perm's sake get down!"

Pat turned and looked back to the west.

Less than a hundred yards away, masses of Merki were advancing out of the smoke, at the run, screaming their battle chants, standards held high, red flags down, pointed forward.

Pat raised his arm up high.

"Take aim!"

He heard the chilling yet reassuring sound of thousands of musket locks clicking back.

"Fire!" and he dropped his arm.

The volley slashed out, and it appeared as if the entire front rank of the Merki charge simply collapsed. artillery, loaded with solid shot and a load of canister on top, kicked off, the deep-throated bellow of the Napoleons counterpointed by the high cracking whine of the light four-pounders.

The charge continued in. From out of the cloud of smoke a darker wall rose up, the unleashing of over twenty thousand bows, fired by the two umens supporting the assault of the two umens going straight in.

Pat leaped back down into the trench, pressing himself up against the wall.

"Volley coming in!" he screamed.

A hail of arrows slammed down onto the overhead roof of earth-covered boards, the iron-tipped hail rattling with a near explosive roar, shafts suddenly raining down to the front and rear. Other arrows started to come in low on a flatter trajectory. A rifleman wordlessly tumbled back from the firing step, the tip of an arrow driven out the back of his skull.

A steady staccato roar of gunfire raced up and down the line. Pat looked up forward. Merki continued to drop, sprays of canister wiping out whole sections at a time. Yet still they continued in, tumbling into pitfalls, tripping and falling on top of sharpened stakes, tumbling and writhing in agony. A steady, near-hysterical screaming thundered up from both sides, the deep-throated booming roar of the Merki, the higher-pitched screams of the men, the pent-up fury and rage of both sides released in a maniacal frenzy of killing.

Yet as fast as they dropped them, more sprang up to take the place of the fallen, archers moving in, crouching low, firing with deadly skill, arrows slicing in through firing ports.

The covered trench was filled with a choking cloud

of smoke, the view forward obscured, men firing at shadows. Pat started to walk up and down the line.

"Feed it to them, God damn their souls, feed it to them!"

He paused, climbing up to where a battery was deployed above the trench, protected by high earthen walls and a roof of planking. The gunners were taking casualties, bolts slamming through the wide firing ports. He pushed a gun sergeant aside and peered down the barrel. Cursing, he grabbed hold of the screw handle under the breech and cranked it up higher so that it seemed as if the shot would almost strike the ground directly in front. The loader finished, the crew ran the gun back up, and Pat sighted once more.

"Stand clear!"

He jerked the lanyard back, the Napoleon leaping, the smoke in front swirling from the load of canister screaming downrange, striking into the Merki line at knee height.

"Keep it up!"

He climbed back down into the main trench and started back to his command bunker, stepping over the bodies of the fallen, moving aside as two stretcher-bearers carried a soldier to the aid station, the old man choking on his own blood, the broken end of an arrow sticking out of his mouth.

"Pressure's building with Morrison's brigade," an aide shouted, looking up from the telegraph station. "Merki into the trenches."

Pat nodded, listening as the key continued to chatter.

"Requests support of the reserve division."

"Not yet, not yet," Pat growled. "The goddam day's only started."

Cursing angrily, Jack paced up and down in front of *China Sea*'s hangar.

"Get the damn engine going, get it going. God-dammit, you never should have come back in. *Republic*'s the only one up there."

The pilot looked up at him, just as angry.

"The piston's cracked! It's got to be replaced!"

Jack knew the man was right—the ship had barely limped in, minutes behind his own—but not now, why did it have to be now?

The warning bugle continued to blow, and Jack looked back at the watchtower. In the distance he could hear the staccato of musketry from the fight on the other side of the river. But there was a closer sound, four-pound artillery, close by.

"They've stopped over the powder mill. *Republic*'s got one of them. The powder mill guns are firing."

The watcher started to jump up and down excitedly.

"They've got one, right over the mill, it's going in!"

Jack started to run back to *Yankee Clipper*. Atop the bag he could see his own crew chief.

"How is it?"

"Broken spar. Some bastard didn't retie it right—it's ripped a hole through bigger than my Aunt Mari's ass. All the hydrogen's gone."

"Get the hell down. We're going back up."

"You're crazy!"

"Get the hell down, or they'll burn us on the ground."

A dull whoosh cut through the air, and he started to turn. From the corner of his eye he saw a tremendous fireball rising up from out of the forest, and a split second later a thunderclap explosion snapped over him, the blow staggering him. The sound of shattering glass washed over the field, the fireball continuing to climb.

He steadied himself and looked back.

"Merciful Perm, it's the powder mill," Feyodor shouted, running up to Jack's side.

"We've got to get her up," Jack shouted, and turned to run to his ship.

He reached the basket, and Feyodor started to climb in.

"Just set the engine on full. I can work the throttle from up front."

"Like hell."

"It's leaked too much gas—it'll never get off the ground with both of us! Now do it!"

Feyodor hesitated, and Jack forced a weak grin.

"You said you were sick of flying with me."

Feyodor stepped out of the cab and took Jack's hand.

"I never meant it."

"Liar."

Jack climbed into the cab, and reaching over into Feyodor's side, he grabbed the engage for the propeller and pulled it forward. He looked to his port side and saw the crew chief sliding down from a support rope and landing heavily.

"Get the hell out," the chief screamed, running up alongside Jack even as he started to taxi *Yankee Clipper II* out onto the field. "You've got no lift—the gas in the forward bag's gone!"

"Out of my way!"

Throttle full open, he pushed the rudder stick forward, the airship bouncing along the ground. There was no need for a ground crew to restrain the ship. He floated up slowly, gaining only a couple of feet. The woods on the east side of the field were straight ahead, coming up fast.

He reached back into Feyodor's cab and disengaged the propeller, pushing the rudder hard to the left. The ship turned ponderously, its nose barely missing the edge of the forest. And as the ship turned around, he looked back to the west and saw them.

To either side of the fireball that had once been the powder mill, two Merki ships were bearing in, the first already over the far side of the field, barely above the trees, coming on fast.

"No, God damn you!"

He grabbed hold of the propeller engage and slammed it, the blades humming up to a blur. With elevator stick full in his stomach he started forward, the nose ever so slowly lifting up as he gained speed.

The Merki ship continued straight on, passing over *China Sea*. He saw the harpoon go down and hit. There was a moment as if nothing had happened, and then the blue flame started to race across the top of the ship, blowing into the tail end, which was still inside the hangar.

China Sea disappeared in a fireball explosion, the victorious Merki ship now turning slightly to come straight on.

Ground crew, armed with crossbows, the flaming tips of the bolts wrapped with kerosene-soaked cotton, ran across the field, aiming up at the enemy ship, firing, the bolts disappearing into the vessel. Jack didn't even see them, he was looking up, the nose of *Yankee Clipper* rising slowly, the cab barely hovering above the ground but slowly gaining height.

The shadow of the enemy ship was racing straight at him, his own vessel now blocking the view. He felt something hit. The shadow of the enemy ship was past, and for a brief second he thought he was going to make it. He looked to one side and saw ground crew, running—away from him, and the ship started to sag down, twisting on its long axis at the same time.

He vaulted up to the side of the basket and leaped out, hitting the ground hard, feeling something in his ankle give way with a crack. He went down and then came back up, feeling the heat of the fireball on his neck. Men to either side were running, but one came straight at him, Feyodor, grabbing him around the waist and bodily picking him off the ground, running hard. The fireball washed out around them, and Feyodor went down, covering Jack with his own body. The scorching flame shot over their heads, not touching the ground, the burning hydrogen racing up into the sky.

Feyodor came back up, grabbed Jack by the collar of his flight overalls, and ran a bit farther before collapsing down to the ground by his side, panting.

"Second time you've done that," Jack gasped.

"If I didn't save your ass I'd have to fly with some other damn fool with even worse luck."

Jack turned to looked back at *Yankee Clipper II* as it collapsed in upon itself, flame soaring to the heavens. Another shadow raced pass, the ship climbing steeply, no targets left on the ground for it to kill.

"They got the bastard," someone shouted, and Jack looked up to see the Merki ship that had hit him buckling up over the forest a half mile to the north, flame gushing out of both ends of the ruptured bag. The Merki ship, which had no internal support, collapsed in upon itself, sections of the paper-and-silk bag spiraling up, the basket underneath and what was left of the ship going down in flames.

All around him was chaos, two ships burning in the field, the powder mill a mile away burning fiercely.

Feyodor helped Jack up, supporting him as he walked on his good leg, and they hobbled across the field back to the headquarters building. High overhead another engine sounded, and he looked up to see *Republic* swinging out in pursuit of the Merki ship.

"One ship left," Jack said, his voice weak.

Feyodor said nothing, helping him along, their crew chief coming up to lend a hand.

They cut a wide circle around the flaming ruins of *China Sea,* half a dozen men lying still around it, blankets already covering their burned and broken bodies. They reached the headquarters, which was filled with wounded.

"Put me outside," Jack gasped as he looked in at

an unrecognizable man writhing on the table, his skin black, the smell of charred flesh thick in the air.

Feyodor got a blanket and laid it out against the far side of the cabin, and together with the crew chief he helped Jack to lie down.

Smoke drifted through the woods, coming up from the burning mill. Ghostlike, from out of the smoke, Chuck Ferguson appeared, walking numbly. He stopped and looked out over the field and then came up to Jack.

"So they got here too."

"They learn quick," Jack said. "What happened back there?"

"I'd just come out of the building. I wanted to get up here because of the alarm. It was the damnedest thing. Their aerosteamer came straight in at the factory, dropping right down on top of it, and four Merki leaped off carrying torches and went in. They blew themselves and the ship up. The damnedest thing."

He shook his head.

"Two hundred people in there," he whispered.

"Theodor?" Feyodor asked anxiously.

"Your brother's all right. He was with me, he's sorting things out now. But not much to sort."

Chuck stood back up, still in shock.

"The damnedest thing."

From out of the smoke, Theodor suddenly appeared, running hard, and his twin brother rushed up to him, hugging him tightly, the two obviously fearful for the safety of the other. Theodor broke away from Feyodor's embrace and cautiously walked up to Chuck.

Chuck looked back at him.

"I told you to stay at the factory."

Feyodor, his features pained, said nothing.

Chuck looked away from him and turned back to Jack.

"Let's get you over to my place, and the other wounded as well. Olivia can help tend them."

"Mr. Ferguson?"

He turned and looked back at Theodor, surprised at the formal tone.

"What is it?"

"She's not at your place."

"What do you mean?" His voice trailed away. "I just left her there an hour ago."

"She came to the factory to look for you."

"What do you mean?" Already his voice was breaking.

"She's alive, sir, but . . ."

"What are you saying? He grabbed hold of Theodor, shaking him.

"She's burned, sir, bad, real bad. They just pulled her out."

He pushed Theodor away and stood silent, swaying.

"Olivia!" It was a drawn-out shriek of pain, and he ran madly off, back into the smoke, Theodor following.

"Here it comes," Andrew said coldly.

A light breeze had finally stirred up from the west, causing the smoke to drift over the battlefield, revealing the opposite shore. A solid column of Merki, a full regiment across and three or more umens deep, started down the hill. Beside them, gunners were limbering up their artillery, ready to push the guns forward. To the rear of the column another umen was forming, mounted warriors, scimitars flashing.

Andrew looked up at the blazing sky, the sun hanging motionless, the heat well above ninety. The hammering had been going on for nearly eight hours without letup. Fourth Corps had almost been overrun twice, fighting raging in the trenches hand to hand, Pat finally committing his entire reserve division.

The charge was coming straight to the left of center. Andrew came out of his headquarters, Schneid following.

"Get your reserve division aboard the trains, move

them directly to the center, position them on the forward slope ready to go in. Now move it."

He ducked low as a shell screamed overhead, slamming into the side of his headquarters, the round detonating with a thunderclap, limestone dust and splinters raking across the yard. He stood up and looked back at his headquarters staff at the back of the bastion.

"Get Barry to shift one of his reserve brigades down here—he's holding his own with what he has. I'll be at Third Corps headquarters."

An orderly brought Mercury up, and he mounted, guidon bearer, messenger staff, and bugler falling in around him.

He nudged Mercury forward, crossing over the tracks, moving through the stake-marked path that guided them out of the line of entrenchments atop the ridge and out into the open valley below. To his right, a quarter mile away, was the main line, still manned by Schneid's first division, the position holding well, protected by the grand battery anchoring its flank atop the bluff.

He gave Mercury a gentle tap with his heels, and the horse leaped forward, heading down across the open field, gaining a narrow dirt road which weaved through a row of vineyards, most of it crushed flat by the barrage. A steady stream of walking wounded filled the road, heading up the hill to the hospital area on the east side of Hispania. He knew Kathleen was there; he didn't want to think about what she must now be doing.

Vincent Hawthorne stood up from the trench, gasping hard for breath, squinting to see through the smoke. The ground before him was black with bodies, the last wave having gained the trench, the battle degenerating into saber, bayonet, and clubbed musket. He opened his hand, the blood still flowing from the saber cut to his arm, trickling over the dried blood of the Merki he had shot in the throat at point-blank range.

It had felt good, and the pain of his own wound was barely noticed.

"Here it comes!"

From up over the edge of the riverbank, he saw the standards, the far bank of the river black with them, wave after wave sliding down, splashing into the river. The grand battery to his left, up on the south hill, plunged in a devastating crossfire, shells bursting over the river, solid shot raking the riverbank, knocking down entire rows, but still they came on.

The first line appeared up over the low edge of the riverbank, two hundred and fifty yards away. Sheets of arrows, fired at long range, arced up high and rained upon the covered trenches.

"Hold fire, hold!" Vincent shouted, his voice hoarse. The men around him were armed with smoothbores. Ramrods were worked feverishly, the brief lull giving them time to run swabs down the barrels to clean the choked bores. The men continued to load, many of them taking handfuls of buckshot out of their pockets and pouring them down the barrels, running down wadding on top.

The enemy lines came up out of the riverbank and held, letting the mass build up behind them. This one was going to be different, not a charge all along the line, but rather a column aiming for one point.

He squatted down, oblivious to the arrows, raising his field glasses. The back end of the Merki column was still pouring down from the opposite slope, limbered guns falling in on the flanks. Forty, maybe fifty thousand of them forming.

The chanting grew, incomprehensible, but filled with explosive rage, growing louder. Artillery opened up, plowing case shot into the ranks, the light four-pounders barking, five to ten Merki going down from a single round. Still they waited.

"Kesus, come on, come on," Vincent hissed, the tension nearly exploding inside of him.

Several riders gained the bank, red signal flags up, and they galloped down the line, standing tall in the stirrups, pointing forward and to their left.

The column started forward at the run.

"They're coming on the oblique," Vincent shouted, standing up again. The charge was angling away from his position, aiming straight at the juncture between his corps and Pat's.

Fourth Corps opened up, all but one brigade armed with rifles. Merki went down as if a scythe had cut the front rank. The next rank plunged forward, the deadfalls and traps now useless, the approach carpeted with bodies. The survivors of the last attack, pinned down in front of Pat's line, stood up to join in the assault, leaping forward, their long legs devouring five yards in a running stride.

Vincent jumped down from the embankment and ran to the bombproof shelter behind his lines.

"Get my horse!"

An orderly led the animal out into the sunlight, and Vincent climbed into the saddle.

"Tell Dimitri that he's in charge of the line. I'm going back to bring third division up to our right flank. Send a message to Marcus on my left that if he hasn't already received orders from Andrew to bring up at least one division to support the rear between my corps and Pat's."

He raked his spurs in and galloped to the rear.

"Feed it to them! Pour it in, pour it in!" Pat screamed.

The charge was fifty yards away, pushing in fast. He pulled his revolver back out to check the load and cocked the pistol.

The battery of Napoleons stood ready, holding fire, triple canister rammed in, gunners crouched down, waiting, gun sergeants standing low, lanyards pulled tight.

The charge pressed in, Merki leaping over the backs of their own fallen, some with bows, others with scimitars up, others with lances poised low.

Musket fire raked up and down the line, but not fast enough, men struggling with fouled pieces that had put out eighty, some a hundred rounds. Men started to fasten bayonets, standing back from the firing line, poising weapons up.

Thirty yards, the screaming line a wall that seemed to block out the sky.

At ten yards the battery fired in salvo, the guns leaping high, one of them flipping over, a thousand iron balls smashing down everything across a thirty-yard-wide front, the charge disintegrating, but to either side the host pressed in.

The first wave went right over the trench and continued on into the rear at a run. Others leaped atop the trench covering of boards, their weight bearing it down, crashing into the trench atop the men. A soldier next to Pat crouched low, bracing his musket butt on the ground; a Merki crashed through from above, impaling himself, and the man scrambled out from underneath.

Pat whirled around as a sword struck down from above. He fired straight into the warrior's face, which exploded from the impact at point-blank range, the Merki's hair catching fire as he tumbled into the trench.

Pat leaned into the command post.

"Out, get out! Signal we're falling back!"

A Merki slid into the trench beside him, no weapons in his hands. Pat fired into his chest, the Merki looking at him, wide-eyed. Pat looked at him, realizing that this one wasn't much more than a child, if such things had children, he thought, and seemed almost to be crying. Astonished at his own feelings, he felt an instant of pity, and put a bullet into the Merki's head to end the agony.

He pushed his way up the trench, climbing over bodies, shooting another Merki in the back as he raised up his sword to cut a cowering gunner down.

One of the Napoleons fired at point-blank range, catching a Merki standing directly in front of the muzzle, and he looked away, sickened.

Grabbing hold of a gunner, he pointed back to the north.

"Retreat up the line! Leave the guns—they're finished!"

The artillerymen dropped their equipment, pulling out revolvers, following Pat as he worked up the line. He drew a bead on a Merki standard-bearer standing above the trench and fired, the gun clicking on an empty chamber. There was no time to reload. A gunner next to him went down, a spear appearing to leap out of his chest. He grabbed the falling man's pistol, turned, and killed the Merki standing above him, his hands still on the butt of the spear, roaring in triumph over his kill.

"Retreat up the line!" His voice was failing. He continued up the trench, grabbing men, pushing them forward, a knot of survivors fighting to get out of the tidal wave of Merki that continued to press forward, straight into the center of the line, the Army of the Republics now split wide open in the middle.

Andrew reined in hard in front of the villa which was the command post for the three brigades of Third Corps. The heavy division was formed up two brigades in front, their line a half mile across. A hundred yards to their rear the third brigade was drawn up in five regimental columns. A quarter mile forward, the breakthrough was widening out, the Merki column coming straight in.

"Get 'em in!" Andrew shouted, and he galloped down the front of the line up to the corps commander.

Mikhail saluted and stood up in his stirrups.

"For Hans Schuder, for Rus!"

The cheer rose up, sending a chill down Andrew's spine, and the vast line started forward at the double, moving across the open field.

Gregory, riding beside Mikhail, looked back at Andrew, gave a cheery salute, and continued on in.

He felt a stirring, wanting to ride with them, but knew he couldn't, not yet. When it's lost, then I'll do it, but not before, he thought.

His staff, who had fallen behind in the dash down to Third Corps, mounted on the far slower Clydesdale-size horses, started to catch up. He felt his blood stirred by the sight of the old Third Corps going in, thirty regimental flags dotting the front of the line across the half-mile front. He looked back beyond them to the spreading wall of Merki.

"Fourth Corps going down," he whispered, the hole in the line already as wide as the advancing Third Corps. He looked back up to the circling hills. Where was Schneid's reserve division?

He looked back to the front. Third Corps was engaged, the thunder of its first volley echoing back over him, a high plume of smoke rising up, its own reserve regiments already running to the northern flank to extend the line, matching the growing width of the Merki breakthrough.

He edged his mount back to the villa that had served as Third Corps headquarters and looked up at several men standing on the roof, field glasses turned to the south.

"The left flank of the breakthrough?"

"Looks like Vincent's reserve division is moving to seal it."

He looked back to the north. No more reserves. Where the hell was Schneid's division?

A telegrapher came running out of the building.

"Train of the reserve division derailed at the switch. The entire line's held up."

Unassisted, he swung back up into the saddle and turned to gallop back to the north.

"Wheel it, wheel it," Vincent screamed, galloping down the line.

The first brigade of his reserve division, which had been deployed to face forward, was now completely out of alignment. Third Corps was already moving up to its right, but directly in front the Merki were starting to mushroom outward, moving to the south, rolling up the entrenched line as they moved. He needed to get the brigade turned ninety degrees to hook the left flank of Third Corps at one side into his other two divisions, which were still in the trenches a quarter mile ahead.

"We've got to put a side to the box, close them off!"

Commands echoed down the line.

"Wheel to the right, in line by brigade!"

The twenty-five hundred men stepped off, the man to the extreme right of the line standing still, the last one on the far left moving at the run, pivoting, the entire formation, a quarter mile across, turning like a gate swinging shut, in a bid to pen in the breakthrough.

The line continued to turn, slowly gaining speed, the men struggling to keep alignment as they moved through fields and vineyards, up and over stone walls, regimental flags guiding them in.

Vincent galloped along the front, hat off, waving it over his head, urging them on. The first regiment to the right of the line engaged, hitting the Merki with a volley at fifty yards, bringing the advance to a crashing halt. The two forces raced toward each other, the

Merki desperate to widen the breech, the turning line running to close it off. The Merki crashed into the second regiment of the line, and then the third, volleys rippling up and down, arrows darkening the sky overhead. The fifth regiment reached the entrenchments, sweeping up behind them, racing to a stone wall, deploying behind it, and firing a scathing volley at point-blank range. The Merki who had been rolling up the trench, confident that the battle was already won, were staggered by the onset.

Vincent, screaming with joy, wheeled his mount and started back up the line, checking the alignment, moving up the second brigade to reinforce the first in a heavy volley line four ranks deep. He looked back at the hills behind them. From over the crest, Marcus's reserve division came down, battle standards flying, sweeping to either side of the grand battery, which had turned its guns and now was pouring a deadly crossfire into the Merki breakthrough.

Vincent rode along the line, his heart bursting with the joy of battle.

"Send up the mounted umen of the black horse," Tamuka shouted, pointing to the smoke-clad battle.

"My Qarth, there is no room," Haga roared. "Eight umens are in there, in a front so narrow that barely one could ride in."

"Their north flank is breaking. I want riders in there now!"

Haga, his features flushed with rage at the slaughter, jerked his mount around and rode off.

Tamuka sat astride his mount in silence, eating the last of the salted meat of the cattle taken more than a week before. It was starting to taste rancid. There would be more than enough fresh food tonight, he thought coldly, watching as the northern edge of the breakthrough again began to spill out like a spreading pool of black.

*   *   *

Riding hard, Andrew came around a bend in the road, a low rise in the ground ahead. He reined back in and turned to look to the southwest, and his heart sank. Third Corps was fully engaged, the last of its reserve regiments filing into the right, the regiment bending back at a right angle to protect its own flank. But there was a gap a quarter mile wide between Third Corps and the forward trench, and a deep block of Merki were turning, moving into the opening, threatening to roll up Second Corps all the way back up to Hispania, and to turn the line of Third Corps as well. He sat watching, the Merki less than three hundred yards away, an occasional arrow fluttering down around him.

He saw horses, the flashes of spokes, and to his horror saw a battery of Merki artillery coming out of the press, preparing to wheel their guns out, to fire straight into the flank of Third Corps. If the hole wasn't plugged now it was over, the forward position gone, the reserve formation flanked, and the Merki able to drive straight across thc valley and up over the undefended ridge beyond.

Desperate, he turned to look back up the slope behind him toward Hispania.

For the want of a horseshoe, for the want of a working train switch.

Up over the crest he saw a flag appear, and a thin line of men coming down on the double, running hard. He turned and galloped toward them, leaping over a low stone wall, angling through an orchard, the flag disappearing from view for a moment, as if it were an apparition, and then coming back into sight, closer.

He galloped up to the flag, an officer beside it.

"What unit is this?"

"First Vazima."

Andrew looked down at the panting officer.

"Mike Homula, isn't it?"

"Yes sir, with the 35th from the beginning."

"Where the hell's the rest of your brigade, the division?"

"The train's stuck. Schneid's driving them like hell. They'll be here in five minutes. We were closest up the line."

Andrew turned and looked back at the Merki. The battery was starting to unlimber, the column continuing to fan out. There wasn't any more time.

"Homula, you see those guns?"

"Yes sir."

"I need five minutes. Now take those guns!"

Homula grinned.

"I'll see you in hell, sir!" He saluted.

The young Maine officer stepped forward, grabbed the regimental flag away from its bearer, and held it aloft.

"First Vazima, fix bayonets!"

The ragged line paused, drawing up along the narrow path, bayonets snicking from scabbards.

Homula looked back at them and held the flag aloft.

"We're taking those guns. Come on, boys, charge!"

Homula leaped forward, holding the colors up, running madly, not even looking back to see if anyone was following him. An insane frenzy seemed to take hold of the men, and they leaped forward with a maniacal roar, running full out, rifles held up, bayonets flashing.

Andrew sat in silence, watching, heart in his throat, filled with a sense of overwhelming pride and yet at the same time horror for what he had done, ordering Homula and his men to certain death.

The young officer's voice could still be heard, a mad joy to it.

"Do you want to live forever?"

The Merki battery, which had been deploying to rake Third Corps, paused. A commander turned, pointing toward the thin line of Homula's regiment running madly across the open field.

Andrew raised his field glasses, unable to tear himself away.

Merki rammers worked madly, running charges home. To the flank of the guns the column charging to the north slowed, turning to meet the assault, a volley of arrows going up, most of them long, a scattering of men dropping, the charge continuing on.

He held his breath.

Fifty yards to go, Homula far out in front, hat gone, hair streaming, blue flag of the regiment snapping.

Ten yards. A gun kicked back, a ragged hole torn into the line, the flag going down, and then he saw Homula come back up, as if driven by some superhuman strength, staggering forward, leaping atop one of the guns, Merki turning, fleeing.

The column of enemy infantry, caught on their own flank, were staggered, the charge pressing on into them, bayonets and scimitars flashing, musket fire rippling. And yet still the flag was up, waving back and forth.

The full weight of the column turned, pressing in, swords flashing, arrows raining down. Smoke drifted over the battle, obscuring the view. It cleared for a moment, and he saw the flag go down, and then there was nothing but the smoke, and the flashing of the swords.

"Sir!"

Andrew turned, wiping the tears from his eyes.

It was Schneid, the full reserve division coming down the hill behind him.

"I'm sorry, sir, the train—"

"Not your fault," Andrew said.

"Something wrong, sir?"

"Nothing wrong. I guess you could say there are worse ways of dying."

"Sir?"

"Never mind, general. Get your men in, close the gap."

Schneid saluted and rode down the line, sword pointed forward. The division swept forward, battle flags up, the veteran formation closing in to seal the gap.

Unable to contain himself, Andrew fell in with the line, his staff finding him, riding to catch up.

"Colonel, what the hell are you doing?" an orderly shouted.

Andrew continued forward, barely noticing the ever increasing rain of arrows sweeping in, men starting to drop, staggering out of the line. Bugles sounded, clarion calls high and clear, and the division raced forward at the double, cheering madly, Andrew angling over toward Schneid, who was still out front, sword drawn.

"Come on, let's take them!" Andrew roared, and the charge swept forward at the run, men yelling hoarsely, the wall of bayonets flashing in the afternoon sun.

The Merki seemed to pause in their advance, a single volley of arrows lashing out low, men stumbling, dropping, most of the shots going high. The charge continued on, and suddenly the Merki, stretched out to the final breaking point, turned, falling back, running, pouring back toward the river, which was clogged with a mounted umen advancing forward.

The press increased, panic in the air, and they were over the Merki guns, pressing on in.

Andrew reined in out of the charge as it continued to sweep forward, slowing his horse to a walk. His orderlies caught up and moved in front, placing themselves between Andrew and the rain of arrows still arcing in.

He stopped. A dazed knot of men stood around the guns, survivors of the 1st Vazima.

Andrew dismounted and walked up to them.

A lieutenant stepped forward, blood pouring from

his scalp, the broken-off end of an arrow still sticking out of his forearm.

"We took the guns, sir," he said, his voice weary but proud. "Just as you told us to."

Andrew nodded, looking around at the group, counting not more than a score of survivors still on their feet. Unable to say anything, he walked away, stepping over the piles of bodies around the battery, pausing for an instant to look at a Merki and Rus locked in a deadly embrace on the ground, each holding a dagger, each having driven it into the heart of the other. The ferocity of the fighting was evident, with few surviving wounded. He walked up to one of the guns and found Homula, lying crumpled on the ground, torn flag still in his hands.

Andrew looked up at an orderly.

"I want his body taken to the rear. Have his grave marked."

The orderly dismounted, and several survivors of the 1st Vazima came up and gently picked up the body. Andrew reached down, took the flag, walked over to the lieutenant, and gave him the colors.

"God be my witness, I'll never forget this," he said softly, and stepping back, he saluted the flag.

He returned to Mercury, mounted, and galloped off to rejoin the fight. The lieutenant, standing alone, holding the flag, looked up at the colors as if seeing them for the first time.

Nearly doubled over, he leaned against the trench wall, gasping, his throat so dry that he thought he was about to suffocate. Another rattle of musketry sounded to his left. He didn't care. A dead Merki was at his feet, a water skin dangling beside the body. He reached down and shook it. There was still some water.

He took the end of a broken bayonet and used it

to cut the water skin's strap, brought it up, and raised it to his lips.

"For Kesus sake, sir, some water."

Pat looked over. In the dusty smoke-choked haze he saw an old soldier, hair gray, sitting on the firing step, blood streaming from half a dozen wounds.

Pat sighed, went over, and raised the bag up for the man, the water trickling down his blackened face, the beads of water leaving white furrows. The man nodded a thanks. Another soldier, one of the men from the Roum division of the Fourth, lay beside the gray soldier, an arrow in his chest, unable to speak, but eyes pleading. Pat knelt down, held his head, and gave him the last of the water in the bag.

A flurry of shots rang out, and he looked up. The men were firing to the east. From out of the smoke and haze he saw several Merki riding back, one of them going down, horse screaming. The other two rode straight over the trench, heading back to the river.

It was impossible to tell what was going on. All he knew was that the sun was getting lower, its red disk barely visible, a fog of smoke, heat, dust choking the field. He couldn't even tell what was going on twenty yards away, whether the trench was theirs or not. All he knew now was this small knot of survivors, a hedgehog defense, the battle no longer a battle, but rather a murdering brawl without any semblance of reason or control.

A musket volley slashed overhead, and from out of the haze a Merki came running back, leaping into the trench as if seeking protection, blood pouring from a wound to his side.

In panic the Merki looked around, suddenly realizing he had landed in the midst of cattle. The men stood in shock as well for a second, and then with wild screams fell on the lone Merki, pinning him to the trench wall with their bayonets.

Pat watched with a growing distaste, remembering the young Merki he had killed earlier. The men, as if releasing their rage, continued to stab the Merki, even though he was dead.

The insane battle continued, and he looked back to the west, understanding now why the Bible said that at Jericho the sun had remained motionless in the sky.

He heard a hoarse cheer, looked up, and saw shadows moving through the smoke. Men!

A flag appeared.

"Third Corps! It's Third Corps!"

Stumbling before the advance, the last of the Merki continued to fall back, the survivors of Fourth Corps staggering up out of the trench, bayoneting the remaining Merki caught now between two sides. Pat climbed up out of the trench and stood in silence as the men of Third Corps swept up past him, their lines thin, many of the men wounded but still in the fight.

"Hold here at the trenches," Pat said, trying to shout, his voice barely above a whisper.

The cheering spread, and Pat staggered down the line, unable to avoid stepping on bodies, so thick did the casualties lie. In the haze he saw a rider.

"Gregory!"

The Rus soldier turned, came up to Pat, and saluted.

"Thank Kesus," Gregory said, sliding off his horse and embracing Pat.

"We thought all of Fourth Corps was dead."

"I guess some of us made it. Sections of trench held out even after we got overrun. Where's Mikhail?"

"Dead," Gregory said. "Killed in the first moments of the charge. I guess I've been running the corps since."

"You did good, son."

Gregory smiled.

"A long way since we did Shakespeare together."

Pat nodded.

"Hell of a fight, by damn, a hell of a fight," Gregory said, his blood still up. "Schneid's division closed on our right, Hawthorne's on the left. We boxed 'em in on three sides, caught the bastards in a crossfire, and murdered them wholesale. Hell of a fight. They were packed so thick you couldn't miss."

"You got a drink?" Pat whispered.

The young officer reached into his tunic and pulled out a flask.

"Not that. Just water, for God's sake."

Gregory went to his saddle, unclipped a canteen, and tossed it over to Pat. The old artilleryman tilted it back, the water going down his throat. He felt for a moment as if he couldn't even swallow it, his throat so raw and choked with dust.

"Oh, thank God," he groaned, feeling as if he might live out the day after all.

Tamuka, unable to speak, paced the crest of the hill.

Not since the first day of Orki, not in far more than a circling, had a charge of the Merki been broken. It was impossible to see, the other side of the river cloaked in a caldron of fire and smoke. Yet it was evident that the attack had been broken. A steady river of warriors, all formation gone, streamed past him, most of them wounded, clutching at their injuries. There were no cries of victory, no chanting of boasts, of deeds accomplished.

It was impossible to believe, and yet it was real.

"And you thought it would be easy."

He turned and saw Muzta looking down at him, an almost mocking smile lighting his features.

"I once paced as you now do. When first we encountered them, the crossing of the ford, and I saw the river choked with my dead as this river now is," and he pointed to the Sangros, the banks of the river and all the way across the shallow ford carpeted, the stream actually tinged pink farther down.

"I lost my youngest son that day," Muzta said.

Tamuka said nothing, the rage still seething.

"And you dared to mock me, to mock my people these last three years, as if we somehow were weak, were fools because we lost. Well, now you as well stare into the rotting face of defeat."

Tamuka pulled his scimitar from its scabbard and for a brief instant prepared to strike Muzta down. He hesitated. No, stay with what you planned, he thought.

He resheathed the blade.

"I am angry," he said almost apologetically, "but not at you."

Muzta smiled. "How many did you lose?"

"Ten umens were engaged, and all were broken. Forty, perhaps fifty thousand are dead or wounded, the formations shattered."

"End it for today," Muzta said. "Your field is so choked with the wounded, the fleeing, there is no hope to press a fresh assault in to win the day. Your water is short, and in this heat the warriors are collapsing from thirst."

Tamuka looked back to the red sun low in the sky.

He did not need this Tugar to tell him that. Already he had lost far more than he had expected. He had believed that once the cattle line was broken, panic would spread. How they maneuvered to seal the line had filled him with wonder, for they had held with a brilliance worthy of any horde foe. And he realized now as well that his own warriors had always fought mounted battles, sweeping across a dozen leagues of steppe. This fighting upon such a narrow front had disorganized them.

"I have lost much, but so have they. I still have twenty umens fresh, and they have without doubt used all. Tomorrow we shall see."

Muzta smiled as if fully agreeing.

"And you shall lead one of the assaults, Muzta Qar Qarth. I am curious to see the vaunted skill of the Tugar against their old foe. Perhaps this time you will fare better."

"I was expecting no less from you," Muzta said, and he rode off.

It was the place he had always feared more than any other, a military hospital.

The long rows of tents were crammed to overflowing, the air filled with shrieks of pain, horror, terror of what was going to be done to them.

Chuck Ferguson weaved his way through the dimly lit tent, looking from cot to cot.

Not here.

He stepped out of the far side of the shelter. A long row of bodies lay to one side, not even covered, a detail loading them like cordwood onto a railroad flatcar to be moved to the burial ground. He wanted to go up to look, to check.

"Chuck?"

He turned. It was Kathleen.

Her white uniform was stained with blood, her perfume now a tincture of lime and alcohol.

"What are you doing here?"

"I'm looking for . . ." He couldn't say the name, terrified that she'd tell him what he feared.

He had carried her to the train that was rushing the survivors of the powder mill explosion to the hospital. She had not even been able to tell it was him; she was unconscious, bleeding and battered, face blackened, hair burned away.

He had wanted to ride with her, to stay, but Theodor had forcibly held him back, screaming that he had work to do.

Well, now it was midnight, and the hell with the duty, and he had taken the train down here to find out the truth.

"Is she . . ."

"She's alive," Kathleen said quietly. "I'll take you to her."

He tried to gasp out a thanks but couldn't, his shoulders shaking with relief.

Kathleen put a soothing arm around him and led him through the hospital.

It was, to his eyes, worse than any hell he had ever imagined. Every wound he could ever imagine was there, and some he had not believed possible. He looked to a side tent as they came out between wards and saw Emil hunched over an operating table, an orderly holding a flaring lantern, Emil cursing for the man to give him more light, his hand moving up and down rhythmically as he stitched, a pile of arms and legs lying outside the open flap.

"Merciful God," Chuck whispered, and he looked back at Kathleen. "This is what you do?"

She nodded, wanting to cry, to blurt out her own agony. At her last operation the Roum soldier had begged in incomprehensible Latin, but his pleas were obvious nevertheless, as she prepared to take off both his legs.

She pulled Chuck along into the next tent, a ward for female casualties, filled now mostly with the survivors of the mill blast.

"She's at the far end," Kathleen whispered. "I've got to get back to my own ward." She kissed him lightly on the forehead, hesitated, and then decided to tell him.

"It's bad, over twenty percent of her body burned. The concussion deafened her, so she won't be able to hear you."

"Will she live?"

"She's got a chance. She's a fighter."

Chuck started to cry openly with relief.

"But Chuck . . ."

He looked at her through his tears.

"She'll be scarred, horribly scarred, especially her face and hands."

"I don't care, I just want her back, I don't care about anything else."

Kathleen forced a smile.

"When I'm done, I'll come here to check on her, I'll personally see to her."

"Thank you."

He turned to go to her, and Kathleen took hold of him, kissing him on the forehead.

"Saints preserve you, Chuck, I'll pray for both of you," and in her emotion her Irish brogue came back strong and clear.

Chuck walked quietly up to Olivia's bed, not sure if she was asleep or not. Her face and hands were heavily swaddled in bandages, one eye covered, the other barely visible. She stirred and looked up at him, and then turned her head away.

He sat down on the edge of her cot, and she started to shake her head back and forth.

"Olivia."

"Go away," she whispered. "Go away, and don't ever come back."

He sat numb, gently reaching out to take a bandaged hand in his.

"I'm ugly, a monster now. Go away, let me die."

He smiled and spoke slowly, hoping that she could read his lips.

"I don't care how you look. Stay with me forever. I love you."

With a muffled cry she sat up, wrapping her arms around him, oblivious to the physical pain, as the other pain within disappeared, the two holding each other and crying with joy and relief.

Rubbing his eyes, Andrew leaned back in his chair, the cup of tea by his side long since gone cold, and looked at the small group of officers around him.

"If they hit the line tomorrow as they did today, we'll crack open like a rotten shell."

A throaty snoring filled the room, and he looked over to where Pat was stretched out on the floor in the corner, fast asleep. Gregory laughed softly and then was still.

"His corps is finished, out of the fight for tomorrow," Andrew said. "He's got less than three thousand effectives. I'm putting him into reserve. Gregory, your boys were gallant today, but you're out tomorrow as well."

Gregory started to raise a protest but fell silent.

"Gentlemen, we took sixteen thousand casualties here, Barry another two thousand up in the woods."

"We did a hell of a lot of killing in return," Vincent said. "Maybe seventy or eighty thousand."

"That still leaves twenty-five or more umens left. If they come at us the same, we'll crack wide open."

He sighed and looked back at the map.

"I'm abandoning the forward line," Andrew said quietly.

"What?"

Vincent was up on his feet, looking at Andrew, incredulous at what he had just heard.

"Any objections Mr. Hawthorne?" Andrew asked quietly.

"Sir, the front across the valley is nearly four miles, and the ridgeline behind is over five miles from the south grand battery to the north, six in all to the river. You're saying we lost over fifteen thousand men and now you want to extend our line by an additional fifty percent. I don't get it."

Andrew more than half agreed with Vincent and had been agonizing over the decision for hours.

"They broke the front when we were at our strongest—we had over twenty thousand men committed to close the gap. Damn near that number of men are gone now. And I think it's fair to assume that tomorrow they'll break us again, and this time they'll keep right on going.

"If we hadn't retaken the trenches, every last man of Fourth Corps would have died and the entire corps artillery would have been lost. Tomorrow I want those sixty guns and every other field piece from the trench line back up on the hills.

"I think they'll open the same way, a bombardment of several hours, thinking to rattle us even more. Remember that when they charge this time the deadfalls will no longer be there, they're covered now by their bodies, and the abatis is down, the trench coverings torn to shreds in the fight. They'll overrun the line in minutes. Well, this time they'll hit empty air. I think that alone will slow them, confuse them. They'll reform, then have to wait for their artillery to be brought across to prepare for the next assault. By then it'll be midday, maybe even afternoon. We'll now have the hills, and clear fields of interlocking fire as they come up the slopes. Remember, they'll be firing uphill, their arrows less effective, while we'll be firing straight down into their damn throats."

The room was silent, the men listening intently.

"If they send their aerosteamers over at dawn, they'll see the lines are empty," Vincent said.

Andrew nodded.

"I think you know we lost the powder mill today to a suicide attack from the air, that two of the three remaining aerosteamers were destroyed."

Most of them had not yet heard, and the news hit hard, the exhausted men not replying.

"We have one ship left. According to our reports they still have two, maybe three. It'll be our one ship's job to keep them back."

"That's the end of the air fleet," Schneid said coldly.

Andrew did not reply, knowing that he had ordered Jack back up again, not willing to let the inexperienced crew of *Republic* to take on the job. He thought of Homula again for a moment and closed his eyes.

"Vincent, pull your corps straight back to the ridge to the east," he began again, his voice quiet. "Anchor your command post on the central grand battery."

Vincent did not reply, but merely looked at the map.

"Marcus, your entire Seventh Corps will deploy to the left of Vincent, plus I want one division of your Fifth Corps as reserve."

"Andrew, what about the river to the south?"

"One division will have to handle it. I think, though, that he's focused here, his blood is up now. We've seen nearly all his warriors on foot—the horses are most likely being held to the rear. We'll have to trust that he doesn't try something to the south. I don't think he will."

Marcus nodded.

"Schneid, you extend your line to hook into Vincent's right, and Barry's reserve division will serve you."

"Andrew, they damn near got across just south of the powder mill early this evening," Barry objected. "I need that reserve."

"You'll have to make do," Andrew replied, and Barry nodded glumly. "Gregory, you and Pat will form to the rear of Vincent. Get your men reorganized, but be ready to act if we have another crisis."

Gregory smiled, relishing the role of acting corps commander, even though his unit was down now to little more than a reenforced brigade.

"Good luck, gentlemen. Now get back to your posts."

The room slowly cleared until finally he was left alone, except for Pat, still sleeping in the corner.

He looked down at the map, the decision made, but still agonizing if it was the right one.

Again that cold chill, and he blocked off the

thoughts of his decision as if sensing that somehow this one could almost read his mind and thus steal his secrets. He stood up and went out the door. One moon was rising low in the eastern sky, the second one just starting to break the horizon.

The encampment was not still, even though it was past midnight. A low uncomfortable murmuring came from the hospital area, and to his right he could hear the sound of digging, men repairing the damage to the grand battery. Down in the valley, cries of the wounded could still be heard, lanterns bobbing up and down as men wandered the fields looking for their fallen comrades. Occasional rifle shots snapped out, pickets on the river edgy about any shadow, or from behind the lines Merki wounded being dispatched without pity.

From across the river came another sound, a steady unearthly howling, what he knew must be cries of rage, mourning, and the moans of their wounded. It was hard at times to realize that they felt pain as well. So easy to understand that with the rebs—after all, the same languages was spoken, the same God prayed to.

He couldn't feel pity, not for them, not when he still sensed the presence lurking. He couldn't weaken. He could sense the despair that was trying to force its way into his soul, a despair he knew it was all too easy to fall to. Tomorrow, tomorrow, the Merki could crack his army wide open and finish it before the sun set. He focused his thoughts.

"Tomorrow you'll get even worse, you bastard," he whispered defiantly.

Chapter 11

Wincing and leaning on a pair of crutches, Jack Petracci hobbled into the hangar. Chuck looked up from under the basket.

"Heard you're flying," Chuck said.

Jack nodded. "How's Olivia?"

"I think she'll make it," Chuck said, the relief in his voice evident.

"I'm sorry I wasn't over the factory to protect her."

Chuck came back up to his feet. "You've done your bit already. You don't have to fly this one today."

"Andrew asked me to."

Chuck sighed, wiping his hands. "I've rigged something special up."

"I heard about it."

"It's really simple to use. I've mounted a crude gunsight to the front of your basket. Remember you have to be pointed straight at them. You'll be able to traverse it ten degrees to either side, but you have to be at the same height as them."

Jack nodded, watching intently as Chuck pointed the system out.

"Your range should be two hundred yards. I've mounted a real sensitive trigger in the nose—it should go off when it hits. But if it doesn't, there's a one-second fuse. You've got three of them, along with the harpoons. That's all I had time for. When you're ready, move the telegraph key to one, then two, and then three over there on the left, press down, and that's it."

The crew chief for *Republic* came into the shed. "Hour and a half to dawn. We'd better get going."

Jack sighed, motioning for help. Chuck and the ground chief lifted him into the basket, and he settled in.

"Take her out," he said.

The ground crew walked the aerosteamer out of its hangar. The thinning crescent of one moon was overhead, the other one twenty degrees closer to the horizon, and the first faint streak of approaching dawn just creased the horizon.

By the starlight he could see the twisted hulks of the two ships at either end of the field.

"Let's get on with it," he said.

Jack looked up to see Feyodor climbing in behind him.

"I told you to stay home. I'm taking this up with Danolov. He's the engineer for this ship."

"And Yuri was the pilot. Besides, if I stay down here I'll get drafted to fight along the river. That's too dangerous."

Feyodor climbed in without waiting for Jack's permission. He bent over to check the engine burner and then looked straight up at the exhaust, which was shimmering up into the hot-air bag.

"Full lift," he said, and the ground crew chief stepped back from the cab to watch his men on the ropes.

Jack raised his hand. "Clear."

The crew let go, and the crew chief saluted as the ship started to float up.

"Try not to get any holes in her," the chief shouted, and Jack absently waved a reply.

As they cleared the tops of the trees, Feyodor engaged the propeller, and with a push forward to the rudder, *Republic* turned to port, heading down to Hispania, the still-burning factory below and to their right.

By now he had expected to be grazing his horses on the far side of the distant ridge barely visible in the early-morning fog. The prayer to the sun was finished, and he looked out across the field and then back up at the Yankee aerosteamer overhead.

"Where are our own ships? I thought all the Yankee machines had been killed."

Sarg stood silent, unable to reply.

Tamuka fumed angrily. His ships were to be over the Yankee lines, to report to him if the cattle army was deployed differently. He scanned the line again with his telescope. It was obvious that most of the guns were still there, and he looked back up to the far ridge, able to see yet more barrels. More there than yesterday. Had the cattle concealed them beyond the far ridge? Did they have still more than they were showing?

It was impossible to tell. All he had to go on at the moment was the angry sense of defiance that Keane so clearly showed, a rage that was coldly shocking, creeping into his own soul. It had a strength far greater than Vuka's. Vuka had been weak, not even aware that his thoughts were being touched, the fears evident. This one somehow knew that the *tu* of the shield-bearer was looking and shouted a defiance in return.

It was troubling.

He looked back at his own lines.

The remains of ten umens were now in the rear, their numbers more than halved, the survivors demoralized, shaken, talking darkly about cattle who were truly possessed by demons. Rumors already had spread of headless cattle that would spring up and still fight, of cattle that crushed with bare hands, of cattle that simply refused to die and submit, as all cattle had in the past.

He had kept them isolated. Ten fresh umens were now ready for today's fight. Extra water bags had been issued to the warriors, but already he could tell that that would not be enough, the day already hot.

There was a stirring. He looked north. A yellow signal flag fluttered on the far horizon, the message writer next to him watching the distant flag, raising his own to repeat the message for confirmation. A flutter in reply indicated that the message had been received correctly.

The flag waver turned to Tamuka with a grin. "A regiment of the red horse has gained the eastern shore of the river ten leagues north. Request another umen."

Tamuka nodded, hesitated.

A single regiment, perhaps a front of but a hundred paces. He had only three mounted umens in reserve, none with remounts. He cursed silently. Nearly a million horses to his army, and the nearest not in use now grazing ten leagues to the rear, others as far back as the last river and even beyond it.

Damn them.

Last evening he had been forced to detach two full umens to go back nearly to the place where Vuka was buried to protect the home yurts, cattle raiders from out of the forest having killed more than three thousand of the women and children.

He pondered the message. A single regiment. He looked forward again.

"Our cloud fliers arrive."

He turned to look back to the west, and on the horizon he saw the three ships, small dark circles in the sky, still a half hour away.

No. The main battle would be here. A breakthrough was possible by the middle of the morning.

"Order the bombardment to begin," he announced.

"But our cloud fliers," Sarg said. "First let them see. There will be smoke."

"The guns can stop firing after the cloud fliers are over the line, but till then let us smash them down. Order it to begin now."

"Has the ball begun?" Pat asked hoarsely, lifting his head as the crashing of the first Merki volley rolled across the plain.

Andrew looked back at him, still stretched out in the corner of headquarters where he had fallen asleep during the staff meeting. He had not awakened Pat, delegating the reorganization and deployment to the rear of Fourth Corps to one of his own staff officers. Fourth Corps might be finished as a fighting entity, but he still needed Pat as second in command and chief of artillery.

Pat groaned, his joints cracking as he sat up and looked around.

"I guess I dozed off. What time is it?"

"Half hour past dawn, a little after five."

"I've got work to do. Why the hell did you let me sleep?"

"You needed it after yesterday."

"My corps—where is it? I've got to get back to the trenches."

"They've been pulled to the rear into reserve. They're off the front today."

"Well, I need to get to them."

Andrew shook his head, bringing over a cup of hot tea and two pieces of hardtack sandwiching a slab of salt pork.

Pat took the tin cup, grimacing slightly from the heat, holding it gingerly at the seams, and took a long drink.

"Thanks."

"I'm taking you off Fourth Corps. I want you with me."

"Why? Did I do something wrong?" Pat asked.

"No. You did everything right."

"But Fourth Corps . . ."

"It doesn't exist as a corps anymore, Pat. You took the brunt yesterday. You've got less than three thousand left."

"God, I had twelve at dawn."

"You did what had to be done. Now you're running artillery and staying as my second."

Pat nodded glumly, shocked by the destruction of the unit he had poured so much work into. He sighed and then started into the sandwich, his teeth cracking the hard bread, chewing noisily, and Andrew walked outside the headquarters to watch the beginning of the bombardment. The trenches below were already wreathed with the detonation of shells, earth geysering up from solid shot. The ten guns he had left on the line started up a rapid fire in return. Each gun was to fire at the beginning as quickly as possible to simulate the action of a full battery, adding their smoke. A single regiment from Second Corps was now occupying the entire front, ready to keep any Merki skirmishers back and to set fire to bundles of damp straw to add to the smoke. Quaker guns, logs painted black or bronze, had been set up along the forward line, their snouts protruding out from the earthworks where yesterday real guns had been emplaced.

Perhaps they'd be more cautious today in coming across, Andrew thought, stretching out the bombardment, using up more ammunition than they could afford, wasting it on an abandoned line. The price of yesterday's assault was readily apparent. Down to the river they had retrieved their wounded and dead. But from the beginning of the east bank and at points nearly a half mile beyond the entrenchments the ground was carpeted with bodies. Few wounded were left. The men had seen to that grisly task with a vengeance, bayoneting or shooting any Merki that were still alive. He tried not to let it bother him, remembering the photo of the burial mound.

When they came on again it wouldn't be pleasant. Already there was the beginning of the faint sickly sweet smell, and as he looked to the east he could sense that today would be even hotter than yesterday.

Good. Let them see what's waiting. He remembered how Stonewall Jackson had a fetish for cleaning up a battlefield that his troops might assault across, not wanting them to see what might very well soon happen to them. Well, today the Merki would see.

"Hot day for a fight."

Andrew looked back as Pat came walking out the door, his gait stiff, as if every muscle in his body were crying out.

"Getting too old for this," Pat said, and he looked to the south. "Merciful God, is that where we fought?"

Andrew nodded.

"Killed a parcel of the bastards, didn't we?"

"They've got something like three hundred thousand more."

The two ducked as a round screamed overhead to detonate in the rail yard behind them, a cry of agony rising up seconds later.

"Going to be a long day," Pat said.

Andrew looked up as a thumping noise grew louder and saw *Republic* turning to run to the west.

"Good luck," he whispered, knowing that yet again he was sending someone out to die.

He could hear Feyodor chanting a soft prayer, and though he was a good Methodist he was tempted to join in the prayer to Perm.

This time there was no backing off. Either three Merki ships would be down or he would be down, and even if he survived it would be far behind their lines.

He pulled his revolver out to check the load. Two rounds would be saved.

He crossed over the long columns of the Merki umens, the sea of faces turning up to watch his passage, scimitars flashing, defiant chants rising up, taunting him to come down.

He didn't even bother to lean out of the cab to give a derisive wave. He was too focused on what was ahead.

The three ships were at different altitudes, one almost at ground level, the second at his own, several thousand feet up, the third angling up a thousand feet higher.

He watched intently, calculating. Go for the top one and the low one goes straight through. Go for either of the other two and the top one comes down.

He decided, nervously opening and closing his fist, perspiration beading up under his goggles.

The ships were getting bigger, coming on, one staggered above the other. He started to pull up slightly, as if going for a climbing match against the topmost ship. The Merki aerosteamer raised its nose even higher, continuing to climb.

"Oh Perm, in our hour of need, heed our prayers to thee."

"Shut up and get ready."

He pulled the elevator full back, nose climbing.

"Dump the hot air!"

Feyodor reached up and grabbed hold of the release cord, pulling it full open.

"Going down hard. Hang on!"

The two aerosteamers straight ahead were pitching up higher in an attempt to outrace his climb.

He slammed the elevator full forward.

"Keep that speed at full bore."

The nose of *Republic* went down, crossing through the horizon, the pitch dropping down and speed increasing as he went through a forty-five-degree dive and then into a sixty, aiming straight ahead of the lowest ship, which was continuing to move straight on in.

He could not help but admire the courage of the crew in the lowest ship, who were obviously putting themselves in the position of bait to give an advantage to the upper two.

He saw a dark form moving atop the ship. "Jesus Christ, they've got someone on top!" Jack shouted.

The Merki, standing in a small basket, swung a swivel gun up, pointed straight at Jack, and fired. Most of the shot screamed to port, but a round of grape cracked into the forward hydrogen bag, a spar cracking from the impact.

"Son of a bitch! Why didn't we think of that?" Feyodor shouted.

"Hang on."

He continued the dive, pushing the nose farther forward, bracing the elevator stick with his knees, and leaned forward to look down the gun sight.

He swung it slightly to starboard, judging the distance. The front of the Merki ship filled the sight. Three hundred yards. A few more seconds.

"Pull the heat vent closed," Jack shouted. It'd be a minute or more before he needed the additional lift, but when he did it had to be there.

The center of the ship was in the sight, the Merki working with a rammer, reloading his gun.

He put his hand on the telegraph key, sparing a quick look down to check that it was over the first terminal. He looked back down the sight.

He pressed the key down, completing the circuit.

He wasn't really sure what to expect, and in the first instant it scared him to death. A rocket, strapped to a swivel mount below, flared to life, shooting out of its launch tube. The bottom of the basket was protected by a thin layer of tin. The rocket snapped forward, racing straight down at the Merki ship, flame and smoke blowing out the rear, and a curse started to form, for surely it would burn a hole right through the bottom of his own ship.

Directly behind the Merki gunner there was a flash of light even as Jack pulled back hard and slammed the rudder over full to port, still keeping the nose down.

The explosion of the ten-pound charge ripped the bag open, spraying it with grapeshot and burning pitch. A fireball leaped up, and as he started into his turn he leaned over to see the Merki ship collapsing into flames.

"Mother of Perm!"

Screaming, Feyodor was standing up, backing into Jack, the basket swaying, and he looked over his shoulder.

A harpoon was dangling out of the bottom of the bag, directly behind the propeller.

He waited for what seemed like an eternity for the explosion to hit, and then the harpoon started to fall again, a broken piece of rope trailing behind it. To the rear of the ship he saw a smoking board tumble off the aft end and fall to the ground.

Still shaking, he looked back forward. The nose was still down, the ground now only a few hundred feet below.

"The harpoon hit, but the rope broke. We're all right."

"It could still be burning!" Feyodor shouted.

"If it was, we'd be dead. Now shut up!"

He started to pull back hard on the elevator, sparing a quick glance at the mushroom of fire racing out over the steppe as the Merki ship impacted. Coming yet lower, he saw his shadow racing far ahead, another shadow moving across it to the rear at a right angle headed south.

He continued the dive then pulled back hard, fearing for an instant that though he knew the characteristics of his old *Yankee Clipper*, he had misjudged how this ship would handle.

The nose started to swing up, even as they continued to drop and then started to level out. The ground came racing up, the ship cutting an arc, the basket sweeping a dozen feet above the ground, the ship running full out, and then it started up into a climb.

He looked at his shadow, seeing the shadow of the Merki ship moving to the south. He pushed the rudder to starboard and started into a spiraling climb, nose now passing through thirty degrees. He realized he was rising a bit too slow; the harpoon hole in the hot air section was letting the lift escape. As he turned he saw the Merki ship leveling out, fifty feet off the ground, now alongside.

"Harpoon!"

Feyodor stood up, striking the friction match, dropping the board over. Continuing to climb, he aimed for the middle of the Merki ship, passing over it. A gunner was atop this one as well, firing, the shot tearing another hole in the bag.

"Harpoon away!"

Jack looked down, groaned as the spear seemed to be heading for the ship and then passed over it, skimming by to one side and continuing on down to the ground.

Another harpoon dropped past, this one forward. The other Merki ship.

He continued to pull back on the elevator and the nose rose yet higher, passing through sixty degrees, Feyodor cursing wildly.

He suddenly saw the bottom of the Merki ship passing overhead, a hundred yards straight ahead. He crouched over the gunsight, lining up. The hell with the range.

He looked down at the key, swung it to the middle terminal, and pressed down.

The rocket snapped out, racing forward, then turning on a long graceful arc straight into the ground, exploding just before it hit.

"Goddamm it, Ferguson!"

He threw the key to the third terminal and pressed down hard.

There was another flash. The rocket climbed straight up, less than a second later slamming into the bottom of the Merki ship forward of the cab. *Republic* continued to climb straight at it, and Jack was tempted to try ramming.

And then ever so slowly the nose of the ship started to crumple up, and he saw the explosions racing along the top, the hydrogen ignited by the rocket's going clean through from bottom to top, even though the warhead had failed to explode.

Jack pushed into a turning corkscrew dive, and as he watched to port, not fifty feet away the Merki ship tumbled down, the screams of the two crew members clearly audible even above the roar of the flames.

Shaking, he watched as it hit the ground several hundred feet below, one of the two crew actually crawling out of the wreckage, writhing in flames, and then collapsing.

The third ship was turning back to the north while he continued south, and he shot past it, not fifty yards away.

The other pilot was clearly visible as they approached, the Merki looking down at the wreckage of the two ships, and then back at Jack.

And to his astonishment the Merki did not shoot. Instead, he raised his hand almost in defiance, and yet almost in salute to a fellow aerosteamer pilot who had won, and then turned his ship away, heading back to the west.

"Did you see that?" Jack shouted.

"Guess he's had it."

"Flying fleets of one to a side," Jack said. "Maybe he wants to keep it that way."

He watched warily, expecting at any moment that the Merki would turn or go into a climb to position himself for another attack. But he continued straight on.

"Let's go home and get repaired," Jack said wearily, aware that he was beginning to shake violently. "The war's over for today."

"They're coming in."

Andrew, who had been dozing in his office, was instantly awake, heading out the door and into the glaring heat of day.

Eyes gummy, he looked up at the station clock, which miraculously had withstood two days of bombardment, its glass panes still intact.

Almost eleven. Six hours. Good.

He crossed the tracks and went up to the line of breastworks. A battery of light four-pounders to his right was kicking into action, adding its weight to the heavy fire of the grand battery that was now going into rapid fire.

It was difficult to see through the smoke. He raised his field glasses, and trained them on the opposite shore.

The checkerboard blocks were coming down the opposite slope at the run, the front lines well past the batteries, advanced skirmishers already into the river, the calf-deep water splashing as they crossed it at a slow run.

He looked back down to the valley. Through the haze he could see several guns being withdrawn to the rear, gunners clinging to the caissons, riders lashing the horses, skirmishers coming up out of the trenches and running for the rear.

"Any more word from the north?"

Pat shook his head.

"Telegraph line's still down. Last report was that

they had two, maybe three regiments across. The rail lines are still cut."

"Damn."

He ran a quick calculation. Sending Barry's reserve division back up would strip the line here. Schneid's entire corps was positioned from a couple of miles north of Hispania all the way down to here and a third of the way out along the ridge, only two regiments pulled to be reserve. Marcus was stretched on the far south and Vincent in the center. The Third and Fourth, both of them shattered, were in the center aboard trains, ready to be shifted.

Damn.

"What do you think?"

"Their mobility's down," Pat said meditatively, leaning over the parapet to eject a thin stream of tobacco juice. "Otherwise we'd be in the manure pile. Detach two regiments by train north, and keep the rest of the division here. That'll still give you eight fresh regiments."

Andrew looked back at the advancing host and then turned to a messenger.

"Send one regiment north from Barry's corps. Have 'em clear the line."

He looked back at Pat.

"The battle's here, and here's where we concentrate. If they cross north we'll deal with that later."

"What about the aerosteamer field, and that other factory of Chuck's?"

He hesitated.

Ferguson was supposed to bring his contraption up today. The damn thing might work, but most likely not. He couldn't wasted more reserves just to try to retrieve it.

"I can't spare the men," Andrew said coldly. "I'll need every regiment, every battery, right here before this day's finished."

*   *   *

The thunder of battle swelled closer.

Chuck Ferguson stood in the doorway of his factory, wiping the sweat from his brow, watching as the columns of smoke rose out of the woods.

"Getting damn close," Theodor said, coming up to join him.

He looked back to the rail siding running parallel to the factory. Three long trains were drawn up, crews working feverishly, bolting the frames down, loading the tubes. Not as many as he wanted, but still enough for one damn good shot. He'd soon be ready, but where the hell to go?

Over by the aerosteamer field a detachment of Merki had burst out of the woods, almost reaching the hangar that held *Republic* before being gunned down. The fight in the woods was insane confusion. Small detachments of both side were lost, and sections of the woods were on fire. Most of Barry's men were assigned to closing the gap to the south of the breakthrough.

He turned and walked back into the factory.

The last scrap of powder had been packed this morning, still far short of what he had fantasized, but that was fantasy and now he was staring a harsh reality in the face.

He was tempted to use it all here, but knew it'd be a waste. All the months of sneaking and planning had been for something far different, and by God he was going to see that it happened that way.

The long building was almost silent, except for the loading crews, the rest standing by the now-empty lathes and presses; even the steam engine that had powered it all had gone still.

He walked through the factory and saw them watching him, five hundred men and women.

"Theodor."

"Here, sir."

"Go back into the back warehouse. We've got fifty

Sharps carbines, a couple of dozen pistols, something like two hundred smoothbores. break them out."

Theodor looked at him and grinned, shouting for some workers to follow.

Chuck climbed up on top of a stamping machine.

"Many of you men got detached from your regiments in Barry's corps, which is now fighting to the south, so you know soldiering. I want you to take twenty, thirty people, form them into your companies. We've worked hard together, now we're going to fight together."

He hesitated.

"We've got something like two hundred and fifty guns, and there's five hundred of you, men and women. Two people to each gun. When one falls the other can still fight."

A defiant cheer went up. He had always wanted a field command, and now he finally had one.

"Magnificent, grim and magnificent," Vincent said, lowering his field glasses and looking over at Dimitri.

Taking off his hat, he raised it over his face to shade his eyes from the glare of the early-afternoon sun. In the plains below, the Merki army continued to deploy out into the open valley. Ten umens, he figured, two of them mounted. Artillery crews were pushing their weapons forward, already into extreme range, forming an arc of over two hundred guns, more still coming across the river, moving slowly, confined to the narrow width of the river that was beyond the range of the grand batteries positioned to the north and south of the arc.

A faint breeze stirred up from the valley, and he suppressed a gag.

"Must be a hundred degrees. Those dead bastards are starting to cook," Vincent said coldly.

"Imagine what it's like down there for them."

He put his hat back on, pulling the brim low, feeling

slightly light-headed, his mouth dry. He was tempted to take a drink but decided not to. It was going to be a very long afternoon, the heat would hold, and water would soon be short, even with the cisterns set up behind the line.

He looked down his line. Again that sense of awe. The men were sitting on the ground, resting, dozing in the heat, the long lines of his three divisions occupying nearly two miles of front, a hundred yards to each regiment. The central grand battery of fifty guns was to his left. He looked over at it, remembering his arrival here only days before. The villa was gone, the limestone blocks now piled up to reinforce the battery position.

The battery commander stood atop the wall, field glasses trained forward, shouting orders to his gunners, the rifled pieces being aimed to hit the Merki artillery pieces, the Napoleons to be used for the infantry and cavalry when they finally came in.

The tension was palpable, as if a safety valve had been jammed shut and the pressure within was building and building.

A battery of horse-drawn Merki artillery started to weave up a narrow lane down in the valley, passing the ruins of a vineyard pressing mill.

Vincent looked back at the battery. He knew that every landmark within range had been paced out.

"Fifteen hundred yards!"

The battery commander leaped down from the bastion, and a second later the first three-inch rifle kicked back, the shell screaming downrange with a high-pitched whine. Vincent trained his glasses forward. The Merki battery, still limbered, continued forward. A puff of smoke detonated to the right of the road next to the mill, long seconds later the distant crack of the exploding shell rolling back over the hill.

The eleven other rifled guns fired in salvo. Seconds later, shells bracketed the Merki, horses going down, soundless at this range, a caisson igniting, smoke rising up. A cheer rose up from the battery, the men leaping to reload.

From the north a distant rumble echoed, the northern battery now starting to engage. Vincent slowly moved his field glasses across the field, watching. The infantry was still back, formations coming into line, waiting, their lines building. Guns moving forward, pressing in closer to the ridge. The battery under fire continued forward at the gallop, moving up the road, coming in closer.

The first rifled piece fired again, this time dropping its shell near the rear of the advance, more horses going down. The front of the battery in column continued, crossing a dry creekbed and then swinging out into line, coming to a stop.

"Right down their throats!" the battery commander shouted. "A thousand yards!"

The rifles fired again. Shells detonated like blossoms around the guns, one of them losing a wheel, spinning around. The three surviving pieces unlimbered, gunners working to load.

Another battery came up the road, swerving to avoid the wreckage of the still-burning caisson. Over in the next field to the south, two more batteries in line abreast came up out of a vineyard, moving forward to support. Guns were now moving up all along the line, spreading outward from the center.

The first battery to advance finally fired a shot. Seconds later the round slammed into the ground fifty yards short of the grand battery, a plume of earth rising up, the solid ball ricocheting up into the air, passing lower over the battery and on into the rear, the gunners laughing disdainfully even as they fired, dismounting another of the enemy guns.

The second Merki battery up finally delivered its first shots, rounds screaming in, a shell exploding with a thunderclap a hundred yards forward, the ground churning up from impacting shots falling short.

The exchange started to flare outward, more and yet more of the Merki guns coming up on line and unlimbering, the arc of fire spreading outward around the valley.

A shot finally screamed overhead, a shell exploding directly over the grand battery. Screaming wounded were dragged to the rear moments later, the gunners now angrily at their work, as if an insult had been offered.

"What the hell is that?"

Vincent turned as Dimitri pointed to three soldiers moving down the line, the uniforms of two of them dark green, the other one wearing a faded blue jacket of the Union Army. Slung over his shoulder was a long rifle, a brass tube glistening atop it.

The three stopped, pointing down the slope as if arguing, and then moved down to a rifle pit, the men occupying it looking up and moving over. Vincent strolled down to watch.

"The only other Whitworth we've got," Vincent said with awe.

"What the hell is that?"

"The same kind of gun that killed Jubadi."

He moved over to the rifle pit. The three soldiers looked up, coming to their feet, saluting, but betraying that at the moment they felt they had better things to do than deal with nosy officers.

"Patrick O'Quinn, isn't it?"

The sniper squinted up at Vincent and smiled.

"The same it is, and you now a general and me still a private with the old 35th."

Vincent shook his head. Dimitri was surprised that Vincent didn't explode at the tone of insolence from Patrick.

"If you'd laid off the bottle and the women you'd have made command."

Patrick laughed.

"Some is born to such things, others to being generals. Me, I'd rather be doing this. Old Keane finally found a job I was suited for. Always was the best shot in the regiment, and now I'm killing officers." He stared at Vincent and smiled. "I like my work."

Vincent shook his head and gestured for them to carry on. He squatted down behind the pit to watch.

An assistant set up a tripod. The gunner rested the muzzle upon it and lay down, bringing the gun to his shoulder squirming slightly.

"Roll up the blanket and get it under me armpit," Patrick said, and his assistant pulled a small blanket out of an oversized haversack and tucked it up under Patrick's right arm, the soldier shifting and settling down.

The other assistant sat on the ground, knees apart, elbows resting upon them, a telescope in his hands.

"The one to the right of the first gun on line—I think that's the bastard."

"Stand still, you son of a whore," Patrick whispered.

Vincent raised his glasses to watch and saw a Merki on foot, arm up, pointing, obviously shouting, an officer. The Merki turned and moved to the next gun, leaning over to look along its barrel, and then stood back up. A shell detonated behind him, and he ducked.

"Tell those bastards to stop shooting. They're ruining me aim," Patrick snapped.

The Merki battery commander moved down the line to the next gun, and the instant he stopped, the Whitworth cracked off.

Vincent sat transfixed, watching. The Merki crouched down slightly, stood back up, and started to turn his head. Then he doubled over, collapsing on the ground. The warriors beside him looked at him with astonishment.

"The fourth damn one today!" Patrick barked.

Vincent looked over at the man with admiration.

"A good kill," he said softly.

"Kill bloody officers, that's what Keane wanted, that's what I'm giving him. It's something I've always wanted to do."

Vincent said nothing. He came back up to his feet.

"Let's go get the next one," Patrick announced, rising up and passing the Whitworth over to his assistant. He looked at Vincent and smiled. "Hell, I might even turn out to be as good a killer as the famous Quaker."

He laughed crudely, spit a stream of juice on the ground, and continued on down the line, Vincent watching him silently.

"Son of a bitch," Dimitri said softly.

"Never mind," Vincent replied. "The bastard's right."

He turned and looked back out at the growing battle.

"Magnificent," he said softly. "Magnificent."

Tamuka Qar Qarth rode along the line, squinting through the smoke. The bombardment was apparently one-sided, the cattle upon the hills having the advantage of height and obviously of skill. Forward he saw several batteries with half their guns smashed or out of action. The two days of bombardment had depleted nearly all the ammunition stocks; he couldn't maintain this rate of fire much longer. There was another report that was almost as disturbing. One after another, since yesterday, battery commanders were being shot from long distance. Most likely by a murder weapon like the one used by Yuri.

He kept his distance from the batteries.

He looked back to the west. From the opposite side of the river the last umen of the spotted black horse was advancing into the river on foot, the midafternoon sun behind it.

The battle was going too slow, far too slow. Two-thirds of the day wasted by this tedious advance on foot, waiting for guns to be moved, for paths for them to be cleared through the corpses, for infantry to move up, all of it taking far too much time.

And the heat. It was almost as bad as the burning sands beyond Constan. Only light breaths of air occasionally stirring, the sky cloudless, the color almost of polished brass.

Water now had become a serious problem. Fetching it from below the crossing was no longer possible because of the rotting corpses in the river. No water could be taken from the few muddy rivulets running in this valley; his warriors refused to drink water that smelled of death and corruption. Already it was reported that thousands in the ranks were sick, some even dying, vomiting or shitting uncontrollably, adding to the general stench of the area. As he rode down the line he could see his warriors, heads lowered in the heat, panting, commanders shouting orders not to drink.

It was almost time. It had to be now.

He crossed over a small creek, water no longer flowing, the bottom churned to mud, bodies pressed into it, bloated, swollen, and distended. His horse, trying to gain the opposite bank, stepped on a corpse, shying away nervously; a puff of air came up from the body.

Tamuka retched, ashamed at his display of a weak stomach, even though more than one on his staff had vomited from the cloying stench. He gained the opposite bank and started to retch again from the smell. Before him, what had once been a cattle house was now a burned-out ruin, charred corpses of his warriors piled around the building, a half-burned body hanging out of a broken flame-scorched window, its insides spilling out onto the ground like a bloody curtain. Upon a stake beside the house the decapitated head of one of his warriors had been set, mouth open, swollen blackened tongue protruding, eyes gouged out.

Drawn up beside the house was a line of warriors on horseback, and he approached them, angry that the sacrilege had not been taken down.

Tamuka snapped his fingers and pointed at the head. A silent one ran up to the head and removed it from the stake, setting it next to a corpse that it might belong to.

Muzta Qar Qarth watched the action with bemused interest. "Sorry, we forgot to clean up around here," he said with a grin.

Tamuka said nothing.

"Merki seem to smell the same as Tugars, maybe a bit worse. Another day of your fighting and you'll even have as many dead."

"There'll be more of you as well," Tamuka said coldly.

"I assumed that."

"You've ridden with the horde of Merki for more than a season now and have done precious little. Today your umen can start the assault," and as he spoke he pointed at the grand battery positioned in front of Hispania.

"And see my remaining people killed on a useless assault?" Muzta snapped. "This battle is all wrong—it's become a madness."

"Are the Tugars afraid to fight?"

"We do not believe in suicide."

"You seemed to do a good job of it once before."

"You do not know about these people at all," Muzta snapped. "You still see them as cattle, but by all my ancestors I've seen cattle fight with a ferocity unimagined," and as he spoke he pointed to the piles of dead that were heaped across the field. "Tamuka, our enemies have become like us, perhaps even better, in the making of war."

Tamuka continued to point at the grand battery.

"I don't mind dying when there's a purpose," Muzta snarled, "but to attack that cannon-covered hill is madness."

"We will attack all along the line, from north to south, the pressure striking everywhere at once."

"You are fighting on the field Keane chose. I heard he slaughtered fifty, maybe sixty thousand yesterday, and he'll do the same today."

"Damn your soul! Attack!" Tamuka snarled.

"You think you have the *ka*," Muzta said coldly. "You have the spirit to kill, yes, you have that, but you have none of the cunning of the true warrior. That is how my people beat yours at Orki when outnumbered more than two to one—we fought with cunning and skill. Keane has walked you straight into this valley, and you batter your head against the wall he has made. You are a fool and your people are fools for letting you rule over them, a weakling who plays at war and does not understand it. A hundred thousand of your people will be dead or wounded before this day is done, and still the cattle will stand. It is a lesson that Qubata finally taught me, but you have no Qubata, only yourself.

"Tamuka, our enemies now excel over us even in the art of killing. Stop this madness now, use your *tu*, not the *ka*, see and find another path to victory."

"Attack, or I'll cut you down myself for your impudence, you Tugar bastard!"

The knot of mounted warriors around Muzta drew their scimitars, edging up to protect their Qar Qarth, the silent ones of Tamuka nocking arrows, standing ready, half-raising their bows toward Muzta.

A thin smile creased Muzta's face.

"Murderer of Jubadi and Vuka, watch how Tugars can die," he snarled, and with a vicious jerk to his mount he turned to gallop down the front of his line, waving his sword and pointing straight up the hill.

Tamuka looked around at his staff, who sat astride their mounts, impassive, no comment made.

"Order the assault to begin," he said, his voice barely a whisper.

Andrew lowered his telescope and looked over at Pat.

"I think that's him, Vuka, the one on the left."

"Where the hell is O'Quinn, the bastard? We could have tried a shot."

"Never mind that now," Andrew said, raising his telescope.

The other one was Muzta Qar Qarth, he was certain of it. Twice he had met him face to face, the first time in the parley just before their final assault, the second when, in a remarkable display, the Tugar had returned Kathleen and Vincent alive.

He braced the telescope on the parapet wall, oblivious to the bombardment raging around him, cursing when a curtain of smoke blocked the view, a wisp of noisome breeze pulling the curtain back again.

He saw the flicker of swords, a circle of warriors on foot surrounding the other one, bows half drawn.

It was the same Merki he had seen before, and somehow he sensed it was the same one who attempted to walk in his thoughts.

Curious.

The standard was nearby, that of the Qar Qarth, but no shield-bearer's emblem.

Muzta turned and galloped off, the circle of warriors around the leader lowering their bows at his departure.

A horn sounded and Muzta rode on, waving his scimitar, pointing straight to where Andrew was.

"Forced to attack," Pat observed. "A bit of trouble in the ranks."

He could hear the excited cries rippling along his line, men standing up, pointing down the long slope, as the umen of the Tugars stepped off, coming straight north toward the grand battery.

"Load case shot, five-second fuses!"

The gunners with the Napoleons leaped to their work, eager to begin, having sat out the entire bombardment and counterbattery fire in order to conserve ammunition, the work left solely to the far more accurate three-inch rifles.

Andrew barely paid attention. Instead he was focused on the other, who was now pointing to the ridge to the east and then to the south, as if drawing a half circle.

"They're going to hit everywhere at once," Andrew said quietly.

More horns sounded, the cry carrying off to the south.

Tamuka, is that you? Are you the Qar Qarth?

The leader turned and looked over his shoulder, his gaze rising up, looking straight at Andrew.

Unable to resist the urge, Andrew lowered his telescope, climbed up atop the parapet, and stood with his one arm extended in full view of the valley below.

He focused his thoughts as if his confidence and rage could somehow strike into Tamuka like a spear.

So now you're the warrior king and no longer the adviser. How do you like it, you bastard? Did you kill Vuka to get it?

"Andrew, what the hell are you doing?"

Pat was standing on the ground beside him, looking up gap-mouthed, shuddering as a shell screamed in, detonating overhead, shards of shrapnel hissing down.

Andrew laughed coldly and leaped back down, his features grim.

"What the hell was that all about?"

"Nothing," Andrew said, still shaken by the focus of rage he had sensed in return.

The Merki guns below started to fall silent, and

from out of the swirls of smoke he saw the advancing lines of the Tugars coming straight at his position.

The thirty Napoleons within the battery fired in salvo. Andrew leaned against the parapet to watch, raising his telescope, searching for Muzta.

Case shot burst over the line, and he found Muzta, his horse rearing, going over and down. He held his breath and saw Muzta stagger back up, his aides running up to him. He shook himself and started back in.

Surprised at his own reaction, Andrew actually felt a flicker of relief. He's the enemy, dammit, he argued to himself. Yet he had spared Kathleen and Vincent, returned them, honoring the memory of a fallen comrade.

"I almost hope you make it," Andrew whispered.

Back along the rest of the line the assault was coming forward, a dark wave moving out in a vast semicircle, horns blaring, chanting rising up. Along the crest he saw the regiments coming to their feet in anticipation, hundreds of puffs of smoke snapping out as all the artillery, which had held back for this moment, opened fire.

He looked over his shoulder at his headquarters building. The clock face was smashed, the hands twisted. He pulled out his own watch to check. A quarter to three—more than five hours of daylight left.

"I'm going over to the central battery. You stay here and keep an eye on the situation to the north."

Pat smiled, looking down the slope at the advancing Tugar charge, shells blossoming over the ranks, the four-pounders now opening up, hurling their solid shot down the slope.

"It'll be some fine killing here."

Andrew nodded, then mounted his horse and galloped off down the line.

*   *   *

It was an insane madness, and he gloried in it. He had lost count after six assaults. Nothing mattered anymore, not even victory, only the killing.

All the way up to his lines the forward slope was blanketed with Merki corpses. To the right of the central battery they had even lapped a hundred yards into his rear, until Gregory had brought up what was left of Third Corps to seal the breach.

He looked back behind his line. A train was rolling north, pulling a dozen flatcars, hundreds of casualties piled aboard, heading to the hospital. On the opposite track, racing south, another train screamed past, whistle shrieking, more flatcars, laden with limber chests filled with artillery ammunition.

Madness, magnificent madness.

He looked to the north, seeing bursts of smoke on the ridge, Merki artillery rolled up, a breach in the line across the crest.

"Here it comes again!"

He looked forward, squinting into the early-evening sun. Another wall advanced out of the smoke, chanting now, a hoarse guttural shrieking.

"Rifles at two hundred and fifty yards, smoothbores at seventy-five!" His voice was barely a whisper, but it didn't matter; the men knew what to do, his men, fighting like tigers.

He looked along the slope. In sections the regimental lines were down to single ranks, torn flags fluttering, 31st Roum to his right, 2nd Capri to his left, anchoring into the grand battery, reinforced now by a regiment from Third Corps.

The battery was in ruins, a sustained barrage of a hundred Merki guns having pounded it now for over four hours. Half the guns were smashed or crewless.

The charge continued forward, coming straight at him.

He grinned.

*   *   *

"Once more, just once more!" Tamuka screamed. Helmet off, black hair streaming, scimitar in hand, he galloped along the front of the line, pointing forward.

Three times they had gained the crest this afternoon, and one breakthrough was still pushing in. He could sense it—their reserves were gone, the lines thinner.

His warriors looked up at him, eyes bloodshot, tongues lolling, panting for breath, gasping in the heat and smoke, moving as if possessed, exhaustion sinking in. Warriors were collapsing from lack of water and the heat. Five fresh umens were supposed to be up, crossing the river even now, struggling forward through the ruins, the wreckage, the streams of casualties staggering to the rear.

He pointed forward, looking up the slope, seeing the thin line atop it.

Now I have you now, he thought, sensing the presence. Look upon me and despair.

The charge lurched forward, warriors stepping over bodies, hoarsely chanting their death songs, breaking into a staggering run, moving slowly, woodenly, yet pressing forward one more time, and he reined in to see the final destruction.

Andrew pulled up hard alongside Vincent, Mercury shivering with exhaustion, dried sweat caking his sides.

"You've got to hold!" Andrew screamed. "You've got to hold!"

Vincent looked up at Andrew, sensing the desperation, his commander on the edge.

"I'm shifting what's left of Third and Fourth Corps to cover the breach to your right," Andrew said.

"I need reserves," Vincent said, pointing forward to the Merki advance, now less than five hundred yards away.

Andrew leaned forward, his vision blurring. He felt

light-headed, on the point of fainting. The hundred-degree heat, the goddam heat—he could never stand it.

Not now, dammit, don't faint, not now.

An orderly came up to Andrew's side, uncorked a canteen, pulled Andrew's open collar back, and poured water down Andrew's neck. He started to shiver, and leaning over Mercury's flank, he vomited, knowing that heat stroke was taking hold. He felt a cold sweat breaking out. Almost in a fatherly fashion the young orderly talked softly, soaked a handkerchief, and draped it around Andrew's neck.

He sat back up, near to swooning.

"You've got to hold, Vincent. We've got to make it to sundown."

"Reserves?" Vincent's voice was cold.

Andrew, squinting, looked to their left. The higher ground held by Marcus's Seventh and the division of the Fifth was still secure, the grand battery at the far end of the line smashing the flank of the Merki assaults.

"I'll bring up Marcus's reserve brigade."

He spurred Mercury and galloped off, swaying, trying to hang on, to keep his mind working. The entire line was set to crack, the pressure unbelievable, the slaughter in five hours as bad as all the day before. The third division of Second Corps had been completely overrun, annihilated. Every other unit had sustained horrific casualties from the long hours of a stand-up toe-to-toe fight that seemed to go on without letup. His only advantage lay in the artillery, the three hundred remaining guns firing downslope, chewing up the charge before they even got into arrow-volley range. And yet enough survived to get forward and to pour in a devastating fire. Everyone was screaming for reserves. Barry, up in the forest, was fighting desperately to close yet another breach, begging for just one more regiment. But there was none left; the army was cracking apart.

He swerved around the back of the central grand battery, riding hard down the road, casualties moving aside at his approach, men looking up to him in blind shock, some in recognition, feebly saluting, shouting encouragement.

Behind him he heard what was left of Sixth Corps cut loose with a thundering volley.

John Mina awoke as if from a dreadful dream. He opened his eyes and looked around weakly.

So it wasn't a dream. All the memories came back of what he had said, all that he had done, the failure at the end of it all.

Shakily he stood up, noticing for the first time that the tent was packed with wounded. A thundering roar outside.

Then the battle was already on.

His trousers and uniform jacket were draped over the edge of his cot, and he pulled them on, not bothering with his boots, and stepped out of the tent.

"My God," he whispered.

At the edge of the hospital area he could see the thin line standing, wrapped in smoke, shadowy forms coming up over the inner line of breastworks.

To his left a pistol shot snapped out, and he turned. A Merki staggered forward into the hospital area where the wounded lay, collapsing.

The wounded by the hundreds stirred, looking up, watching as the line forward started to buckle in. A boy came out of the smoke, wide-eyed.

"Ammunition, ammunition," he chanted hysterically and disappeared to the rear.

Overhead a flurry of arrows arced past, some of them coming down into the tents, men screaming inside.

John looked around. How long had this been going

on? There was still powder to get, trains to move, ammunition to send out, all of it.

No, not now, and then he remembered the rest.

It was finished, all of it finished, but there was still one last thing to do, to retrieve it all in the end.

He saw a discarded musket on the ground, barrel bent, bayonet still attached, dried blood on the gleaming shaft. He picked it up and looked forward, and then back at the wounded that carpeted the field.

"Come on!" John screamed, and the men looked at him.

"Do you want to die lying down or standing up? Come on!"

Men started to stand back up, picking up their weapons, slowly moving back toward the crumbling line. He looked down at his gun. Ammunition? It was .58 caliber, wasn't it, or was it? Cartridge box—where was that? Where was any of it? And then he started to laugh. It simply didn't matter anymore.

"Give 'em the cold steel!" John screamed, and lowering his musket he ran into the smoke, disappearing from view.

"Stand, boys, you've got to stand!"

Vincent walked along the back of the line, peering forward through the smoke, trying to gauge what was happening.

Arrows were streaking in low, hissing past, the ground a forest of shafts sticking out of the ground. The dead lay in a long row directly behind the firing line. Open gaps were evident everywhere, sections of twenty, thirty feet or more where not a single man was left standing, the regiments dressing to the center, contracting in around their flags, tight knots of beleaguered survivors. He looked to his rear. The plateau behind him was empty, the vast open plain stretching on to the far horizon. He could see it clearly now, the

horde riding straight on east, spreading out, mushrooming far into the rear.

"Dimitri!"

The old man came up to him, limping badly, blood
trickling from his thigh, the wooden end of a broken-
off shaft sticking out.

"Get to the tracks. Stop any trains, any of them, I
don't give a fuck if they've got wounded, take some
men, and stop them and keep them there, directly
behind us."

Dimitri saluted and hobbled off.

The arc of fire continued to slash out from his line,
four-pound guns leaping up, their four-man crews
working feverishly. A soldier staggered out of the line
in front of him, clutching his stomach, turning to look
back at Vincent, and went to the ground, twisting and
gasping. Vincent picked up his musket and stepped
over the wounded soldier, two arrows in his leg. He
was sitting numbly, watching the blood spurt out.

"You can load, dammit, load for someone who can
shoot!"

It all started to seem surreal as thoughts, images,
and memories mixed. A Roum boy stood rigid before
him, mechanically beating his drum, tears streaming
down his face. An old man, cursing, finished loading,
jammed his ramrod into the ground, leaned forward,
aiming carefully, firing, and then pulled his cartridge
box open for another round, the curses never stopping. A captain, bandage covering his blood-soaked
eyes, continued to stand, leaning against the flag
bearer of the regiment, shouting encouragement. Two
young soldiers, both wounded, crawled along the line
dragging an ammunition box between them, pulling
out ten-round packages, passing them up, then continuing on, one dragging, one pushing. A young soldier
jammed a round into a barrel that was filled to the
muzzle with unexpended rounds, raised his gun, and
squeezed, completely forgetting to put on a percussion

cap, and then started to load again, oblivious to the fact that he was not even shooting.

Vincent heard a whistle shrieking, and he looked back to see several of his men standing on the track, Dimitri alongside the engine, pistol raised as if threatening to shoot the engineer, two more trains behind him, flatcars heading south to pick up the wounded of the Seventh. The hell with them—there was more important work.

From out of the smoke he saw the Merki coming. An angry hoarse shout of rage rose up from the men as the line came on at a run, scimitars and lances flashing.

The men staggered up from out of the shallow trench, bayonets gleaming. Vincent unholstered his pistol, checking the load. The charge bore in, a last flurry of shots dropping many at point-blank range, the men still armed with smoothbores doing the worst damage with loads of buckshot.

They sagged backward from the weight of the impact, men jabbing upward to strike their taller foes, scimitars coming down with such strength that bodies were split from shoulder to sternum, arms cut off, heads severed or crushed.

Vincent found himself looking straight up at a warrior who seemed to be moving far too slowly, his panting breath washing over him with a fetid stench, eyes bulging. He put a round into the Merki's face and turned, backing up. A flash to his left and he fell back, feeling the icy slice of the scimitar as the tip of the blade laid his arm open. Hitting the ground, he raised his pistol, pressing it into the Merki's groin and firing. The Merki tumbled backward, shrieking in agony.

The line was buckling, losing the crest of the hill. But the Merki were coming on too slowly, their line too thin, many of them staggering forward, moving barely faster than a slow walk. None fell back, however; they pressed forward, dying, trading life for life. And then there were none left standing.

Gasping, Vincent looked around.

There were hardly any of his own left standing either. The men pushed their way back to the forward edge of the ridge, bayonets rising and falling as they killed the Merki wounded.

A breeze was stirring up, smoke clearing momentarily. To the north the sound of battle was like a hurricane, a perpetual thunder as if the world were being ripped apart, flashes lighting the ridge, what he assumed to be Third and Fourth Corps pressing in on the flank of the breakthrough in a desperate bid to close it off.

He heard something else, this time forward, and it reminded him suddenly of long ago when with the 7th Suzdal he had held the pass while the army retreated. It was the sound of cavalry advancing.

Through shifts in the smoke he saw a dark wall of Merki cavalry deploying out directly in front of his position a thousand yards away. His entire front was gone, not one man in four still left standing.

He looked to his rear. Dimitri had done his job. It was a last chance.

"Fall back behind the trains!" he shouted, his voice cracking, and he pointed toward the three trains that were backed up on the track behind him, their flatcars and boxcars forming a wall several hundred yards long. The regiment to his left, responding to the command, started to the rear, picking up their wounded as they pulled out. He looked up at the young Rus major now commanding the grand battery, who was watching with growing alarm as the infantry to his right turned and started to run.

Vincent pointed to the train, and the officer suddenly understood, ordering that some of the Napoleons were to be deployed to the right.

From the grand battery north the line started to the rear.

"Now, now in and after them!" Tamuka shouted, swinging his mount around, his *ka* at last taking possession. With scimitar drawn, he fell in with the umen of the black horse and started into the charge.

Andrew turned and saw the heavy block formation starting forward, the front of Vincent's line giving way, heading to the rear.

"What the hell is he doing?" Andrew screamed, unable to see the line of trains to the rear.

He felt, with a sickening certainty, that the war had just been lost.

"He must have a reason. That madman would die rather than retreat."

Andrew turned and saw Marcus coming up beside him, nearly a full division of reserve troops emerging from the smoke on the double.

"Let's go," Andrew gasped, certain that by the time they arrived, the entire front of his line would be gone.

"Behind the railroad cars, get behind and under the cars!"

The thin line of soldiers climbed over the trains, still dragging their wounded, pulling on the men even as they screamed in agony. Vincent climbed up into the cab of the middle train, the engineer looking over at him.

"This plays hell with the schedule," the engineer growled, and Vincent started to explode until he realized that the man was grinning, reaching for a revolver, and then putting his hand to an icon of Saint Malady to say a quick prayer. The thunder of hooves grew louder and yet louder.

Forward on the edge of the ridge the grand battery

continued its work, the first gun on the flank opening up, firing across the slope.

The first rider appeared over the crest of the hill, and then a wall of riders, moving forward at the gallop. Another gun in the battery fired, slicing down an entire line at nearly point-blank range, but the charge continued forward.

Vincent leaned out of the engine cab. His men were standing ready.

The charge closed in, and as the first of the Merki riders reached the side of the train the men opened fire. A mad seething explosion of noise rose up, horses screaming, Merki and humans roaring their anger and defiance. The forward line went down, more piling up behind them.

But there was no place to go forward, the three-hundred-yard front of trains blocking them. The rear ranks still pressed up the slope, believing that they were riding to victory. The press forward increased, riders jamming up against the side of the train, infantry standing behind the cars, shooting up. Merki started to leap off their horses, running across the width of the cars, men shooting them, pitchforking them with bayonets. The entire train started to shake beneath Vincent's feet as if it could somehow be upended.

The engineer, screaming madly, leaned out of the cabin window, shooting, and then reached up and yanked the steam vent cord. Hot steam sliced out, and wild shrieks rose up.

Vincent, standing in the cab doorway, emptied his revolver into the press and then drew back, drawing his sword, suddenly and very painfully aware of a cut to his arm.

The engineer staggered backward, a lance buried in his chest, and collapsed. He reached up to grab hold of his icon, pulled it down, and died.

A roar of a musket exploded behind Vincent, and

he turned to see a Merki who was trying to climb through the cab window tumble backward, his face gone, the fireman crouching low beside his engineer, a sawed-off musket braced against his side. Throwing the weapon away, the fireman picked up a shovel, tore open the door into the firebox, pulled out a load of gleaming coals, and threw them out the doorway, laughing maniacally.

He went down, an arrow in his chest.

A Merki rode up next to the door and jumped from his mount, filling the world before Vincent. Vincent leaped forward and drove his sword into the Merki's stomach. The Merki looked at him wide-eyed, dropping his own blade, hands feebly grasping around Vincent's blade.

Vincent tried to pull the sword out; it was stuck.

The Merki continued to look straight into his eyes.

Vincent backed up, pulling hard, screaming hysterically, and the sword slid out, the Merki falling to his side. The Merki continued to look at him and slowly grinned.

"A good fight, human. You have *ka*," he gasped in broken Rus.

Vincent stared at him, speechless, and then in the distance he heard the bugles.

Tamuka, screaming with rage, pushed himself out of the charge.

He needed infantry, infantry and guns. He could see other units down in the valley, broken formations, shattered guns, thousands of disorganized warriors staggering toward the rear, some struggling with each other for possession of water skins taken from the dead. Forward, the press was impossible, Merki jammed up against the side of the trains. The warriors to the rear had nothing to fire upon and were unable to advance or retreat. The guns to his flank were tearing the charge to shreds, the warriors unable to ride up into the bastion.

A thunderous volley rose up on his right, and he saw the thin line of cattle infantry advancing.

And yet forward, forward and to the left. He could see it all so clearly as darkness began to settle. Except for the thin line here behind the train, there was nothing left, nothing at all, not a single cattle left in reserve. If it had not been for this final trick, even now his warriors would be far to the rear, victory complete.

He turned, and for a brief instant he saw him, riding along the line, his one hand up, pointing. He could sense the panic, the fear, all his thoughts at this second so clear, the dreadful certainty that he had already lost and was riding to die, a final redemption for himself, and then he was lost to view.

"I have you, damn you, I have you!" Tamuka screamed, even as the charge around him started to break. "One more charge and I have you!"

He turned his mount and started to the rear.

Reaching the edge of the battery, Andrew reined in, stunned. Before him the Merki riders were jammed up in confusion, hundreds of them down around the guns, horses screaming, the charge at a complete halt, pressed up around the trains.

A wild shout rose up around him, the infantry, staggering from exhaustion, from the forced march and the final run, coming up, all formation lost, leaping past Andrew and going in.

Andrew turned to see Marcus riding up, the old Roum standing up tall in his stirrups, short sword pointed forward, shouting with a fierce exultation.

The flanking charge hit with a mad fury, the men wading in, shooting down Merki at point-blank range, horses kicking, riderless mounts dashing through the line, heading into the rear.

"By the gods, that boy did it again," Marcus shouted.

Andrew slumped forward in his saddle, numbed.

He had thought it already finished, felt a cold sense of release almost taking over, as if nothing remained but die. And yet it was still going on, another staving-off at the very last moment. He felt completely used up. The strain of the last two days of desperation had gone deep into his soul, deeper than he had ever known before. He sat watching, and yet not seeing, as Marcus's soldiers broke the Merki charge and sent it streaming to the rear.

Vincent sat slumped in the corner of the engine cab, the dead engineer and fireman beside him. Outside he could hear hoarse triumphal shouts, the screams of wounded animals, guttural shouts of pain, the roar of battle starting to drift away.

"Thought we had won," the Merki said, between gasps of pain. Blood was now flowing freely from his mouth, dripping onto the iron floor of the engine cab.

"You speak Rus," Vincent whispered.

"Rus pet when child, loyal, good."

The Merki coughed, doubling up in a spasm.

"Kill me, end this."

A dark flash of memory filled him, the Merki hanging on the cross, dying. He looked down at the revolver in the corner of the cab. It was empty. Still clutching his sword, he came to his knees, and the Merki nodded.

"Wait." He started to cough again. "Fathers, see me now, accept my spirit, forgive me my sins, let me ride beside you through the everlasting sky, and grant to me the power to protect my wife, my sons, though I am gone."

Stunned, Vincent looked at the Merki.

"Those are our words at death." The Merki grinned,

seeing the shock on Vincent's face. "Now kill me, cattle."

"We are not cattle," Vincent hissed. "We are men."

"Perhaps you are right, but I die hating you nevertheless for what you've done to us."

"And what you have done to me!" Vincent shrieked, and he leaned forward, driving his sword into the Merki's throat.

A spasm went through the Merki's body, and blood sprayed out across Vincent's face.

The Merki continued to look at him, almost smiling. The breathing stopped, the blood in a vast pool around him, eyes still open.

Vincent Hawthorne fell back against the far side of the cab, still looking at the Merki.

And what we have done to each other, he thought.

Protect my wife, my sons, though I am gone.

Tanya, little Andrew, the twins. What are we doing to each other?

All of it flooded over him, the tiny cab now his entire universe, the engineer dead, icon of a old friend clutched to his chest, the fireman beside him, the dead Merki by the door, the blood of all three flowing together, outside the sound of battle drifting away, the world becoming dark, and over all the smell of death heavy in the air.

He leaned forward, shoulders shaking.

Oh my God, what have I become? What am I doing? Am I truly like them now?

God help me.

Sobs started to rack his body, sobs he had not known since he was a child, a time that inside his heart he knew was not so long ago.

He heard someone approach, but he no longer cared. Face buried in his hands, he cried, the fresh tears mingling with the blood, washing it away.

He felt an arm go around his shoulder.

"It's all right, son. Let it out, cry it out."

It was Marcus.

Leaning into the old soldier's shoulder, he cried, his friend holding him tightly.

If this is field command, Chuck thought grimly, they can keep it. Crawling forward, he stuck his head into a small pool of muddy water, and drank deeply. He heard a twig snap.

He jerked up and rolled, raising his carbine, and pulled the trigger.

The chamber was empty.

A rifle cracked behind him, and the Merki crumpled up, crashing into the water. He looked at the body, still twitching, realizing that the lone Merki had approached the muddy pond with the same intent as he had.

He looked back over his shoulder. An old woman crouched down behind a tree, hands shaking.

"Good shot, mother," he said, and crawled back to her.

Still shaking, she clicked the breech of the Sharps carbine open and chambered another round. This time he remembered to do the same.

A slow but steady crackle of gunfire boomed through the forest. It was hard to tell exactly what was going on. The fight was a mad confusion of small groups hunting and being hunted. To his right, down by the river, he could hear a more steady thunder, a straggler having told him that First Corps was sealing the breech.

That was all well and good, but there could still be hundreds, perhaps thousands, of the bastards in the woods.

He looked over at the only soldier in his entire unit he was now in touch with.

"Olga, isn't it?"

"Yes, your excellency."

"I'm not your excellency, dammit."

"No, your excellency," and she smiled weakly.

"That was a good shot. Thank you."

"It was an honor to kill him," she said, showing him a toothless grin.

"Well, let's go get another."

"You've got other work to do," she said. "We'll hold things here. Now get the hell back and get that train moving, before its too late."

Andrew walked through the hospital ward, trying to project a sense of calm, a sense that somehow it was still under control and victory was possible.

The world was a nightmare. He knew that something like thirty thousand had been wounded. Another ten thousand were already dead, and thousands more were missing.

The army as a fighting unit was finished. Third and Fourth Corps together wouldn't make a strong brigade between them. Vincent's Sixth was not much better, Schneid's Second had lost half its men, Marcus's Seventh almost as many. It was a shambles and here was the aftermath, the mangled wreckage chewed out and left behind. In the lantern light it looked as if the etching of a Dürer nightmare had come to life. Limbless men were stretched out in row after row. He passed through a ward of stomach wounds, men whom Emil, Kathleen, or two or three other doctors might have saved if given the time, but who were now left to die, so many were the casualties.

He weaved his way through the tents, stopping occasionally as a hand reached up to grab him.

"We licked 'em good today, didn't we colonel?"

He'd nod and smile.

"We'll win, won't we?"

Again he'd smile.

A young man grabbed hold of his arm, reaching up

from the floor, and he looked down. The face was familiar, from the old 35th.

"Billy, how are you?" Andrew said softly, stopping and kneeling down on the bloody floor.

"Not good, colonel," he whispered.

"I saw your brigade fight today. You did good, son, very good."

The young brigadier smiled weakly.

"I'm afraid, sir," he whispered.

Andrew didn't know what to say, feeling already the coldness in the young veteran's hand.

"What should I do now?"

Andrew lowered his head.

"Remember back home, on earth?"

Billy smiled sadly.

"Remember the prayer your mother taught you when you went to sleep?"

Billy nodded.

"Let's say it."

His voice came out, barely a whisper, and Andrew joined him.

"Now I lay me down to sleep . . ."

Andrew finished the prayer alone, the soldier's hand slipping out of his.

Andrew pulled the blanket up over the boy's head and heard crying behind him.

It was Kathleen.

She wiped the tears away.

"That poor boy. He kept calling for his mother, and then you came."

"Most of them do call for their mothers in the end," he said softly.

"I keep realizing how much more I love you," she whispered. "Andrew, thank God you're still alive."

"Where's Emil?"

"Next tent. Why?"

"I need to talk to him."

She fell silent, as if knowing. Then she asked, "How are we doing? I've been hearing things all day, and I don't know what to believe."

"Take me to Emil," he said softly.

Taking his hand, she led him into the next tent, where Emil was finishing up a surgery, extracting an arrow from a boy's chest, laying a bandage across the wound, turning away to wash his hands while an assistant finished bandaging the wound. Emil looked up to see Andrew, and his eyes were dark circles of exhaustion.

"We need to talk," Andrew said.

Emil motioned for him to wait. The assistant and orderly picked up the stretcher and carried it out of the tent. Emil followed them and then came back a moment later, pulling the flap shut behind him.

"How bad is it?" Emil asked.

Andrew looked over at Kathleen and tried to form the words but couldn't.

"It's finished, isn't it?" Kathleen said softly.

Andrew nodded, unable to speak.

Emil exhaled noisily and sat down in a chair in the corner.

"And you're here to tell me I should kill the wounded."

Andrew hesitated, wishing somehow that Kathleen weren't here, wanting to tell her to leave. He looked back at her. There was a sad gentle smile on her lips. No tears, no anguish or hysteria, only a vast hidden strength.

"Even if it all ends tomorrow, it was still worth it," she whispered, coming up and putting her arm around him.

He nodded, kissing her on the forehead.

"At least Maddie will be safe awhile longer," she said softly. "For that only it was worth it all."

He tried not to think of his daughter; he knew if he

did it would finish him. He had to keep his thoughts focused. He looked back at Emil.

"You know how many casualties we've had. I've got less than thirty thousand men left able to fight, and not even enough ammunition to get us through another day. The artillery's almost been depleted. First charge tomorrow and they'll be through us. And then . . ."

His voice trailed off.

"My God, Emil, you know what they'll do to those poor men out there," and he nodded toward the madness just outside the tent.

Emil reached over to a side table. With hands shaking he poured himself a drink and downed it.

"For forty years I've been trying to save lives, and now you're telling me to kill all those men."

"Emil, you know how the Merki will make them suffer first."

Emil nodded. "Fucking animals." He looked up at Kathleen, suddenly ashamed of his profanity.

"Oh, I agree," she whispered, a smile coming to her lips.

"Come dawn, I'll detach a regiment to this hospital. We've got some extra revolvers, and your orderlies have weapons. Any wounded that can fight should be sent back up, or have them stay here as a guard.

"I'll have the order in writing in my breast pocket. My aides will know it's there if something should happen to me. I'll only send it when I know it is truly finished and not before. God help me, I don't want any mistakes on this. But if they start to overrun you first, you know what you'll have to do."

Emil nodded, hands still shaking.

"Is there any chance?"

Andrew looked back at Kathleen.

"There's always a chance," he whispered, and she looked back at him, knowing the truth.

He looked back at Emil. "Thank you for everything, Dr. Weiss—for your friendship, your advice." He paused and tapped his empty sleeve. "And for my life."

He let go of Kathleen and stepped forward, taking Emil's hand in his.

The old doctor smiled, shaking his head softly.

"Next year Jerusalem," Emil said in Hebrew.

"What?"

"Oh, just an old promise I always wanted to keep."

Andrew smiled and turned away. "Maybe someday you will."

He walked out of the tent, Kathleen by his side.

"I've got to go back."

She said nothing, watching from the corner of her eye as a fresh casualty was brought into her tent.

"I've got to go too."

He hesitated.

"You know I want you to live, to try to escape, there's still time . . ." His voice trailed off; he was ashamed of what he was saying when so many others were standing and dying. But this was his wife. He looked over at her.

She shook her head. "I have my duty as well," she whispered. "Tanya and Ludmilla will see that our baby is safe."

He looked at her, filled with pain and yet also with a deep pride.

"If I had it to do all over again, even the losing in the end, it would be worth it," Andrew said softly. "It'd be worth it because for at least one moment I had you."

He kissed her gently on the mouth and then backed away, the lingering touch between the two dropping, arms lowering.

He turned and walked into the night.

"I'll wait for you," she whispered, and then went back into the tent.

* * *

"That's him right there."

He could barely understand the words; it had been long since he had learned the cattle language of the Rus.

He felt someone grab his shoulder, rolling him over, and the cold touch of steel at his throat.

Muzta Qar Qarth waited for death, but it did not come.

Rough hands grabbed hold of him, pulling him up. By the light of the lantern he saw a short burly man, red-haired, hair on his face growing out of either cheek and over his lip.

The man looked at him and grinned coldly.

"Muzta of the Tugars?"

Muzta remained silent, sparing a glance to either side. The field was covered yet again with his own dead, dying yet another time. But this time he felt it was not the cattle who had killed them, it was Tamuka.

"Will you kill me now?" Muzta asked, struggling to form the strange words.

The red-haired one looked up at him and slowly smiled.

"I think there's someone you might talk to first."

He felt the nick of a sword at his back. But he needed no urging to go forward. The wall of the parapet was but a dozen strides away. His head ached, and he reached up to his helmet, feeling the dent on the side, from whatever it was that had knocked him senseless.

He paused for a moment and looked down.

Jamadu, his last son, lay upon the ground, unconscious, a gaping wound in his chest.

Muzta paused and looked over at Pat.

"My son," he whispered. "Please help him."

Pat nodded, and motioned for a detail to bring the youth in. Muzta knelt down beside Jamadu, touching his brow, smoothing the hair back, praying silently, and then stood back up, going over the parapet wall, no longer needing any urging.

"Once more, only one more charge," Tamuka shouted, looking at the silent forms around him. "I was there, I was atop the ridge, and it was near to empty."

"Then why were we defeated?" Haga asked, his voice cold. "By all the gods, Tamuka, a hundred and fifty thousand or more of our warriors are dead or hurt. If you claim this to be victory, I dread the specter of defeat."

"And yet it is victory," Tamuka shouted in reply. "Three times today our host gained the ridge."

"And three times driven back," Haga replied.

"Yet each time it was closer to the final victory. I tell you, if that last charge had been but five hundred paces to the north it would have broken through into empty air and tonight we would already be feasting."

Several in the circle nodded their heads, but the others stood silent.

"If! I hear nothing but ifs," Haga said coldly. "If we had extra skins of water so our warriors did not drop of thirst, if we had charged only a few hundred paces to one side, if the cloud fliers had not been defeated. All of it ifs, and I see the certainty of over one in three of our warriors gone, one in three no longer fit to fight. Our arrows are near gone, the flashing powder for the cannons all but used, and still the cattle stand upon the hills."

"How many of theirs do you think are left standing?" Gubta snarled. "Their numbers have never been as great as ours. Even if they have struck us down three for their one, there are few left. Though my umen did not attack today, I rode forward into the breakthrough upon our left. I saw open steppe beyond and clear sky, and nothing but one thin wall of cattle.

If you, Haga of the black horse, had supported that charge, it would have gone clean through to victory."

Tamuka turned to Haga.

"He is right," Tamuka said coldly. "Thirteen umens finally were across the river, two of them yours, and they did not fight."

"How were they even to get in?" Haga snarled. "The signal flags could not be seen for the smoke."

"The cattle fight in smoke, not in clean air for all to see valor and to see the flags," snapped Yimak, umen commander under Haga. "By the time the bell rider had come to me with my commands, the assault was already repulsed, the field before me clogged with retreat."

Tamuka held up his hand for silence, and slowly the arguments died away.

"I tell you this from my *ka,*" he whispered, deliberately keeping his voice low so that all were forced into silence to listen. "Today I saw into the heart of Keane, just before the setting of the sun. And he was afraid, he saw defeat before him. Never have I felt such fear within him. I was atop the ridge and I saw the light of victory beyond."

There was a murmur from some, others yet silent.

"My brothers, have we ridden so far, fought them so many times, to now turn away as Haga would wish, only to hear their laughter of scorn?

"I tell you now this. Our fate rest upon tomorrow. Behind us our women, the old ones, the young, move across the steppe, expecting that by the passage of another moon we shall spread before them the fat, the wealth, of this land to feed their hungry stomachs. Are we now to ride back, heads lowered, and whine that a few remaining cattle have frightened us away?"

"At least we shall ride back and not have them come to seek our bleached bones," Haga said.

"Are you of the blood of the Merki?" Tamuka snarled, looking over at Haga.

Haga bristled, hand resting on the hilt of his sword.

"If you did not bear the helm of the Qar Qarth I would strike you dead for that."

The circle about the fire was deathly quiet.

"I should ask," Haga said low, his voice a sinister hiss, "if you are even our Qar Qarth."

No one spoke. Tamuka gazed at Haga, seeing his deadly resolve, his desire to offer challenge of sword, perhaps even here, at this very moment, and he knew in his heart that Haga would win. Yet his anger boiled and his hand came to rest upon the hilt of the sword of the Qar Qarth, ready to draw it out.

"It is forbidden for there to be blood challenge in time of war." Sarg came into the circle to stand before the fire. He looked around at the clan chieftains and commanders.

"It is forbidden," Gubta said, coming to stand by Tamuka, half-drawing his blade.

With a low snarl, Haga turned and walked out of the circle.

Tamuka watched him depart, knowing that in Haga's mind it was not settled.

He looked back at the others.

"I tell you this from all that I know, that you cannot even see," and his voice was low but insistent. "If we turn away now, there shall come a day when it will be the cattle who will come in search of us, armed with weapons beyond our darkest nightmares. Three seasons back they were but infants in the ways of war, and the Tugars in their foolishness allowed themselves to be defeated."

He looked around the circle. Muzta was not present, and he smiled inwardly, having heard the report that the Qar Qarth of the Tugars and his son had fallen at the head of the assault. The survivors of his two umens were gathered together singing their death songs even now, vowing to die at dawn and thus end their disgrace. The world would be best rid of them anyhow.

"I tell you now that if we suffer the cattle to live, there will be endless war. They will rebuild, become yet stronger, forge new weapons, spreading their madness to all the cattle of this world. Tonight, upon that ridge," and he pointing to the low surrounding hills, "their broken army stands, knowing they cannot retreat, knowing as well that they cannot win. Yet if we ride away now, in years to come it will be war after war, our sons struggling against theirs, a war across the world, and we shall lose ten times what we have lost here, until in the end the Merki will be no more.

"We must do, we have to do, this."

He could see nods of reluctant agreement.

"I tell you this now as well. As Qar Qarth I promise you victory at dawn. Already I have ordered remounts brought forth. Six umens of horse I shall have placed in the center at dawn, four umens of warriors afoot behind them and to either side."

He picked up a broken musket, and using the attached bayonet he drew a half circle on the ground and a block in the middle. Then he drew an arrow straight forward from the block to pierce the half circle.

"This is how it will be. By tomorrow evening our riders will already be to the gates of Roum, which stand defenseless, their army here, what little is left smashed and captured. The day after, the rest of the horses will be brought up, and after we have feasted upon the cattle we take, we shall ride eastward and feast some more upon the city.

"I swear this as Qar Qarth, I swear this upon the *ka* of my spirit, which can see such things and bring them to be. I tell you now they are already beaten and at the first charge we shall slice through them with ease.

"Tomorrow I promise you victory."

*   *   *

Andrew Lawrence Keane walked along the lines, his thoughts no longer on the war; they seemed to take in so much more, all the dreams he had ever had since coming to this place, and he saw them reflected in the eyes of those who looked up at him.

The field was quiet now, a few fires sparkling low, men sitting around them, cooking what little they had, sharing the last of the rations.

There were no songs tonight; it was beyond that. He stopped, looking out across the fields. The Great Wheel of the heavens was moving westward; soon it would be dawn.

A fire flared up, and he turned to look at a knot of men gathered around a ruined villa. He drew closer.

"A hard day."

It was Marcus, Rick Schneid beside him.

"A hard day," Andrew whispered.

"And tomorrow?"

Andrew smiled sadly, and then shook his head.

"We're played out. Over twenty thousand more casualties today. It was a miracle that we held them at all—they started too late, or they would have finished it. Tomorrow they'll come in at dawn."

He shook his head again and looked off.

"A miracle," Marcus said. "A miracle we made ourselves today, perhaps tomorrow another."

"We'll see."

"What's over there?" Andrew asked, nodding toward the fire.

"Gregory, some of the boys," Rick said, limping along, nursing the saber cut to his leg. "Word kind of spread that Gregory wants to say something, so I thought I'd come over."

"How's Vincent?" Andrew said, looking over at Marcus.

"He's fine now. I think he'll be all right."

Andrew smiled sadly, having seen Vincent, Marcus

holding him; he had quietly withdrawn, not even capable of helping.

He started over toward the fire. The villa had served as the anchor point for Third and Fourth Corps sealing off the breach to the line. The ground was still carpeted with Merki dead. A roaring fire was blazing in front of the ruined building. More and more men were coming up, many with bandaged wounds. Leaning against the wall were the battle standards, and as Andrew approached he stopped to look at them. Proud flags, Suzdalian regiments, Kev, Novrod, Murom, and Vazima. Old names of ancient Russia, now upon this world, the army instilled with all the valor and traditions of the Army of the Potomac. In the middle of the stand he saw the colors of the 35th Maine, the men of the unit deployed to help seal the breach, and already he had heard more names said softly, men who would never answer another roll.

He looked around at the gathering crowd, seeing many of his comrades from the beginning. To one side he saw Gates, sketch pad in hand, as if he would actually turn out another newspaper, Bill Webster beside him, no longer the financial planner of the country, now again in the ranks for this fight. So many of the familiar faces.

Several men came out of the villa carrying a table and set it up in front of the fire, and Gregory, now commander of the corps, one that wasn't much more than a small brigade, came out, features set with a grim purpose. He climbed up on the table, extending his hands to silence the growing crowd.

Andrew moved to the back of the group, Marcus beside him, old friends of the 35th moving up around them. He felt the old bonds again, comrades of such times together, and he felt the first glimmer of a returning strength, even though he knew with a dreadful certainty that it was finished, that come morning all was over. He looked about the group, their faces shining in the firelight, and he felt a bond of love and comradeship that for the moment transcended all pain.

"I asked you men, my comrades, to gather around," Gregory began, "because I wanted to talk with all of you. You brothers of mine of Third Corps, and all you others that now gather in to this circle." He paused, looking out at the gathering, waiting for a moment as more and yet more came in from other parts of the line, drawn by curiosity, until more than a thousand had gathered around.

"We have fought upon many a field, you and I," he said, his voice carrying high and clear, "and tonight we know we are brothers. Our tradition goes back far into the misty past, our battles together many, starting with Antietam."

Andrew stirred, looking around at the few around him who had once stood upon that desperate field.

"And then to Gettysburg, and the Wilderness. And then here at the Ford," and the men of Rus nodded. He continued to recite the long list of honors, bringing them all closer together through the shared memory of pain and glory.

"And now so few of us are left to face the greatest fight of all."

The men around him were silent. He lowered his head for a moment and then looked back up, eyes gleaming, head raised.

> "If we are marked to die, we are enow
> To do our country loss: and if to live,
> The fewer men, the greater share of honor."

Andrew stirred, looking over at Gates, smiling. Gregory, a Rus peasant, was reciting *Henry V*, and he felt a stirring within at the words.

The young man's voice cut through the night air

like a clarion call. Those assembled were silent, faces raised, shining in the firelight.

> "This day is called the feast of Crispian:
> He that outlives this day and comes safe home,
> Will stand a tiptoe when this day is named,
> And rouse him at the name of Crispian.
> He that shall live this day, and see old age,
> Will yearly on the vigil feast his neighbors,
> And say, 'Tomorrow is Saint Crispian':
> Then will he strip his sleeve and show his scars,
> and say, 'These wounds I had on Crispin's day.' "

Andrew, stunned, looked out across the assembly, men standing transfixed, eyes shining, headings nodding, an electric like thrill running through all of them.

> "This story shall the good man teach his son;
> And Crispin Crispian shall ne'er go by,
> From this day to the ending of the world,
> But we in it shall be remembered . . .

Gregory paused, lowering his head for a moment, and then looked back up, tears streaming from his eyes, his voice choked but clear.

> "We few, we happy few, we band of brothers . . ."

His words were barely a whisper, yet ringing and clear, many in the group joining in with him, reciting, Andrew, his voice choked, reciting as well.

> "For he today that sheds his blood with me
> Shall be my brother; be he ne'er so vile
> This day shall gentle his condition:
> And gentlemen in England, now abed,
> Shall think themselves accursed they were not here,
> And hold their manhoods cheap whiles any speaks
> That fought with us upon Saint Crispin's day!"

The words soared out, as if defiantly flung to the world, and when they were finished a wild cheer thundered up, men pressing forward, crying, fists raised to the heavens, shouting their approval, their passion finding voice, words created so long ago leaping across time and space to give spirit yet again in an hour of desperate need.

Head raised high, Andrew Lawrence Keane wept unashamedly, men pushing past him, not even aware that he was there, struggling to get closer to the center. Battle flags were pulled from the wall, held aloft, waved in the firelight.

He backed away, standing alone at the edge, watching. Gates came out of the press, eyes shining. He came up to Andrew as if to say something and then couldn't, just extended his hand as if to touch Andrew, and then he turned away and ran into the darkness back toward the city.

Andrew looked up to the heavens.

"Merciful God, please let them win," he whispered.

He turned and started to walk away.

"Andrew."

He looked up and saw Pat standing in the shadows. Andrew went up to him.

"Did you hear that?" Andrew whispered, still awestruck.

Pat nodded clearing his throat. "Even though he was a bloody Englishman he had a way with words, he did."

"God, if only we could win tomorrow," Andrew said, the euphoria still inside him, yet the cold reality pushing in, as if begging to seize hold again.

"There's someone here I want you to talk to," Pat said, and he motioned for Andrew to draw farther away from the celebration.

Andrew followed Pat into the darkness, and then he saw him and came up short.

"Andrew Keane, is it not?"

"Muzta," Andrew whispered in reply.

FATEFUL LIGHTNING   427

Merris prefled. "But so honored his wand as you

Chapter 12

Dawn broke on the third day of battle. The chanting from down in the fog-cloaked valley rolled upward, sound distorted, echoing nearer, and then farther away.

Andrew stood upon the crest of the ridge, looking down into the valley.

Gazing down from a thousand feet, Jack Petracci leaned out the cab, engine throttled back to idle, propeller thumping over lazily. To the east the red disk of the sun was breaking the horizon, bearing with it the threat of another day of scalding heat. He looked back at Feyodor and smiled grimly.

They had agreed upon their plan. As they floated southward in the predawn light he was not even sure if he would find the army still there. The telegraph lines had been cut in the breakthrough, the track overrun. At the first sight of the fires burning low along the ridge, the forms of men gathered around them, he had almost wept with relief.

But as he circled out over the lines he could see that all hope was gone. Where divisions had stood two days before, broken remnants of brigades now stood. Troops were on the move, shifting into the center, as if Andrew had somehow guessed the intent of the Merki, a guess which Jack could see was right. Centered in the valley, a vast block had been drawn up, tens of thousands, their standards and spear tips visi-

425

ble through the ground fog, which even as he watched
was starting to melt away. To either flank, other units
were drawing up, ready to strike to north and south,
but the main assault was poised to drive straight east,
as if driven by an instinct which had propelled the
hordes about the world for thousands of years, to per-
petually ride toward the rising sun.

Tamuka Qar Qarth stood up tall in his stirrups,
watching as the wisps of fog started to burn away. He
would wait a bit longer. There would be no smoke,
no fog, today. He wanted the cattle to see clearly what
was coming up out of the valley, ten umens arrayed
in battle order. He felt a certain confidence as he
looked up the long slope, sensing the presence of
Keane, sensing the growing knowledge that all was
finished, and he laughed.

Andrew turned and looked at his corps commanders, who were gathered around him.

"It will be here. I want every regiment, every company that can be spared, here. If we are to die, let it
be together on this ground."

He looked around the circle, at the men whom he
had been with for so long, and smiled.

"And we are but warriors for the working day," he
said with a smile, and Gregory nodded.

A courier came riding up, handed down a sheet of
paper to Andrew from the bundle in his arm, saluted,
and rode on down the line.

Andrew smiled. It was *Gates's Illustrated*, reduced
now to a single sheet, upon the front a crude etching
of Gregory giving his speech, the words he had spoken
written underneath, printed in Rus and Latin, upon
the back of it a rough quick etching of the battle standard of the Army of the Republics. Already he could
hear others back in the line reciting the words, cheers
rising up.

"Gentlemen, I have never been so proud of this army and of you as I am at this moment. No matter what happens here this day, whether we win or lose, we shall be remembered. If we achieve victory, it will be, as Gregory said, a day to remember, an anniversary on which to turn back our sleeves and show our scars of honor."

He hesitated, his voice lowering.

"And if at the end of this day we meet again in another world, we shall look upon each other and smile, our fellowship continued in a far better place, I am sure. In the world we leave behind we shall not be forgotten, for we have started something here that will never end. Our spirits will come back, and we shall be millions, who will rise up and call our names once more. The dream we have for this world, the dream some of us once fought for upon another world, can never die. It will exist as long as man exists, a dream of freedom, of equality, of liberty. That has always been worth dying for, and I promise you that dream shall never die."

A horn sounded in the valley below, its brazen cry rising up, echoing, others joining in.

"God be with you all this day."

He turned and walked back across the field, the army waiting, a cheer starting at the center of the line where the 35th and 44th were drawn up, their flags held high.

"Keane, Keane!"

The shout started to race to either side, spreading outward, rising in the still morning air till it rolled like thunder.

He came before the colors, looked up, and saluted, the cheers still echoing, and turned to stand in front of the line, drawing out his saber.

From the far side of the ridge the thunder of the charge came in.

* * *

Kathleen stood by the open flap of the tent. To the southeast the battle was plainly in view, smoke rising up into the heavy morning air, the thunder of artillery crashing across the hills. The vast field of wounded around the tents was quiet, those who were able sitting up or standing to watch in silence. A steady trickle of new casualties was already coming back.

A man brushed past her coming out of the tent, a Roum soldier, leaning on the shoulder of a Rus artilleryman, each helping the other, muskets over their shoulders, heading back into the fight, the one trailing a bloodstained bandage behind him. Others were rising up, a growing river of them moving painfully back into the line.

"How can we lose?" she whispered. "How can we ever lose?"

And yet as she watched she saw the dark clouds of arrows rising up into the heavens and pouring back down, smothering the line under, and ever so gradually the sound of musketry diminishing, the chants of the Merki growing louder and yet louder.

She reached into her apron and felt the cold handle of the revolver, remembering that she would have to save the last round for herself.

The high piercing shriek of a whistle cut the air, and she watched as a long train came through the switchyard, whistle tied down, the train slowing for a moment as it switched into the main line heading south. Long boxes draped in canvas were piled upon the flatcars, and soldiers stood at the ends of the cars, shouting.

She looked around the tent and saw Emil behind her, cleaning his spectacles as if he were about to settle down and read.

"Catch the train, go to him. I think he'd want you beside him."

She turned back to the old doctor.

"I'll see you later," he whispered. "You don't want to be here for what's next."

She grabbed hold of him, hugging him fiercely, then turned and ran toward the train as it continued slowly through the switchyard. As she came up alongside the last car, a soldier looked down at her, and she held her hand up.

"You don't want to come with us," he shouted. "We're heading to hell."

"Keane, I'm Colonel Keane's wife, I want to be with him."

The soldier leaned over, extended his hand, and lifted her off her feet, even as the train started to gather speed again.

Winded by the run, she sat down on the bed of the flatcar as it swayed and rattled down the track, the engine forward still shrieking, two more trains behind her doing the same.

The first two charges had broken at the crest, the Merki infantry dropping by the thousands, yet ever so slowly the line started to buckle back from the ridge, Merki archers sending sheets of arrows in.

Vincent Hawthorne stood with the tiny knot of what was left of the 7th Suzdal, Dimitri at his side.

He felt somehow purified, as if the dark sickness of war had left his soul. He would fight now, and he knew with a sad finality that he would die here, but he would die with the men he loved.

The words of Andrew still rang in his ears, telling him what he had been searching for all this time, an understanding of why he would fight and die this day. It had nothing to do with hatred, though he knew he could hate what his enemies did. He would fight now for a promise of what could be, even if he no longer was alive to see it. He believed now that there would be generations born that he would never know, and would never know him, who might live in freedom and in peace for what he sacrificed this day. For that he was content.

As he looked to the south he could see that to the flank of the grand battery the line was broken clean open, Merki already fanning out into the rear, turning southward to roll up the rest of the line, turning toward him to destroy what was left of his line as well. It would not be long now. The flag bearer beside him suddenly crumpled up, collapsing wordlessly to the ground.

Vincent reached down and picked up the banner of the 7th Suzdal.

Directly below in the valley he saw the heavy block formation of horse-mounted Merki start to move forward at a walk, nargas cutting the air with their brazen cry, hundreds of drums setting up a bone-chilling beat.

To his right the line started to fall back toward the line of trains, and his command followed, the Merki infantry shadowing them. They crossed over the first line of open track and then climbed over and onto the second line, a dozen trains parked along its length. Battle flags went up, tied off to smokestacks and guard rails, glass shattering as men moved into passenger cars. As he climbed atop a flatcar he looked down the line, seeing that they were now so pitifully few, a thin line waiting for the final blow. To the right of the trains he saw the center of the line formed around a ruined villa, the flag of the army and the 35th and 44th flying alongside. He knew that's where Andrew was taking his stand, along with the men of Third and Fourth Corps. He was tempted to go over to them, to die at Andrew's side.

But no, his duty was here, with his men, the men he had trained, the men he had taken as peasants and slaves and turned into soldiers and comrades.

It was as good a place as any, and he planted the flag in the middle of the car, his men gathering around, and waited for what was coming.

*   *   *

Tamuka Qar Qarth, his heart beating with a fierce joy, stood tall in the stirrups, looking up at the ridge, as the cattle started to withdraw. They were doing the same as yesterday, pulling back to the line of trains, the cars and engines barely visible. He pointed his sword to the left, to where a ruined building of limestone stood back a short distance from the crest of the ridge, flags flying above it. He knew with a final certainty that Keane was there. And above all else he wanted to see Keane die.

Chuck Ferguson leaned out of the cab of the engine. In the valley below they were already starting their advance. He cursed madly. But for a few minutes more, damm it to hell, but for a few minutes more!

It had taken hours to move the train from the factory to north of Hispania. Barry's men had finally sealed the breach, but sections of track had been damaged, and more than half a dozen times small units of Merki had put up a fight to block their way. In the corner of the cab he saw Andre, the train engineer, dead. Never again would Andre play his favorite ballad about the boyar's daughter.

Still holding the whistle down, he ran the train forward at full throttle, wounded on the track ahead scattering. Around a shallow curve, a Napoleon was still half on the track, its crew bodily lifting the weapon up and pushing it off the roadbed, cursing wildly as the train thundered past.

Chuck looked back down into the valley. The head of the charge was already moving forward, a thousand yards away, he estimated, and he cursed madly, tempted to slam the brakes on now but deciding not to, realizing the front of the advance was aiming half a mile ahead.

The curve straightened out, and directly ahead he

saw a ruined building, flags atop it, a long line of trains farther ahead and on the same track.

He released the whistle, giving three short blasts, and slammed the throttle back, the fireman putting his foot up against the side of the cab and leaning with all his weight against the brake. The wheels beneath him started to shriek, sparks raining out, and he grimaced at the thought that if they ever made it out of this the wheels would most certainly be out of round and have to be reground, and the thought made him laugh.

The train continued to slide forward, the last car on the train parked straight ahead coming closer and closer. A line of infantry drawn up across the track scattered, the men on the last car leaping down, shouting a warning.

The train slowed, passing in front of the building, and with a rendering crash slammed into the last car of the train ahead, lifting it up into the air, knocking it sideways. Chuck fell forward, his hands hitting the hot firebox. Barely noticing the pain, he pulled back, scrambled into the tender car, and leaped up on top.

"Clear the canvas!"

Men on the cars behind him came back up to their feet, ripping the canvas back from one car after another. Behind them the second train slid to a stop, and behind that one the third, crews already working on the protective covers.

He turned to Theodor as he released the break.

"Fuses are set at one thousand yards. Set Elevation at one thousand yards as planned. Run to the next train, make sure it's twelve hundred, and on the last train eight hundred. Now move! Make sure the wire gets connected between the trains. If it fails to set 'em off, have the individual crews fire them!"

Theodor leaped from the train and ran back up the line.

"Ferguson!"

Chuck looked over his shoulder and saw Andrew climbing up into the cab of the engine.

Chuck ignored him and turned back forward.

"Ferguson, what the hell are you doing?" Andrew shouted. "Their charge is coming in!"

"Sorry, sir," Chuck said, his voice almost boyish. "I'll explain in a minute."

"Damn you, Ferguson," and Andrew stepped to the back of the tender, looked down the length of the train, and fell silent in awe.

Chuck cupped his hands. "Everybody clear from the rear of the train! Everybody clear and get down!"

Chuck leaped down on the first car. The side facing the approaching charge was armored up to waist height. A heavy canvas covered a protruding barrel beside him, and two men were working to clear it. The next ten cars down the line were now fully cleared of canvas and crews were working at the elevation cranks, the rocket launchers slowly pointing skyward. Bolted to each of the cars were racks, six tubes high and twenty-five long, filling the flatcars from one end to the other, a hundred and fifty rockets per car, thirty-two carloads behind three trains.

"One thousand yards and ready!"

The crew of the first car stood up and leaped from the car, running toward the rear, their action causing the infantry that had stood gawking to fall back. Down the length of the train the other crews jumped off, running.

Chuck looked forward, raising his field glasses.

The crest of the ridge blocked the view for several hundred yards down the slope, but beyond for well over a mile back into the valley he could see them clearly, the massed formation of mounted umens a half mile across, advancing straight toward him at the gallop. The elevation difference, dammit!

He did a quick calculation. Directly on the crest

forward he saw the first line of the charge coming into view. It was too late to change things now.

"Duck, you bastards!" Chuck screamed, and he looked back at Andrew.

"Better get down, sir," he shouted with a grin, and he reached over to a wooden control box and flipped the lid open. Inside was a brass key connected to half a dozen telegraph batteries.

He crossed his fingers and pressed down on the key.

There was a moment, a brief instant, when he felt as if his heart would stop, but it was only for a second.

With a throaty roar the first rocket slashed out of its launch tube, rising upward, trailing a plume of fire and smoke, shrieking with a banshee scream. An instant later a long salvo started to flash down the length of the train, six rockets a second rising up from each car, the other two train loads igniting as well, thirty-two cars in all, over a hundred and eighty rockets a second.

The thunder of their rising filled the air, the unearthly screaming of the rockets drowning out even the thunder of their launching, the flatcars rattling on the tracks, leaping up and down. For second after second their long plumes rose heavenward, nearly all flying true, yet some others turning straight up, or arcing back over the train, or skimming low across the ground and smashing straight into the front rank, which was still advancing.

A car on the second train went up with a thunder-clap roar, half a carload detonating at once from a rocket that exploded in its tube, setting off a chain reaction, loads going off in every direction.

And yet still the salvo continued.

Andrew stood awestruck, not even bothering to duck, mouth open in wonder, forgetting all else, watching with a growing elation as over four thousand rounds soared upward, arced over, and started to plummet down upon the Merki horde.

* * *

"Jesus and Perm!" Jack gasped. "That idiot's done it!"

Looking straight down, he saw the wall of fire rising upward from the sides of the trains, the ground instantly blanketed with smoke, sheet after sheet of fire rising upward. The first volley reached apogee off to his right and then started to curve downward, still trailing sparks and smoke, the salvos spreading out, covering nearly half a mile of Merki advance.

Snaps of light started to detonate over the Merki line, first one, an instant later another, and then in the blink of an eye hundreds of detonations. Seconds later the sound washed over him, a continual thunderous roar, joining in with the shrieking screams of the rockets still leaping from the launchers.

A high piercing shriek snapped by the balloon, but he didn't even notice.

Shouting with maniacal joy, he watched as four thousand rounds of case shot smothered the Merki charge, the world below disappearing from view in a boiling caldron of fire and smoke.

Tamuka Qar Qarth reined in his terrified mount. For the first time in his life he felt truly terrified as well. The world ahead had suddenly disappeared, the air around him filled with the mad howling of demons.

It had to be a machine, part of his mind was screaming, another damned Yankee machine, but the shrieks of the rockets drowned out all other thoughts, as if the riders of the night sky had come down in judgment, the ancestors falling from the heavens, either in damnation or now to join the cattle in vengeance upon their own.

The charge around him ground to a halt, horses rearing in panic, throwing their riders, warriors covering their ears, howling in terror.

He turned and looked back, seeing the smoke trails

die and then the sparks of light, hundreds of them coming down, down directly over the center of the advancing horde. A red flash and puff of smoke ignited over the line, then, within seconds, thousands of explosions, silent at first, but the thunder started to build, growing louder into a sustained world-shattering cataclysm of destruction.

Stunned beyond all comprehension, Tamuka watched the destruction of his umens, and then his horse bolted, breaking from the front of the van, pulling him back into the rear. Around him was mad confusion, riders caught under the salvo looking heavenward, roaring in terror, seeing the destruction behind them, unable to move in the press.

A howling shriek filled the air, and Tamuka, terrified, looked up as a rocket seemed to come straight down out of the smoke, exploding before him with a thunderclap.

The blow nearly lifted him from the saddle, and he reeled, aware that a frightening coldness had seized his arm. He looked down in horror to see blood spurting from his mangled hand. His horse, screaming, turned and bolted for the rear, Tamuka struggling to hang on.

The panic took hold; the sight of Tamuka, horse rearing and bucking, riding to the rear finished anything that was left.

Screaming in terror, the lines forward wavered.

The last rocket leaped out and away, the thunder of the detonations forward roaring against the hills.

An awed silence was the response. Many of the men were almost as terrified as their enemies, not understanding what had happened. A dawning realization started to arrive that whatever it was, it was destroying the Merki in the valley below, and a desperate cheer of hope started to rise up.

Chuck jumped up and down like a small boy at a

Fourth of July finale and then suddenly remembered his one other surprise. His two assistants had finished pulling the canvas cover off the Gatling gun. Chuck reached down and opened the steam power line that was hooked back into the locomotive, then stepped behind the gun, aiming it straight at the Merki line on the ridge, which was milling about in terror.

He pulled the trigger back.

A single round snapped off, and then with a moaning hiss the gun seized up, steam pouring out in every direction.

Chuck stepped back from the machine and shook his head.

"Well, I'll be damned," he whispered.

Andrew, not even aware of the gun's failure, still stood in awestruck silence as the clouds of smoke billowed around him.

Chuck looked back at Andrew, grinning.

"He hath loosened the fateful lightning of his terrible swift sword," Andrew said, his voice filled with awe.

"At least the rockets worked," Chuck said quietly.

"If I ever say no again, tell me to go to hell."

"Can I have that in writing, sir?"

Andrew threw back his head and laughed. He slapped Chuck on the shoulder and stood up on top of the launching car.

"Soldiers of the Army of Republics," he began, his voice sharp and clear, thousands of men looking to the trains, many of them now seeing Keane, who stood tall, sword in one hand, half-empty sleeve outstretched deliberately so that all would know who he was. Behind Andrew the flag bearers for the 35th Maine and the Army of the Republics stepped up to join him.

"Charge!"

He leaped from the car, striking the ground hard, losing his footing for a moment and then coming back up. Flag bearers came forward, standards of the 35th and the Army of the Republics by Andrew's side, men streaming out of the trains to his left, the line to the right struggling to get under or over the still-smoking launch cars, cheering wildly. The cry went up all along the line.

"Charge, men, charge!"

The cry was a thunderous release of rage and frustration, and now of growing hope.

Andrew swept forward, running hard, not even looking back, unaware that from out of the smoke a vast arc of men were rushing forward to the edge of the ridge. Forward, the line of Merki seemed transfixed, as if torn between the horror below in the valley and that before them. Riders turned, horses bolting. The Merki horde broke and started to run.

A warrior turned, raising his bow, aiming straight for Andrew, and a musket shot lifted him from his saddle, Andrew not even aware of what happened. Men paused for a second, pouring fire in, and then rushed forward with empty guns, bayonets lowered.

Andrew gained the crest of the ridge. And below he saw madness.

Across a front of half a mile and to a depth of nearly a quarter, a caldron of smoke was rising upward. To either side and the rear, Merki by the tens of thousands were fleeing, heading to the river. Forward was a writhing sea of confusion, Merki no longer fighting but turning, trying to flee, warriors losing their mounts, falling to be crushed, a wild insane deafening cry filling the air.

Directly overhead and not a hundred feet above, *Republic* came out of the smoke, a rocket detaching, arcing down into the confusion, exploding, and the sight of the machine coming out of the curtain of darkness added to the madness, riders crouching low in terror.

Along the rim of the hill the army paused, men

working feverishly, reloading their muskets. A spattering of musket fire rattled out, growing to a continuous concussion of sound, men firing into the packed mass, unable to miss, the grand battery to his left, which had continued to fire throughout the long minutes before, adding its weight. Along the ridge beyond the battery, Merki were now streaming back, running in panic after witnessing the destruction in the valley.

Volleys continued to thunder out and across the ridge, and in the smoke Andrew could see that nothing was now in front except the dead, the dying, and those still trying to flee.

"Push them into the river!"

The cry rose up, and the army started down from the crest, men leaping forward, battle flags forward.

He started into the charge and felt a hand on his arm.

He turned and looked back, ready to shake the restraining grip off.

"I don't want to lose you now," Kathleen said. "A commander should direct from here."

He felt the battle fury in him, the desire to drive them all the way back to the river and see it to the end.

She looked up at him pleadingly.

And he felt the fury die away.

He stopped, watching as the colors of the 35th went forward, flanked on one side by the red and white stripes of a flag he had once fought for so long ago, and in a way still did fight for, the old national colors flanked by the flags of Rus and Roum and the Army of the Republic.

They swept down the slope and disappeared into the smoke. He felt her arm go around his waist, and he pulled her close beside him.

"Well, you dark devil, will you look at that!" Pat O'Donald shouted, looking over at Muzta. The two of them were standing transfixed as the Merki host turned and started for the rear.

Muzta turned and faced Pat.

"Let me go."

Astonished, Pat could not reply.

"My horde is down there, all that is left of it. You heard what I said to Keane, of my hatred of the Merki. Let me go now."

"Why?"

"Because I wish to save my people."

Pat laughed darkly, looking over at the sentry who had orders to shoot Muzta if he so much as made a threatening move. Muzta had made the same offer to Andrew, an offer which was refused when Andrew realized that Muzta had undoubtedly seen just how truly weak they now were.

"Human, I will strike a bargain with you."

"And that is?"

"I will fight the Merki and not just pull my people out of the fight."

Pat looked at him in astonishment, and Muzta grinned coldly.

"The Merki still might rally at the river. My horde is there," and he pointed to a block of warriors drawn up just beyond the range of the northern grand battery.

"You have but a handful of a hundred or more here, and your wounded are behind us. My son in there as well," he continued, and he pointed back to the hospital area to the rear. "In their madness they might flee this way and slaughter all of them in vengeance. I will stop them."

"In exchange for what?"

"I expect nothing, but I wish to die with sword in hand, fighting those who have always been my enemy, even before you."

Pat looked up at the Tugar, remembering the sight of Kathleen running into Andrew's embrace, young

Vincent beside her, freed by a strange act of chivalry from this hated foe.

He looked back into the valley. Though the stampede of the horde was moving straight back toward the river, still others were running blindly, some moving up the slope, and all too quickly they could learn that this section of the line was all but defenseless.

"There's my horse," Pat said.

Muzta grinned.

"Tell Keane I believe he is a warrior after all," Muzta said. "Perhaps even you and the others as well."

He ran to Pat's mount and leaped to the saddle, the horse nickering at the strange but yet somehow familiar scent and feel of the one now riding him.

Muzta jerked the reins around and started the horse forward, moving faster, scrambling up over the side of the parapet and then started down the slope, weaving his way through the deadfalls. Pat shouted an order to hold fire and stood grinning.

"By Jesus I actually hope he does make it," Pat said, leaning on the parapet to watch.

Muzta reached the bottom of the hill, riding hard. The block formation of Tugar infantry, which had turned to watch the destruction, now noticed who was approaching, and a deep guttural cheer rose up to greet him.

Pat raised his field glasses to watch. Muzta had taken a sword from a warrior, was standing up in his stirrups, speaking. A deeper cheer sounded, and the block turned, spreading outward, some moving back toward the river and the line of the Merki retreat, others moving along the edge of the slope back to the east. Merki, not yet comprehending, rode toward them. Arrows snapped out, Merki going down.

"I'll be damned," Pat roared, passing the word to hold fire along his front. The Tugars swept forward and in their movement blocked the hospital from any last attack.

Tugars started to edge up the hill, sweeping eastward, their joyful shouts ringing up, as once again, they fought against a foe they understood, a foe already in panic, a foe they could take glory from in killing.

He looked at his watch. It was still an hour before sunset, but the world was dark. From the western horizon to far eastward the sky was green-black, thunderstorms marching in from the west. Already a cold wind was whipping in, the flags behind him standing straight out, snapping.

He looked back across the valley. The stench was now being driven away, and the air was almost breathable again.

Occasional musket shots still sounded as lone Merki refused to surrender and were hunted down. He had passed the order shortly before noon that surrender was to be accepted when offered, for to his amazement he had seen warriors throw down their weapons and go to their knees, heads lowered, as if they had reached the conclusion that fate had turned her back upon them and death was now unavoidable.

The frenzy of the last three days had been such that many were more than willing to comply with this final wish of a hated foe, but many more had seen enough of killing, and prisoners by the thousands were being herded to the rear.

He looked back across the river.

A warrior was upon the opposite bank, a rider beside him holding a white flag, waving it back and forth. Andrew nodded, and an orderly tied a dirty towel to the tip of his sword and waved it overhead. The warrior and his flag bearer started forward, his horse splashing up spray, moving gingerly to weave its way around the corpses.

They gained the opposite bank and stopped a dozen feet away. The warrior looked straight at Andrew and began to speak, his voice low, his words incomprehensible, and then he stopped, the flag bearer translating in broken Rus.

"I am Haga, Qarth of the black horse clan of the Merki horde. I come to speak of terms."

Andrew felt a ripple of excitement behind him. Though they had driven the Merki clear across the river, slaughtering tens of thousands, still there were others, and they could always try again tomorrow, or a week later, or a month.

"Where is your Qar Qarth, the one called Tamuka?" Andrew asked, and the flag bearer translated.

Haga growled angrily, spitting upon the ground, and then replied.

"He is a usurper of the rightful title of Qar Qarth and only holds such rank until the flag of war over the golden yurt is lowered, and the flag of peace flies. Then we are free to choose another. Until then I speak for the council of Qarths. Tamuka is now an outcast."

The implications of it all caught him by surprise, and already he could see the political weakness. They needed peace to select their new leader, but then what?

"Why should we speak of peace to you?" Andrew said coldly. "You are on our land. It never even was the land of the Merki—before we freed ourselves it was Tugar land. You are usurpers yourselves."

At the mention of the word "Tugar" he saw a spasm of anger cross Haga's features. Good, he thought, it stings them that even now near to ten thousand Tugars are in the middle of the valley, guarded to be sure, but there nevertheless.

Haga sat silent for a moment and then began to speak, his voice low.

"This is not our land. It was the wish of Jubadi,

whom you killed through sorcery, and Tamuka. It is no longer my wish or that of the council."

"Then leave it," Andrew snapped in reply, "or we shall unleash more of our sorcery so that the sky will rain fire, not only upon you but upon the yurts of your families as well, until the land is a smoking ruin, filled with the stench of your dead."

A peal of thunder rolled in from off the plain, and Andrew smiled, as if he somehow had control over the fortunate coincidence.

Haga, unable to restrain himself, looked over his shoulder and then back at Andrew.

"Peace then," he said. "We ask that we might pass through the land of the Roum to the great steppe beyond."

Andrew looked over his shoulder at Marcus, who was listening while Vincent translated the conversation into Latin. There was a flicker in Marcus's eyes, but he said nothing.

It would be simple to grant this request. A month from now they would be gone. Gone to unleash their pent-up fury on someone else, or to reconsider and still turn to fight again. No. Here was the choke point. He was glad Kal was not present, for he could well imagine that the president might be tempted otherwise.

"No."

Haga stirred, not sure what to say next.

"Turn around, go back to whence you came."

He paused, not sure of what was occurring five hundred miles to the south, suddenly realizing that if he prevented them from going east they might very well turn back upon Cartha yet again.

"And Cartha as well we now claim as part of our alliance."

Haga bristled. "That land is ours."

"Not any longer," Andrew snapped, inwardly nervous that he might have pressed too far, backing them into a corner that might drive them to the desperation of deciding to die fighting.

Haga was silent, glaring coldly at Andrew.

"We shall give you free passage back through the land of the Rus, and you may graze your horses as you move."

He did a quick mental calculation.

"At the end of sixty days you must be to the west of the river we call the Neiper, where our city of Suzdal rests. You are free to graze your mounts, but not one building is to be molested. All cities are forbidden and not to be entered. If but one more town is burned, we shall fight. If you agree, then you are free to pass. From there you are free to move as you please, but Cartha is not to be molested, though the grazing of your horses upon the land to the west of them is yours."

Haga sat in silence, this time barely flinching when another snap of thunder sounded even closer.

"This we also demand. That all humans who might be prisoners are to be released and none who are of Cartha, or Roum, or Rus are to be taken by you.

"If you do not accept, then the war must continue and we at least know how it shall end. I should add that if you honor these terms, when the last of your people cross the Neiper we will release back to you, unharmed, the prisoners we have taken, who number over ten thousand."

Haga lowered his head.

"It is agreed," he whispered.

"Swear it upon your blood."

Haga looked up at Andrew in surprise. He unsheathed his short blade and cut his arm, holding it up for Andrew to see the blood. Andrew looked over at Marcus.

"Could you help me?"

Marcus edged his mount up and with his sword traced a light cut across Andrew's arm. Andrew held it up. Haga was clearly shocked that a cattle would give blood oath.

"We still hate you," Haga said coldly.

"And we you. I doubt if it is finished here between us. But for now there is peace, and that is enough."

Haga nodded. "You have *ka,* the soul of a warrior, Keane, even if you are a cattle."

"I am no different from any of my comrades who stood with me today," Andrew replied.

Haga's eyes, filled with sadness, looked past Andrew to the fields of dead behind him. "In three days we lost all that was best upon this field. Its memory will be cursed. A hundred thousand yurts will be filled with mourning."

He jerked his horse around and galloped off.

A cold drop of rain splashed Andrew's face, and within seconds a downpour came swirling in from the southwest, lashing across the river, a snap of lightning arcing the sky.

It always rains after a battle, he thought, looking back across the valley. Perhaps the heavens wish to wash the earth clean, to soak the blood into the ground, so that life can grow again.

He turned his back to the storm and rode silently back up the hill, to Hispania, Kathleen, and a night of sleep.

The Merki war was over.

Chapter 13

Overhead the church bell started to peal, and was picked up by the other churches of the city of the Rus, the city of Suzdal. Andrew Lawrence Keane stepped out of the cathedral.

The procession was drawn up in the town square, waiting, the men of the 35th Maine in front, flanked by those of the 44th New York. He stepped down from the steps of the cathedral, the men snapping to attention. He paused to return the salute and then walked down the line, looking into their faces. Some of them were old familiar comrades, men who had served with him since Antietam and Gettysburg. So many were new, Rus and Roum, and so many, all too many, were missing.

He thought of them, his first colonel, Estes, his brother, John, and then all the others lost, the Malady, Kindred, Mina, the list going on and yet on, three hundred and fifty of the six hundred who had come to this world now gone forever. And yet their sacrifice was not in vain. Today of all days that was clear to him. He looked back to the flag of Maine with a sadness mingled with joy and saluted once more. Next he passed the 44th New York, Pat O'Donald before the four guns of the battery, the barrels of the Napoleons polished to a gleaming brilliance.

Pat stepped forward and shook his hand.

"A fine day, me bucko, a glorious day."

Andrew smiled, putting an affectionate hand on

Pat's shoulder, and continued on, Pat stepping out and falling in beside him.

Drawn up behind the two units were men of the other seven corps, representatives of each regiment standing at attention, their colors held high.

He walked down the lines, looking up at the banners, eyes bright. Barry's First Corps was before him, the first unit of the army, the old guard as they now called themselves, the men who had held the northern flank in the three days of the battle of Hispania. The flag of the 1st Suzdal was to the right of the line, the very first regiment of the army which had seen the first action in the war against the Tugars. He continued on to the Second Corps, Rick Schneid standing proudly before his men.

Andrew paused for a moment, looking up at the torn standard of the 1st Vazima, the haunting words "I need five minutes" hovering around him.

Emblazoned on the flag in gold letters was the rest of his command: "Take the guns." He stopped and directly saluted the flag and then continued on.

Before the Third Corps was Gregory, new stars of a major general on his shoulders. The Rus officer proudly saluted as Andrew approached.

"We few, we happy few, we band of brothers," Gregory said with a smile, and Andrew nodded, unable to reply.

Fourth Corps was next, Pat stopped for a moment to look at the standards, eyes moist, grinning with pride. Next were the men of the Fifth, who had fought a near-unknown war to the south of Roum, distant skirmishing to hold back the Merki detachments that had crossed the inland sea and come north. Finally there were the men of the Sixth and Seventh, Vincent standing before them, eyes clear and bright, the young officer saluting.

"A fine day," Vincent said with a smile.

"A day to tell our grandchildren about," Andrew replied, shaking Vincent's hand.

"I'm proud of you, son," Andrew said.

"And I'm proud to have served under you, sir. Thank you."

Beside Vincent's command were half a dozen mounted troopers, a sergeant carrying the guidon of the 1st Cavalry Brigade of the Republics, the flag recovered by some of Barry's men from a Merki unit caught in the forest.

Finally there was the naval detachment, Bullfinch drawn up stiffly in front of his men, behind him the flags of the marine detachment and ensigns of the ships now anchored in the river. On the flags of the marine brigade were emblazoned "Defense of Cartha" and "Battle of the Bantag Pass."

Two days after the end of the war, Bullfinch's ship had dropped anchor at Roum and he had taken a train north to Hispania to report. Andrew looked at the young admiral, remembering again that nothing protects a soldier more than good luck and above all else success. Bullfinch had organized the Cartha and then moved his ships two hundred miles south to cover the main coastal pass through which the Bantag were advancing. The marines had deployed, coming up behind them tens of thousands of Cartha militia pushing before them cannons that were nothing more than wagon wheels and logs painted black, carrying muskets that were poles painted black and tipped with knives. A bombardment from the ships and the sight of the army arrayed across the pass had been convincing argument enough for the Bantag, who had not seen such weapons but had heard far too much about what the cattle were capable of doing. They had turned back, the battle a near-bloodless coup.

Next they had turned north to shield Cartha from the Merki umens which were still west of the city and the additional units coming down from the north,

Bullfinch and his men getting a factory back on line to start producing smoothbore muskets and powder. The Merki had probed but not attacked.

The situation was still tense with Cartha, especially after Hamilcar had learned the contents of the treaty struck on the Sangros. His hatred for Andrew was stronger than ever, but at least for Bullfinch he held a clear affection, an affection however that did not extend to the returning of the ironclad he had taken. Four weeks after the end of the war, Bullfinch had brought the fleet back north to cover the Neiper River and shadow the Merki as they started the recrossing to the west, a constant reminder of a power that could cut them off from even that retreat if the treaty was violated. It was with the ironclad fleet that Andrew, along with a brigade of infantry and representatives of all the other regiments, had finally come back to Suzdal.

Bullfinch, still slightly nervous around Andrew over his venture into diplomacy and independent command, stood stiffly at attention while Andrew stared at him for a long moment. A grin gradually creased Andrew's features, and he extended his hand.

"Good job, admiral, a damn good job."

Bullfinch beamed with delight as Andrew continued down the line, turning to come back to the front. In the distance they all heard the high piercing cry of a train whistle, and a spontaneous cheer went up from the assembly.

Andrew went over to Mercury and mounted, Pat and the other corps commanders coming up to join him. Andrew turned his mount toward the broad road that led down to the east gate of the city. Behind him a band started to play, the regiments forming into columns, the thunder of their marching echoing across the square, the men picking up the song, the deep bass so beloved by the Rus starting the opening refrain.

"Yes, we'll rally round the flag, boys,
We'll rally once again,
Shouting the battle cry of freedom!"

Andrew hummed along, turning to look back over his shoulder, the street behind him packed with the standards that seemed to float in the air.

"I'm proud of you, son."

He felt as if the voice had actually spoken, and he turned to look. Pat was beside him, looking straight ahead, bellowing the song off key.

Hans, damn it all, Hans, I wish you were here.

They passed through the gate, the first train to make the run from Roum and Hispania turning through the outer earthen wall, bell ringing, whistle playing out the first bar of "The Battle Hymn of the Republic," the engine and cab decorated with bunting.

Even as the Merki retreated across the steppe, the work crews had started forward, advance units repairing the track, rebuilding bridges from prefabricated stock that Mina had hidden away. It had taken two and a half months of hard work through the heat of the summer and now into the early fall. Already trains were running on a regular schedule to what was left of Kev and the ruins of Vazima, refugees returning home, standing first in shock at the wreckage and then starting into the task of rebuilding. Now at last the first train back to Suzdal was arriving, the whistle sounding high and clear.

He turned in his saddle to watch. Through the glade of trees the city was barely visible on the other side of the river, but the sound of the singing and cheering was unmistakable. He felt as if his hatred would burn out of his soul and consume the world around him.

Tamuka, who had once been Qar Qarth and was now known as One Hand, sat astride his horse, his followers around him.

Civil war was now the reality of the Merki horde, which was fracturing into three parts, the clans of Roaka, who even now harried the borders of Cartha, not acknowledging the treaty. Then there was the traitor Haga, who had cast him down from his power at the council of Qarths, daring to proclaim himself Qar Qarth and leader of the Merki horde. There was no horde any longer. But someday there would be, he thought bitterly.

The numbers who had perished were uncountable, some said a hundred thousand, others a hundred and fifty thousand just in the battles, tens of thousands more dying now from disease, hunger, thirst on the retreat across the steppe, and lingering wounds. By the council of Qarths it was agreed that there would be no fighting for now, peace and the finding of enough food for winter the sole concern, the three parts of the horde spreading out and away from each other after crossing the river. Two umen commanders had elected to stay with Tamuka, those of the Vushka Hush and of the Kartu. It was enough.

He watched, his heart cold, as the train came down the slope, heading toward the city. He could see all so clearly what it heralded, and suspected that Haga saw it as well but would not face such a thing. But he would. If need be he would go to the Bantag, to the Nan, or to whatever hordes rode even farther south. If need be he would take a circling of twenty seasons but he would prepare and return. They could have their peace for now, but there would be another time yet to come.

The rest of the horde was already heading southwestward. He would go straight west and then decide where to go from there. This morning the last of his riders and their pitifully few yurts had crossed the river. Behind them, coming last of all, were the humiliated ones, those who had allowed themselves to be taken prisoner. Many had joined him, too ashamed to return to their own yurts, where the death songs had already been sung for them. The outcasts joining the outcast. It was strength to him, and that was all that mattered.

Haga had released those few pets spared from the sacrifice that were still with the hordes as well, but he was not aware, he would never be aware, that there were two who were not released this day.

He jerked his horse around and looked at the two cattle standing to one side, kept well separated, for the old one had tried repeatedly to kill the other.

"Look long, cattle, it is the last you'll ever see of your home."

Hans Schuder smiled, spitting a stream of tobacco juice on the ground.

"He beat you, that's all I need to know. He beat you and they're free."

Tamuka was tempted yet again to kill him. This one had refused to partake of the flesh of his own kind, starving nearly to death, fighting, struggling, his thoughts sealed away. And yet he felt some reason to keep him alive, for what he was not sure, but he would find it.

The other looked around nervously, his own dreams of vengeance and power gone. Yet still he was alive and he would survive no matter what. Dale Hinsen looked over nervously at Hans, ready to move quickly if the old sergeant tried yet again to kill him.

Tamuka turned his horse and rode back into the forest, disappearing from view, his warriors following behind him.

"I'm proud of you, son!" Hans cried, still smiling. "Proud of all you bastards!"

The halter around his neck jerked tight, and he looked up at Sarg, eyes defiant. He spit a stream of juice against the rump of the shaman's horse and then turned away as well, shoulders and back straight, and disappeared into the forest.

*   *   *

The train rolled into the station, bell ringing, the church bells in the city tolling in joyful reply, the regiments drawn up in columns beside the platform.

Steam hissing out, the train came to a stop, and Chuck Ferguson leaned out of the cab, grinning with delight, and leaped down to the platform.

He turned and reached up. Olivia was climbing down slowly, still moving painfully. Andrew looked at the couple and smiled. If she had lost her beauty it had been replaced by something far stronger and deeper. Chuck walked by her side, arm around her waist, helping her as she walked, still limping slightly.

"Track's bumpy as hell but we've got a railroad again," Chuck announced, coming up and saluting. "The Maine, Fort Lincoln, and Suzdal Railroad's back in operation."

Andrew smiled and shook his head and then took Olivia's hand, bending over formally to kiss it. She smiled, lowering her eyes, which had lost none of their luster.

"When you've got the time, sir, Jack and I have come up with a couple ideas about flying, but it's kind of expensive."

"Later son, later," Andrew said, a grin lighting his features. He patted Chuck on the shoulder and turned away.

The band struck up "Hail to the Chief," and Andrew turned, walking down the platform, motioning for Vincent to follow him, Pat by his side.

From the last car, President Kalencka of the Republic of Rus emerged, stovepipe hat on, black suit as baggy and rumpled as ever. Tears streaming down his face, he looked out at the assembly, Father Casmar coming out behind him. Kal stood at attention until the last note was played, and then ever so slowly he walked down the stairs and stepped to the platform, Andrew rushed forward to grab his hand, but Kal smiled and turned away. Stepping off the platform, he went down upon his knees, bent over, and kissed the earth. He reached into his pocket and pulled out a small lacquered box and opened it. Inside was nothing more than a handful of dust, earth that he had scooped up and borne away on the day he went into exile. Lovingly he turned the box over, letting the dust return, and bent low again, making the sign of the cross, openly weeping.

Andrew heard the Rus soldiers around him starting to weep, and he lowered his own head, emotion taking him as well.

"To the earth from which we came, to the earth to which we now return," Kal said, his words barely heard.

He stood up and looked at Andrew, tears still streaming down his face. He rushed up to Andrew and embraced him.

"Thank Kesus for this day, my friend," Kal said, "and thank Kesus for the day I first met you."

Andrew returned the embrace, remembering well the night Kal, a frightened Rus peasant, had been shown into his tent, the first contact with this strange and wondrous world.

"Welcome home, Mr. President," Andrew replied, his voice choked. "We've got our country back again."

Kal nodded, stepping back from the embrace, and he saw Vincent rushing up to hug him as well, Vincent laughing with delight, grabbing hold of Kal and lifting him in the air in a bear hug.

"I'm proud of you, son."

"I'm proud of you, Father. Welcome home."

Kal turned and looked then at the regiments drawn up, flags snapping in the breeze.

He extended his arm.

"My brothers, my sons . . ." His words trailed off; he was unable to speak.

A wild spontaneous cheer soared up, the men breaking ranks, pushing forward, all order now lost, crowding in around Kal, raising him up on their shoulders, flags waving about him, the cheers echoing against the city walls.

Andrew made his way through the press, laughing with delight, accepting a blessing from Father Casmar, who suddenly was swept off his feet and borne away by the crowd. Others were now coming off the train, reunions around him, Gregory pushing his way through to grab his wife, the two kissing passionately. From out of the last car Vincent saw Tanya and the children and rushed up to them, kneeling down to grab hold of young Andrew, crying with delight as Tanya came into his arms, the twins clutching at their father's legs.

He saw Marcus come down off the platform, and he went up and saluted.

"Welcome, Mr. President," Andrew said, saluting smartly and grinning.

"It's going to be an interesting party," Marcus said, his Rus still halting, but improving. "How's the situation?" he asked, trying to be serious even now.

"The last of them were released this morning, some ragged bands moving west out of the woods across the river."

"Tamuka's people."

"The same."

"We've not heard the last of him."

"It'll be years, maybe never. It'll mean we can't stop now. There'll be railroads to build, linking more and yet more people, freeing them from tyranny, freeing an entire world one day. We've got a lifetime of work ahead of us, your people and ours."

"Our people together," Marcus said, and Andrew grinned broadly.

"The Tugars?"

"Still riding east. They crossed through our lands without incident, though that move had me worried,"

Marcus replied. "But he honored his word as you thought he would, and pledged to stop the killing of people farther on in his march eastward wherever they might go. He told me to say to you that Qubata was right about you after all, perhaps right about all of us, and then he rode on."

The turning of the Tugars had been crucial, increasing the terror of the Merki, adding strength to his bargaining with Haga, and, perhaps most important, protecting the wounded, who still might have been killed. In the days to come, many of those wounded would be coming back home who would not have been alive if it had not been for Muzta. He was glad that Emil had managed to save Muzta's son's life. He hoped that somehow what was left of Muzta's people would survive.

Marcus looked past Andrew as the men of the three corps of Roum came pressing through the crowd, and he stepped down to them, arms extended, laughing as they swept him up into the air, cheering loudly, holding him aloft.

Behind Marcus, Emil came out of the car and looked around at the chaos.

"I bet the city's a mess," Emil said, lowering his head, taking off his spectacles to clean them, and then putting them back on.

"How are the boys at the hospital?"

"Still losing some, but most of those still with me are on the mend," Emil said quietly. "I'll tell you something, though, Andrew. I'm retiring."

Andrew looked at him, a bit startled.

Emil forced a smile. "I guess the last time did me in," he whispered sadly. "One operation too many, one sacrifice too many, one too many boys of war dying on me."

He paused and looked back at the crowd.

"But I can see it was worth it in the end," he whispered. "Plan to do research," he said, his voice brightening again. "Doing some experiments with carbolic acid—seems to work better than tincture of lime to stop infection. Want to do some more work on what my old mentor Semmelweis was on to. I think there's a connection between those microscopic creatures I told you about and infection. A lot to do, and I'm looking forward to it, by damn."

"But who's going to run the medical service?" Andrew asked.

"Hell, without a war we won't need what we had, thank the Almighty. But I've got a replacement already picked," and he pointed into the car, "and she's in there. She'll tell you all about it, and something else as well."

He grinned and climbed down from the car. Pat O'Donald grabbed hold of him, pulling out a flask, and the two shared a drink until they were picked up by the crowd and swept away.

Andrew climbed up the platform and onto the train. Kathleen was standing inside the car, to his delight wearing the one dress she still had from earth, Maddie asleep in her arms in spite of the turmoil outside. Beside her was a small trunk, holding in it the few possessions they had taken with them into exile.

He went up to her almost hesitantly, not having seen her for over a month. Maddie stirred and he kissed her lightly on the forehead, and then Kathleen set the baby down to sleep on one of the chairs.

Andrew pulled her in close, kissing her, the two of them laughing, and then he held her tight.

"Welcome home, Kathleen darling."

"Our house?"

"Dusty, some windows broken, but still there."

She smiled.

"We're really safe, it's over with?"

"It's over, they're gone. It'll be years before we ever hear of their likes again, maybe even never."

"Thank God."

"I heard about your promotion to chief surgeon."

She laughed as he stepped back to salute her formally, and then she was back in his arms.

"Let's go out and join the celebration."

"I don't think so," she whispered shyly, looking up at him.

"Why not?"

"The crowds and all the pushing. I've got to be careful."

He felt his heart skip over.

"A baby?" he whispered.

She smiled and nodded.

He held her close to his side, and together they went out to the back platform to watch as the crowd cheered and sang, and wept with joy. And over them floated the flags of the regiments.

Above them all, Colonel Andrew Lawrence Keane saw two standards that seemed somehow to float above the others—the flag of the Army of the Republics, and beside it, shining in the glory of a new day, the faded colors of the 35th Maine.

If you and/or a friend would like to receive the *ROC Advance*, a bimonthly newsletter featuring all the newest and hottest ROC books and authors, on a complimentary basis, please fill out this form and return it to:

ROC Books/Penguin USA
375 Hudson Street
New York, NY 10014

Your Address
Name _____
Street _____ Apt. # _____
City _____ State _____ Zip _____

Friend's Address
Name _____
Street _____ Apt. # _____
City _____ State _____ Zip _____

There's an epidemic with 27 million victims. And no visible symptoms.

It's an epidemic of people who can't read.

Believe it or not, 27 million Americans are functionally illiterate, about one adult in five.

The solution to this problem is you... when you join the fight against illiteracy. So call the Coalition for Literacy at toll-free **1-800-228-8813** and volunteer.

Volunteer Against Illiteracy. The only degree you need is a degree of caring.